WILD STREETS

WILD STREETS

Tales of the Frontier Towns
by Members of
the Western Writers
of America

Edited with an Introduction by Don Ward

DOUBLEDAY & COMPANY, INC., GARDEN CITY, NEW YORK

1958

Library of Congress Catalog Card Number 58–12058
Copyright © 1958 by Western Writers of America
All Rights Reserved
Printed in the United States of America
First Edition

To
Harry Sinclair Drago
who fathered the WWA anthology idea and
has nurtured it through many successive
volumes

NOTE

The Western Writers of America is an organization of professional authors whose aims are to promote their common interests, encourage the writing of better quality Westerns, and bring them more effectively to the attention of the reading public. One part of WWA's extensive program has been the publication of an annual collection of stories by its members. There have been five such volumes prior to this one: *Bad Men and Good, Holsters and Heroes, The Fall Roundup, Branded West,* and *Hoof Trails and Wagon Tracks.*

Introduction

Don Ward

NEW Orleans . . . Santa Fe . . . Dodge City . . . Tascosa . . .
Tombstone . . . names on the land. Names that conjure up scenes of
danger and violence and romance, a vision of lusty life moving ever
westward as the tide of settlement swept remorselessly toward the
Pacific.

Names bestowed first on tent hamlets, on clusters of shacks and huts
huddled together where a trail crossed a river, or where one trail met
another, or where gold was dug, or cattle loaded, or hides bought and
sold. Some of them persist as significant place names of present-day
American geography. Dodge City, for instance: once the "wickedest
little city in America," the "Beautiful Bibulous Babylon of the Frontier," successively army trading post, hide hunters' town (they called
it "Buffalo City" then) and, for a raucous decade, veritable Cowboy
Capital of the Southwest. Today it's a neat, spruce, thriving community,
the little metropolis of southwest Kansas. Take Fair Play—in the 1870's
Fair Play was the most important mining town on the stage road from
Denver to Leadville; today it's still a lively spot—its de luxe motels and
cocktail bars a far cry from the unpainted false fronts of long ago—
although most of its dozen gold and silver tributary camps are now
ghost towns, like the one in Allan Vaughan Elston's story.

Virginia City, Nevada, now a quiet place basking in the memory of past glory, was once the booming, brawling site of muscular exploits chronicled so vividly in Mark Twain's *Roughing It*. The first twenty-six graves in Virginia's cemetery were occupied by murdered men, and when a stranger arrived they didn't ask if he was capable or honest—they asked if he'd killed his man! If he hadn't, his position was that of a man of "small consequence," but if he had, "the cordiality of his reception was graduated according to the number of his dead. It was tedious work, struggling up to a position of influence with bloodless hands; but when a man came with the blood of half a dozen men on his soul his worth was recognized at once and his acquaintance sought." The best-known names in the territory belonged to accomplished pistoleers like Sam Brown, Sugarfoot Mike, Pock-Marked Jake, El Dorado Johnny and Six-Fingered Pete.

Another roaring silver-mining town was Tombstone, today a dot on Arizona's map, entitled to rest on its historic laurels even though it's not content to, as evidenced by its lively, still-going-strong newspaper, the Tombstone *Epitaph*. It's the scene of Thomas Thompson's novelette, "Trail's End in Tombstone." John Myers Myers, who did homage to the town's hell-raising days in his book, *The Last Chance,* asks us not to overlook what he calls "that zany among boom towns," Calabasas, in Arizona ranked second only to Tombstone as a burg with alarmingly eruptive tendencies. Most maps don't show Calabasas today, but—if you can find a copy of the book—you can read all about it in John Cabell Brown's *Calabazas* (he spelled it with a "z"), which was published in 1892; and now Jack Myers has spun a riotous tale of its doom in his verse-novelette, "The Sack of Calabasas."

But you're not to imagine that the Southwest's towns had any monopoly of lusty action and dido-cutting. Politicking up in old Montana, for example, had a gamey quality all its own, and Dan Cushman has done it justice—or maybe even more than justice—in his book, *The Old Copper Collar,* which follows the hilarious course of a senatorial election in Helena, the state capital. If the excerpt included here whets your appetite—well, there's a paper-bound edition extant and available, under the Ballantine imprint. Montana Territory had its Virginia City too, just as wild and woolly as Nevada's, and a glimpse of its own variety of wildness is furnished us in "The Proud Diggers."

There was Bannack, too, in Montana, and Norman Fox's story introduces us again to that smoothest of all frontier scoundrels, Mr. Henry Plummer. Speaking of personalities, that fellow James Butler

Hickok pops up in the Abilene story, of course; as does Wyatt Earp, just as naturally, in the Dodge City yarn. And that smiling, buck-toothed killer, Billy the Kid, gets a nod in Omar Barker's poem, "Old Lincoln Town."

Oh, the old towns were wild, all right. Even in Texas. Brownwood may be little known today but it was a rough, tough cow town in its early days, the scene of Elmer Kelton's "Coward." Sitting at the edge of the Cross Timbers section in West Texas, it was once the center of the state's fence wars, where the struggle between free-grass men and fence men went to the verge of civil strife as a mob of armed and desperate fence cutters rode into Brownwood with the ungentle aim of burning down the town. There was a citizens' party forted up in the opera house, determined to fight it out . . . but that's another story, and one we can't tell here and now. Texas had its rough and ready buffalo towns too: Sweet Water and Fort Worth and Fort Griffin— this Griffin was a raw and lusty place, one that rivaled Dodge as a hide hunters' rendezvous, with its crowded streets and sprawling low buildings and those flesh-peddling shacks along the river (known as "Hunters' Heaven"); it was in Griffin that Doc Halliday, who was to win enduring fame later on in Tombstone as a pard of Wyatt Earp's, took up with Kate Fisher, the dance-hall gal they called Big-Nose Kate, who saved him from a lynch mob after he shot and killed Ed Bailey. We don't have a story about Griffin, more's the pity, but you can read about the town in WWA member Mari Sandoz's fine book, *The Buffalo Hunters.*

Santa Fe, with its narrow streets drenched by sun and history, its 'dobe buildings and dark-eyed senoritas—now a great resort town and convention city. Visit there, and you're apt to stay at La Fonda, where fur trader Tony Ferrar plunges into strange adventure in Les Savage's stirring novelette, "Traitor Town." And Denver, Colorado's mile-high city, is much in evidence today, even more so than it was back when Tom Blackburn's "Buckskin Pensioner" roamed its streets. New Orleans, teeming cosmopolitan port city of 1958, was a lawless frontier town back in 1803, when the action of Noel Loomis's "City of Sin" takes place.

Yes, we can sing the towns of the frontier full as much as we do its mountains and its plains. Sing their dusty streets, where cowboys and hide men, muckers and gamblers, gunmen and lawmen stood and strode and looked death in the face—and, often enough, laughed at it.

Yes, sing the frontier towns, sing all the wild streets, sing the danger
that lurked among the low buildings under the blazing sky, sing the
courage of those who took over that raw country and somehow made
it civilized. . . .

My thanks for help in making this book go to the many members of
WWA who ransacked their files and contributed scores of stories for
me to read and choose from. But special thanks for special help have
to go to Norman Fox, Harry Sinclair Drago, Bill Gulick, Omar Barker,
and to Tommy Thompson. Without them, the task would have been
much more difficult.

CONTENTS

WILD STREETS

Old Lincoln Town

S. Omar Barker

LINCOLN Town, old Lincoln Town, by time's sun grayed and browned,
What gunsmoke spells your history, what bloodstains rust your ground?
The talking wind recites what tales of hoofbeats in your street,
And which the ancient cottonwood where ghostly gunmen meet?
What heroes' names are written on your scroll of sudden death—
Bold men who faced the music to their last lead-silenced breath?
O Lincoln Town, old Lincoln Town, rimmed by the quiet hills,
Do you hear voices in the night, or only whippoorwills?

I hear them, yes, I hear them in the moon dusk and the dark,
As ghostly as the echo of a phantom coyote's bark.
Within my old adobe walls they speak in every room;
They whisper where the cottonwoods ensomber night with gloom.

O Lincoln Town, old Lincoln Town, what names from long ago
Are heard upon the night wind when the yellow moon is low?

New Mexico born and raised, OMAR BARKER's ingratiating cowboy stories
and poems have been appearing in the magazines, both Western and general
interest, for the last thirty years. An active member of WWA from its inception, Omar now lives and works with his wife Elsa (another Western writer
and WWA member) in Las Vegas, New Mexico.

What names? . . . What can names matter when the bones of
     men are dust,
And hot blood spilled in anger is but unremembered rust?
Yes, ghostly names are whispered here, one more than all the rest,
But if adobe walls could speak, they would remember best
That of my hardy horseback crew, sons of the cowboy breed,
Each was a man who lived and died according to his creed;
And in this quiet village, with my days of gunsmoke past,
Old enemies hold rendezvous in ghostly peace at last!

Lincoln Town, old Lincoln Town, how quiet sleeps the street
Beneath those ancient cottonwoods where phantom gunmen meet!

Buckskin Pensioner

Tom W. Blackburn

MIKE McGeehee was wearing a new suit of buckskins. Wearing them
on this *pasear* to Denver was, in a way, a fool thing and a waste. He'd
left a passable outfit at his cabin in the hills, and if he'd stayed in his
own bailiwick he wouldn't have had to break out this new suit for maybe
a couple of seasons yet. A good thing too. Decent leather gear was hard
to get these days. But he was going to visit Molly, and Molly had always been finicky, even when she was a kid. She wouldn't like him in
an old outfit, stained with use and a mite frayed here and there, regardless of how much use might still be left in it.

This going to see Molly—that is, making this haul down to Denver
just to see her—was kind of a fool notion. Mike was sheepish about it.
Not that going to see Molly wasn't all right. Mike had been doing that,
off and on, for near a score of years, dropping in for chow and a "hello"
every couple of seasons or so when he hit Denver for new gear and sup-

The name Tom Blackburn has been one of the big ones in Western writing
for many years. He's had literally hundreds of stories in the magazines and
several books, the most recent of them a historical novel, *Sierra Baron*.
Several years of screen work have been topped off by a long run as chief
script-writer for Walt Disney Productions. Born and raised in the Mountain states, Tom now lives on the West Coast with his wife, Juanita.

plies or to peddle a few bales of the plew he still took regularly in the hills. But dragging his carcass two hundred miles down off of Grand Mesa for a visit—hell!

It was just something he wanted to do and up and did. In the back of his mind he figured it was tied up with his cutting his trap line down from thirty-five miles a day to nearer eighteen, the last season. He figured it was tied up with him getting old and maybe thinking—without doing it a-purpose or ever admitting it—that maybe he wouldn't be seeing Molly too many more times.

Mike sat on the back seat of the horsecar lugging up Barnum Hill, ignoring the stares and smirks of his fellow passengers—a pasty-faced outfit without a decent pair of shoulders or a respectable head of hair in the lot—and stared at the sorry animal plodding along between the rails ahead. He had never been especially a saddle man. Horses didn't do as good as shanks' mares in the timber country, and a fur man wouldn't be caught dead more'n a day's hike from a place where big sticks grew.

It took white water and green timber to grow prime plew. But he'd seen horses do a sight of chores for men, and damned if this wasn't the sorriest and the most disgusting of them all. He heaved a sigh of relief when the car squeaked past the head of Molly's street, and when he was afoot and shut of the contraption he spat with feeling. There'd been a time when Denver had been a right decent town, with honest mud in its streets, and folks got about afoot without a passel of gadgets like carriages and these horse things and the like to clutter up their way, but that had been a long time ago.

Going up the walk to Molly's neat green-and-white house, Mike tried to get time settled in his mind. Near's he could remember, it had been in the seventies that he found Molly. She'd just been big enough to talk, then, and when he'd first seen her, she was jawing the hell out of a couple of Cheyenne braves who'd been prowling the ruins of a gutted wagon train on the sand flats edging the Dawson Hills north and east of Cherry Creek. The Cheyennes had got a lot of hair off the members of the train and were right ugly. There'd been only these two left—the rest had pulled out—and Mike McGeehee had been a fair-to-middling man in a quarrel when he was young. There was a tangle and then Molly'd had only him to talk to.

He'd never been able to rightly tell which of the bodies among the charred wagons had been her father and mother. Whoever they were, they weren't smart, riding a train that'd take the Dawson Hill route in those days. He'd worried, off and on, about Molly's brains, account of that. He'd turned her over to some Sisters in Denver and sent money regular for her keep and things and she'd turned out all right after a while, smart and pretty as a picture.

Thinking now, he decided it must be between fifteen and twenty years since she'd married a young jigger with nice eyes but a damned thin mustache and practically no beard, who claimed to be a medico. Considering this gent was quiet and almighty peaceable, he had done pretty good. They had this house and Molly'd been refusing Mike's money almost from the day they got married. They had a couple of kids. One of 'em looked just like Molly and made the seventies seem no longer ago than yesterday, every time Mike looked at her. The other was a boy with a slim, long-geared build to him and eyes as level as a Winchester's sights with a dash of hell 'twixt the notch and the bead, and Mike doubted if he'd be a medico—a peaceful one, anyways. All in all, Molly had done right well.

There was a push-pull jigger on the casement beside Molly's door. There was a lock set in the door itself. It made Mike think of the leather thong that'd been hanging through his door on Grand Mesa for half a century. When a man had to put a key between him and folks coming to his door, things were bad off. Mike scorned the jigger on the casement and the lock and took hold of the handle and walked into the house.

There was a front room, and Molly and young Molly were in it, looking up, startled like and curious, and maybe a little bit mad that somebody would hump right in on them like that. Then the two of them were squealing, and young Molly had got her arms about Mike's neck, which was quite a reach, because Mike had been poured into the old mold that made men duck their heads under the lintel of most doors, and old Molly was standing, hands on hips that hadn't fatted up too much yet, just looking and squealing surprise.

There was quite a ruckus for a spell, and Mike stomped a bit himself, and then old Molly—and that was a funny way to think of her—got hold of Mike's arm and dragged him to a padded-up chair that was like sitting on a woman's lap, arms around both sides, and she frowned at him.

"Mike, are you feeling all right?" she asked.

"Pert," Mike said emphatically.

"You look peaked," Molly said. "It's been a bad winter in the mountains. It's flushed half the riffraff out of the hills. There's been a lot of trouble with them down here since Christmas."

Mike snorted. "It'd be a bad winter that'd flush me out!" he said dryly.

Young Molly saw the mistake. "Oh, Mike!" she said hurriedly. "Mom didn't mean you were riffraff!"

Old Molly laughed. "I did so!" she said flatly. "The worst in the hills. Hungry?"

"Tolerable," Mike agreed.

"I've got broth makings in the pantry."

Mike snorted again but he had broth, and it was flavorable enough and filling, but damned poor eating for a man that still had his teeth. And he didn't like the padded chair; still, he had to sit in it.

Old Molly and young Molly kept to the front room with him, and talked hell afire and gave him news and asked of his, though there wasn't any since old Jules Rondeau had got the pneumonia a season before and left Mike without any neighbors worth talking to on the mesa. It was a good warm greeting. It was what Mike had expected. It was good to look at Molly and her little one and see where she'd come to in the world and all. But the two women kept looking at him. There wasn't the sly joking in their talk that he was used to. They were more gentle than there was any need with a grown man. It got under his skin.

Directly he got him a chance, he got up and looked in the mirror over Molly's little kindling pot of a fireplace. It gave him a turn. Looking square, by thunder if he didn't seem a little peaked!

There was a stiff chair by the door, and he could have dropped into it when he turned back from the mantel but he didn't. He dropped again into the padded contraption and wondered if maybe he was a mite off on his feed, at that.

Come nightfall, Doc came home. Young Hank was off someplace for a couple days. Mike missed him. He figured he needed a man, and somehow he'd never quite convinced himself that Dr. Henry McGowan was hair-chested, in spite of the fact he'd married Molly and done right by her and the kids they'd had.

Doc was thickening up and losing what hair he'd had. He shook Mike's hand and gave him a middling clap on the back and then went out in the kitchen. Mike heard the women talking to him, quiet like.

Doc came back in directly and drew a chair up close to the padded one and put a hand on Mike's knee.

"About time you showed sense, Mike," he said. "Man isn't a clock. You can't expect to keep winding the old carcass up and have it keep on going forever."

He got out his little black satchel that he'd left by the door and he hung a jigger from his ears and shoved the other end of it up under Mike's leather shirt and punched around in the gray brush on his chest and cocked his head one way and the other and made little squirrel sounds with his tongue against his teeth, like he knew a hell of a lot about what he was doing and none of it was good.

Mike didn't care for any of this, but a man couldn't be a fool for more'n seventy-five years of his life. After that, like it or lump it, he had to look to himself. Mike could see that. And when he came to think of it, he couldn't lug forty pounds of traps up the Devil's Slide without once stopping for breath, like he used to. That was a fact.

Then there was that Creek arrowhead alongside his spine. Seemed as though the blamed thing moved around some of late, sort of digging in a bit when he hoisted a fair lift. And one foot had got frostbit maybe four-five times back along and was a mite touchy when contrary weather turned up. The ribs he bunged up on the White River three springs back had been kind of troubling him if he stuck to his lines more'n ten-twelve hours or so.

Mike had never thought directly about these things. A man went along, and one thing and another happened to him, and he grunted a bit or swore if he was where he could and felt the notion, and directly he was on about his business again. If he was lamed a little, it didn't amount to anything and he could still get around, and that was that. Now it seemed there was more to it.

Mike put up a good fight, considering. But Doc was a howling heller when he got on medics. He got Mike down on the mattress in the front bedroom and near to naked, and he pounded and he punched and kept on making squirrel sounds, and finally he came out and let Mike get dressed again.

The three of them were waiting in the front room—Doc and Molly and young Molly. The two women looked at Doc, and Doc looked at his toes, and Mike sat down in the padded chair.

"Mike," Doc said—but he was talking to his toes, shoved out in front of him. "Mike, you know how all of us feel about you. You've been Molly's father and mother for thirty years. You've been my friend. And you've been grandfather to the kids. We've never tried to bring you down out of the hills. You're too stubborn to see the old days are gone, and we've known better than to try persuading you."

Mike nodded solemnly. This was, he supposed, Doc's way of putting into words things Mike could not put into words himself. There was a lot of affection and one thing and another mixed up in it.

"The point is, Mike," Doc went on, "you've got to the end of a trail."

Mike swallowed with astonishment. It must have showed on his face.

Doc went on hurriedly. "Oh, Lord, no!" he said. "You're not going to die! Not tomorrow, anyhow, if you use some sense. But look, man, you're seventy-five years old if you're a day. And after the kind of life you've led——"

"What's the matter with my kind of life?" Mike growled ominously.

"Nothing! Nothing!" Doc said, looking up hurriedly. "What I'm trying to tell you is that although you are in remarkable shape for a man your age, you can't go on bucking the winters on the mesa and tracking your lines indefinitely without collapsing and going out suddenly one day like a lamp in the wind. You owe it to yourself and to the women here—and to me too—to take care of yourself from here on. You've got more money than a banker's widow, and it's time you got some use and pleasure out of it. Molly and I have done well. Our children won't need more than we can give them. The fur trade's done. Admit it. Give up the hills."

Doc sounded like he was giving advice, but it was more than that, and Mike knew it. These were orders.

He shrugged wearily. "You ain't going to put me to bed?" he asked hopefully.

Molly laughed then, the first time since Doc had got home, and it was a good sound.

"You, in bed!" she snorted. "Mike McGeehee, do you think we're crazy? I'd rather have a locomotive in the house! You wouldn't stay in bed. There's no need of that—yet. Henry and I have talked it over. You should take a trip. Spend some of your money. You're a restless kind. Travel, look at the country and the people. You told me, when I was a little girl, that someday you reckoned you'd take a look at California, seeing as there was an ocean there and you could go west to get to it. Why not go now?"

They put store-bought clothes on Mike, clothes that cost twice what a man could pick up a beaded ceremonial outfit for and itched something fierce and made him look a foot more than his unbent six-and-six in height. They put a white sombrero on his head, and the brim kept getting in his way every time he wanted to look out sidewise right quick. They laughed when he made them pack his buckskins in his grip but they knew better than to laugh when he wouldn't let them cut the hair that had been to his shoulders since he could remember.

Doc did right handsome by him with a carved stick of some black hardwood. It was pretty to look at, and Mike could see the chore whittling it out had been but he felt like a fool, carrying it along with him. Still, Doc had done a passel of worrying about this, and if he'd done it for hire, it would have cost a bale of money, because Doc was doing a good business these days and his prices ran high. Doc was apt to be sensitive, and hurting him wouldn't do. He'd been a fair man for Molly, and his kids set a store by him.

Mike got kissed in the open by old Molly and young Molly, and young Hank near smashed his fingers, and Doc gave him a cigar, and a mess of folks around the station grinned like hell, and Mike got on the train. He was right glad when the shebang bucked a mite and started rolling. He wasn't happy, but he was glad, all right.

The train lugged out past Castle Rock and Twin Peaks and hiked up over the pass betwixt Trinidad and Raton, and Mike looked out the window at all this familiar old ground which was familiar no longer. He got to feeling downright cussed. Things had sure happened fast. He'd come down off the mesa for a gossip and, Lord A'mighty, here he was riding springs south'ards!

He didn't care much for this train travel. It was maybe a mite more steady than a freight wagon or a long-shanked mule, but it sure lacked a lot. For one thing, there wasn't any air past a man's ears. When Mike opened the window, he got whiffing of smoke and cinders, and folks that were near looked so ornery he closed it again.

He reckoned it would be a hell of a long ways to California on this contraption, and he tried to stretch his legs and wait for it to be over with, but it was slow work. There was a young jigger come along somewheres between Raton and Las Vegas and plunked his breeches down alongside Mike. The young jigger seen right off somehow that Mike didn't know for'ard from rear'ard of a train and he made talk about coaches and trucks and grades and semaphores and the like for quite a spell.

It wasn't what a man could call a powerful interesting conversation, and Mike napped along here and there. Wasn't but one thing that struck him about this train. There was a hunk of rope came in one end of the car he was riding, and out the other, and this young jigger said it was an "emergency cord." Seems as though a gent off east had built up a gadget to put the bit on the locomotives that hauled these trains, a gent named Westinghouse. You just up and pulled that cord, anywhere on the train, and this air brake Westinghouse had built would clamp on and the whole blasted train would rear back on its hocks in a hurry.

It was kind of comforting, looking up at that hunk of rope and thinking any time things got too bad, a man could haul on it and drag the works to a stop, so's he could get off and be shut of smoke and cinders and red-plush seats all at once.

Night came while the train was poking up the first leg of Glorieta Pass out of Las Vegas, bound for Santa Fe. It came dark, no moon, and a train jigger came along touching lamps afire in the ceiling. Mike began to get drowsy and wished to hell for leg room, but the young jigger beside him turned restless. Didn't seem as though he wanted to talk; just appeared to have a passel of squirming and twisting around in him that had to get out.

It was maybe three hours after dark and the train had got itself into a tolerably deep and dark canyon, when the young jigger stood up. Seemed as though several gents had a like notion, all at once. There was three that Mike could see in his car, all of them straightening up in the aisle and looking of a sudden like business was on their minds. Mike saw one of them had a gun in his hand before he rightly knew what was happening, and by that time the young jigger who'd been riding with him had stooped over him.

"All right, grandpa," the young jigger said very thinly and nervously. "This is where we get off. Shell out—and fast!"

Mike McGeehee smelled the wind then. This was what Molly had been talking about. This was the riffraff the winter had flushed out of the hills. These buckos figured on making a good take the easy way. It was funny. If this one hadn't bent over him, chances were Mike would have let them be. A man's business, setting reasonable limits, was his own. And there was Doc McGowan's promise that getting rambunctious at seventy-five wasn't a smart way to live a long time. But there was a nasty sort of snarling note in this young jigger's voice and he looked like he might stick his hand into one of Mike's pockets right sudden, and Mike just plain didn't like the look to his face.

He didn't mean to be rough about it or do any great hurt. He sort of wiped out with his near hand, kind of curling his knuckles up as he wiped, and the young jigger hit the back of the seat across and bounced farther than a man'd think he would, and he landed with his feet on an arm rest and his head in the middle of the aisle.

Farther up the car, the other two gents had got maybe three-four people up out of their seats, hands high, and were commencing to shake them down. When Mike's seat mate upended, one of the other two bellowed like a bullet-burned elk and belted out the door into the next car. The other shoved the customers he'd lined up back out of the way and dropped to one knee.

Something came howling down over ducked heads and kited Mike's new hat clean across the car. There was smoke in front of the kneeling gent and a hammering against the windows Mike reckoned was the racket of a shot. That did the trick proper.

It had been ten-twelve years since anybody had shot at Mike McGee-hee, and twice that since anybody had meant it right out honest. That shot made Mike feel like a bob-tailed buck on virgin grass. Who was it had said the old days were dead? Doc, it was. Doc was crazy. He was crazy as hell, and about a lot of things. Tarnation, if this was the new days, what in thunder did Doc think the old ones were like?

The jigger with his head in the aisle wasn't even kicking. His gun was spilling out of his belt. Mike hooked it up and folded his carcass behind a red-plush seat and made sure he had good brass to work with. Then he shoved his shoulder high, so it'd look like he was coming up, and his head low, so's he could get a sight without getting tagged, and he sent a slug smoking up the aisle near snug against the carpet.

The slug went between one of the kneeling gent's knees and the other, and made him jump some, and it gave Mike range and he sort of got the feel of things. He hunched low, like he was going to try another on the floor, then popped up above the seat back, set for a quick one. But the kneeling gent had got up, and his partner, who had run into the next car, was back with a couple more lads and they laced him proper.

Red plush splattered all over the place, and Mike got something against his cheek that didn't split the hide but stung like hell, and every soul in the car that wasn't holding a gun was caterwauling like a bobcat in a beaver set. This wasn't going to do. Mike could see that. These boys were bushed up pretty bad, and a nervous gent was a hard one to handle. The seats of this palace car might stop the first couple of rounds of slugs, but they wouldn't do permanent, and Mike had an aversion to being smoked out slow.

He took a good look at the piece in his hand and decided it was reliable and got his knees folded up under him where he could use them. He sucked in a good breath, so's it'd last and taking another at the wrong time wouldn't spoil his eye, and he came up from between the seats where he was crouching like a scared ptarmigan out of a snow-bank.

He came up howling and his gun level. He swung into the aisle and started up it. One of the four at the end of the car let fly. It hummed pretty close and Mike shot where there was smoke, and there were only three men left standing. He shot again, and one of the others took a sick look on and backed half into the vestibule before he fell. The other two milled, and their guns snapped like a pair of cheated women, and Mike kind of rocked around on his heels and wasted another shot and then got one that counted. And all the time he kept moving ahead steady.

The one bucko that was left was kind of flat against the end wall of the car. His gun was sort of up and down, kind of wiggling, like he wasn't right sure.

Mike called at him, persuasive like, "Dang it, son, don't make me do it!" And he still kept walking.

The last bucko still couldn't make up his mind. Finally, Mike saw him brace suddenly. But it was too late. Mike's legs were long. A stride and a reach could cover a lot of ground. He rapped the barrel of the pistol in his hand down on the bucko's head an instant before the man's gun fired, and all that happened was that the railroad company lost a pretty lamp. The way Mike looked at it, they could afford it.

He prodded the last man's limp belly with his toe.

"You damned fool!" he said quietly. "Couldn't you count?"

There was a stupid-looking customer with a bald head and plenty of sweat on his face came crawling out of a space between seats which ought to have been too narrow for his pudgy carcass. Still on his hands and knees, and with his eyes big as cheater dollars, he looked up at Mike.

"Count?" he said stupidly.

Mike tossed the gun in his hand down beside the pudgy man.

"Sure!" he snapped. "This ain't no Winchester with a five-foot magazine! I'd busted my last cap, and he should have knowed it, instead of standing there wavin' one way and another, like grass in the wind!"

The man on his hands and knees picked up the gun very gingerly, like it maybe had teeth, and he looked at it.

"Empty!" he said in the same kind of stupid way.

Mike figured maybe he was scared to death. In fact, the way the rest of the folks crawling out here and there in the car were acting, he guessed they were all scared to death. He could see too, by the way the eyes of one and another of the women were looking, that right sudden he was going to get thanked.

Mike had a right warm place in him for Molly and young Molly, but come by and large, he'd never been one to truck with women and he wanted none now. Matter of fact, what he wanted was a long ways from this train. Seemed of a sudden that burning a little powder and scrunching down and jumping up and whacking a gent on the point of his chin and another on the top of his head had all been pert tonics. Seemed as though he'd let Doc and the two Mollys and young Hank talk him into something he hadn't ought to have any part of.

He hadn't thought of the emergency cord overhead and how he could have crossed up the buckos that aimed to empty this train of cash, just by reaching up and giving a pull, but he thought about it now.

He hooked his finger over the hunk of rope and gave it a little tug that made it come slack, like maybe it had broken somewhere up the line. Sure enough, this Westinghouse customer had him a good gadget, all right. The whole blamed train sort of squatted like a short-legged horse refusing a jump. There was considerable grinding and clanking, and folks were a mite spilled around, and Mike was jostled into the vestibule at the end of the car. Then the works was sitting still, sort of panting like.

Mike had just got the vestibule door open and had sorted his bag out of the tangle which had dumped onto the floor from the rack over the seats when the conductor showed up from the other car, all pasty and heaving like the bellows on a smith's forge. He took a look at the clutter in the end of the car and turned a touch more pasty and kind of squeaked twice before he could get his voice, and then stiffened his back up and scowled at Mike. "This isn't a stop!"

"We ain't moving," Mike countered.

The conductor looked at the buckos kind of lumped together on the floor.

"This is a bad mess," he said sort of importantly, but weak. "We've got to get this holdup straightened out."

"Looks straight enough to me now!" Mike said with satisfaction.

The conductor did not like the looks of the men on the floor.

"You couldn't have done that!" he said unsteadily.

Mike shrugged. "Maybe not, but I sure tried, son," he said kindly. "Now look, any law says I can't get off here?"

The conductor shook his head. "But don't be a fool, man!" he protested. "We're in the middle of the mountains!"

A kind of holy light came up in Mike McGeehee's eyes. He grinned more widely than he had since he'd caught the stage at the foot of Grand Mesa on his way to Denver. He felt wonderful! He fished a sizable bill from his pocket and handed it to the slack-lipped trainman.

"Son, you pedal this here train on to California. When you get there, do me a chore, and the rest of that's yours. Drop a card to Molly McGowan in Denver, tellin' her I'm having a tolerable time. Pick up a coconut or a goldfish or something for Molly's kids and something for Doc, and ship 'em back. And if I've got bunions or lamed up the while, I'll be waitin' up the line yonder somewheres for a lift back to Denver."

The trainman took an envelope and a pencil out of his pocket and, with his eyes kind of popping out on his cheeks and his hand almighty slow, like he was asleep or something, he wrote down the names and the address Mike gave him. Mike looked over his shoulder till he saw the writing was right, then he clapped the conductor on the shoulder and pulled open the door and dropped to the ground with his bag in his hand.

He backed off from the tracks a ways. The man up in the locomotive thing at the front squalled a whistle. The conductor sort of came to in the vestibule and tied the broken rope together and tugged on it, and the train started moving.

Mike watched it go, then he sat down where he could look at one peak on one side of the canyon and another peak on the other side of the canyon, and he sucked in air. Figuring rough, it seemed likely he could make Las Vegas over the ridges, come noon tomorrow. After that—well, hell, there were mountains all the way north to the mesa, and a man that was traveling for his health could take his time.

Man From Texas

W. Edmunds Claussen

A SUDDEN twist of the wrist sent pain darting through John Giddings's arm all the way to his shoulder. He drew his horse back to level prairie, letting no acknowledgment of the passing agony reach his long brown Texas face.

He pulled the bandanna over his nostrils for the hundredth time that long day. They were crowding close to the pens of the Kansas Pacific—he could see the long gray fences through the dust. He'd hold the cattle here, ride into Dodge City tonight, and make arrangements with Kirk Goodman to have the stock turned over to a buyer in the morning. Then a day—two full days!—with Vance. After the dust and turmoil of the trail two days was hardly enough time to spend in a woman's company.

He sat his horse on a little knoll, watching the chuck wagon pull up and the men break into a camp. The cattle drifted a little, then picked a dry slant for their bed-ground. No different from any other spot on this hard, sable prairie. A frail smile pulled John Giddings's mouth. They knew what they wanted, all right. Perhaps some cloying

BILL CLAUSSEN and his wife are highly successful professional photographers in Boyerstown, Pennsylvania, where they make their home. Sentimentally, though, Bill is trans-Mississippi; and all his fiction—scores of magazine stories, plus several books—has been Westerns.

odor was different from a hundred yards yonder, perhaps the grass held a sweet shading of flavor.

He too knew what he wanted. He hadn't been able to get Vance out of his blood. He shaped a cigarette and tosssed it away unsmoked. He was restless, irritable. A dance-hall queen! What would the old man have said if he still lived?

Maybe it was best old Jeff Giddings had died before this wild northern cattle market had opened. This was the second herd over the trail for John. The last trip, last year, he had met Vance.

His father had been hard as a boil, but righteous living. One of the Texans the history books would someday write about as the founding pioneers. He would have bent a lass rope over his kids' rear ends if they hadn't gone to church of a Sunday.

Jeff Giddings hadn't built his Four-Aces spread to be inherited by any honky-tonk breed. Even this far north and with the old man under the Texas sod, John Giddings could visualize his father's roaring protests. The idea pulled John's mouth tight. He'd gone over every angle of this for a year. Still he yearned for Vance with a longing that made itself felt all over.

He rode in on his riders and drew rein, letting his eyes sort over the ones that could be depended upon. He picked the men who'd been most faithful, the ones too old to give a hoot for Dodge City's pleasures. He named them off slowly.

"Swenson—Buckley—Beahl—Carmody. You four ride herd. Be an extra ten in tomorrow's pay. Rest of you hit the breeze for town. Get goin' before you lose your sight staring at that old helltown!"

They let out yells, fierce and unruly, and raced toward the distant stock pens. The men he had named fell into well-known, familiar tasks. Swenson and Buckley, with saddles on fresh horses, would night-ride the cattle. Carmody, the night hawk, would guard the horse string. Beahl, the old cook, was already pulling the last of the firewood from a sling fashioned between the wagon's wheels. Next came his Dutch ovens.

He was a gnarled, stooped old man, wearing a dusty hickory shirt streaked with grime and wet with sweat about the arm sockets. His eyes lifted to John, and then he spat juice. The dust in his windpipe made his voice crack.

"Gord's pulled in with his critters."

It was a statement, not idle speculation. God alone knew how news traveled along the empty plains, but it did, and old Beahl knew. John nodded, rolled a fresh smoke. Idly he lifted a glance, wondering how much Beahl understood about that Red River fight with Taylor Gord. He said edgily, "I don't count on more trouble from Gord."

"You don't?"

John Giddings sat easily atop his roan horse, a pair of cool blue eyes on Beahl, and Beahl stepped mechanically a bit nearer and laid his hand on the roan's neck.

"Then you're a damned fool, John. You near killed him at Red River!"

"And so I should have. If there hadn't been an easy spot in me, Gord would be down the trail now—sleeping."

Beahl ejected another stream of brown spittle. "Soft spot in every Giddings."

John turned that over and dismissed it. The old cook was one of his earliest recollections of his father's ranch; together, he and Jeff Giddings had torn it from the redskins' grasp. Familiarity could be overlooked in Beahl's case.

He lifted his hand, touching his roan with spurs. "Don't let anything spook the beef!"

"An', young fella, you keep outa the clip-joints!" Beahl yelled.

He rode on, and the herd's dust thinned until the backs of Dodge's South Side buildings took definition in the failing light. He was rubbing his right hand as he rode, a frown piling deep in his face. When he found himself nursing the hand, he dropped it quickly to his side. The fight with Taylor Gord along the Red had shown him how close he stood to death. He could have shot Gord instead of pistol-whipping him. He should have done it. Then the jarring impact of that fight would not have weakened the old bone fracture.

The shock of that blow against Gord's head had traveled along his whole arm, blinding him with pain. As it turned out, not a man of his outfit knew how he suffered. Not a one but respected him as the quickest trigger man to come up the trail. That had probably been true—last year. . . .

Darkness was settling over the holding lots. There was no one to observe him, and to satisfy the nagging dread inside he let his hand slide to his holstered Colt. His fingers fitted around the handle in a stiff grasp. Then he groaned. White light filtered in front of his eyes, and he pulled the gun by will power alone. He would have been killed in that draw before the muzzle started its outward course. The only reason he had whipped Taylor Gord at all was because Gord had been drunk.

It was a good thing for him Vance was the only one in Dodge who knew his wrist had been smashed last year. Vance and that old infantry Doc in his blue surgeon's coat.

As he neared the rows of gray South Side buildings his thoughts went to his sister, Susan. She had kissed him twice when she saw him in the yard ready to leave. Twice she had warned him: not to get into a fight; and second, not to forget their good name. . . .

He pondered the threat of ambush as his roan stepped into the long, dust-cushioned street. A wild Yankee town, born of the railroad and of Texas cattle; a town that didn't give a hoot how many Texas men were buried in its unfenced boot-hill.

Taylor Gord might shoot from the dark alleys, if he meant to carry on the fight. The law of the trail boss had given John the right to kill Gord back there along the Red. But John had preferred to spare a Texas herder's life. They had cut their herds after the fight, and Gord had headed north. And Gord was in Dodge now, his mind festering and sore.

South of the railroad tracks, below the Dead Line, Dodge City's Texas town held a stench of whiskey halls. Even this early, men staggered from the saloons, holding fast to the curb railings. The blare of hurdy-gurdy and piano lay on this street, the shrill song of a woman entertaining behind slatted bar doors. A hell of a place, John thought, for Vance to live and breathe and have her roots.

He had beaten the life out of one hardcase last year over her. That was how he had broken his hand. She had asked him to take her out of there. He should have done it then, but he hadn't.

Kerosene lamps picked out a sign, and he turned his roan in toward the curb. The saloon board held a painted sketch of a girl in dancing costume, and underneath were the words The Lady Gay.

He went inside, and the riotous sounds closed around him. A woman got to him before his smarting eyes grew accustomed to the blaze of light. She had a white face that had once been young, a mouth that seemed too red, and her eyes held a touch of sadness.

"You want a dance, mister?"

He shook his head.

"Come on, mister!"

When she saw how it was, she spun away. He touched her arm and slipped a silver coin inside her fingers. At once the smile returned.

"I'm looking for Vance," he said.

The girl hunched a bare shoulder. "Never heard of her."

She gave him a cracked bending of her lips as he turned aside. Another man's arms slipped around her back. That was the last he saw of her in the press of bodies that closed between them. Texas herders up the dry trail from south, gamblers in black, cattle buyers anxious to make a quick deal, buffalo hunters. . . . John walked up to the bar, and a busy bartender set him up. He lifted his glass, thinking this was the way he had found Vance. She had been singing on the stage, the way this girl up there was singing now, and when he turned he'd looked into her face. Stars in the night, they had been. Stars in the soft sky after the hell of a prairie storm. He could still catch the throbbing, warm echoes of her voice. . . . Slowly he turned.

But this one was rouged, plump, disappointing. She was singing harshly:

> You're wild and woolly
> And full of fleas;
> Ain't never been curried
> Below your knees.

He wheeled back and stared into the steel-hard eyes of the bartender. He laid a second silver dollar on the counter.

"I'm looking for Vance."

The bartender's eyes lidded—a cagey, watchful man. "Friend of his?"

"*Her*. She used to sing here." His hand lifted to about shoulder high; he was seeing her smile as she stood beneath those downturned fingers.

"Vance will be glad to see me," he said.

"All right." The bartender grinned. "She left here and went back into the millinery business. She was a milliner before her husband brought her out here. Eleven and a half Railroad Avenue." The bartender scowled. "She'll kill me if you ain't the one she's been expectin'."

John went out and got onto his roan. He felt his veins fill with the sweep of fresh blood. Vance had left this place because of what lay between them, because she had believed he would be back. . . .

He found the number on Railroad Avenue and put his roan to the hitch rack. It was a small shop, and a quick doubt struck him. Could Vance make a living here? Was millinery the only trade at which she worked? It was dark along the front quarter, and he went up the side alley and found a faint light at the rear. He paused, with his fingers poised to rap.

This town was a baited trap; the warning lay in the empty wind, the motionless shadows steeped against the yard fence. It would have been more sensible to have put his roan into a livery; here on the street before Vance's shop, Taylor Gord would be watching for the roan.

Then he shrugged and knocked. She opened the door a few inches. When lamplight brushed his shoulders she flung the door wide. He thought first she meant to come into his arms, but then she drifted deeper into her kichen. The color left her cheeks.

He put out a hand. She came to him, and he knew she had waited for this, wanted it. A soft cloud spun around him, a strumming of his senses. And yet there was no response from her lips.

She was the same, with her red hair let down and lying in a fold against her shoulders. It was only the look behind her eyes that stilled him. A dread that stole her luster.

"Vance," he said, "I've been dreaming of this. It's been a whole year."

She nodded, but vaguely. Her voice was throaty, sweet, as he remembered.

"John, there are men in Dodge who say you cheated a herder on the trail."

He drew a long breath. "Taylor Gord!"

"He says you pooled herds and then stole four hundred of his cattle."

His voice went flat. "You believe it, Vance?"

She pulled on his arm, irritated. "John, I'm merely warning you!"

"Do you believe it?" he repeated.

"Marshal Earp may believe it. He'll make you trouble!"

He shook his head. "It's you I'm interested in," he said.

"I'm ready to listen to you, John. We've been through a great deal—I want to be careful now. I—I've missed you. And now I've got to know."

Anger pulled him. He snatched his hat from the table. So this was it. She was doubting him—asking him to explain. A dance-hall woman!

Her voice broke against him, pained and sharp and brittle, "John, please!"

He went on out. He thought again of Susan, and a flush crept up his cheeks. Yes, that shop in front—too small for a girl to make an honest living! He'd dreamed himself into an ugly mess—like a kid with a wild first crush on a girl.

"They'll kill you, John!" she sobbed. She was running beside him, trying to keep step in the narrow alley. "This could be a trap—to draw you into a fight."

"They wouldn't tempt a Giddings that way."

"What about your hand?"

He wheeled, let his palms run out to touch her shoulders. "Just what do you mean by that?"

She whispered, "The doctor told me. Sometimes a man can't draw a gun after his hand is broken."

"Did you tell anyone that?"

"No, but Rath's still in town, that man you whipped in the dance hall."

"You been seeing that one again?"

"No, John! There hasn't been anyone."

"Don't lie to me, Vance," he said harshly.

Her breath came in a sudden rush. "I waited a year—hoping, praying you hadn't forgotten. Now you come in like the wrath of God and treat me like—like a cheap woman!"

He stalked on, a dull emptiness in him. It was sooty dark beneath the front awning, and she clung close to his side when he struck the boardwalk. Then a sudden, somber warning swept through his senses. She was close to him, keeping pace, pleading for him to listen. He put his hand against her shoulder and sent her spinning backward. The first shot rang out while he was still shoving her into the darkened alley.

The ball spanged past his head and splintered the gallery post. From the corner of his eye John noted a balcony of Deacon Cox's hotel across Railroad Avenue at Front. What a fool he'd been! Of course they'd watch Vance's place. For days Rath had been planning, and perhaps Taylor Gord had run into Rath. Rath knew his fist had been smashed that night. If they didn't kill him, Wyatt Earp would run him in—the marshal allowed no shooting north of the tracks.

He was conscious of Vance's soft cry behind him. He yanked his gun as his boots struck the wagon-rutted dust. His pull seemed deliberate, slow. The gun was a long while coming up. Sweat seeped around his forehead, and pain etched a white light in front of his eyes. Lead was splintering the boardwalk planks behind him.

He lifted the Colt a little above his waist and fired. Four swift shots, all grouped around that last muzzle flare from the balcony.

Now he leaped for the hotel entrance. He went upstairs two steps at a time. He spun onto the balcony, Colt foremost, and found it empty. He went back into a gray hall with cracked plaster and found a table pulled into the passageway at the rear. Above it was an open trap leading to the roof.

He went up, expecting a gun's blast at his head, but he found the roof empty. He walked the edges, found a gutter where a man might have climbed down. And yet he doubted it. They had outsmarted him. The table, the trap above it, had been carefully arranged before the ambush, but the bushwhacker had not used either. While he was up here wasting time the killer had returned to the street.

He came down and met Vance on the walk.

He asked sharply, "Who came out?"

"Rath," she said numbly.

"Which direction did he go?"

She didn't reply for a moment, then, "John, I saw that draw. They'll kill you!"

"Which way, Vance?"

"Let him go. Please, John. Come back to my house."

His mouth was a firm line. "I'll find Gord first. A woman can't very well love a man when she thinks he'd steal a herd. I guess the man can't respect her when he thinks she'd believe it."

She whispered low, "It's what they want. You can't shoot. You can't win!"

He wheeled off and turned and entered Front Street. His shoulders were squared, his head erect, ears alert to catch the sound of death. His hand was swinging close to his holstered Colt. He knew he couldn't get the gun out fast enough to down Gord, but there was no fear in him. He walked into the first saloon.

"I'm looking for Gord," he told the bartender. "When you see him, tell him Giddings wants him."

He walked on down the Plaza. There was a saloon in nearly every building along that hell-packed, roaring strip. The news of his coming ran far in advance. In the Alhambra he stayed a little longer. He saw his buyer, Kirk Goodman, at the bar counter.

Kirk said quietly, "There's a lien against your cattle. Earp will have to impound them until the brands are examined. I'm sorry, John."

John Giddings shrugged, the frown deep in his brown face. "Tomorrow's still another day."

"But why are they trying anything like this? I know the herd is straight. Earp will find that out in the morning, of course. What will it gain Taylor Gord?"

John Giddings knew. Even Vance had known and tried to warn him. A cold anger gnawed at him as he stared into the bar mirror. Gord had planned this knowing he wouldn't take it lying down. A Texas man would come up fighting.

And he had a hand that couldn't pull a gun.

Kirk Goodman talked some more. "I overheard Gord say some things. It might add up and make sense to you. He boasted when this was over he was going back to Susan and to hell with John Giddings. It sounded like he wanted you out of the way."

It made sense to John. He'd more than suspected all this before, and now he realized it had been crawling around in Gord's brain, driving him. The way Gord had looked at his sister; the way she'd avoided being with the man.

"Is it as bad as that?" Kirk Goodman murmured.

John walked out of the Alhambra, searching the shadows between the frame and tin buildings. Ab Webster's Alamo Saloon was next. He felt a man bump him lightly, swung swiftly on the balls of his feet.

The man was tall and straight and wore a special Colt against dark trousers pulled down over the tops of his boots. Surveying John, his cool blue eyes were like opaque glass.

"I'd like a little talk, Texan. I'm Wyatt Earp."

There was no expression about his tight mouth—no malice, no trust. John Giddings's eye ran to that Buntline Special. Earp was a master in the way he could let the long barrel drop on a man's head.

John said softly, "I want you to ride out in the morning. Count my brands carefully. Don't miss anything."

The marshal nodded. "I'm riding out," he said. "But that's not what I want now. Step inside so I can buy you a drink. We'll talk."

They edged up to the bar. Men made room and pretended to show no interest. The marshal ordered coffee, stirred it, and had John's whiskey glass refilled before the first shot warmed John's belly.

"This town has got a gun law," he said. "If you mean to keep walking down the Plaza I want your gun."

John said, "I don't give up my gun. Not even to you."

Earp's eyes slitted. "Nor do I let Texans get away with that sort of thing, Giddings."

John's mouth tilted in a frugal smile, and Earp said calmly, "Suppose, Giddings, you don't walk down Front any farther. Go back to your herd. I'll buy you a bottle."

John still shook his head. "I'm walking where I want."

"All right. Then you'll walk to jail." His hand dropped against John's arm.

John looked sharply at Wyatt Earp and knew the marshal was giving it straight. He knew one other thing clearly in that moment. A man did not go against the town boss of Dodge City—especially a man who couldn't shoot.

He said tightly, "You make it hard on a man."

Wyatt Earp shook his head. "I don't want a duel when the walks are crowded. A bullet might hit a drunk, an innocent man. It's my job, Texan. I fill it the best way I can."

John thought a while longer, his chest a tight, constricted knot. It was not much different than it was on the trail. The trail boss had his way there, and his word was law. He had split with Taylor Gord because Gord wouldn't acknowledge this fact.

He said, then, "We'll let it go till morning."

Earp's face broke in a rare smile. "Glad you see it my way. I'll ride out to your holding ground in the morning about that lien. I know how you feel. I wouldn't want any man calling me a thief. If you duel on the prairie I won't interfere."

He walked outside with John, and they moved along the walk together. Standing beside the hitching rail the marshal watched him swing atop his horse, watched him ride slowly out of Dodge City.

John rode in on his herd and saw that the outriders were with the cattle. He hadn't seen a single one of his punchers in Dodge but he knew there would be stiff heads in camp in the morning.

Old man Beahl was asleep in his blankets, and a fire glowed near the wagon. John took his suggans and tossed them the other side of the fire. But first he filled a basin with water and sloshed it over his head and washed his arms, his neck. He took off his boots, unbuckled his gun belt. Then he froze with the Colt's handle against his palm.

A rider was threading his uncertain way between the ground swells. He crouched, waiting, thinking that either Gord or Rath was bringing the fight to him.

The rider came up and called his name. A soft, throaty whisper.

He ran to Vance's horse, and she fell lightly into his arms. He held her off, the pale moon light touching her face.

"We haven't been fair to each other. John, I don't give a *damn* about the cattle!"

His arms pulled her to him, and he searched out her lips. Her cheeks were moist, and he knew the year had been long on them both.

"Vance," he said. "About what happened along the Red——"

She tried to silence him with her arms tight about his neck. But he wouldn't be stopped.

"Gord brought in whiskey from the trail saloon at the crossing. Some drifters set up a shanty along the riverbanks and sell rotgut to the herders. It doesn't matter what a trail puncher does when he's in town, on his own time. But on the trail there's no liquor for my men. I ordered Gord to break his bottles, and he got ugly. When he reached for his gun I slugged him."

"I knew it would have to be something like that."

He said, "Vance, is it true you were married before?"

Her eyes fell to the campfire, avoiding him. "Do you want me to tell you about it?"

"I wouldn't mind listening."

She looked up full into his face. "Stephen wasn't well when we came West. When we got this far he grew worse. We stayed here until our money gave out. And then Steve died. I—I was still working to pay for his funeral the time you heard me sing in that place."

"Then you haven't had any men around since you opened the shop?"

"Why, of course! I've been waiting for spring. For you to come up with another herd!"

He could almost hear Susan give a sigh, across all those barren miles.

He watched Vance a moment longer and then he reached out his arms and pulled her to him.

Beahl was surly in the morning. His sidelong glance shifted to John, and he was grumbling, "Soft spot in every Giddings."

Had he been aware last night of Vance riding into camp? Had he kept one eye open while he snored?

John caught a dust trail stirring the prairie and called Swenson beside him. Squinting, he gazed toward the stock pens.

"It's Wyatt Earp," he decided presently. "When he rides up make sure he sees every brand in our herd."

"How about you, boss?"

"I'll be heading for Dodge."

He slipped his toe into a wide stirrup and climbed into saddle. Carmody had roped him a gray horse that hadn't been saddled for a few days. It got him to Dodge in a hurry.

The South Side was slumbering the dull sleep of the exhausted. There was no heat in the morning sun, and Bridge Street was empty and without dust. Only a few drays were in motion along Front where it widened to form the Plaza. He thought to himself, *It's not as dead as it looks.* Gord would be waiting.

He put his gray to an empty rack below the Dead Line and quit saddle. The quiet Plaza beckoned him on. He moved down the center of the still dust, glance drifting to each hushed saloon. A few men were inside; he could feel their restless eyes.

He got to the middle of the block and could look along the railroad track and see Vance's place on the fringe of the respectable section of town. Her shop was closed tight, and he was glad she was not yet up.

He could feel the tension begin to mount within him. His hand edged closer to his gun butt. The sun's rays sent a man's shadow stretching out across the boards. Then Gord followed, out into open sight and into the Plaza. He was grinning. He knew John Giddings couldn't pull a gun.

They were thirty paces apart when John said, "That'll do!"

He waited until Gord's hand slid after his gun and then he reached. Blinding pain shot through his hand before he got the big Colt out.

Another shadow was running into the middle of the Plaza. He heard Gord's gun bang, and it turned his heart to stone. A woman had run between them, he saw her sag and go down under Gord's slug. He knew then Vance had been watching every move Gord made.

Now Gord was looking directly at him, his face white, too stunned to lift his Colt for a second shot. John shot him then.

He ran forward and bent above Vance. She smiled at him around her pain. "We could get it done—together!" she murmured.

He lifted her gently against his arm and found the slug had torn through her shoulder. It was high above her chest, staining her white shirtwaist, making it appear worse than it was. She'd be all right if he got her to the doctor. That Yankee sawbones wasn't much good at setting fractures, but Dodge and the war had taught him how to dress bullet wounds. Vance would be all right.

He got her into his arms and started down the center of the wagon track. Men were crowding the front doorways, watching, but he paid no heed.

"You can put your gun away," Vance told him meekly. "Wyatt Earp ran Rath into jail last night for starting a fight above the Dead Line. He meant to tell you that this morning."

He said slowly, "You think you can stand a stage trip after the doc fixes you up? Sue'll take wonderful care of you as soon as we get to Texas."

She was silent a moment. "Will your sister like me, John?"

"She'll love you, Vance. Almost as much as me."

It wasn't true. Nobody could love her anywhere near as much as he did.

The Old Copper Collar

Dan Cushman

THE FIRST balloting for United States Senator had been scheduled for noon at the joint session. Shortly after ten o'clock word came down that the investigating committee, after working throughout the night, was ready to present its preliminary report to that same session. This was fast action, and it sent rumors through the city. Business came to a standstill. Many places closed their doors as clerks and owners alike hurried to the Capitol. At 12:14, when the joint session was called to order, the galleries were jammed and crowds filled the corridors beyond.

The first ballot for Senator proceeded as expected, with O'Hanlon scoring 32, Bennett 14, Bundy 12, Gleason 9, and the remainder split widely, with no candidate garnering more than three. Senator Stockman then rose, straight as a broom, with his stiff pompadour adding to the resemblance, and announced to Lieutenant Governor Cherill, pre-

Dan Cushman has written of Africa's steaming jungles with just about as much verve and credibility as he has of America's arid mountains and plains. But his best and most characteristic work has been done in Western settings: *Badlands Justice* and *Tall Wyoming, Stay Away, Joe* and *The Old Copper Collar*, and an excellent historical novel, *The Silver Mountain*. Dan lives in Great Falls, Montana, with his wife and children.

siding, that a preliminary report of the Special Joint Committee to Investigate Allegations of Bribery had been written. This, he said, the Secretary of the Senate was prepared to read. Senator Havinghurst at that moment rose and obtained recognition. Havinghurst's success with the Chair caused a stir of surprise, because the presiding officer was most favorably disposed toward the Company while Havinghurst had become identified with the Bennett faction. The Chair however allowed Havinghurst to address the joint session on a point of personal privilege.

Havinghurst advanced to the front, struck a pose reminiscent of the Revolutionary War statesman in schoolroom prints, and launched forth into what was to be the great scene of his life.

"Mr. Chairman," he said. "Gentlemen of the joint session." He looked around the galleries with men filling every square foot of space and drifting cigar smoke indicating more hundreds in the open corridors beyond. "Gentlemen of the State of Montana. My fellow citizens. From the moment I stepped off the Northern Pacific passenger train on the thirtieth of December last, arriving here to assume the office to which the voters of my county elected me, I was aware of reports to the effect that Mr. H. B. Bennett was offering large amounts of cash in his attempt to persuade this legislature to elect him United States Senator. Specifically, I heard charges of attempts at bribery, and in order to test the truth of these rumors I decided to offer myself as a likely recipient of such bribes. This I did . . ."

The crowd quieted. It heard with fascinated attention how, working inside the Bennett camp, Havinghurst had secured "documented evidence" of bribery. To *prove* Bennett bribery "beyond the peradventure of a doubt," was how he chose to put it. He soon realized this was too much for one man. He therefore elected to enlist the aid of certain public-spirited statesmen whose honesty was beyond all question, being associated with no faction or group. These men were Senators H. V. Gill of Virginia City, W. R. Cox of Mineral Springs, and Representative Scott Hensman of Great Falls. Each of these men, he said, made known his willingness to vote for H. B. Bennett provided the price was right. In due course meetings were set up with Mr. Walker Lorenz in room 302 and in other rooms of the Grand Western Hotel. The result of these meetings was an agreement to deliver the votes for a sum of $10,000 each.

To an audience now breathless, Havinghurst described how ten one-thousand-dollar bills had been placed in each of three manila envelopes, each sealed within sight of the pretended bribetaker, his name inscribed, and each marked with an ink blot for future identification. This done, Havinghurst had himself, as a middleman, taken charge of the envelopes, it being agreed that he should hold them until Gill, Cox, and Hensman had carried out their agreements to vote for H. B. Bennett each time they were called on to do so in that session.

At this point the galleries packed with Bennett sympathizers commenced heckling him with suggestions that he wore the Copper Collar, but these hoots and catcalls he contemptuously ignored, reiterated his freedom from all cliques, factions, and corporations and that his purpose had been purely and simply to prove or disprove unlawful practices, and sat down.

The report of the joint committee was then read. This proved anticlimactic until the Secretary of the Senate produced the three ink-blotted manila envelopes previously described by Havinghurst, opened them, and removed a total of thirty thousand dollars, all in thousand-dollar bills, and stacked them on a table for all to see. On the audience, most of whom saw little more than a thousand dollars in a year of earning, it produced quite an effect.

Excitement long pent now slipped its bonds. The floor became a scene of turmoil. Spectators mingled in equality with senators and representatives, all crowding forward to get a look at the money. Jarvis, a representative from Silver Bow County, attempted to move for a ballot on the senatorship which, in view of the demoralization of Bennett's forces, might have produced a quick Company victory. He could not be heard in the uproar. He was still screaming, "Mr. Chairman! Mr. Chairman!" when Kingsley, a Republican, shouted, "I move for adjournment!" The chairman, beating his gavel, tried to recognize "The gentleman from Silver Bow," but others were yelling "Aye!" for adjournment and thought that the gavel had ended the session. Jarvis kept trying, but by the time Bleeker and O'Keefe had rallied assistance there was no longer a quorum nor hope of securing one that day.

Fred Bennett had not gone to the Capitol. At 12:30 he talked to H.B. on the phone. He did not mention his conversation with Maureen. He felt unpleasantly keyed up. He was unable to eat lunch. Outside, the street was ominously deserted. A phone rang and his bones nearly leaped from his body. It was Campbell, with the result of the first ballot. Campbell was quite gratified with the initial support for H.B.

"What of the joint committee?"

"I'm not a bit worried."

Fred moved through the empty rooms. The phone lay quiet as a fossil in the sea. He rolled and smoked cigarettes, leaving dead butts on the edges of furniture and in the ash trays. When he could endure it no longer he went to the street. Most of the stores and saloons were locked. Through a window at the corner of Sixth and Main, he could see Levi Goodman with a magnifier over one eye, working through the bowels of a watch. He went inside, looked at a rather unsatisfactory selection of solitaire rings, and chose instead a lapel watch of green gold set with crescent-cut rubies. Levi had a card and promised to deliver the watch to Miss Maureen O'Keefe at the Western. Fred had been out half an hour. The street was still deserted. He wanted to remain longer and kill the hours of waiting, but he felt the counterurge to hurry back, the alarm of the telephone ringing.

It was not ringing. Two bartenders killed time in the reception room. The phone had not rung. He was tempted to have just one brandy. He resisted it. He smoked. His mouth was like a burned-over prairie.

At a quarter past three Cletus appeared and drew up, popeyed, to look at him.

"What the devil's wrong with you?"

"I heard it! I heard the state militia is out. It's out and they coming."

"What are you talking about?"

"I hear they comin' to arrest Mist' Lorenz. I hear he's sentenced to forty years in the penitentiary."

"Quit jibbering!"

"They do it! They send 'em to the penitentiary for it."

"For what?"

"Bribery."

"Who told you all this?"

"Red the bellboy! He heard it."

Fred said, "To hell with Red the bellboy." He started rolling another cigarette. He wadded it and flung it at a spittoon. Cletus remained staring at him.

"Mist' Freddy, you don't suppose they'll come up here and git you?"

"I haven't bribed anybody." He tried to laugh.

"No, you ain't! You're innocent. When a man's innocent he's got nothing to be afraid of. That's true. An innocent man he's got *nothing* to be afraid of."

"Did Red say they were after me too?"

"Well, he said something. But he's such a liar. That's what he is. He's a little redheaded liar. And he did say something about arresting your fatha!"

Fred produced a laugh. That would be something to behold—the old man behind bars.

"No sir, they wouldn't *dare* arrest Mist' Freddy and his fatha! Ol' militia try and arrest any Bennetts and Colonel Roosevelt he'd hear about it and call out his Rough Riders, and they'd come rearing out here——"

"Oh, keep quiet."

"Yessah."

He was quiet. All the hotel lay quiet. Cletus tiptoed to the window. There was nothing out there. No militia.

Fred said, "I never saw the town so quiet. What the hell do you suppose they're doing up there?"

There was nothing to do but wait. Wait. He lit an old cigarette. He lay on the couch with hands clasped back of his head. He could hear the bartenders tinkling bottles, waiting. Distantly, through walls, a telephone bell. It rang and rang. Nobody answered it. It stopped. The quiet was long. The elevator door rumbled open and shut. Someone entered the reception room. Fred sat up.

"With ice?" asked the bartender.

"No, no." It was Judge Gibbons. He was taking a drink straight. He looked and saw Fred. "Very rough. I've been standing. Very rough."

"What happened?"

He downed the whiskey. It gave him the needed energy. In brief, uncompromising sentences he told Fred what had happened.

"Havinghurst!" Fred could not prevent a bitter gloat of gratification. Lorenz's great friend! "Well, now what?"

"Nothing more today. They were trying for a ballot, but there was some very quick thinking on the part of a Republican forestalled it."

"The militia?" asked Fred, not listening.

"What's that?"

"Cletus informed me that there was talk of calling out the militia."

"I believe they will try criminal procedure."

"The militia would be flattering, anyway."

"Actually, I believe this will be their key error."

"To bring charges? Why? They have evidence and testimony."

"My boy, it will call for the grand jury. That will of necessity be a

Lewis and Clark County venire. This county can always be depended upon to treat H. B. Bennett with justice."

The Judge meant that Helena would countenance anything as long as it was committed against Regan and Cobra Copper.

"Anyhow, it finishes us. You certainly had it right about the Ides of January."

"I had—an inkling."

"Thanks, Judge. I'll see to it you're not forgotten."

They would be all climbing on the O'Hanlon bandwagon tomorrow. He would have to tell H.B. The Butte line was open. He said, "Hello," and whistled into the mouthpiece until the incisive voice of his father came in answer.

"Dad, have you heard what happened? That smart Lorenz, with all his valuable contacts——"

"Now, wait!"

"Yes?"

"Let's have no more of that. This is no time to quarrel among ourselves. It happened to Walker. It might have happened to anyone. He's not the first man betrayed by his friends."

"You've heard about this afternoon?"

"Lewis has been in touch with me."

"Well——"

"Wait a moment!"

He could hear H.B. talking on another phone. Details crowded his mind. He would wire Minneapolis in an attempt to stop Raffles. And there was the Duryea Motor Wagon. He might as well have it shipped back to New York. And Maureen—he would have to find her. They would leave together. Tonight, perhaps. Yes, it must be tonight. There was nothing to be gained remaining in Helena any longer.

H.B. again, "Are you there, son?"

Wearily, "Yes."

"Now, I was just talking to Lewis at the Capitol. They tried to push through another roll call on Senator and it failed. The Republicans blocked it. That is very hopeful news. Very."

"Great gods, Dad, we only had fourteen votes to begin with, and after this——"

"Don't let this setback discourage you."

"Discourage me! I'm looking at the facts!"

"The facts are that I do not accept defeat this easily."

"Let's face——"

"Are you trying to tell me that you're licked?"

The brittle scorn of H.B.'s tone made him draw back and say, "I didn't mention being licked."

"If you are, admit it." He waited. "Are you or are you not *licked?*"

"No, I'm not licked, but——"

"Very well. You're not licked. I am not licked. Today has been theirs. I hope they celebrate it in a suitable manner. I hope Pat Regan so celebrates it. The final result may not provide such an amply propitious occasion."

"If they go to court——"

"Son, we must not allow the legislature to be stampeded by these untrue allegations."

"Untrue? They had that thirty thousand dollars stacked up on a table for everyone to look at."

"Did *you* give them that thirty thousand dollars?"

"Of course not! Lorenz——"

"You saw Lorenz give it?"

"No."

"Then what do you have but the unsupported word of the Cobra Copper Company?"

"You mean that the Company provided the money?"

"I believe they are capable of raising such an amount."

Fred did not know. He just did not know.

"Son, are you listening?"

"Yes."

"Their big move will be tomorrow. Tomorrow they will make every effort to bring about the election of O'Hanlon. At all costs that must be blocked. Tonight, the next few hours, may be decisive. It makes no difference how, they must be stopped."

"Yes, Dad."

Campbell came in. He looked beaten out. He had fallen somewhere, and there was dirt all down one leg of his blue broadcloth trousers.

"That H.B.?"

"Yes."

"I'll talk."

He was glad to give up the phone.

The hotel had suddenly filled. Exultant voices came through from the Company floor above. Newsboys outside screamed *The Citizen.* Already it had the full story. Obviously the story had been set in type ready to roll while the session was still in progress. The Company had indeed been well advised. "Bennett bribers caught red-handed!" cried a shrill newsboy on the sidewalk below. "Thirty thousand dollars stacked up for all to see!"

Bennett campaign workers were in the reception room, silently bracing themselves with whiskey. Lorenz arrived with White, Longfelt, and two members of the Helena police force. Lorenz had been in the Capitol gallery all afternoon. At adjournment he had tried to escape down a side corridor. Someone saw him and almost knocked him down with a huge, watersoaked lump of newspaper. Fearing for his life, he waited at a rear entrance until the police hack could come for him. His pink complexion had vanished. His face looked hollow. He looked gaunt, with fat that hung on him in bags and pouches. He tossed off a whiskey, and another. His breathing was audibly distraught. Fred sent Cletus to bring him to the office. He nodded without hearing and controlled his nerves while pouring still another drink. The first two commenced having an effect, he heard Cletus, and at last, carrying the third drink, walked to Fred's tiny office.

"Close the door."

He did. "Havinghurst!" he whispered. He commenced to curse. He cursed with an unusually vile choice of epithets, fervently, like an incantation of evil, naming Havinghurst.

"You *did*," said Fred. "You did give him that money."

Lorenz turned on him. Spots of color had appeared in the grayness of his cheeks. With shaking fingers he put his glass of whiskey down. He opened and closed his fists, using a stiff contraction of muscles that made his knuckles pop. He lifted a fist and drove it straight down to the table with a force that made his whiskey jump.

"I did *not* give them money, sir! I gave them not one penny! Allow me to make that fact plain to you, my bright young sir! You've been waiting here to crow at me, haven't you? In this room, safe and snug from their abuse, you've been waiting, haven't you? All the time I was there facing them! Facing them, listening to their jibes and their sneers, being pelted with wet balls of paper, risking my life to a mob. That is where I have been, my brave young sir, while you have waited here. Well, let me tell you this—that which took place this afternoon was a swinish trick engendered in the fertile brain of Mr. Archy O'Keefe, the parent of your much trusted sweetheart——"

"That's enough!"

"No, it is not enough. You will let me be the judge of what is or is not enough!"

"Leave Maureen out of this."

"I will not leave her out of it, because she is most definitely in it. I propose to talk straight to you, young sir. I'll tell you what is obvious to every worker in this campaign—that she was thrown in your path for the purpose of gaining information."

"That's a lie!"

"It is not a lie. They have tried to use you. In fact they have used you. And laughed behind your back while they were using you. Are you aware of her actions over the weekend? Did you know that she traveled alone and unescorted with Mr. Leroy Stockman to some unknown destination——"

"She went with him to Bakerville to meet his mother, who returned with them, and there was no secret about it."

"She is engaged to marry him, but you will notice that she has not announced *that!*"

"Oh, the hell——"

"I have heard it on the good authority of his mother."

"That's ridiculous."

"Oh, is it? Is it indeed! You have been hoodwinked in one transparent manner after another from the moment you arrived. You have . . ." Lorenz checked himself. It took an effort. He shuddered and breathed very deeply. His knuckles oozed blood where the skin had been bruised against the table. He whispered, "You accused me, Fred. You accused me unjustly."

He had shocked Fred into believing him. "I have your word on that?"

"My solemn word as a gentleman."

"The thirty thousand did not come from you?"

"It did not. Look at the holes in their story! Observe that *he* wrote the names Hensman, Cox, and Gill on those ridiculous ink-blot envelopes. If I had directed it, wouldn't I have written their names? But no, Havinghurst wrote the names. And were I to bribe someone, would I be such a fool as to do so in the presence of witnesses? Were I a scoundrel, I would still know better than that!"

"That's all right, Walker. I believe you."

"Thanks, Fred. Thank you, Fred."

"I was just talking to H.B. We can't stand around pitying ourselves.

We have to hold the line. We have to deadlock that joint session to-morrow."

"That's talking, Fred. Now you're talking like a *Bennett!*"

He felt they had made a fool of him. Slowly anger tingled through him, a hot hate and anger for the Company and all its double-dealing hypocritical cohorts. He doubled his fists and vowed yes, he would hold them. He would deadlock that joint session tomorrow if it was the last act of his life.

He counted the votes he could be sure of. They were precious few. He was glad for the index file. It was one firm rock in the rapids of chaos. He called a meeting. Everyone was there except for Joe Duncan who was at the Capitol talking to State Senator Bradbury.

"All right," he said, pulling Bradbury's card, "he's Joe's man."

He assigned all the votes. The Company men were staging a stamping, whooping celebration on the floor above. He wished them glad spirits. He wished them hours of thoughtless joy while he fought for time through a deadlock.

"For you, Fred," said Judge Gibbons, whom he had put in charge of the telephone. "It's Joe Duncan."

"Let me talk to him."

Bradbury, said Duncan, was convinced that the Company would win. He could not afford to antagonize them.

"What's his ambition in life?"

"He wants to be agent at the Blackfoot Reservation."

"Tell him the job is his. H.B. will set it up with Dickert."

"I did tell him that. He's still afraid."

"Where is he now?"

"In the bathroom."

"Bring him here."

"I don't dare. Those Company fellows are outside with a hack."

"Which Company fellows?"

"Hale and Garrity."

"I'll call the cops." He hung up and said to Gibbons, "Judge, you know about these things; I want Hale and Garrity arrested. Think of something that will make a good news story."

Gleason and White arrived with Representative Wallace between them. "Now, Eddie," Gleason was saying to him, "I know everything you're going to say, but it won't hurt to have a couple of drinks of good eighteen-year-old bourbon whiskey."

"I can't be seen here. I can't afford it."

"What do you mean, can't afford it? You can't afford not to. We're the winning side."

"If they do bring charges, and the jury finds Bennett guilty, then———"

"Yes, Eddie, but suppose they're a bunch of conniving liars, and we prove it, and H.B. ends up in Washington, and the honest Democrats get hold of the state administration, then what? The point is, Eddie, you're in a hell of a spot if you make the wrong stand either way. So my advice to you is stand pat and don't vote for us or the Company until you can see which way the cat's going to jump."

Wallace stood and thought about it.

The Judge, one hand over the telephone, called, "Hey, Fred, how about charging them with indecent exposure?"

"Oh no! Make it lewd and lascivious conduct." He got White to one side. "Where's Whittaker?"

"I couldn't locate him."

"Do those Company sappers have him?"

"I don't know!"

Lewis came in. He was in a hurry. He waited for the telephone. The Judge was saying, "That's right, Byron. Don't you worry about that. You go ahead with the arrest, we'll produce the witness."

Lewis waited. He heard them talking about Whittaker. He said, "Put a copper on that blond knock-kneed Ginny up at Belle's place and before the night's out you'll find Whittaker."

"I think the Company has him."

"It'll take more than the Company to keep him away from Ginny."

White wanted to use the telephone too. He got in line.

"Why can't we have more than one phone? The Company has four."

The Judge hung up, but before Lewis could get Central, a call came in from Major Chapman. Fred answered it while Lewis and White still waited.

"Is Flaherty good for a three-thousand loan?"

"Yes, but bring him up here. We have to work through Mulligan."

"God damn it," said Lewis, "get off the phone."

They had to have at least one more telephone. Fred went downstairs and found Charlie Monroe. Monroe had lost all his hotel manager's obsequiousness. He was just barely civil. There were no more phone lines available.

"The Company has four of them!"

"And arranged for them far in advance. The Company gets no favored treatment here."

Fred wanted to climb over the counter after him.

"Get me at least one more line."

"I tell you there are no more lines available."

"Pull one from the Company!" shouted Fred.

Monroe indicated with a smirk that Fred's demands no longer meant a thing to him. "You Bennetts! You think you can just walk through the world telling everyone how to run his business and people will jump and say 'yes, sir,' and 'no, sir,' but as far as this place is concerned that day has passed. Let me tell you something—being a Bennett cuts no ice with me. Wake up, Freddy! You Bennetts are on your way out as far as this state is concerned."

In a charging anger Fred headed for the elevator. He found it so jammed full of Company men that the operator could not get the door closed. They hooted and waved. "H'ray for Fred Bennett! H'ray! H'ray!" They were half drunk and having one hell of a time. He answered unprintably and went up the stairs three at a stride, reaching his floor as the elevator labored past.

"H'ray! H'ray!" they were yelling.

"H.B. from Butte, Fred! H.B.'s on the phone."

"Tell him Holtcamp has withdrawn," said Campbell. Holtcamp of Deer Lodge had received two votes in that day's balloting.

"Withdrawn in whose favor?"

"Nobody's. He just withdrew."

"Who voted for him besides Pete Vining?"

"Deeves."

He picked up the phone.

"Now, Fred, listen. Both Vining and Deeves can be controlled——"

"That's just it. They can be controlled by the Company too, and where in hell are they?"

"You don't know?"

"No! And there's a dozen more we've lost track of."

"You must find them!"

"I know. Good God, Dad, you don't have to telephone to tell me that. In fact, all this telephoning is just wasting my time. If——"

"Very well, I merely wanted to inform you that I have contacted Dickert, and the agency job is definitely Bradbury's if he stays with us. Now, is Lorenz there?"

"Walker!"

All through the room men shouted, "Walker!"

Four men were lined up waiting for the city phone. That bastardly Charlie Monroe! He had hamstrung them on the telephones. Fred wished he had his .30–40 Krag rifle. If he had his good old .30–40 Krag he would go down there and get another line from Charlie Monroe. Gleason was pleading for just half a minute's time on the phone. He had to call Belle's.

"This is no time to think about women," said Longfelt.

"I'm not thinking about women. Lewis told me to get Ginny up here and stake her out because it's probably the only chance we have of getting Whittaker away from the Company."

Ed Vaney came in and said, "Fred, we ought to have somebody on the doors at the lobby so we'll know who goes in and out. I'm sure I just saw Fowell."

"Who with?"

"Little Chief Richards."

He cursed. Fowell was one of the doubtful votes. He wondered how many more the Company had upstairs. He could hear the celebration booming along. With voices and stamping feet now came the sounds of music—a piano, a cornet, a fiddle . . .

"I'm going up there," he said. "They can't hold a man prisoner."

"I tried going up there. They got that punch-drunk wrestler named Cowboy Brown on guard, and he gave me the bum's rush into the elevator."

"Then call the cops."

The telephone miraculously stood idle. He made a dive for it but he lifted the receiver and there was Dugan on the other end of the line.

"Get off, Dugan, I have to call the bobbies."

"I have O'Mara in tow."

"Fine! Where's Mulligan?"

"That's just it. He's gone over to the Company. He says to hell with you and your bribery, he's going to vote for a good Irishman tomorrow —O'Hanlon."

"Bring O'Mara here. I've thought of something."

What he'd do was give O'Mara ten thousand dollars out of the suitcase and turn him loose. Once Mulligan got a look at all that money . . .

Sutton had learned from Neil the bellboy that nine men, key votes every one of them, were being held upstairs by the Company. Fowell was one, and Cully and Howard, and Neil had promised on his next trip with chipped ice to learn the identity of the others.

Fred knew without looking at his card index that these defections would almost be enough to beat them.

He strode to the hall. The music and shouting came plainly down the stairway. He started up, but Cowboy Brown blocked his way. Brown looked like Neanderthal man, with ball-shaped ears and eyes almost hidden beneath growths of scar tissue.

"Move aside," said Fred.

"You got to have a card."

"Wait!" said a voice from the top of the stairs. It was Little Chief Richards. "Hello, Fred. How's the boy? Sorry I can't ask you up. Another time and you'd be sure as hell welcome, but——"

"Listen, Chief, I know who you're holding up there and——"

"Don't start any trouble."

Fred tried to get past, but Richards gave the sign and Brown flung him down again. Fred lay sprawling. He got up and shook his fist. "I'll run you out of there if I have to burn the place down."

"We got witnesses you said that!"

Lewis and the boys were all around Fred arguing him back to the reception room. H.B. was on the phone again. "Oh, the hell with him," said Fred. Great gods, what was he going to do? He couldn't do much without telephones. Or even *with* phones, as long as the Company held those nine votes. . . .

Longfelt said he had seen Vining. Vining promised to keep voting for Connell. It cost him a five-thousand-dollar loan. He needed ten thousand more. Fred gave it to him. Campbell got through on the wire. He said the Republicans were still holding solid for the party. And H.B. insisted that he come to the Butte phone.

"Now, son, I have purchased Bob Work's overdue chattel and all his land mortgages from the Heston State Bank," H.B. said in his cold-chisel voice. "Let him be advised of that, and let him further be advised that should he vote for O'Hanlon tomorrow I will sell him out, every stick, cow, and clod of dirt."

"If I can find him."

"We got Whittaker!" H. T. Lewis yelled, striding in. "He followed Ginny right into the elevator."

"Tell her to keep him there. It's worth a fur coat with a thousand-dollar bill in the pocket if she keeps him there."

"Oh, make it fifty bucks. She understands that kind of money."

Still, all was lost, all lost with those ten pivotal votes upstairs.

He asked for coffee. He sat rubbing his forehead, trying to concentrate. "Does Herb Sislow still own this hotel?"

He did. Campbell knew where to find him. Fred got hat, coat, and checkbook. The weather had turned cold again. It was twenty-two degrees below zero by the thermometer under the marquee. They stamped in the cold, waiting as bellboys raced the streets searching for a hack. None could be found. At last they secured a rig from the Apex livery stables—an open buggy with an old gray team the driver refused to extend past a dreary jog in the frigid temperature.

Sislow lived in a big red-brick house beyond the electric lines. All the front windows had been boarded up. They went around back, hammering and shouting, until he finally came to the door in his long underwear.

"It wasn't locked," he said, holding a kerosene lamp and squinting out their identity. "All you needed to do was walk right in."

He was a leathery old bachelor with a home-roached beard and quick blue eyes.

"What's the matter?" he asked. "Is there something gone wrong down at the hotel? I only show up there once a month to look through the books. I just leave everything to Charlie Monroe."

"Fine hotel," Fred told him. "I'd like to own it."

"Why, it *is* a good hotel. A real money-maker. I'd be glad to show you Bennetts the accounts."

"Give you one hundred and fifty thousand," Fred said.

"No-o, I wouldn't part with that select property for much shy of half a million. Cleared forty-one thousand on it last year. You know how much money forty-one thousand is six per cent of? Almost seven hundred thousand dollars!"

"I'll give you two hundred and fifty thousand dollars, and that's more than it cost to build."

Sislow was crafty now. There was a large bowl of eggs on the kitchen table. He chose one fine specimen and turned it in his hands.

"Finest food in the world," he said. "I eat fourteen, fifteen eggs a day."

Look at me. I can climb up any of these hills, just as good as in '63 when I first came to the country. Came same year as your daddy. Remember him well. Both lit in Chinytown, other side of Bannack. I had a piece of a claim on Jeff Davis Gulch. Your daddy was a miner too, only he more mined the miner. Tell you about H.B.—he was a wonder. Do you know that he could look at the way the smoke drifted from a man's chimney and tell what he'd be short on next winter? He'd meet the freight outfits away over in Idaho, buy up every lick of something, keep mum, not say a word, and all of a sudden when you went to buy some next winter he was the only man that had it. And would he heap the price on! He never got me only once, and that time I paid him three ounces of gold for a pound of chewing tobacco. Just common old Kentucky dogleg. That Jeff Davis dust was nine hundred fine except for the big nuggets that didn't run so high, and close as I could figure it cost me twenty-five cents a chew for that tobacco. At a price like that a man will keep chewing and chewing until it spits the color of cabbage, and then if there's some left he'll dry it and smoke it."

Fred knew time was running right along, but he also knew it was better not to hurry Sislow because all this would conclude with the price of his hotel.

Sislow got to laughing and shaking his head. "Oh, you got to watch your step with H.B.! I remember there was a fellow in that same Chinytown by the name of Hoss Rawnig who *did* find that out. He was a great betting man, Hoss was. He'd get to arguing about something at the top of his voice and you'd think he was the most ignorant man alive. For instance, he'd admit the world was round, not round like a ball but like a saucer. He said it *had* to be round like a saucer with mountains for a rim or else all the oceans would run over the edge and leave it dry as a bone. He'd get people to arguing with him and he had a terrible loud voice and he'd just shout 'em down. He'd claim to be so damned smart it'd make people mad, and then they'd bet with him. Of course that was what he wanted. He might claim he was able to guess the weight of a rock closer than any man in the whole country. He'd say, 'Take that piece of quartz out there. How much you say it weighs?' And he'd get the other fellow to guessing and arguing about who was the closer and of course he knew what it was right to the ounce, because maybe a month before he'd weighed it and left it there.

"Well, one night H.B. came in real late. He'd been out peddling pots and pans, lending fellows money at twenty-per-cent interest on good security, things like that. There was a pole awning along one side of this little sort of store he had, and he pulled in under it but he didn't put up right away; it was real fine at that hour, two or three in the morning; you can smell the pines, and the stars seem real close there in the hills, and I suppose he was figuring who he could do out of a bit of cash the next day, when all of a sudden he noticed somebody come around quiet, leading a cow. It was Mrs. Mulvaney's milk cow, the only one in camp. Now, most fellows would probably gone over to see who was stealing that poor widow woman's cow, but not H.B. He stayed right where he was, not moving a muscle, and it turned out to be Hoss Rawnig. Hoss had a halter on that cow and he led her up a little ramp to weigh her on some scales that the California-Idaho Company had installed in front of its freight house.

"Next day, of course, H.B. didn't go out with his stuff at all. He stayed around town and pretty soon he got in this terrible argument with Rawnig. You could hear Rawnig all over town saying it was true, he was the only man in the territory that could guess the weight of a *cow* right to the ten pounds. They bet and bet and bet and Hoss thought he was going to get it back for all that chewing tobacco H.B. had sold him, but he didn't. Your father had him. He'd slipped around and fed that cow salt oatmeal so she was holding about thirty pounds of water in her, and by the God he taught Rawnig a lesson he never forgot. And so, I'm going to think for a while about selling you my hotel."

They settled on a price of $327,000. Fred wrote the check. He asked Sislow to come and verify his ownership to Monroe. It was after 1 A.M. Men still formed groups in the lobby and the bar. Charlie Monroe stood alert behind the desk.

"Charlie, old boy," said Fred with hearty benevolence, "I got a surprise for you. You're fired."

"He can do it," said Sislow. "He can if he wants to, Charlie. He owns the joint."

Monroe looked as if he had been shot.

"Hurry up," Fred told him. "Get your hat and coat. Get from behind my counter. I won't have you on my premises." He motioned to the night clerk. "Come on, Archy. Put a carnation in your buttonhole, you're the manager now. Get a move on. Call the janitor. Tell him to shut off the heat on the fourth floor. Turn off the water. Turn everything off. Turn off the electricity. Cut the phones. Open the skylights.

We got to air out the joint. If they complain, tell 'em to vacate. I'll not put up with rowdy tenants."

"I wouldn't have missed this for five hundred dollars!" cried Sislow.

"No, I'll not give up my job on this kind of notice," cried Monroe, recovering from shock.

"Don't look at me. It's out of my hands. It's between you and Fred. My obligation to you came to an end at 12:45 A.M. tonight. Legally I'm not beholden to you for one penny beyond that time. But I'm willing to do the right thing. I'll pay you your wages clear through to the end of the week."

Fred rode up in the elevator with Sislow still beside him. Little Chief Richards stood halfway down the stairs from the fourth floor.

"Hey, you fellows got any lights down there?"

"Lighter than ever."

"Ours went off, every damn one. Fuse must have popped. Can I use your phone?"

"You need *five* phones now?" asked Fred.

"Ours all went dead. It must have had something to do with the lights."

"Help yourself."

Embarrassed and apologetic after the way he had treated Fred, Richards waited his turn to use the phone. He finally got it and called the office. He listened to what was apparently a long explanation from downstairs and his eyes grew steadily protruding. Finally he cried, "Wait! What the hell do you mean we got to vacate the fourth floor?" He slammed the phone. He turned on Fred. "Did you buy this place?"

"Yah," said Fred. "I did. It seemed to be a good, going business. Did you know that this hotel netted forty-one thousand last year?"

"It was you shut off our lights and phone."

Sislow could not contain himself. "And have you laid your hand on the radiator lately?"

In near-inarticulate rage, Richards waved a finger at Fred. "Why, you son of a bitch! You'd stand there while I used your telephone and— listen here, if you think—— Now let me tell you something——"

"Sorry, but you'll have to vacate. We're going to remodel. Hereafter this will be known as a three-story building."

The janitor came in with his nightshirt making a big roll inside his overalls and said to Sislow, "Which one of them skylights you wanted open? I can't find 'em if the juice isn't turned on. I got the fire doors to the roof all open, though. They let in one hell of a blast. What's wrong? Is it coal gas? I couldn't smell any coal gas."

Richards charged to the stairs. "Stay back!" he said to the janitor. "Stay back or I'll brain you with this bottle."

"Lights! Lights! Turn the lights on!" they were shouting all over the fourth floor. A little while later they commenced pounding the pipes for heat.

"I'm hungry!" said Fred. "Hey, we own the joint, don't we? Let's open the dining room."

"Steak for me," said Campbell.

Everyone wanted steak. The steam pipes were being banged in drum tempo. Senator Cap Watterson groped in from his room on the second floor. "What's going on here? Why all this racket? You fellows ought to use some common sense. You're keeping everybody awake. They can hear you over in the annex even."

"Have a steak?"

"Steak?"

"We opened the kitchen."

Cap poured himself a drink. He decided he would have a steak. A sound of smashing wood came from upstairs.

"What are they doing up there?"

Sislow said, "There's a fireplace in 407."

"Why, they're smashing up your furniture! You seem to be pretty calm about it."

"It's not my joint. This is the new owner."

"You?"

"Yah," said Fred. "Maybe we ought to go up on the roof and stuff pillows down their chimney."

"I've paid the coal bill in this joint long enough to know they'll do little enough heating with a fireplace."

On rolling serve tables the steaks commenced to arrive. An urn of coffee appeared fragrantly. Great platters were heaped with golden-greasy French fried potatoes. The odors wafted upstairs. A man roared hoarsely, "No son-of-a-bitching has-been wrestler is stopping *me!*" It was Representative Donnelly. He came pantsless, wrapped to the top of his head in a quilt. He stood by a radiator shuddering cold from his spine while waiting for a hot toddy. "It's ten below zero up there!"

Fowell, Cully, and Anson followed him. Howard and Work arrived.

Big Jake Hovalt, the Senator from Flatwillow, stalked in baggy-eyed and truculent and said, "I wouldn't vote Bennett dogcatcher after this." But he stayed for a steak. Conroy and Arnets deserted the Company, as did Wagner, Highshaw, and McKerrow.

"We're not asking a single man here to vote for Bennett," Lewis kept assuring them. "Just don't vote O'Hanlon before the grand jury passes on the guilt or innocence of our candidate."

To this, over T bone, even Senator Hovalt agreed.

Dawn grew above the mountains. The town commenced to stir. *The News* arrived headlined:

COMPANY PLOT FAILS!

BENNETT DEMANDS GRAND JURY CONVENE TO INVESTIGATE THE TRUE SOURCE OF THE $30,000

Men were still phoning with news about Davis, Rowley, Bracker, Haupt, and twenty others. The reception room was strewn with dishes containing the fat, gnawed bones, and congealing grease of steaks. Fred was groggy from fatigue. His coffee was cold. Judge Gibbons lay on a couch snoring. The sun made a bright slash across the snow of Mount Helena. Cletus came in.

"Mist' Freddy!"

"What's wrong now?"

"I don't know! They's some man to see you. And he ain't *alone!* He's got a whole bunch of women."

Longfelt had been talking about moving some of Maude Brubaker's girls to the fourth floor now that the Company had vacated, but this was much too soon.

"He say he's Raffles," said Cletus.

Fred got to his feet. It *was* Raffles. He was an ageless man, all knuckles and tendons, with the desiccated face of a burlesque comedian. His clothes were strongly redolent of train smoke. He cried Fred's name. They shook hands and clapped each other on the back.

"We'd have been here an hour ago," said Raffles, "only we couldn't get transportation from the depot."

"Wasn't there a hack?"

"Sure there was a hack. What good was one hack? Couldn't walk in this cold. It must be thirty below out there."

"What do you mean, 'what good was one hack?' "

"Look for yourself!" Raffles said proudly.

Crowded near the door of the reception room were young women. More women were revealed by waving plumes in the hall. He still could not shake it from his excitement-glazed mind that they were Maude Brubaker's girls. "What were they doing at the depot?"

"Are you rummy? I brought them to the depot, of course."

"All those girls?"

"Sure, these are the ones you wanted. I had one hell of a time, too! I got them all but six. Six, I couldn't talk into it. I had to give these a raise in salary, transportation, everything. I'm strapped. I just barely made it here."

"What are you talking about?"

"I'm talking about those girls out there, the ones you telegraphed for me to bring."

"I never telegraphed for any girls."

Raffles stared at him. "The hell you didn't!" He commenced going through his pockets, tossing aside envelopes and pieces of paper until he found a telegram almost worn out from carrying. "Listen to this: *Get chorus at Gayety! Come in haste! First train!* So there you are. Look at 'em. The whole damn chorus except for six girls!"

"Oh, ye gods!" Fred sat down and propped his head in his hands. "You didn't send this telegram?"

"Yes, I sent the telegram! I wanted the chorus that closed Act One of *Countess Katinka!* We left it backstage at the Gayety that night we took it over for the quartet."

"You didn't want the girls at all?"

"No!"

Raffles stood in shock, but a large, handsome woman, somewhat older than the others and apparently their boss, came elbowing through and shouted, "What do you mean, you don't want us?" She turned on Raffles. "What kind of a waltz did you take us on, you rummy-dumb piano player? You think you can drag us out here five thousand miles leaving a good engagement, and ditch us in the middle of some prairie-dog town, ninety degrees below zero——"

"Now, Madge!" said Raffles, pleading for calm heads. "Madge, this is Freddy. Freddy will fix everything."

"He'd better! If you think——"

"You're getting paid, aren't you?" shouted Raffles. "You haven't missed any meals, have you? You ate all the tenderloin on the train, didn't you? All right, now keep your mouth shut until we straighten this out."

H. T. Lewis was there, pulling Freddy by the arm. "Who are they? You bring these girls, Fred? You bring all these girls from New York?"

He found strength enough to nod.

"You mean they're ours?"

"Yah."

"Fred, let me shake your hand. This is the best idea you had yet. We *got* to hold that Company today! We got to do it, Fred. Oh! if we can come through today, nothing can stop us!"

Ghost Town

Allan Vaughan Elston

THE TOWN of Smeed lay grotesque and weirdly desolate in the dusk, its crumbling walls resembling gray specters. Its shapes and shadows startled Everett Gregg. A roof of black cloud hung low, spanning the canyon from timberline to timberline, and beneath it those skeletons of stone and iron loomed in strangely forbidding ranks. A smokestack arose crazily from the ruins of a forsaken smelter. A derrick, from whose crossarm swung a rusting cable, gave against the oncoming night the fleeting impression of a gibbet. The streets of the town were deserted and had been, Gregg knew, for twenty-five years.

He knew that much because Ed Patterson, at Fair Play, had informed him:

"On the way up to Soupdish Pass, young fella, you'll go through Smeed. They ain't nobody there. Smeed died with its boots on 'bout the year you was born."

One of the real old-timers in Western fiction, Allan Elston began publishing stories way back in the early twenties and he's still going strong. Readers of the old *Adventure* and *Short Stories* remember his rousing magazine tales; today's fans enjoy such fine books as *Stage Road to Denver*. Allan headquarters in Santa Ana, California, but does a great deal of traveling throughout the West in an unremitting search for story material.

Thunder now rolled out of the black cloud. Rain was due, and plenty of it. It meant, Gregg decided, that he'd have to make camp here in the deserted town.

He eyed the prospect with small relish. Most of the roofs were caved in; but he noted one square two-story structure of limestone rock which seemed to offer ample shelter. Winds had blown the doors from it, and most of the window glass was smashed by hailstones; nevertheless it should provide a sanctuary for the night.

After watering his saddle horse and pack mare at the creek, Gregg tethered them. Then, lugging his bedroll through the gloom, he approached the chosen structure. At its doorless entrance he stopped with a presentiment that rats, reptiles, or worse might infest the dark room.

A zigzag flash and the groan of a riven pine on the slope above him decided Gregg. Rain was already beginning to strike him in cold, fat drops. Pushing his bedroll through that black portal, Gregg stumbled in after it. A minute later he was shining his pocket flash down the length of a thirty-foot mahogany bar.

These quarters, he saw, were the old saloon of the boom days of Smeed. Although the small fixtures had been stripped away by vandals, the bar was still in place. In spite of age and scars, Gregg noted that it had once been more than commonly handsome. A score of thirsty muckers might have breasted it. Beyond was a marble-topped back-bar, and above it a massive mirror. These ornate relics recalled to Gregg certain facts mentioned by Patterson at Fair Play. Smeed in the old days, it seemed, was a one-mine camp. Samuel Smeed, better known as Silver Sam, owned and developed both mine and town. He was lavish with his funds and with them had erected every stick and stone of the town.

"The best," according to Patterson, "was only half good enough for Silver Sam. Money came his way easy, and he spent it like water."

That, Gregg thought, would explain a rich mahogany bar.

Cobwebs in stringy festoons dripped from the ceiling. Inches of dust, presumably blown through the entrance, covered the floor. On it lay an old playing card. Gregg picked it up; it was so faded that he could barely recognize the jack of spades.

The customers' floor space was, the intruder judged, about forty feet long by half as wide. At the rear a sagging stairway ascended to the upper floor.

Everett Gregg unrolled his blankets. Then, after a minute of indecision, he made his bed squarely atop the bar. By that means he hoped to keep pack rats from galloping back and forth over his recumbent form through the night. Next he produced a candle from his kit, lighted it, and stood it in its grease on the bar. He went to the door and peered out; it was raining briskly now. He came back disconsolately. There was no use sitting up in this gloom, so he blew out the candle, mounted the bar, and turned in.

For an hour or so the hardness of his bed cheated sleep. Yet it might have been worse. He heard no scamper of pack rats—only the steady drumming of rain. There'd be a muddy trail over Soupdish Pass tomorrow, of course, but he'd make it. By noon he'd be snugly housed in Cunningham's cabin at Steelhead Lake.

His first idea had been to go via a roundabout route on the narrow gauge. But at Fair Play, Ed Patterson, to whom he had presented a letter of introduction, had tipped him that he'd see more of the country by packing over the pass. Patterson himself had furnished an outfit for the trip.

Now, after a restless period on that hardwood bar, Gregg fell asleep. He was dreaming about Smeed in its heyday, or rather about Silver Sam Smeed as sketched by Patterson, when he was awakened by some sound which was neither rain nor pack rat. When he opened his eyes his first impression was that the candle was burning.

That was all wrong. Most certainly he had blown the candle out before turning in. Raising himself sleepily on one elbow, he looked about. Yes, the candle was still burning. Above he saw the stringy strands of cobweb. Below, on the dust-littered floor, he saw the faded jack of spades. He heard nothing. The rain had stopped, and the place was like a tomb.

Then, from a gloomy corner of Smeed's barroom, came a voice.

"Don't let me disturb you none, mister. Was just aimin' to turn in myself."

A figure advanced into the light. It was inhumanly lean and its frightfully deep-sunken eyes alone would have been enough to startle Gregg. Gregg threw off his blankets and leaped to the floor. He stood there staring widely.

"Slaughter's the name," the lean man said. "Ike Slaughter."

The voice was squeaky. The intruder himself was old yet spry, and advanced with a springy step. He was grinning hideously with teeth closed tightly together. The grin, the man's deep eye sockets and sunken cheeks, gave an effect not unlike a death's-head. Gregg stood there blinking. Was he dreaming?

He saw that he who called himself Ike Slaughter wore gum boots; his ears heard the thump of those boots on the barroom floor. And there were two burnt matches near the candle. Gregg himself had used only one. This human scarecrow must have used the other to relight the wick during Gregg's sleep. Therefore he could be no dream-born illusion of the ghost town.

The other, still grinning his ghastly grin, stopped directly in front of Gregg. He towered there, tall but thin to the point of emaciation. His face was wide at the forehead, narrow at the chin. On his long, skinny neck the Adam's apple stood out as sharply as the breastbone of a starved turkey, and Gregg, noting a linear scar which receded each way from it, wondered whether whiplash, rope, or hook had ever encircled that throat.

"Slaughter's the name. If it's any of my business, young feller, who might you be?"

Gregg steadied himself against the bar. His fingers, rubbing his eyes, felt the dampness of his brow. He answered huskily:

"I'm Everett Gregg, a geologist. The rain drove me in here."

"Any port in a storm, eh?" cackled Slaughter. "Well, I reckon you got as much business here as anybody else. Me, I'm beddin' down upstairs."

He made, however, no move toward the stairs at the rear. Instead he sprang spryly to the bar and perched there, swinging his booted legs and grinning at Gregg. Wide awake now, the younger man was less apprehensive. No doubt this was some broken-down prospector, perhaps some derelict denizen of the old Smeed who had wandered back to peck rock on familiar ground.

"Glad to know you, Mr. Slaughter. Been here long?" he probed.

"Off and on all my life," the oldster wheezed.

The sunken eyes kept a steady stare on Gregg. It was disconcerting, that stare, and Gregg, seeing his own face in the mirror beyond, was startled by the tension of his features. He tried to relax. To prove that he wasn't in the least afraid he lighted a cigarette and inquired casually:

"An old-timer around here, are you? Were you here when Smeed was a live camp?"

"Was I here when Smeed was a live camp?" shrilled Slaughter. "Did you hear that? He asts if I, Ike Slaughter, was around in them days, an' the answer is I sure as hell was. And not six feet from where I am now, young feller. I was Sam Smeed's friend and bartender."

In the last announcement a note of pride colored the squeak of Ike Slaughter.

"In that case," Gregg prompted genially, "you didn't need to be ashamed of your bar. This must have been something of a swell layout for a mining camp."

"It was for a fact," agreed Slaughter. "It sure was one swell set-up, even if Sam never did git it paved with them silver dollars."

The fellow was still staring like a death's-head. The last phrase gave Gregg his first reason to suspect that Slaughter might be crazy as a loon. Certainly the remark made no sense. However Gregg inquired politely—

"The Silver Dollar was the name of Smeed's mine, wasn't it?"

"It was that," Slaughter agreed with a wag of his head, "an' Sam was danged proud of it. He was a proud man, Sam was. And a fast spender. When he built this barroom in order to keep his men from driftin' down to Fair Play on Sattidy nights he aimed to outdazzle every barroom in five States. Spent a mint on it, he did, and it sure was a beaut."

"Rich, was he?"

"Rich?" Slaughter looked sorrowfully at Gregg, as if in pity at the listener's complete ignorance. "Sure he was rich. A hunerd thousand dollars was small change to Silver Sam Smeed. He hearn about a bar on Broadway, New York, or maybe it was Chicagy, where the floor was paved with silver dollars. Some sport come in an' told about it. Sam was drunk that night, an' right away he said he'd pave *his* barroom the same way. Them Easterners couldn't top no bets of his, he said. He made the brag in public, and when he sobered up he had to make good."

"You mean," Gregg echoed in amazement, "that he actually paved this floor with silver dollars?"

"No, but he aimed to," Slaughter insisted. "Fact is, the idear was made to order fer Silver Sam Smeed, drunk or sober. It fit the name of his mine too, the Silver Dollar, like a buckskin glove. Top o' that, the stunt would make Sam talked about from Denver to Frisco, and Sam sure liked to be talked about. So he measured the barroom floor and figgered out how many coins it'd take; then he ordered his Denver bank to ship 'em by narrer gauge to Fair Play."

Gregg no longer suspected that Slaughter was crazy. But he found himself leaning strongly to a theory that he, Gregg, was being made sport of. Surely this old derelict was pulling his leg. However, Everett Gregg chose to voice no doubt. Instead he inquired:

"Wasn't Smeed afraid somebody'd steal dollars off his floor?"

"Not with them dollars grouted in cement," Slaughter wheezed. "Them coins was to lay 'bout a quarter inch apart edge to edge, countersunk, y'understand, in a concrete floor. Some shifty gent might gouge one or two out on the sly but he couldn't hardly snitch 'em in bulk."

Gregg looked toward the floor and pursued amiably:

"How many silver dollars would it take?"

"This floor's forty foot by twenty, bar to wall," Slaughter said. "Figger it out yourself."

Gregg did some rapid mental calculation. Silver dollars in a row with about a quarter of an inch between adjacent rims would run, he estimated, perhaps six to the foot. Multiplying six by six by twenty by forty, the result astonished him.

"It would take something like twenty-eight thousand, eight hundred dollars," he announced.

"Go to the head of the class," cackled Ike Slaughter. "Twenty-eight thousand silver dollars was zackly what Sam Smeed had shipped in sacks, from his Denver bank to Fair Play. But he never did git 'em up here to Smeed."

"What seemed to be the trouble?" Gregg inquired more at ease now. This foolery, he decided, was a good way to while away a bit of time, even if the man was cracked.

"Sam," Slaughter squeaked at him, "kept his plans as secret as he could. Coupla gents named Higgins and Smith, masons and handy men around here, was to do the actual groutin' in of them dollars. Naturally they had to know all about it. Me too, seein' as I was his friend, knew the plans. Smeed picked Higgins and Smith fer guards, and he picked a dark night to freight them sacks up from Fair Play. Smeed made the run hisself, and the three of 'em had four fast mules hitched to a stout wagon. They started with the coin all right, close to a ton of it, but they never got here. Smeed, Higgins, and Smith was found dead by the trail halfway up the canyon. The mules and a empty wagon was found loose in the woods."

"And the twenty-eight thousand dollars?" Gregg prompted.

"It," Slaughter assured him, "just didn't show up nowhere. That was twenty-six year ago, and sheriffs 've been huntin' fer them coins ever since."

"Did the mine keep running after Smeed's death?"

"A year or so. Then it played out, and the town went to pot."

Ike Slaughter yawned. Then he stretched his bony arms, jumped to the floor, and started shambling toward the foot of the stairs.

"Time to turn in," he squeaked. Turning suddenly, he added, "But hold on. Maybe you'd like a drink." He cocked one hairless eyebrow inquiringly at Gregg.

Then, without waiting for a response, he moved around the end of the bar to a position behind it. From beneath it he produced a quart bottle of liquor. Then up came an old rag and two cracked glasses.

With his rag the man mopped the bar for a space in front of him. The celerity of his gesture half convinced Gregg that indeed he had once been a bartender.

"Just like old times, huh?" Slaughter cackled. He poured two drinks, pushed one of them toward Gregg. "It's on the house, young feller. Step up."

The pitch of this invitation was wild and shrill. Slaughter was again grinning like a death's-head, and the frightful stare was again fixed in those deep-sunk eyes. He looked crazy. Was he? The candle, now burned almost to the bar, flickered in its grease. In the mirror, Everett Gregg again saw the tension on his own face.

With an effort he righted his mood and faced Slaughter with a smile. The oldster continued to stare fixedly, without friendliness or menace, at Gregg.

Not to offend him, Gregg took up a glass.

"Did they ever catch up with whoever got away with that coin?" he inquired.

Now a sly look came to the narrow visage of Slaughter. His voice lowered to a husky whisper.

"Sure, they caught him," he whispered. "They not only caught him, but they hanged him."

"Served him right," echoed Gregg, and drained his dram. It was powerful. After making a wry face Gregg added, "Him you say? Did one man get away with those dollars single-handed?"

"He sure did, and they hanged him high," insisted Slaughter.

"Who was it?" asked Gregg.

Slaughter's lean face now became slyer than ever. His lips twisted to a leer of confidence. Leaning far out over the bar, he beckoned Gregg nearer. Then he whispered:

"You're lookin' right at him, young feller. It was me they hanged." Ghoulishly, the old scamp drew a finger across the scar encircling his long skinny neck. "See?"

Was he crazy? Or, having sized Gregg up as a tenderfoot dupe, was he merely making sport? Between those possible answers Gregg wavered.

"They sure hanged me," Slaughter said. "And it hurt like hell."

It was all too raw to be mere foolery, Gregg decided, so the man must be mad. To humor him he answered:

"O.K. They caught you, hanged you, and it hurt like hell. Speaking of hell, how come you to leave there?"

"Well," Slaughter wheezed, still leaning far and confidently over the bar and looking crazier than ever, "somethin' had to be done with that coin, didn't it? It was still hid in the woods."

"I see," Gregg rejoined sympathetically. "The load of coin was still cached in the woods. So twenty-six years after they hanged you, you came back to dispose of it. Put it in a bank, did you?"

"In a bank?" mocked Slaughter. "Why would I put it in a bank? It wasn't my money, was it? It was Sam Smeed's. He was my friend. He meant to put those dollars right here in this floor. It would have done him proud, and it was his last wish. He died trying to carry it out, didn't he? So that's what I done. Only last month I paved the whole floor of this room with that silver. And you're standin' right on it now, young feller!"

Immediately Gregg reverted to his theory that this old-timer, far from being crazy, was merely trying to make a fool of his audience. Gregg no doubt was now expected to stoop and scratch wildly in the inches of dust littering the floor. That would be the cue for a hoarse laugh from Slaughter.

Such being the play, Everett Gregg declined to scratch on the floor. He declined even to look downward. Instead, in a voice elaborately casual, he said:

"Well, thanks for the drink. It must be pretty late by now, so what do you say we turn in?"

A flicker of disappointment crossed Slaughter's face. With his voice pitched to a peevish whine he asked:

"You wouldn't call me a liar, would you, young feller?"

"By no means," Gregg assured him solemnly.

"And you wouldn't go so far's to claim I'm loony, wouldja?"

"Absurd!" Gregg echoed.

It seemed to satisfy Slaughter. He picked up his own untasted glass and drained the liquor therefrom at a gulp. With his old rag he again mopped the bar. He wiped the glasses and put them away with the bottle. Then he emerged from behind the bar and clumped, in his gum boots, to the foot of the stairs.

There he turned and for another long minute his hollow eyes bored a stare through Gregg. The lips were parted; teeth were locked tight in a horrible grin. In spite of himself Gregg winced.

Gregg was glad when the old scamp turned his back and mounted the steps. The candle was nearly spent, and in the dim light Gregg could barely see him. Yet he heard each thump of those boots as the figure ascended. When Slaughter had reached the upper floor and passed entirely from sight, Gregg could still hear the steps. The man was clumping across a plank floor just over the barroom. He stopped at a spot directly above Gregg.

Then Gregg heard, or thought he heard, the creak of a cot. Followed a brief interval of silence. Then came one loud thump on the floor above. Gregg divined that the fellow must have seated himself on a cot, pulled off one of his boots, and dropped it to the floor.

"Since he's gone to bed," Gregg thought, "I might as well make it unanimous." He moved toward that end of the bar on which his blankets were still stretched, more than a little pleased at having resisted the bait offered by Slaughter. He looked at his watch. It was 11:15 P.M. He was on the point of blowing out the candle, when something made him hesitate. He had heard the thud of only one boot. Weirdly he found himself tense, his ears straining expectantly, waiting for the fall of the other boot.

Five minutes later he was still waiting. It was an infinitesimally small detail, but as the seconds passed it assumed for Gregg an overwhelming importance. The strange tension enmeshed him like a cord.

He began to imagine things. He began to wonder. Was he, Gregg, walking in his sleep? Had he dreamed Slaughter? No, because Slaughter, flesh and blood, had just gone to bed. The seal of proof would come any instant now—his ears would hear Slaughter's second boot drop with a plop on the loft floor.

For that trifling detail of ultimate reassurance Gregg waited. He waited one minute, two, three. The house was like a tomb. The second boot did *not* drop. There was not so much as the creaking of a cot. There was no shuffle, no stirring, not even a breath, and most certainly that last boot was not kicked off on the floor.

Again his reflection in the bar mirror shocked Gregg. He saw himself painfully alert, his face drawn in lines of taut anxiety, head inclined sidewise. Had a pin dropped up there Gregg would, he was sure, have heard it.

Neither pin nor boot dropped.

At length Gregg could stand the suspense no longer. The thing to do, he decided, was to take his flash and have a look upstairs. No doubt everything was all right. But sight of Slaughter, recumbent on a cot above, was the only way to prove it.

Gregg drew his pocket flash and went to the steps at the rear. A bit sheepishly he mounted them, projecting his flash ahead. When he reached the top he saw a long, dusty room, bare except for a disreputable cot at its center.

On the cot were a few old blankets. Ike Slaughter was not under or among those blankets. Under the cot there was nothing. Gregg's flash explored every corner of the room. He saw that there was no egress other than the steps. Yet Slaughter was gone.

Had he *ever* been there? Yes; of that there was proof. On the floor beside the cot lay one gum boot.

It took the breath from Gregg. He stared at the boot. Then he advanced to all quarters of the room, exploring with his flash. He made sure that Slaughter was not hiding. He made certain that no door or other stairway or trap in the roof existed to explain his disappearance. All he found was a window, the glass of which was cracked and punctured by hailstones. It was shut and latched on the inside. No single hole in the glass pane was large enough to permit Slaughter's exit. The man had positively evaporated. All that remained of him was one gum boot.

Breathlessly Gregg descended to the barroom below. His heart was thumping; his face was bathed in cold sweat. Desperately he reassembled his wits. He must clear away the cobwebs and stick to the facts. What were the facts? Fact number one was that Slaughter had ascended to the loft and removed a boot, which was still there. Fact number two was that there was no egress from the loft except these visible steps. Fact number three was that Slaughter was not now in the loft. Did that mean that Slaughter, prowling resident of a ghost town, was himself a——?

"A ghost? Bunk. A dream? No!" Gregg spoke aloud. "I talked to him, didn't I? He stood here and lied his head off for an hour, didn't he? He not only exists, but he's the biggest liar that ever——"

No epithet which Gregg could summon seemed fit to measure Slaughter's prowess as a liar. To prove that he *was* a liar it was only necessary to establish that this same barroom floor was not paved with silver dollars.

Standing on it now, Gregg raked his foot edgewise in a swath through the dirt on the floor. Having done so, he stooped. With his fingers he felt of the exposed floor surface, contemptuously sure that he would touch only old and rotting wood.

Instead, the surface seemed to be cement. The candle, having burned to its grease on the bar, went out suddenly. Thumbing his flash, Gregg directed it along the space which his fingers stroked. Instantly he stiffened to the rigidity of a rock. He saw rows of silver dollars. They lay flat, grouted flush in concrete. Ghost or wraith of a dream, Slaughter in at least one respect was no liar. Smeed's barroom floor was paved with silver dollars!

The monstrous fact stupefied Gregg. Was the entire area of the floor like this? He moved ten feet to the right and raked again with his foot. Yes, there were more rows of dollars. Gregg tried many spots, found them all the same. The job was complete. The coins lay only about a quarter of an inch apart. Some one had actually carried out the original specifications for Samuel Smeed's barroom floor.

Examining carefully, Gregg came to three conclusions: First, the job had been executed by an amateur; this was suggested by certain irregularities and by areas of improperly troweled surface. Second, the job did not date from the old days of Smeed; it had the look and smell of fresh cement; most likely it was not over a month or two old. Third, the inch and a half of dirt on top of it, which Gregg had mistaken for wind-blown dust, was too even in depth to be dust naturally deposited. A human hand had sprinkled it there—perhaps, Gregg thought, to hide the job till it was firmly set; or perhaps to let it cure without cracking, as contractors often cover new concrete roads.

But what, wondered Gregg, was the motive? Slaughter's story was, of course, out. Certainly Smeed's murderer had not returned, twenty-six years after his hanging, to pave this barroom with the loot. Here, nevertheless, it lay. Or were these metallic circles, laid in a mosaic pattern, really coins? To settle that, Gregg produced his knife and began gouging for a sample.

After three minutes of work he had still failed to dig out one, proving that Smeed's original plan had not been so vulnerable after all. No stealthy thief could have stolen any considerable section of the floor.

With patience Gregg at last pried out a sample. It was, he found, a genuine dollar minted thirty years before. His next step was clear: He must take this sample and report the entire business to Sheriff Ed Patterson at Fair Play.

He immediately began rerolling his blankets. In order to use both hands at the chore, he pocketed the flashlight. Awkwardly in the dark he completed the roll, wondering whether he would find that some grim ghost of a horse thief had stolen his horses. It would almost require such a touch as that, he thought, to top off this night at Smeed.

Weird fancies haunted him, yet in the midst of them a sound emerged, or seemed to. He thought he heard a step on the gravel outside the building. He stiffened to attention. Sternly he tried to assure himself that he had heard nothing at all. All his senses must be affected by a riot of tricky imaginings.

In the dark, he shouldered his bedroll. But after one groping step toward the exit he again heard a tread on the gravel without. This time he was sure of it. It was an approaching step. Distinctly he heard it coming nearer, and ahead of it came a pale glimmer of light. Someone with a lantern was moving directly toward the barroom door.

Who could it be but Slaughter? Slaughter, having made a mysterious exit from the loft, must be stalking him. What trick was he up to now? Gregg quickly decided to spy on him. Quietly therefore he groped his way around to the rear side of the bar. He set the blanket roll down and stooped.

Half a minute later he heard some one enter by the front entrance. With the intruder came a mellow light. Rising a trifle, Gregg peered cautiously over the bar. He saw a man with a lantern. The man was bent forward, looking down, and Gregg could not see his face; but he was of a stout, stocky build and therefore could not be Ike Slaughter.

Gregg dodged down behind his shelter. He listened. He heard wary footsteps reach the center of the room. Then Gregg peered again. This time he had to raise his head higher, for the intruder was now on his knees. With gloved hands the newcomer was scooping dirt to one side. In a moment Gregg heard his gasp of astonishment.

Taking no chances, Gregg remained hidden. This fellow, he had noticed, wore a holstered gun. If suddenly startled, he might shoot. On the other hand, he might be only a curious rancher, here to spike or confirm a rumor that the floor was paved with coins.

Gregg could now hear the scratching of the man's knife. Obviously the man was digging out a sample of the dollars. For a minute or more the blade scraped. Holding his breath, Gregg listened. Suddenly the other man, with a cement-crusted dollar in his hand, stood to full height. His awe-struck comment came plainly to Gregg:

"Shoot me fer a walleyed sheepherder if this ain't real money!"

Limp and speechless, Gregg arose. Sheer relief left him weak. The other man whirled suddenly and was snatching at his holster when Gregg managed to protest hoarsely:

"Don't shoot, please. You know me. I'm Everett Gregg."

The face across the bar relaxed into a grim smile. Here was the man of all men whom Gregg wanted most to see. He was Ed Patterson, sheriff from Fair Play.

Reciting his story to Ed Patterson helped vastly to steady Gregg. Patterson was a dependable, comfortable sort of man—broad, stolid, of even temper. His granite-gray eyes were more often inclined to bore into the truth than to doubt or rebuke.

When Gregg finished his story the sheriff removed his Stetson from his round, bald head. After twirling it on his finger, he stared thoughtfully into its depths.

"It checks with a yarn brought in by Doc Asa Cutler of Como," he announced. "That's why I'm here."

"But why," Gregg puzzled, "did Ike Slaughter feed me that pack of lies?"

"As far as I know," Patterson answered gruffly, "he didn't feed you anything but straight goods. Anyway, the deal twenty-six year ago was just like he said."

"You mean that Sam Smeed actually did plan to pave this floor with silver dollars?"

"Yeah, and while haulin' the coin up here to the mine, him and his two guards was murdered by Bartender Slaughter. Slaughter was caught, but they couldn't make him tell where he'd stashed that load o' coin."

"But Slaughter," Gregg protested, "claims he was hanged."

"He was, but not quite long enough," the sheriff explained dryly. "The jury acquitted him and he walked outa court a free man. In the street a mob roped him, picked out a tall pine, and strung him to the top limb. My dad, who was sheriff in those days, loped up just in time to cut the rascal down. Slaughter rambled off and ain't showed up since."

"What did they have on him?" Gregg inquired.

"Plenty. Only four men knew the night the coin was to be freighted and the route it was comin' on. Three of 'em were shot dead off the wagon, and the other one was Slaughter. The three dead men were riddled with buckshot. Slaughter had a shotgun he always kept at his bar. A couple of his empty homemade shells was found at the spot. All the same, Slaughter had a smart lawyer and was acquitted."

"But why should he come back after twenty-five years," Gregg puzzled, "and pave the Smeed barroom with his loot?"

Patterson was no less puzzled. All he could hazard was:

"Slaughter must've gone screwy. Crazy with remorse, maybe. So finally he comes back and puts the coin right where Smeed aimed to put it himself, and then aims to crack down on any one who gouges one of 'em out."

Gregg was unconvinced. A man mean enough to kill three associates in cold blood would not, he felt certain, go mad with remorse. Too, he would have spent the money long ago.

"You mentioned a Dr. Cutler," Gregg reminded the sheriff.

"Doc Cutler," Patterson explained, "came by here day before yesterday, fishing. Wading down the creek, he heard sounds from this barroom. Sounded like a hammer pounding on a concrete floor. Curious, Doc came for a look. He was just in time to see a tramp dodge out the back door. A hammer, a chisel, and an empty sack lay on the floor. Looked like this tramp had been chippin' out pieces of concrete. Looking closer, Doc seen the floor was paved with dollars. He went to Como with the story, which same just reached my office late this evening."

"The tramp," Gregg guessed, "was Slaughter. Needing a dollar for spending money, he was chipping it from his own floor. My own hunch is that he's not crazy, and that a key motive is still missing."

Taking the lantern with them, they went out behind the building. There they discovered an old tub in which mortar had been mixed. A pile of empty cement sacks lay nearby, as well as a heap of creek sand.

"Maybe he stole the cement," Patterson hazarded. "Then, usin' creek sand, he just needed to mix a lean mortar and flood the floor with a one-inch layer. While it was wet, he could lay the dollars out in rows, and they'd sink flush of their own weight. When the mortar set, he had a silver-dollar floor. What do you say we have a look upstairs?"

They ascended to the loft, finding it as Gregg had last seen it. One boot, and one only, lay on the floor. But as to the mystery of Slaughter's disappearance, Patterson quickly scored. For when he examined the cracked and hail-pitted windowpane he discovered a large section of loose glass.

It covered the lower half of the window. With small effort, the sheriff took this loose pane bodily from its grooves and set it upright on the floor. He could now thrust his head and broad shoulders through the hole. The roof of a lean-to was only a few feet below.

"The window was probably like this when Slaughter sneaked out on you," Patterson guessed. "Then he reached his hand back in, picked up the triangle of broken glass, and set it in its groove."

"And so stealthily that I couldn't hear him," added Gregg.

The two went back down to the barroom. There Patterson examined the floor at many spots and made certain it was completely paved with dollars. Gregg, absorbed with vain wonderings, moved toward the rear and peered through stringy strands of cobwebs into an area beneath the stairs. He saw a closed door, which he guessed gave to a mop and broom closet.

Patterson joined him. They brushed the cobwebs aside, went to the closet door and tried to open it. It was locked.

"I know where the key is, if you gents want in there!" shrilled a voice back of them.

Gregg, whirling about, saw a tall bag of bones with deep hollows under hairless brows. The teeth were locked in the same frightfully skull-like grin that Gregg knew. It was Ike Slaughter himself, and he was approaching across the barroom.

He seemed to be limping. But that, Gregg saw, was merely because he had one boot off and one on.

Instantly Patterson's gun was out and on him.

"Hands up, Ike Slaughter!"

"You ain't pinchin' me, are you, Sheriff?" Slaughter whined. "If so, what fer?"

Patterson stared coldly for a moment and then reluctantly sheathed his weapon. A second's reflection reminded him that he could not arrest Slaughter. Having once been tried for the murder of Smeed and and the two guards, the acquitted man could not be tried again for the same crime.

Slaughter stood for a moment in a pose of ghoulish insolence. Then he wheeled and limped to the end of the bar. He moved to a position back of it, and once again Gregg saw him mop the bar top with an old rag. Again out came the bottle of liquor and two glasses.

Patterson had advanced sternly to the front of the bar and stood facing Slaughter across it. Slaughter poured two drinks. One he pushed toward the sheriff.

"It's on the house, Sheriff."

Patterson shook his head.

"I'm not drinking with a murderer," he said.

Slaughter rested his bony elbows on the bar. Across it his white and fleshless face leered mockery at Patterson.

"And suppose," he cackled shrilly, "I didn't kill Smeed?"

"No good," Gregg cut in. "You confessed that much to me."

"I did no such thing," echoed Slaughter. "I said they hanged me fer it, and that I was the gent got away with them silver dollars, but I didn't say I killed Smeed. And I didn't say just when and how I got away with said dollars. What's more, I didn't kill Sam Smeed."

"Prove it," Patterson challenged stonily.

"I sure will and this time I'm pickin' my own judge and jury," Slaughter shrilled.

He looked eagerly up and down the bar, as if a crew of thirsty miners were assembled there instead of only Patterson and Gregg.

"If you did not kill Smeed and his two guards, prove it," again challenged Patterson.

"If I do, will you drink with me, Sheriff?" wheezed Slaughter. His eyes, rheumy and deep-sunk, seemed to plead with Patterson.

Patterson rested his own blunt elbows on that same bar, faced Slaughter across it, and said:

"Shoot."

Gregg stood by in a suspenseful mood much like that in which, earlier this same night, he had waited in vain for a second boot to hit the loft floor.

"After they hung me," Slaughter squeaked, "I put in twenty-five year ramblin' from hell to breakfast. Mostly prospectin'. Finally I wanders back to the old diggings. I come right here and got in the habit of campin' in the loft over this bar. Daytimes I chip rock in all the old stopes and tunnels. In one of 'em I find bags of silver dollars 'longside of a gent who's been a long time dead."

"Found a dead man, did you?" Patterson prompted. "What did he die of?"

"Lead poisoning. And I seen right away howcome."

"Yeah?" Patterson's face was still uncompromisingly grim.

From beneath the bar Slaughter now produced an old and tarnished liquor flask. It was apparently of silver, and the engraved work on its sides was richly ornate.

"Coupla nights before Smeed and his guards went fer the coin," Slaughter said, "a dude stranger come in here and bought drinks for all hands. Seemed like a harmless little feller. After buyin' a few rounds, he pulled out this here flask. Filled it from a bottle, he did, and then put it in his inside right breast pocket. Betcher they's old-timers alive today who'll remember him fillin' this same flask, sech fancy pocket jugs not bein' common in them days. In fact, it's the only one of its kind I ever saw, and I never forgot the design on it. Well, twenty-five years later I find this same flask in a stope, 'longside a load o' coin and a man who's a long time dead."

"Proving what?" countered Patterson.

"You notice a bullet hole plumb through it?" Slaughter piped.

The sheriff nodded. Gregg himself saw that a bullet had once perforated the flask.

"That dude," cackled Slaughter, "died from that bullet. I remember that he and Sam Smeed got quite chummy after a while. I know he talked big an' dressed the part. He must 'a' impressed Sam; and when he got liquored up Sam must 'a' told him about the silver dollars. That's the way I figger it. An' I figger the day Sam died, this dude stranger stepped from behind a tree with a double-barreled shotgun. He let fly with both barrels, potting Smeed and his two guards as they sat on the seat of the coin wagon. One of the guards must 'a' snatched his .45 in time to sling one slug. He made a right breast hit, but it went through the flask first. After he was holed up in the stope, that wound must've festered. It finished him."

"You're claimin' he died from it?" Patterson asked.

Slaughter nodded. And to Gregg it seemed fairly reasonable. With a bullet in his body, a bandit might well have chosen to hole up with his loot in the nearest deserted stope. There, lacking proper treatment— if even that might have helped him—he died.

"No good," Patterson argued. "Because it was your shotgun, Slaughter, that did the shooting. They found two of your homemade shells there, empty. In court you claimed you loaned the shotgun to Smeed for the freighting trip, but you couldn't prove it."

"I can prove it now," Slaughter echoed in shrill triumph. " 'Cause in that same stope I found these."

He opened a drawer back of the bar and brought out two rusty, double-barreled shotguns. One was hammerless. One was not.

"This here one's mine." Slaughter tapped the hammer gun. "The other one must 'a' belonged to the dude stranger."

"Why would he take both of them to the stope?" challenged Patterson.

"Why wouldn't he? Maybe he expected to stand siege there. If so, two scatter-guns would be better than one. Anyway, there they were and here they are. It boils down to this: Either I shot Smeed with my shotgun, or the stranger done it with his'n."

"I'll admit that much," Patterson said. "Either you did it with your shotgun or somebody else did it with another. We've known that for twenty-six years, because all three victims were riddled with buckshot."

A delighted grin formed on Slaughter's bony old face. He rubbed his hands together gleefully, then spat on them.

"All right. It was either me or him. It was either me, his friend, that Sam always trusted and aimed to put in charge of a silver-dollar barroom, or a stranger. Take your choice, Sheriff. Say it was me if you wanter—and say I done it with this same old two-bore barroom bouncer what Sam hisself give me fer a present. 'Take it, Ike,' Sam said, 'and shoot hell outa any and all bums and crooks. Stand flatfooted on my silver-dollar floor, Ike,' he said, 'an' let 'em have it!' Them was Sam's very words, Sheriff."

Slaughter picked up the hammer gun and displayed its butt plate to Patterson. On it was engraved: *"From Sam to Ike."*

The old bartender's eyes were now swimming with rheumy tears, and his face was flushed. Gregg sensed that the old-timer was pressing hard toward some climax which had long seethed in his mind. Patterson must have caught that too. For he invited gravely:

"I ain't interruptin' none, am I, Slaughter? Shoot."

Slaughter nudged the other shotgun toward the sheriff.

"Look it over," he cackled. "It's the kind you've potted ducks with many a time. It wasn't made like mine was, fer close range in a barroom where they's no chance to miss."

Slaughter then tossed a key to Gregg.

"Young feller, unlock that broom closet under the stairs."

Gregg went to the rear of the room and unlocked the door of the broom closet. When he opened the door, he staggered back, shocked.

In the narrow closet was a chair. Seated in the chair was a human skeleton, the bones of a smallish man. It was crudely wired together and it sat upright, without a shred or rag on it and without a knuckle or a rib missing. The arch of bleached ribs, the round, empty eye sockets and the grinning teeth surprised Gregg so that his backward leap almost toppled him in a sprawl on the silver-dollar floor.

When he turned, Slaughter stood at the far end of the bar and about forty feet from the closet. He was aiming with the "Sam-to-Ike" shotgun. A single roar detonated as the old bartender fired both barrels.

Amazed, Gregg again faced the skeleton. The arch of ribs was still there; so were the arms and legs. But the skull was gone. *Only* the skull was gone. A headless skeleton sat upright in the closet. And Gregg saw that on the wall back of the position occupied a moment ago by the skull there was a sheet of white paper. Buckshot had perforated this paper, albeit the perforations were limited to an area no larger than the palm of a hand.

Patterson's jaw dropped. He realized, as did Gregg, that Slaughter's gun had *two choke barrels*. And that most shotguns have one choker and one spread or scatter barrel. Not conceivably had three men seated abreast on a wagon seat been riddled by a volley from two choke barrels. Smeed himself, in a futile snatch for his borrowed weapon, must have fired those twin chokers.

"Sam missed him, but I didn't!" came in shrill exultation from Slaughter. He was again at mid-bar and facing Patterson.

With calm deliberation the sheriff picked up the glass of liquor which, a few minutes ago, he had declined.

"To Silver Sam Smeed!" he offered.

Ike Slaughter drank with him, tears streaming down his cheeks. That ritual complete, the old scalawag wiped both glasses and put them away. With a proud and professional celerity he mopped his bar. Then he limped out and to the stairs. With one boot on and one off, he ascended to the loft.

Gregg heard him tramp across the room above. Came next the creaking of a cot. Then there was a single loud thump. With it Everett Gregg sighed and relaxed. At last that other boot was off, and the ghost had gone to bed.

Bannack Doctor

Norman A. Fox

ALWAYS the thing that had amazed Jason Weir was the swiftness with which news traveled in this wilderness that was Montana. Today the excitement had seeped into Bannack, destroying the Sabbath's comparative calm and giving men a studied alertness and a grim intensity. It had sent Jason out of Grissman's store in midafternoon, the blandishments of the wood stove in that favorite gathering place turned sour by the intrusion of a reality that was no concern of his. Let others worry about road agent and vigilante and guess where the ax would fall. And so he trudged toward his cabin on the camp's outskirt, a young man if you only counted the years, a tall man when his shoulders were straightened. And January's snow, hard packed, crunched beneath his boots, speaking of cold, speaking of loneliness, speaking of exile unending.

There have been plenty of notable ones among Norman Fox's twenty-odd Western novels, but the reader who chooses either *Tall Man Riding* or *The Badlands Beyond* will certainly be well rewarded. The best of his short fiction has been collected in *The Valiant Ones,* a jackpot-for-the-reader volume. Prominent in WWA affairs, Norman and his wife have a residence in Great Falls and a summer home in Montana's history-dripping Virginia City.

Around him the camp sprawled, sod-roofed cabin and gaunt frame shoulder to shoulder, the hasty habitations of the Argonauts crowding to Grasshopper Creek. A year ago, when Jason had first looked upon this hurly-burly, Bannack had scarcely had its inception: the flotsam of forlorn hopes, the debris of blasted dreams had just begun to backwash northward, a wave of emigration that had once made of Pike's Peak a beacon and found only disappointment in California's golden sands. Bannack had swelled and ebbed; last summer Jason had witnessed an exodus to Alder Gulch, eighty miles to the east, to the greater gold strike that had reared chaotic Virginia City almost overnight. Now, with 1864 less than a dozen days old, Jason wondered what another year would bring and found the thought strange. A man given to looking backward, he had looked ahead for an instant.

He shrugged this fancy aside, his tireless stride unbroken, and when he came to his cabin on Yankee Flat, he saw the trampled snow before the doorway, and this gave him pause, but only for an instant. Bannack's alarm had become a contagion, but he'd kept immune. The terror that rode this land, manifesting itself in robbed stage coaches and murdered wayfarers and hinting at an organization far from haphazard, had left him untouched. What interest could the road-agent band have in a man who panned only enough gold to provide himself with food and tobacco plus a change of clothes in the season when the Mormon freighters fetched wares from distant Salt Lake? So thinking, he swung the door inward and found three men who were awaiting him.

They were big enough to crowd the single, puncheon-floored room, and one of them he knew by name: Marty Breen, late of the Oro Fino diggings and given to much roistering in Virginia City's hurdy-gurdy houses, those roaring dance halls with the obvious side lines. The three wore mustaches and goatees in the style that Buffalo Bill Cody was to make famous, and all wore their neckerchiefs tied in a sailor's flat knot. Their heavy coats, thrown open, revealed Navy Colts at their belts, and Breen carried a sawed-off ten-gauge shotgun in the crook of his arm. By armament and insignia, they were of the road-agent band, if rumor had it right, but Jason's lean face stayed rigid at the sight of them.

He merely said, "Well, gentlemen?"

Breen shuffled his big feet. "We've heard tell that you're a doctor, Weir."

Jason shrugged, looking down at his worn boots, his homespun trousers, his flannel shirt—garb as rough as their own. "It's no secret that I once practiced," he said. "Back in the States. I'm a prospector now, sir. You'd better get Dr. Glick."

"Glick's made himself hard to find today," Breen said. "Where's your black bag, doc? We've got a horse ready for you."

This imperativeness put a great distaste in Jason, and he said, "I make it a point to mind my own business. I've no interest in your troubles."

Breen moved the shotgun, a movement almost imperceptible but tremendously eloquent, and said, "Better change your mind, Doc."

Jason shrugged again. "I promised to stop in at the Webb cabin this afternoon. The little girl is sick. I'll have to do that before I leave."

He watched their exchange of glances and would have placed his bet that there'd be a refusal, but Breen said thoughtfully, "Cora's safe. Cora wouldn't talk." And the familiarity with which he used the name tightened Jason's jaw, but some of the tension went out of the pair who'd stood silently listening.

Jason put his back to them, quit the cabin and went through the snow to the slope of the hill beyond Yankee Flat to where a tiny well-chinked cabin perched. When he raised his knuckles to the door, Cora Webb opened it and said breathlessly, "I saw you coming through the window. She's worse, Jason."

Cora was a tall woman, and a plenitude of petticoats could not conceal her lissome grace—any more than the shadow of worry could dim a beauty that to Jason Weir was like a flame in the wilderness. He had come here often as a neighbor, making this one exception to his rule of aloofness; and he moved now to the robe-covered bunk where a girl, a blue-eyed, six-year-old miniature of her mother, lay writhing.

Jason bent his browned face close to the child and said, "Where does it hurt, Sue?"

"My tummy," the child cried. "It's like knives sticking in me."

His hand explored gently, and his face was graver when he faced Cora. "Luke in town?" he asked.

She brushed a wisp of brown hair from her forehead. "Henry Plummer sent him to Virginia City again. Some business for the sheriff. Jason, she's—she's bad?"

He didn't answer, and that was answer enough. "I've got to leave camp for a while," he said. "If her fever gets worse, you'd better find Dr. Glick."

She followed him to the door and laid a hand upon his arm. And when he looked into her eyes, it was like being free again; and it would have been easy to forget that she was Luke Webb's wife. He'd told himself he came here only because of the child, but the deception was never thinner than at this moment. Cora's fingers held him, and she said, "You're good medicine for Sue. She trusts you, and that's half the cure. Couldn't you come back, Jason?"

An ancient pain turned his face bleaker. "She wouldn't be safe in my hands. Not under a knife, if it comes to that. Get Dr. Glick, Cora."

He left then, following his own footprints back to his cabin; and when he shouldered inside, the three still awaited him. Marty Breen scowled and said, "You could have stepped livelier, Doc. Time counts with a gunshot wound."

Jason got down to his knees beside his bunk and delved under it for his bag. "I'm ready," he said.

They walked to the horses; the animals stood back in the concealment of the brittle willows fringing Grasshopper Creek, and he was surprised to find that the mount for him was a rangy American horse, tall by contrast to the Indian cayuses and California broncos commonly used in the section. A certain George Ives had ridden such a horse as this, but Ives had been tried and hanged for murder in distant Nevada City about three weeks before, and thereafter the whisper had started of an organization, the vigilantes, that would meet the road agents' ruthlessness with a greater ruthlessness.

The saddle leather was so cold that Jason winced as he mounted. There was no gauging the temperature, but this was the bitterest weather of a bitter winter, holding consistently from twenty to forty degrees below zero since New Year's Day. The three pocketing him as the horses instinctively bunched together, Jason involuntarily looked back to Bannack and wondered if a bullet, insuring secrecy, would be his fee for this day's work. That would be irony for you—subjecting himself to this cold ride in order to die! He wondered than why he'd not long since thrown away the black bag that was his single bridge to the past; and he wondered too if there could be any real escaping from reality as long as he possessed it.

The ride was like something remembered from a nightmare when the blankets get kicked aside and cold seeps through the cabin's chinking and desolation haunts all dreaming. There was an endlessness of alder thickets and snow and the steaming breath of horses and men.

The chill wind whined a threnody through the brush; branches crackled with metallic sharpness to its passage. Jason judged that they were less than four miles out of Bannack when he smelled wood smoke and saw the thin, wavering lift of it. They had never been far from Grasshopper Creek and now they looped back to its frozen rim and found a camp of sorts. Three more men, flailing their arms and stamping their feet when their restless pacing took them away from the fire, stiffened to alertness. The fourth man lay upon the ground, blanket-wrapped and shapeless.

Marty Breen swore a long and savage oath and said, "So he's a goner, eh? Doc, I told you to step livelier!"

Jason came stiffly from his saddle and peeled back the blanket and had his look at the bearded face, and that was all that was needed. He had two thoughts then; the first was that Sue Webb was half an orphan now; and the second that it was better this way, for these were indeed road agents. The third was merely in passing—he understood now why he'd been allowed to stop at the Webb cabin.

The surprise came when he lifted his eyes to a man who approached him, one of the three who'd been waiting here. For that man was Bannack's choice for sheriff of the district—Henry Plummer.

He knew Plummer, of course. Every prospector in the diggings knew this slender, graceful man, so meticulous in dress and person, so eternally gracious. Popular vote had put the law in Plummer's affable hands; and if, of late, rumor had cast a shadow across his name, most people had laughed at the suggestion that Plummer was affiliated with the road agents. Yet Plummer's very presence here was the damning proof that rumor had not lied; and Jason, suddenly conscious of the knowledge now his, felt a stiffness between his shoulder blades and a dryness in his mouth.

Plummer said, "You seem to have had a cold ride for nothing, Doctor. What is your fee?"

In a whiskered era, Plummer kept himself clean-shaven except for a neatly trimmed brown mustache, and on his face today lay the first real shadow of worry. Looking at him, Jason thought of Lucifer fallen. But in Plummer's question there was a half promise of safe return; and this too was surprising and left Jason without answer. His fee? How did a man charge for his services in a country where a newspaper fetched two dollars in gold dust, and a cat was worth a hundred dollars to those who had need for one?

He said, "Whatever you think my time's worth."

Plummer put a buckskin poke in Jason's stiffened hand, and Jason pocketed this without looking at it. He got laboriously to his feet, his body clamoring to move nearer to the fire but his churning mind telling him to climb onto the horse and head away from here. He made it to the saddle, and the stabbing cold was welcome now, but Plummer put a hand to the saddle horn and smiled up at Jason.

"Leave the horse at the Bannack Hotel," Plummer said. "There'll be no questions asked. It has been obvious to me that you are a man of education and refinement, Doctor. And of discretion too, I trust. Discreet enough to realize that the dust I've given you will more than pay your fare out of these diggings. One of Oliver's coaches may be leaving for Virginia City tonight. Be on it, Doctor."

Here was the threat, silk-gloved but like the bite of steel, and Jason remembered Grissman's store and his leaving it today because he had no interest in talk of road agent and vigilante, and it was his bitter reflection that he'd chosen a poor way to escape the intrusion of reality.

He said stiffly, "Can't you believe that your affairs are no concern of mine?"

Marty Breen, dismounted and hovering near the fire, again shifted his shotgun. A swift savagery in his eyes, he said, "Are you fool enough to put your trust in him, Plummer? There are cheaper ways of buying a closed mouth."

Plummer said, "Shut up, Marty! We may all be running before the night's over. This is an affair between gentlemen. Doctor, be gone from Bannack tonight."

Whereupon Jason Weir, reading death in a man's eyes, brought the horse around and prodded it to a gallop. The brush rattled as he forced through it, and he held to a hard pace until he saw the lights of Bannack through the early dusk. The horse was taken from him at the Bannack Hotel by a surly-eyed man with a sailor's flat knot in his neckerchief, and, his mount led off into the gathering gloom, Jason had a quick drink at Percy & Hacker's saloon to take the chill out of him; and when he left the place, there was no conscious prompting of his footsteps, but they brought him to the Bannack office of A. J. Oliver & Company. The office was closed, but he found a man at the stables.

"No stage out tonight," Jason was told. "Schedule's all snarled on account of a holdup this side of Virginia."

"A holdup? Anybody hurt?"

"The driver got nicked. But the shotgun guard brought back word he nailed one road agent neat."

To Jason came the quick memory of Luke Webb's stiffened face, and he knew now how the man had come by his wound and why Webb hadn't been fetched into Bannack. He said, "Any chance of getting out of here tonight?"

"Some miners are taking a wagon through to Virginia. They'd give you a lift. Better be at the hotel no later than nine."

Nodding, Jason turned toward his cabin, drawing his coat closer about him, for the temperature had dropped with sundown. Again the hard-packed snow crunched beneath his feet, speaking of cold, speaking of loneliness and endless exile; and his first rebellion grew with that walk. He was used to putting his back to places; in a sense he'd been running ever since he'd come West, and Plummer's order had merely set the wheels in motion again. He'd long since ceased fighting against destiny, had Jason Weir; yet if a man was to be an exile, the place of his banishment should be of his own choosing.

Such was the run of his thoughts as he neared the cabin; but before he put his hand to the door, he knew he'd be catching that wagon out of Bannack at nine. After all, what was the difference between one camp and another? And what would be the gain in risking road-agent wrath for a principle? He'd had principles once, and they hadn't saved him.

Then he was in the cabin, and again he found someone awaiting him, sitting here in the darkness and the silence and the cold—a short, sturdy man, broad of shoulder and slow of speech. This man said bluntly, "You had visitors this afternoon, Weir. Three of 'em. I could give you their names, likely. You rode away with 'em. Where? And for what reason?"

Some spark of that momentary rebellion still burned, and from it flared a new flame, born of weariness and a sense that all the world was closing in on him. This feeling gave truculence to Jason's tone as he said, "And why should I answer?"

"You're a doctor," the little man said. "You don't work at it often, but we think you worked at it today. A man stopped a bullet in a holdup out of Virginia City the other night. We want the name of that man. And the names of any of his friends you happened to meet."

Jason said, "So you're one of those vigilantes the whole camp's talking about. You don't need my help. The whisper is going around that your stranglers caught Red Yeager, the messenger of the road agents, and George Brown, their corresponding secretary, and hanged the pair of them at Laurin's ranch on the Stinking Water. Talk has it that Yeager named the whole band before he died. Isn't that right?"

"In this business we want to be sure—very sure. We haven't hanged an innocent man yet. Did you look at a gunshot wound today, Doc?"

"And if I won't answer?"

A faint stirring of this strange visitor in the gloom—a stirring that might have been a shrug. "We've got a thankless job to do. But we'll have to remember that them that ain't for us is ag'in us. How do you stand?"

"I stand on neither side," Jason said, his voice a whiplash. "Can't any of you get that through your heads? All I've wanted here is the privilege of panning a little color—and of being left alone. Now get out; I've got things to do. If it makes you any happier, you can report that the man I attended was dead when I reached him. There's one new rope you won't have to spoil!"

The man came wordlessly to his feet and made his departure, and Jason stood waiting until the sound of boots, crunching in the snow, had faded away. Lighting a lamp, he stirred up a fire and began throwing his possessions into a trunk, and he was mindful that the time might be growing short, when he again heard footfalls. He got the door open, and Cora staggered inside, a shawl drawn tightly about her. She had never come here before; and in the first moment of surprise he could only say, incongruously, "You should have worn a coat. It's a bitter night."

"I ran," she said, and her voice told him how close to hysteria she was. "I ran all the way. Jason, she's worse—lots worse. You've got to come quickly."

The lamplight was not kind to her face; it made her drawn and haggard, and he wondered how long she'd been without sleep.

"I told you to get Dr. Glick," he said.

"He's not at his cabin. Jason, there's something wrong in town tonight. Choir practice was called off, and some of the women say the order's gone out that they're to stay in their homes tonight. The vigilantes are up to something. Maybe Dr. Glick is with them. You've got to go with me."

He almost laughed; but there was no humor in him, nor any emotion, but only the ancient pain and the feeling that destiny had woven this web and allowed for no escaping. Go to Cora's cabin and attend a sick child? Go, when Henry Plummer and his road-agent band would consider this disobedience of their order a challenge and a threat? Go, and thereby miss that wagon to Virginia City and seal his own death? Yet he knew that more than this tied his hands—that bowing to her wish would be crossing the bridge to the yesterdays.

But he knew no words to tell her that her faith was misplaced. How could he explain all this to a woman who looked at him with harassed eyes, a mother's wild fear in her? A woman who would still have to be told of her husband?

He said, "I have to leave Bannack tonight. But it wouldn't matter anyway. I'm no doctor. Not any more. I told you today she wouldn't be safe in my hands."

Cora said, "Sue's been calling only one name. Not mine. No, nor her father's. Yours, Jason."

He said then, frantically, "Hear me out. There were two men and a woman, once; that's an old story, as old as the Bible. I was one of those men, the other was my best friend, and he was the one the woman chose. I knew how to be a good loser—then. But one night he had to have an emergency operation and mine was the name he called too. I performed that operation, and he died under my knife. That was when the whispering started. David and Uriah. Maybe you don't know what whispering can do in a small city. They said foul and savage things, and the din of them got into my ears whenever I took up a scalpel. There came a time when I wondered if maybe they were telling the truth—that my mind had willed one thing and my heart another that night. It finished me. That's why you find me in Bannack, panning enough color to survive. That's why I've lived aloof. And that's why Sue wouldn't be safe with me."

It seemed to him that she'd grown taller while he talked and that the fear was gone from her eyes, but he didn't like the thing that had taken its place. She said, "So that's your story! That's why you threw away a fine skill and a fine future. Because you made one mistake—the mistake of running. My story's simpler, Jason. It has to do with only two people—a girl who tired of a bound girl's life on an Ohio farm, and a man named Luke Webb who talked wealth and had the romance of the West about him. I married Luke and I've lived with that mistake for eight years. Do you know how many times I was tempted to take Sue and start running too?"

So she knew at least a part of it.

He said, "This makes one thing easier to tell you. Luke died today."

"I know," she said. "Marty Breen stopped off at the cabin and told me. I can guess how Luke died. I haven't been altogether blind. But it's not Luke I'm thinking about tonight. It's Sue."

Her hand came from beneath the shawl, and a dragoon pistol that must once have belonged to Luke Webb, road agent, looked ponderous in her tiny fist. "I carried this tonight, not knowing what might be abroad in Bannack. I didn't think I'd need it beyond your doorstep. You'll have to go with me, Jason. I fight for what I love."

He stared at the gun in her hand, but it was not the weapon that moved him. The gun was part of it, but the rest was Cora; and he found it odd that in this instant he should at long last realize why he'd never thrown his black bag away. There was to have been a day when he would need the bridge to what he'd once been. There was an inevitability to all this that was more commanding than Marty Breen's shotgun, more compelling than a vigilante's wish.

He was smiling as he reached for his coat and draped it about her shoulders. "You can put the gun away," he said. "A man can learn many things from a woman. I didn't suppose that courage was one of them."

For a moment he thought she was going to faint; but when he moved to steady her, she took his arm. And so they went out into the bitter night together, the ominous night with its strange stirrings and its unspoken secrets. And they came to the cabin beyond Yankee Flat and to the side of the child who lay moaning. Jason made another examination and said afterwards, "It's what I feared when I told you to fetch Glick. An inflammation that's led to infection. Peritonitis. There's no choice now but to operate."

Cora faltered, then steadied herself. "Here?"

"Too risky to move her. You can help me. You've got water on the stove, I see. Good. Bring it to a boil and take all the instruments out of my bag and drop them into the water. Then rustle up all the lamps in the place, and all the candles too. And clear that table. We'll have to use it."

He was all medico now; he knew this woman's courage—he had borrowed from it tonight—but he also knew it was best to give her things to busy her hands and mind. The table was cleared and scrubbed; he lifted Sue from her bed to the table top and prepared her for the operation. The child watched him in silence, listless, no longer moaning; and shortly Jason said, "Cora, fetch the flask from my bag. Yes, that one. It's chloroform. We'll have to fashion our own means of administering it, but thank heavens I've enough.

And now a lamp and candles were clustered about the table, perched upon boxes and chairs; and Cora was standing by, another lamp held high; and the fireplace threw its lurid glow on log walls and slabbed floor. Jason frowned. The vapors of the chloroform, exposed to the flames of the lamps, would produce a choking gas, but he had to have light. Therefore he had to perform this operation quickly. He'd scrubbed himself, and when the chloroform had done its work, he stood with scalpel poised. And it was in this breathless moment that he had the fleeting thought that there was still time to catch the wagon at the Bannack Hotel. He looked at Cora across the table; their eyes locked and held, and Jason placed his hand on the swollen abdomen of the child and carefully began to make what he considered a sufficient incision.

After that the silence closed in, the strained, endless, nerve-wracking silence, broken only by his occasional requests for instruments, each request couched in words Cora would understand. Time ran on, and at first Jason feared his own clumsiness, and that put the sweat in his eyes. But this was an old and familiar performance, and heart and hand and mind were one with him tonight, and the surety came back with each motion. Once the child began to twitch, and Jason's hasty command fetched more chloroform. Then, at long last, came the time when the call was for the needle. And afterward Jason moved back from the table and gently took the lamp from Cora's hand and placed it upon a bench.

"We'll cover her and let her lie where she is. She'll be coming out of the chloroform soon," he said.

"She's going to be well, Jason?"

Her wan, strained face, was, he supposed, a reflection of his own; he felt unutterably weary of body, and yet a strange new strength was in him too, a strength of spirit. Smiling, he said, "She's in God's hands now, but he will treat her kindly, I know. We've done all we can do. There is nothing more to worry about, Cora."

And somewhere in his own words, he found the taste of irony. Nothing to worry about? Nothing but the fact that it must be well after nine o'clock and a wagon had departed from Bannack and Henry Plummer's band would have learned that Dr. Jason Weir had not been aboard that wagon. Nothing to worry about except that the hour was coming when he'd have to pay the price for his choice tonight. But he'd known that all along, and the price had made no real difference. The price of running from reality was greater, he had discovered, for that price stripped a man of principle and took from him the work that his hands were meant to do.

And in the midst of his thought, he heard the footsteps, the wild and floundering footsteps, the footsteps of a man lurching frantically through the snow. There was no knock. The door banged inward, and Marty Breen stood there, his hair tousled and his eyes aflame and his shotgun held in readiness. He said, "Thought you'd be here, Doc, when you weren't at your cabin. So you sold us out!"

Jason's glance went quickly to the child. "Close that door, you confounded fool!" he snapped.

"Worry about your own skin, Doc!" Breen said savagely. "The game's up here, but I'll leave you dead before I run. The vigilantes struck tonight. Got Henry Plummer asleep; and they got his deputies, Stinson and Ray, too. Hung all three of them on the gallows at the edge of camp. Now they'll be hunting down the rest of us. You peached, damn you! And I'll drag you to hell for it!"

The man was mad with fear and anger—and there could be no making him believe that somebody else had named Plummer's crew and brought Plummer to such an end. There could be no stopping that leveling shotgun, no dodging the charge of buckshot that would pour from it. Jason couldn't even raise his hands in protest; he felt too weary for that and too proud to beg, now that he had learned again the way that a man walked. And then he heard the gun go off. Not the shotgun. The shotgun was slipping from Breen's fingers and falling to the puncheon floor, and Breen had been slammed backward out through the doorway and into the snow by the force of a bullet.

Turning, Jason saw Cora; and he saw her gun again. . . .

He got through the doorway and bent over Breen and had a look. He raised his eyes when he heard the ringing beat of boots through the snow.

Jason got back into the cabin and closed the door and said, "You only wounded Breen, and that leaves the real job to a vigilante rope." And the lie tasted clean, for it would save her harsh nights of remembrance.

Again he thought she was going to faint; she reeled toward him, and he got his arms around her neck and took the gun from her hand. She said weakly, "Remember that man—back East—the one who died on your operating table? You lost a life, but you gave one back tonight —and almost at the cost of your own. Does that square things with yourself, Jason?"

But he was only remembering that once she had said, *"I fight for what I love."* Remembering that, and Marty Breen dead by her hand, and Luke Webb dead too, and the warmth of her against him, he knew now that there was an inevitability about this too. Sooner or later there was to have been this hour when he would open his arms and she would come into them.

Outside, he could hear the movement of many men, the dragging sound of a body being hauled away; and just for an instant a face was framed at the cabin window, the face of a short and sturdy man, broad of shoulder and slow of speech. This man looked from Jason's eyes to Jason's hand that still held the gun; and then the face was gone. But that brief glance told Jason that the man now knew how Dr. Jason Weir stood and would always stand—a man who had never lost his principles, though he had seemingly mislaid them.

Boots crunched in the snow again, the sound diminishing until it was lost in an immensity of silence; and there were only the room and the night and the sleeping child and the woman held close in his arms.

High Wind

Ernest Haycox

WHEN Abbie saw his big, easy-going shape press through the crowd on the platform, she stepped down from the car vestibule and went directly to him, excitement turning her dark and definite New England face quite lovely. He was enormously smiling; he simply absorbed her inside his arms. They were not particularly demonstrative people, but this was the climax of two years' waiting and two thousand miles of westward travel and it made them quite indifferent to the crowd roundabout.

Buck LaGrange said, "It's been a long time, Abbie," and kissed her in a way that erased for a moment her faint dread. Afterward he stepped back, his deeply pleased glance absorbing this girl who had come from their common home in Connecticut to marry him.

"You've changed," she said.

One of Western fiction's all-time greats, Ernest Haycox was equally adept at writing a range yarn like *Man In the Saddle*, a mining-camp novel like *Alder Gulch*, or a pioneer epic like *The Earthbreakers*. Further, he had few peers as a writer of Western shorts: "Stage to Lordsburg" is perhaps the best known, but there were many other outstanding ones—"High Wind," for example.

From PRAIRIE GUNS by Ernest Haycox, by permission of Little, Brown & Company.
Copyright, 1934, by Jill Marie Haycox

"Better or worse?"

"You're bigger—you're different."

The train porter had piled her luggage on the platform. Buck LaGrange said to a nearby man, "Put this stuff in my buggy, Pete," and drew Abbie over the platform.

Across the way Abilene's frame buildings made a raw, ragged line. There was a high wind blowing up from the south, dust-laden, hot, steady. When they left the lee shelter of the depot it threw her against Buck LaGrange and at once smothered her breathing.

She put a hand on her hat, gasping, "It's been like this all the way from Omaha. Does it never stop?"

He had to shout his answer against the wind. "Can't tell about a dust storm."

They beat across the street, following a weather-warped boardwalk as far as a small building on a corner; Buck LaGrange opened its door and pushed her in and closed the door again. Two men were standing in the narrow room, and a third man rose from a plain pine table. Buck LaGrange's amusement rolled out of his throat. "She's getting an immediate introduction to our prairie zephyr. Abbie, this is Mayor Henry, and Steve Gearin—and Wild Bill Hickok."

She acknowledged their slow nods with the briefest tilt of her own dark head, knowing nothing better to do. The wind shouldered against the walls and set up a squeezing protest of the boards. Something outside cracked like a pistol's shot. A man's yell whipped down the street, and suddenly she remembered Wild Bill Hickok's name with a start. Even in Connecticut, where the reports of the world seemed to be heard only as muffled echoes, this man's reputation had penetrated, and his deeds had become a legend out of the Wild West.

She recalled one thing she had read about him in a magazine—that he had killed nine men single-handed in one bloody fight. It caused her to draw faintly back against Buck LaGrange, but she made her eyes remain on Wild Bill. He was very tall and symmetrical, with light hair falling full length to his shoulders and a stringy mustache bordering full, broad lips. All his features were big and bold; yet they were soft, almost as soft as a woman's.

Buck LaGrange's deeply pleased words broke in: "Theodore"—pointing to Mayor Henry—"is a justice of the peace and can perform the ceremony. I asked Bill and Steve to be witnesses. These are my best friends. Well, I left Connecticut and this girl two years ago. It has been a long wait for both of us. Go ahead, Theodore."

The drumming of the wind, the eerie yellow color of the daylight, the strangeness of the town—these things confused her. Buck took her hand, and Mayor Henry, not much more than a boy behind his beard, said something about the authority of the state of Kansas. She heard herself whisper, "Yes." Then Buck turned her about in his big arms and kissed her. Wild Bill was watching all this with his heavy, winkless glance. His voice was musical and infinitely courteous. "It is not an easy country on women. Use your friends, Mrs. LaGrange, when you need them. Buck is to be congratulated."

The other two men shook hands with her, but it was all hazy and hurried, with Buck guiding her through the door. Somebody had brought the buggy around and she climbed to the seat and felt the blast of the wind. A square sheet of paper curled through the half gale, so weirdly that the nervous horses began bucking. Buck's voice lifted. "Steady—steady." He was laughing. He bent over, shouting:

"Write and tell your people the greatest gunman in the West was a witness at the ceremony!"

"A desperado!"

He didn't hear. He said, "What?" She didn't answer. They were careening around a corner, enveloped by a whirling wave of dust and sand. A row of houses, all unpainted and angular, sat along the short street; and beyond lay the howling open country, lost behind the dust. They stopped. Buck tied the reins and got down, handing her out. He led her across a yard faintly marked by tufts of scorched buffalo grass to a house standing square and uncompromising in the yellow light. Nothing distinguished it from the other houses, nothing relieved its barren outline. Buck opened the door quickly.

A hot, trapped air rolled into her face. The smell of dust and baked lumber was overpowering. It moved her backward against him, and he had to propel her gently across the threshold. When he closed the door the eternal rush of the wind died to a groaning, rubbing sibilance. A few pieces of furniture partially relieved the gauntness of the room. There was a white cloth on a center table, slowly turning gray.

"This is our home?"

"This is it," he said.

She turned toward him, and the sight of her eyes instantly sobered him. He delayed speaking a moment, seeking the right words. He said:

"I tried not to lead you to expect too much in my letters. It isn't the sort of house you came from. There are no such houses in Abilene. This town's only four years old. About all I can say is that nobody else here lives in any better house."

She came against him, putting her head down. He steadied her. "The zephyr's on your nerves, honey."

"Does it never stop?"

"Maybe tonight. Maybe a month from tonight. Nobody knows."

He went out for her luggage, making several trips of it; and afterward stabled his horses and rig in the barn behind the house. When he came back he found her in the kitchen, staring darkly at the stove. Wind gushed down the pipe, throwing ashes out through the grating. There was a mat of ashes on the floor.

He said, inexpressibly gentle: "One thing all of us have been forced to learn out here. We haven't the time nor the strength yet to fight the temper of the weather. The land won't change for us. We have to change with the land."

She was still watching the stove. "You have changed, Buck."

"In Connecticut I was a grocery clerk. I never would have been anything better. There's a chance for everybody out here. I mean to take my chance—and make a go of it."

She turned then. His deep pleasure was gone, and a shadow hovered faintly across his eyes. She knew what that was— it was the reflection of the doubt he had seen on her face. She had disappointed him. In this first hour of hope and happiness her faint withdrawing had made it less than perfect; and because he was a New Englander she knew the flaw would lie in his memory. The situation had slipped out of her hands. She didn't know how to set the shadow aside.

She said, with a faint laconic drawl: "I had better begin to work."

It continued to lie between them and to chill the intimacy which should have been theirs—the memory of that single instant in which her faith had wavered. Across the breakfast table she felt how easy it would be to bridge that gap with one warm word—and could not find the word; at night she knew he had only to put his arms around her in the rough, hot way of a man and kill the coldness forever. But he did not. In his slow, quiet talk was a perception of her reserve and a memory of his hurt.

This was the fourth day of their marriage, this was the fourth day of the wind. Walking with him toward the stores of Abilene, holding her skirts resolutely against the gusty plucking of that southern blast, she stared at the smoldering yellow sky and the sand-shot air with a feeling of unreality. It was as though she had been transplanted from a familiar world to the howling vacuum of another planet. The train was in from Omaha, spilling out its load of settlers and increasing the confusion in this bustling town. Men on the street spoke cordially to Buck. Everybody knew him, everybody seemed glad to see him. It reminded her more sharply of the fact that this genial, chuckling man was not the diffident Connecticut youth she once had known.

At Herrick's store he stopped. "I'm taking a couple of Dutchmen out to see some land. It looks like a sale. Real estate is on the boom, Abbie. I knew it would come some day." Then his solid pleasure broadened. "Land is our wealth."

Wild Bill came by and spoke. It was morning, with the dust rolling against all the building fronts. Up and down the uneven sidewalks cruised cattle hands in from the Texas trail, restless and reckless in their brief stay here. Steady traffic rolled through the saloon doors studding this street, and men's voices were high and rough against the wail of the wind. The smell of the stockyards on the southern edge of town covered everything unpleasantly.

"Just one thing, Abbie. We make our money from cattle driven here, and from the cowhands that come along. They're free spenders—and they're all wild. It's a rule that decent women stay out of this district after dark. But you're safe enough by daylight. No cowhand will presume to speak to you."

He lifted his hat and walked away; she turned into the grateful shelter of the store. She knew some of the women already there and acknowledged their greetings. Flora Gearin, the wife of that Steve Gearin who had been a witness at the mayor's office, came over to talk. She was a comfortably plump woman full of aimless gossip. In a little while Abbie went out, her arms full. Three cowhands rolled toward her and for a moment she felt fear; but it was strange how all of them instantly left the walk and passed by her without looking. Crossing the tracks, she saw Buck standing with a party of new settlers, his big shape rising above them. She had a doormat rolled under her arm. It dropped, and she struggled with her skirts and got it again and went on, the wind-driven sand stinging her fresh cheeks. Dust lay thick along her porch. It rose in powdery waves when she arranged the mat in front of the door;

it clung to her shoes and left prints across the bare boards of the living room.

Coming home late in the afternoon, Buck LaGrange found her on her knees with a scrub brush and a bucket of water. She had a towel tied around her head, and against its whiteness her face was very dark, very slim. She looked at him, not stopping her work. "Please brush your shoes on the mat before coming in."

He obeyed and closed the door and stood against it, observing the flush of her cheeks, the fire of energy that glowed through her. He didn't protest. He understood the driving zeal for order and cleanliness that impelled this New England girl to toil on her knees. But he said quietly:

"Don't try to do it all at once, Abbie."

She sat back on her legs, small and indomitable in the center of the floor. "The Gearins are coming tonight. I won't receive them in a dirty house."

"There are no clean houses in Abilene. You'll have to compromise with the dust. It will creep back as soon as you scrub it away. It will be in your clothes and your hair and in your food."

Her shoulders suddenly sloped, bereft of vigor. Her voice ran low. "Always?"

"No. In twenty years we'll have trees around Abilene to break this wind."

She murmured: "We'll be old people in twenty years, Buck."

He dissented cheerfully. "It will be a grown town in a settled country then. Such riches and comforts as there are, we shall share." He stopped, waiting for an answer that didn't come, then added gently, "The first years are hardest. Don't make them harder than necessary."

She rose and went into the kitchen, not speaking.

After supper the Gearins came. Hands folded across a fresh dress, Abbie sat quietly in her chair and could not make her words seem more than civil. Faint antagonism stirred in her, though she did not know exactly why. Nothing, it seemed, would ever disturb Flora Gearin's placid acceptance of things; her nerves were buried in her large, untidy body and her enigmatic smile repulsed all trouble. There was an indifference to what came along in both Flora and the bony, sprawling Steve that was to Abbie unforgivably close to laziness. Gearin seemed to possess a secret amusement at the world; and his talk was consistently ironical. "Heard you sold a Dutchman some land today, Buck."

"Part of Mike Olin's ranch."

"Another poor devil comes out here to starve."

"Someday you'll see all that section filled with big red barns," Buck drawled. He was in his shirt sleeves; his body comfortably filled the chair. Abbie watched him closely, this stranger she had married.

"If the wind don't blow the barns away," said Gearin.

"It will pass. It always has." His glance touched his wife and dropped. "I bought the rest of Olin's place for myself. Mitch Sullivan's stringing fence wire around it today. There's a brand of winter wheat being worked out in Minnesota. I'm seeding a hundred acres of it this fall."

Gearin leaned forward. "That's on the trail. You fenced across the trail?"

There was something here, unsaid but expressive. Abbie watched her husband's face tighten. "I know the trail drivers hate fences. But Abilene will outgrow the trail soon enough. When the herds quit coming from Texas we'll have something else better—farms."

"They'll tear out your fence—the first outfit that runs into it."

"I'll have something to say about that."

The Gearins left after an hour. Abbie said, formally, "It was very kind of you to call," and there was a moment then in which the Gearins looked quietly at her and Buck LaGrange stared solemnly at the floor. Mrs. Gearin said, "Come over to our place any time," and turned into the thick, swirling dark. Abbie watched them bend against the rising wind. Dust beat into the room; Buck LaGrange closed the door and filled his pipe, eyes striking across the bowl to his wife, poised rigidly by the table. Her head came around, and she thrust a still, questioning glance at him.

"You need all the friends you can get out here Abbie. Don't lose any."

Her lips barely moved. "Why do you say that?"

"You froze the Gearins out, honey. They won't come again."

She said, "I'm——" and closed her mouth definitely. Her shoulders were very straight; yellow lamplight ran smoothly across her black head. Gunshots raced out of the dark, a halfdozen explosions running together, dying together. Buck saw her flinch. "Texas cowhands," he said. "They're a wild bunch. But," he added patiently, "they will never touch you."

Her hands slowly reached the table's edge and gripped it. "Doesn't anybody care?"

"The house covers us. We're where we want to be. Those men out on the street are where they want to be. A man's his own master. He can take that gamble if he wants to. If he suffers, it is his own fault."

"You've changed. You're gambling too. In other things. In land and a new kind of wheat—and trees that may or may not grow in twenty years. With the dust and the wind. With your whole life to come, and mine." She pulled up her head. Her arms pushed against the table. "Isn't there anything certain at all here?"

He drew his pipe from his mouth, fist closing around the hot bowl. He scrubbed a broad palm across his jet, unruly hair. He dropped his chin, and the light of his eyes was ruffled and harassed. The calmness of his voice minutely broke.

"Well, there is one thing between a husband and wife that ought to be certain. One thing, Abbie—in spite of hell and high wind." His tone had turned harder. He stopped himself instantly and put the pipe between his teeth. She hadn't moved; her lips were set as though against pain. He said very quietly: "Don't let things ride you too hard."

She went through the bedroom door and closed it. Undressing in the dark, she crept between the sheets and lay straight and unyielding on the far edge of the bed, against the house wall. The wind struck the boards solidly, the sound of it like the rush of water. All the corners of the house were howling, and above her and around her was the moan of a terrific and overwhelming emptiness—the insane laughter of space. She closed her eyes and pressed her hands against her ears, but the reverberations of the wall came through the bed and into her body and scraped across her nerves. She clenched her teeth together, thinking of the soft, still twilight of Connecticut.

Buck came quietly in, and she pulled her hands from her ears and remained still. When he laid himself beside her he was careful not to touch her. Her fingernails bit into her palms; she cried silently, and her tremors shook the bed a little. But the frenzy of the mad world outside overbore this small disturbance, and he wasn't hearing her. She stared at the black ceiling. "I have failed him," she told herself. None of his warmth reached across the distance between them.

It was the fourteenth day of the wind. Going toward Herrick's store, she bowed her head against this insistent misery and tried to remember how it felt not to have that sullen crying in her ears.

It was a relief to be in Herrick's store, but only a momentary relief. Coming upon the women gathered there for the morning's shopping, she felt a dread at their reserve. In the beginning she had not known how to meet their friendliness; now she had no way of overcoming their chilling judgment. They thought her cold and proud. There was some polite talk, yet it was only by effort that she could relax the tight set of her lips to answer. Watching them, she was suddenly aware of a weariness, a premature oldness in each. The storm had done something to their faces.

She made her purchases and went out again into the driving smother. At the corner of the Alamo saloon, partially sheltered against the blast racing down the railroad tracks, she stopped to grip her bundles more securely. Men were swinging the Alamo's doors wide as they moved through, letting out the strong stench of tobacco and whiskey. Her glance traveled in a moment—and identified the tall figure of Buck standing by the bar, surrounded by a group of settlers. A high gust of laughter rushed at her, the doors swung shut. Abbie's teeth bit into her lower lip. She hurried on home. Somebody was moving into the adjoining house, for there was a clutter of furniture in the yard and five children running around the yard while a man, violently swearing, tried to move a heavy bureau through the front door. A woman stood in the flailing dust of the street and held the heads of a nervous team, the loose shape of her body describing an unutterable weariness.

Coming home in the premature six-o'clock darkness, Buck LaGrange found his wife standing at the stove, pouring jelly into glasses. The room was filled with a stifling heat; Abbie's cheeks were flushed and wet. She didn't look at him. "Supper's late. The wind comes down the chimney, and the oven won't heat."

"Never mind. Let's go over to the Drover's Rest and have supper."

Her voice was flat, stubborn. "I won't spend your money that way."

"Don't drive yourself so hard, Abbie."

She said: "Do you drink?"

"You'll never need worry about that. I do my business where I find men. The saloon is a good place to find them."

Lamplight shone against a window turned black by the weird night. Out of the steady, beating tempo of the storm rushed a sudden furious attack. It smote the house wall with a long, hollow booming and shuddered every board. The walls definitely swayed. Abbie stepped back from the stove. She looked at Buck, alarm widening her eyes. Her lips moved.

"In the center of it now," he said, and watched the elbow of the stove pipe bend from the wall. Soot gushed down the wall, its fine powder spreading darkly. Above the roar lifted the passionate yelling of a woman, the frightened cry of children. Then a man's outraged voice rode over this.

Abbie said: "They've been quarreling all afternoon. The words have been horrible."

"They're settlers, without any money. It's tough on them."

"They're vulgar!"

He looked at her carefully. "People like that can't afford to be polite and repressed." His words struck her more pronouncedly. "Maybe it's a good idea to quarrel and get it out of your system."

On the third Sunday she sat in the gaunt little room that was Abilene's church and bowed her head and remembered the lost gentleness of her Connecticut home. She could have cried then, had the bitter wind left any tears in her. Beside her, Buck stirred his big brown hands restlessly on his knees while the man in the pulpit shook a fist at the sparse congregation and spoke of the hell-fire and damnation to come. His voice was as strident as an auctioneer's. He had no pity and no gentleness in him, and his long, hungry face seemed to exult in the misery he pictured for them. When he had finished he strode down the narrow aisle, blotting the sweat from his face. Abbie was glad to leave. All the faces around her were tired, all talk was low.

She brought up her handkerchief and held it against her nose. The rank odor of the stockyards came on with the wind again, and all the sidewalk sweepings from the nearby saloons were whipping up into the air. A little beyond the church three narrow buildings sat side by side with drawn blinds; abreast them, Buck LaGrange moved around, placing himself between Abbie and the buildings. Nearby stood the school.

"Must the school and the church be here—beside *those?*" murmured Abbie.

"We do the best we can."

But she shook her head, speaking with suppressed vehemence. "Never—never!"

Buck said, "Hello, Bill." Abbie raised her head and found Wild Bill

Hickok, hat lifted, standing in the dust to let them pass, his long locks flung out behind his shoulders. She nodded only, made afraid again by that bold, womanish face. Above her the hidden sun made a round orange stain in the clogged air. In her own house once more, she put away her bonnet and stood a moment in the bedroom, feeling the tremble of her nerves. When Buck spoke, directly behind her, she started. She wheeled about, her fists doubled, her hands rising.

He said, concerned: "Didn't mean to scare you."

"I hate that man. Why do all of you go out of your way to show him your respect?"

"Wild Bill? He's my friend. Whatever else he is, he's that."

"A killer," she breathed in a minutely uncontrolled voice.

It brought his head down. "In the East," he said, "we'd be showing respect to the banker—for his money. Here we show our respect to Bill—for his courage. It's the thing we look up to. It's the thing we've all got to have. Just courage."

"Do you think I'd tell anybody at home he was at our wedding? Do you think I'd even tell them the kind of a wedding I had? I'm ashamed of it!"

"You're upset."

"Won't the wind ever stop?"

He scrubbed his hand along the sudden dampness of his face; worry cut quick lines across his brow. His eyes showed a ragged light. "Abbie," he said, "you're not happy."

"How can I be?"

He turned away from her. He went into the front room. His voice came back after a while, without emotion. "I had better send you home."

She came after him; she stood across the table from him, white and small. "You wouldn't go back with me?"

"I should be nothing but a clerk there. It isn't enough. I can't live that sort of a life any more. I'm not that sort of a man any more."

"Ambition has made you wild."

He said in a careful, dull voice: "The time to correct this mistake is now. I should be no happier there than you are here."

"There's something between us. There has been since the first day."

"Yes," he said.

Her lips stiffened. "I hate to think I can't be a good wife. Let's go back."

He spoke bleakly. "We'd carry this back with us. It would be in your head and in mine. Twenty years from now we'd be middle-aged people living in a house that had no warmth, no hope in it. That sort of starvation is worse than hunger for food."

She said: "Why do you——?"

Someone knocked rapidly on the door; someone said, in an excited voice, "Buck!" Abbie's lips went narrow and still again. She stood defensively in the center of the room, chin up and shoulders lifted. Buck's big frame blocked a half-open doorway and a man outside was speaking in swift phrases rendered unintelligible by the pound of the wind. In a moment he was gone. Buck closed the door. He stood with his hand on the knob, staring at the panel; when he swung about she saw the change in his face. It was darker, with a rising anger whipping up in his eyes. She said, "What is it, Buck?"

He crossed the room to a closet, reaching into it with an abrupt twist of his shoulders. Inexpressibly startled, she found he had a rifle in his hand when he turned again. Her voice lifted; it was breathless and peremptory: "Buck!"

"Well," he said evenly, "this had to come sometime. There's a trail herd coming toward my fence. They could travel another mile and go around it, but they're Texans and they hate fences. They intend to cut my wire." He stopped speaking and stared at the strangeness on her pale cheeks. He said, spuriously quiet, "I didn't put up that fence just for fun," and left the room. A little later, rooted to her place by the table, she saw him carried past a window in a buckboard driven by another man, who had whipped the horses to a run.

Something in that haste struck fear entirely through her. She moved over to the window and watched the buckboard swing at the railroad track and continue at a dead gallop on down toward the livestock yards, toward Buck's ranch two miles beyond town; she watched it fade into the yellow pall of dust. Afterward, for perhaps ten minutes, she remained in this position, her hands on the sill, the steady pounding of the storm vibrating through her arms. Her heart beat small and fast, and her lungs began to oppress her; and she thought in sudden despair she would never get enough air. There was some malignant, cruel force squeezing the breath out of her.

She turned and went into the kitchen. The stove had gone cold, and there was a roast half cooked in the oven; she rekindled the fire stolidly, matching her bitter anger against a draught which poured down the chimney and blew smoke out of the stove into her face. Her eyes, heavy with the constant dust, smarted unbearably. She gasped, "Won't it ever stop?" She held the stove-lid lifter in her hand. Suddenly she threw it blindly from her and went into the bedroom to change out of her Sunday clothes.

But she didn't change. Seated on the edge of the bed, she closed her eyes and put her hands over her face. Dust smell poured through the room. She got up and closed the bedroom door, hoping to shut off the strong current of wind leaking around her. It was no better. She said, on the edge of screaming: "Won't it ever stop?" There was a hard, long report sailing over her house; it dragged her back to a front window. All her muscles were taut, and her nerves were thin and raw, yet nothing was to be seen on the windy street beyond the railroad track, nothing but one humped-over figure beating his way against the wind into the clouded emptiness surrounding farther Abilene.

She let out a quick, gasping sound and ran across the room and left the house, bareheaded. She had to support herself for a little while against the picket fence; and then pushed on toward the center of town. Past the railroad tracks it occurred to her that Wild Bill would be in his saloon, where she couldn't go. But she could go to Theodore Henry, who would fetch him. Beyond the shanty depot the wind, racing up the open length of the street, struck her fully and wickedly. She had to push herself against it; she had to cover her nose to breathe. Over against the wall of the Alamo she stopped to catch her wind. Theodore Henry's real estate office was a few doors farther along a walk swept bare of life.

She pushed on; and then was halted by a voice coming curiously at her. Lifting her head she saw the buckboard coming back, veering to the walk's edge. Buck got out, holding to his rifle. The other man stayed up on the seat and turned to look behind.

"What have you done?" said Abbie.

He had done something, she knew. His face had no warmth in it. "They'll go around the fence. I shot one of them. Go home, Abbie——"

The man on the buckboard yelled. "Hey——"

Buck LaGrange pushed his wife away. He wheeled slowly, and the snout of his rifle lifted. "Go home, Abbie——"

A column of cowhands rode out of vagueness into the walk. Dust rolled enormously up. They were dismounting; and they were coming along the walk at a set and deliberate stride—one heavy man leading them. She had her fingers around Buck's arm; she felt his muscles go tight. That leading man stopped a pace away, his crew collecting around him. She knew they meant to kill Buck. Violence was in them, hatred poured out of them. The man said in a lashing voice:

"Put your woman aside! Put your gun down! We'll settle this fence business in a hurry. You'll shoot no more trail hands!"

Buck's arm swept out. It threw her across the walk into the side of the buckboard against the feet of the driver, who had never moved. There was a shout behind her, a scuffling of feet, and a deep cursing. She turned her head and saw a man drop under Buck's fist; she saw them coming on, smothering him. The man in the wagon yelled, "My God, lady, get out of here!" Her eyes went up to him and knew he wouldn't be any good. But there was a whip standing in its holder. She saw it and seized it and whirled back. Buck's shoulders rose in the middle of the mass bearing against him; he was silent in this pack which howled and struck and tried to bear him down. She raised the whip, slashing blindly out. She walked on, felt it strike them; she closed her eyes and kept striking and opened her eyes and saw men cringing away.

Behind her a cold voice commanded: "Stop that, boys!"

She was exhausted; and one of the crew had snatched the whip away. But there was no further need of it. For the cowhands had sprung back from Buck LaGrange, who was still on his feet, whose big arms swung and were ready to hit again. One man lay on the walk with blood dripping from his face. The voice behind her spoke again, chilly and monotonous.

"Looking for a little trouble, boys?" Turning, then, Abbie found Wild Bill standing behind her. His big body made an indolent shape in the mealy yellow light. One half-risen hand poised a burning cigar. But there was something greedy and deadly in the man's round, winkless eyes. He said, never changing his level tone: "Get out of Abilene."

The silence behind her was absolute; it was strange to her. She swung around—and witnessed then the power that belonged to one man and the fear he placed in other men's hearts. The cowhand struck down by Buck's fists got awkwardly to his feet, saying nothing. He simply turned and lifted an arm at his crew, and they all walked back to their horses. Her glance followed them until Buck's voice broke in. He was standing beside her, looking down with an intent interest. Wild Bill said:

"What are friends for, Buck? If you had a fight on your hands, why didn't you call me?"

He had taken off his hat, the wind whipping his long hair around his shoulders. He had put the cigar between his big lips and he was remotely smiling. "You're a fighter, ma'am. I admire courage. If there is anything you want me to do for you——"

The power of speech was out of her; she had nothing to say. Buck's hand took her arm and swayed her gently forward. They went out into the street and across the tracks toward home. He said something she didn't hear and braced her against the risen relentlessness of the wind. On the porch he opened the door for her. But he wasn't following. He had stopped at the threshold and was slowly brushing his boot against the mat. Weariness pulled his shoulders down and he braced one arm against the doorway.

Abbie's voice was stony; it was vehement; it was outraged. "Never mind, Buck. Come in here!"

His heavy eyes stared at her. She had to reach out and pull him forward; she had to close the door behind him. He seemed to have no strength left in him. There was a quickness in her breathing, a sudden graphic emotion across her dark face.

"You think I'm cold—everybody thinks I'm cold! I'm not—I never was! I have been a poor wife, Buck! But I love you!"

There was in his eyes the quick burst of hope. He reached out and he brought her against him, heavy arms pressing her hard. A flicker of humor loosened his lips. She felt the soft stir of his chuckle.

"I thought you'd never change, Abbie. It's been tough for us all. But the wind will stop. It will stop—and it doesn't matter any more."

Coward

Elmer Kelton

HIS HANDS tense on the leather lines, Dick Fladness flicked a quick, searching glance at the two women who shared the tight buckboard seat with him.

"Brownwood just ahead," he said.

He might as well have said nothing, for the women sat in dusty, tight-lipped silence, their eyes brittle on the scattering of frame buildings that spread out across the open prairie west of Pecan Bayou.

Dick's mouth went hard again, and he flipped the reins at the ill-matched team to pick them up a little. He had hoped the long, hot ride might wear down the contempt which stood like an adobe wall between the women and himself. But it had not.

He turned the corner by the blacksmith shop, and the trailing dust from the buckboard wheels caught up with him for a moment. Nora

Young, up-and-coming writer Elmer Kelton is a reporter and columnist for the San Angelo, Texas, *Standard-Times*. He has three novels to his credit: *Hot Iron, Buffalo Wagons,* and *Barbed Wire,* besides a respectable number of magazine stories. Every June, Elmer vacations by bundling his wife into the family car and heading for the current WWA convention— he's obviously prone to busman-type holidays.

Matson sneezed. It was the first sound the girl had made the whole way in, except that she had sobbed quietly when they first pulled away from the stark pile of gray ashes and charred wood that had been the Matson ranch home.

Dick pulled up in front of the hotel on Center Street and climbed down, wrapping the reins around the right front wheel. He held up his calloused hands to help Nora's mother down from the buckboard. Her eyes lashed him in scorn. She was a tall, graying woman with a stiff, Puritan kind of pride.

"I can get down by myself."

Her daughter followed her. Nora was eighteen, slender and pretty, with wide brown eyes that used to dance with laughter. Nora's eyes never touched Dick's face now, not while he was looking.

"I'll bring in your things," he said, nodding toward the small bundle of clothing under the buckboard seat.

Mrs. Matson cut him short. "We can manage that too. There's not much of it, since the fire."

Wincing, Dick stood silently by the buckboard wheel while the two women climbed the steps to the high plank gallery of the frame hotel. The balding proprietor hurried out and took the bundle from Nora Matson's hands. He turned solemnly around to the girl's mother.

"We heard about your son, Mrs. Matson. I'm terribly sorry."

She acknowledged his sympathy with a quick nod of her chin, which suddenly was set harder than ever. Stiffly she went on into the hotel, Nora right behind her. The hotel man paused for a quick glance at Dick. His frown showed that he knew. The whole town must know.

Head down, Dick stepped up into the buckboard and flipped the reins. He pulled the team back around and rolled down to the livery barn at the end of the dusty street. He was conscious of idle eyes following him. He drew up within himself and tried to convince himself that he didn't care.

Mike Lavender walked out through the big open door of the frame livery barn and stood waiting for him. Mike was a stiff old cowhand who had had to seek an easier way to round out his days. His leather-dry face was expressionless, but Dick could feel a quiet friendliness in the faded blue eyes. He leaned eagerly toward that friendliness, needing it for strength.

"Walter Matson's buckboard and team, Mike," Dick spoke. "Walter said let you take care of them."

Dick took his war bag and bedroll out of the buckboard and started out. He walked with a faint limp.

Mike Lavender's eyes followed him. "What about you, Dick? What you goin' to do?"

Dick stopped in the open doorway, his saddle slung over his shoulder. "Leave, I reckon. Go someplace where people haven't heard of me. Then maybe I can start over."

Mike Lavender shook his head. "You can't run away from a thing like this, Dick. It'll follow you. Take my advice and stay right here."

Dick dropped the saddle heavily, desperation raising the color in his face. "Look, Mike, don't you know? I'm a coward. Anybody can tell you. I lost my head in a fight, turned tail, and deserted my friends. And a man died."

He lifted his hands. "Mike, do you think I could stay here and have people looking at me the way they will, like I was a coyote or something? Snickering at me, maybe calling me a coward to my face?"

Mike's pale eyes were patient. "Talk's cheap, Dick. You don't have to listen to it." The old cowpuncher's voice softened. "Dick, son, these things have a way of workin' themselves out if you just give them a chance. Now you pitch your bedroll on that spare cot back yonder. You're stayin' with me for a spell."

Dick stood uncertainly, weighing Mike's words. It was going to be tough, staying here with the name the town would give him. But it would be tougher leaving, for the memory would be with him always, haunting him with the image of what might have been, the futile knowledge of things left undone.

If he left now, there would never be any coming back. He thought of Nora Matson, the tinkling magic of her voice, the warmth of her cheek against his as they stood in the moonlight, the cool evening breeze searching leisurely across the bayou.

Leave, and anything there might have been between them would be finished. Maybe if . . .

He picked up the bedroll then and carried it to the empty cot.

Mike slouched in a cane-bottomed chair, idly whittling a stick of kindling wood down to a sliver. His pale eyes lifted as Dick came back. After a while he said, "I've heard the story the way it's been told around town. I'd like to hear it your way."

Squatting on the ground, Dick stared hollowly at the pile of pine shavings that was growing around Mike's big, worn-out boots.

"You've probably heard it just the way it happened," he said. "It's the barbed-wire fences that caused it. Ansel Hornby and his freegrassers have been cutting Walter Matson's fence, and we've been patching it right up again. Three nights ago they cut it and left a placard hanging on a fence post. They said if the fence went back up they would end the fight once and for all. Walter tore the placard to shreds, and we fixed the fence.

"They waited till the sheriff had to be out of the county for a couple of days. Then last night they came. They were masked, but I know Ansel Hornby was leading them. And I recognized the voice of Branch Collin, that foreman of his. They didn't stop at the fence. They came right on to the house. We were putting up a pretty good fight, Walter and his son Lindy and three of us cowboys. Then they got the house to burning."

Dick's hands began to tremble, and his eyes misted. "I tried, Mike. I tried to stay there and fight. But those flames got to licking up around me. My clothes got to smoking. I couldn't stand it. I jumped out the door and broke into a run. All I could think of was to get away from that blaze. I didn't quit running till I fell. I laid there awhile and finally got a grip on myself. I could tell that the shooting had stopped. I went on back. The fence cutters had gone. The house was burned down. And Lindy Matson was dead."

Dick's head was in his hands. "There wasn't a one of them would speak to me. They all looked at me like I had killed Lindy myself. Came daylight, the cowboys rode after some neighbor help. Everybody went up on the hill to bury Lindy. They wouldn't let me help carry him. They wouldn't even let me help dig the grave.

"And when it was all over, Walter told me he wanted me to go. So I brought the women to town, where they would be safe. Walter stayed. He swore he was going to put the fence back up and fight Hornby's free-grass men till he was dead."

Dick's face was grim. "He meant it, Mike. He's got the guts of a Mexican bull. But Hornby'll kill him. He knows the county's watching Walter. He knows if Walter's fence stays up, there'll be others, and the free-grass men will be fenced out. He won't quit till Walter's dead."

Sitting on the edge of his cot, trying to figure out what to do, Dick

Fladness heard the clatter of horses' hoofs coming up from behind the barn. He caught the unintelligible conversation and the raucous lift of laughter. Dick glanced at Mike Lavender and saw that old cowboy bent over in an uneasy nap.

Stiffly, Dick stood up and walked toward the front of the barn. The limp was momentarily heavy because he had been sitting down. He heard riders hauling up on their reins and swinging to the ground in a jingling of spurs.

"Hey, Lavender," a voice called roughly, "how about us throwin' our horses in a corral here for a little while?"

Dick's heartbeat quickened. He would know that voice anywhere. It belonged to gunman Branch Collin. Dick hesitated, looking back at the sleeping Mike Lavender. Then he walked on to the door. Facing Collin, he jerked a thumb toward Lavender's pens.

"Mike's asleep," he said, "but I reckon it's all right."

Branch Collin was a medium-tall, slender man with a quick, easy movement and a sharp, sensitive face. There was a hint of green in his eyes that seemed always to contain a devilish kind of laughter. Ansel Hornby was boss of the ranch. But Branch Collin was undisputed boss when it came to trouble.

At the sight of Dick, Collin dropped his hand toward his gun. Then his mouth broke in a broad grin. "Hey, Ansel," he exclaimed, scorn in his voice, "look who's swampin' for Mike Lavender now. It's Richard the Lion-Hearted."

Dick flared, but he gritted his teeth and held the temper down.

Ansel Hornby kneed his big roan up closer. Hornby had a narrow, intense face. Dick had never seen him smile. Hornby's voice was flat and grim. "Dick Fladness. You should never have quit running last night. You should have kept going till you were clear out of the country. I advise you to move on now."

Anger beat against Dick, but his throat was tight. He could not speak.

Branch Collin said, "He'll leave, Ansel." Collin's smile still lingered. His eyes dwelt heavily on Dick's. "But not till he puts up our horses for us."

Dick opened the gate for the men to ride in. There were five of them, beside Hornby and Collin. They unsaddled and turned their horses loose in the corral.

Collin shook his finger under Dick's nose. "You feed them horses good, you hear? If you don't, you'll find yourself runnin' faster than you did last night."

A couple of the men chuckled. Enjoying the approval of his little audience, Collin suddenly pulled Dick's hat down over his eyes, hard. "There, that's just to be sure your hat don't blow off while you're runnin'."

Trembling with anger and humiliation, Dick pulled his hat up. Collin and the men were walking away, laughing. But Ansel Hornby still stood there, his humorless eyes on Dick's blazing face.

"Man down the road said you brought the Matson women in. They put up at the hotel?"

Dick's answer came brittle and sharp. "You leave the women alone!"

Hornby's eyes widened in speculation at this unexpected hardness in the cowboy who had run away. "I'm not here to hurt the women, Fladness. But sometimes you can reason with a woman when you can't talk to her men." His eyes narrowed again. "You better consider what I told you, Fladness. You can ride a good way between now and dark."

Ansel turned and broke into a brisk stride to catch up with his men. Their spurred boots raised puffs of dry dust in the street. Dick watched Hornby point toward the hotel. But Collin shook his head and jerked his thumb at the saloon. They would take a drink or two first.

Dick's mind turned to Nora Matson and her mother. If only Sheriff Adams were in town . . .

Dick stepped hurriedly back into the barn. In his haste he almost knocked down Mike Lavender. The old man had awakened to the lift of voices and he had seen at least part of this.

Dick limped back to his war bag and took out his belt and gun.

Lavender watched him worriedly. "You sure you know what you're doin'?"

Dick's glance touched him, then dropped away. "I don't know, Mike. I only know I've got to do something."

Summer heat clung heavily over the empty street as Dick hurriedly walked up Center. He sensed men watching him. He heard a snicker and felt the blood rising warm to his face. He held his eyes straight ahead.

An idler leaning against the door at the smoky blacksmith shop pointed a crooked finger and hooted at him. "You're runnin' the wrong way. They're in front of you, not behind you."

Choking down anger, Dick stepped up onto the long hotel gallery.

A backward glance showed him Hornby and Collin pushing out of the saloon. Dick moved on in. The proprietor eyed him suspiciously.

"I've got to see Mrs. Matson and Nora," Dick told him.

The hotel man frowned. "Don't you think you'd better move on, Fladness? I don't believe they will care to see you."

Dick's nervous hands gripped the desk edge. "I know what you think of me. I know what the town thinks. But that doesn't matter right now. Ansel Hornby and Branch Collin are on their way here to see Mrs. Matson. She ought to know."

The man's eyes widened. "They're upstairs in Room seven. I'll go with you."

Dick rapped insistently on the door. Mrs. Matson pulled it inward. Her grieved eyes hardened at the sight of Dick Fladness. "I thought you'd be gone by now. What do you want?"

He told her. Mrs. Matson's jaw set like carved stone.

Dick finished, "I'll be here if you need me." He tried vainly to see past Mrs. Matson, perhaps catch a glimpse of Nora.

Winter ice was in the tall woman's voice. "We needed you last night. We can do without you now."

Through the open door he watched her move back to a wooden dresser and reach into the drawer. Then Dick turned away. Slowly he walked down the stairs, the hotel man behind him. At the foot of the steps Dick stopped and waited. Ansel Hornby strode through the open front door and stood a moment, adjusting his eyes to the dark interior. Branch Collin came in behind him and stood at his side, mouth fixed in his usual hard grin. Dick felt the gunman's eyes raking him in contempt.

A soft, feminine tread on the stairs behind him made Dick step aside. Mrs. Matson came down, and Nora. Dick glanced quickly at Nora. Her brown eyes sharply met his, then fell away. Her lips trembled.

In an empty gesture of politeness, Ansel Hornby removed his broad-brimmed hat and bowed slightly. Branch Collin never moved or changed expression. "Good afternoon, Mrs. Matson, Miss Matson," Hornby said. "I heard about your son. I want to tell you how deeply I regret it, ma'am."

Hatred darkened Mrs. Matson's face.

"It wasn't necessary, Mrs. Matson," Hornby went on. "It isn't necessary that there be any more deaths, either. You could stop it."

Dick saw that her hands were trembling. One of them was covered by a dark brown shawl.

Hornby's voice intensified. "It's only the barbed wire, ma'am. I think I could talk to the fence cutters, if I had your assurance that the wire would not go up again. Your husband would listen. That's all it would take, just a word from you."

Mrs. Matson's voice was quiet and flat. "It's our land. We have the right to fence it. We'll still be there when you're dead."

Hornby's face began to cloud. "There'll be more killings, Mrs. Matson. A word from you could save your men. Keep silent, and they may die."

Mrs. Matson's lips curved downward. "No, Ansel. It's *you* who will die!"

The shawl fell away. Gun metal winked a reflection from the window. For just an instant Dick froze. He saw Branch Collin's hand streak upward from his holster.

Dick leaped at Mrs. Matson. He grabbed her hand and forced it down. The barrel blazed in his grip as the gun thundered and a bullet bored through the plank floor. In fury Mrs. Matson threw her body against him, struggling for the gun. But Dick got a grip on the hot barrel and wrenched it away. It clattered to the floor at Hornby's feet. Mrs. Matson fell back against her daughter, sobbing. Her face was splotched red, and her eyes blazed.

"You *are* a coward. Get out of my sight. If I ever see you again, Dick Fladness, I'll kill you!"

She whirled and tromped back up the stairs. Dick flinched under the lash of contempt in Nora's dark eyes. The girl hurried up after her mother.

Branch Collin's eyes followed the women. "Another second and I'd've shot the old witch," he said coldly. "Good thing for her you did what you did, Fladness."

Dick's face twisted. "I wish she'd killed you, Ansel. One way or another, you're going to die."

Hornby's face blackened. But Branch Collin was cool. That hard, set grin came back to his mouth, and suddenly he was a cat stalking a mouse. "You talk big for a man who can run so fast, Fladness. Maybe you better apologize for that."

Dick clenched his fists. "I apologize for nothing."

Collin's hand toyed at the butt of his gun. "That's a good-lookin' gun you got in your holster, Fladness. Maybe you'd like to try to use it."

Dick went cold. He knew what Collin was after. Thwarted once, the blood lust was still on the man.

"I couldn't match you, Collin," Dick said.

Collin's eyes remained on him, hard as steel. Finally they dulled in disappointment. "Crawfished again."

Impatiently, Ansel Hornby spoke, "What did you expect, Branch? You knew he was a coward. We'll give the boys another hour at the saloon. Then we'll take another ride around the bayou and see about that wire. We're going to finish this thing tonight, once and for all."

He turned on his heel and strode out, his spurs ringing dully to the strike of his heavy boots. Collin faced Dick a moment more.

"Another hour," he said grimly, "then we'll leave. But you better be gone before that, Fladness. If you're still here, I'll leave you hangin' on the fence like any dead coyote."

A chill on his shoulders, Dick stood and listened to the fading tread of Collin's boots as the man stepped down from the gallery. Cold sweat broke on Dick's forehead and on his suddenly weak hands.

The hotel man's shaky voice broke the stillness of the room. "That was better than I expected of you, Fladness. But you'd better move on. You can get a far piece in an hour."

Woodenly, Dick picked up Mrs. Matson's gun where it still lay on the freshly swept floor. He handed it to the hotel man. "Take it to her. She's liable to need it."

Dick stood on the hotel porch, steadying himself against a post. The heat of late afternoon rushed against him, stifling him, crushing his lungs. The street seemed to be stretched out of shape. It swayed back and forth before him and it looked a mile long. He knew it was his nerves. They tingled like telegraph wires.

Two men stood in front of the nearby saloon. One of them pointed to him with a wry grin. The man's words came down the street to Dick like the slap of a swinging rope.

"Bet you the drinks he lights off that porch in a high lope."

Dick swallowed hard. Deliberately then, he stepped down into the street. He started back toward Lavender's barn, his steps measured and slow. Scared? Sure he was scared. But he told himself he wasn't going to run.

It seemed an hour before he gained the door of the barn. Mike Lavender's chair was empty. Dick sagged into it. Lavender hobbled up, braced his long arm against the door and leaned on it, looking out across the town and saying nothing.

"You've heard about it?" Dick asked him finally.

Mike nodded gravely. "Collin means it, Dick. I told you while ago that you ought to stay. Well, now I've changed my mind. You better go, son. I got you a horse in the pen back yonder."

Dick sat staring at the ground. A thousand things hummed through his mind, memories of people he had known and ridden with and liked. He had especially liked Lindy Matson. Now Lindy was dead. Maybe it was Dick's fault, and maybe it wasn't.

"Are you goin' or ain't you?" Mike queried anxiously.

Dick shook his head. "I don't know, Mike. Give me time to think."

For a long time he sat there staring vacantly across the town. He watched a lazy cur dog make its leisurely way down the street, checking under high porches, sniffing at every corner. He watched a brown hen out back of a washerwoman's house, scratching around in the thin shade of a mesquite, seeking a cool place to sit.

But most of all he watched the saloon where Collin and the Hornby crew were. Occasionally he would see one or two of them come out, look around, and go back in. He could feel speculative eyes appraising him from a distance, and he wondered what the betting odds were that he was going to run.

Mike Lavender tromped back and forth in the barn like a stallion in a small corral. Now and then he would stop in the door and look up the street with Dick. Once he reached into his pocket and drew out an old stem-winding watch.

"It's been half an hour already, Dick."

Dick nodded dully.

Mike said, "Son, I know that on a thing like this a man has got to make up his mind for himself. But anybody would know you ain't got much chance against a man like Branch Collin. Supposin' you leave now, there's not much people can say that they ain't said already."

Dick never answered. He just sat in the doorway, watching.

Eventually he saw the flare of a long skirt on the gallery of the hotel. The girl stood looking down the street toward the barn. Her shoulders squared as she saw Dick sitting there in the doorway. Quickly she lifted the hem of her skirt and rushed down the steps and onto the street. In a few moments Nora Matson stood in front of him. Her pretty face was pale.

"Dick," she said huskily, "are you a fool? I thought you'd be gone by now."

Bitterness coiled in him. "Like last night?"

She flushed. "Dick, it won't help anything for you to stay here and get killed. It's too late to bring back Lindy."

He searched her eyes for some sign of the love he had seen there before. "Does it still matter to you, Nora?"

Her soft lips trembled. "Yes, Dick. Last night changed a lot of things, but I can't forget everything that was between us. I'm begging you to go. Please."

Dick watched her walk hurriedly back toward the hotel, drawing upon her stout pride to keep her shoulders straight and her head high. Dick looked down, staring fixedly at the ground in front of his brush-scarred boots. He heard Mike Lavender stomping around behind him.

"Mike," he said, "is that horse still out there?"

A sigh of relief passed the old cowhand's lips. "He is, Dick. And it's high time for you to go."

Stiffly Dick stood up. He glanced at the saloon long enough to know he was being watched from there. Then he moved back into the barn and picked up his saddle and bridle. He flipped a loop over the horse's head, pulled him in, and bridled and saddled him. The pen had an outside gate opening west. Going out through it, a man could leave town without going into the street. But it wouldn't keep him from being seen.

Mike strode out of the barn with Dick's war bag. "Here's your gear," he said. "Good luck to you."

"Thanks, Mike," Dick replied. "But it's not me that's going. It's you!"

Lavender stepped back, jaw sagging. "Me? But what in the——"

Dick said, "Look, Mike, you know I couldn't beat Collin if he came looking for me. But still, I'm a pretty fair shot. If I had surprise on my side to slow him down, I might beat him.

"You're about my size, Mike. You're going to spur out of this gate and head west in a lope. They'll all think it's me. When Collin comes, he won't be expecting me. Maybe that'll be enough to give me the edge."

The old man's face drew sharp with anxiety.

"Mike," Dick said, "in case it doesn't work out, I sure appreciate the way you've stuck by me."

Lavender placed his knotty hand on Dick's shoulder. "I knew why you ran last night, Dick. I knew you weren't a coward. Good luck to you."

Dick opened the gate for him. The old man spurred out and swung westward, the dust rising beneath the horse's hoofs.

Dick watched him a minute. Then he latched the gate and hurried once again through the back door of the barn. In the shadowed interior he picked his spot, about twenty feet inside the barn door, where he would not readily be seen from outside. He pulled up a chair and sat down to wait. Holding the gun, he sat back, his hands cold with sweat, nervousness playing through him like lightning in a stormy sky. His eyes set on the open door, he waited. . . .

He heard the voices before he saw the men. They were laughing voices, lifted high by the warmth of liquor. Dick heard the easy jingling of spurs. Then Branch Collin and Ansel Hornby swung into view, their men trailing a little behind them. Collin was laughing, and even Hornby's normally somber face was showing a little humor. The sight of the horseman spurring out the back way had been a joke even Hornby could enjoy.

Still in the sunlight, Collin threw back his head and roared, "Hey, Lavender, I see we flushed your quail."

Collin and Hornby walked in through the door and passed into the shadow. Collin blinked away the momentary blindness and sought out Dick Fladness's form in the dark of the barn. Dick stood up and took one step forward from the chair.

Collin's jaw dropped in amazement as recognition hit him like the lash of a whip. His hand dipped.

But the surprise had delayed him a moment, and in that moment Dick was bringing his own gun up into line. It exploded twice. Collin's weapon cracked once, raising a puff of dust at the gunman's toes just before the man buckled at the knees.

Paralyzed, Ansel Hornby stared foolishly at Collin's sprawled form. Then he grabbed at his own gun. But that was foolish too, for Dick put a bullet through his chest just as Hornby's .45 cleared the holster.

Deafened by the thundering echo of gunfire within the walls of the big barn, Dick Fladness stood still, peering through the cloud of gun-smoke to see if any of Hornby's men wanted to take up the fight.

None of them did. Muddled with drink, they had been sobered quickly by the sudden and deadly roar of guns. Without their bosses, there seemed little reason for them to carry on the fight. Hands high and neutral, one of the Hornby men ventured in the door, his eyes wide with amazement and shock. He knelt beside the fallen men and touched each of them. His gaze touched Dick Fladness a second and dropped to the smoking gun that Dick still held in his hand.

"Dead," Dick heard him say incredulously. "Both dead."

Dick moved cautiously toward the door and watched. When he was satisfied that the Hornby men were gone, he dropped his gun back into its holster and sagged weakly into Mike Lavender's chair.

Dusk gathered heavily. Dick sat on the broad gallery of the hotel, the cool evening breeze bringing him relief from the heat and ordeal of the day. From inside the lobby, Mike Lavender's voice drifted out to him.

"You see, Mrs. Matson," Mike was saying, "Dick never was a coward. It was the fire chased him away last night. It was several years ago that Dick and me were both workin' on the same ranch. One night one of the cowboys got careless with a cigarette. We woke up with the bunkhouse burnin' down around us. The smoke had already knocked out a couple of the boys in their sleep.

"There wasn't time for us to do anything but run. Dick tried to drag out one of the boys who was unconscious. But part of the roof fell in on him. Dick was pinned under a burnin' timber that broke his leg. He had to lie there and see that other cowboy burn to death. Dick finally managed to pull loose and drag himself out before the whole building caved in.

"That's where he got his limp. And that's where he got his fear of fire. He's no coward. Most anything else he could have stood. But when those flames got to burnin' him last night, he couldn't hold out."

Presently Mrs. Matson came out onto the gallery. Nora was with her.

"Dick," Mrs. Matson said, "I wish there was some way to tell you——"

Crushing his hat awkwardly in his hands, Dick forced a smile. "I know."

Mrs. Matson reached out and gripped his arm. "Dick, I wish you would go hitch the team to the buckboard. I want you to take us home."

Dick shook his head. "There's not much home left out there."

Her shoulders braced with pride. "No house, perhaps, but a house can be rebuilt. It takes more than a fire to destroy a home."

Dick stepped down off the porch and started toward the livery barn.

"Wait for me, Dick," Nora Matson called. She hurried down off the porch and ran to him. Then, arm in arm, they walked on. It was the way it used to be. And they were going home together.

The Rancher's Lady

Elmore Leonard

THEY came to Anton Chico on the morning stage, Willis Calender and his son, Jim; the man getting out of the coach first, stretching the stiffness from his back and squaring the curled-brim hat lower over his eyes, and then the boy, hesitating, squinting, rubbing his eyes before jumping down to stand close to his dad. It had been a long, all-night trip from the Puerto de Luna station and a six-hour ride in the wagon before that up from the Calender place in the Yeso Creek country.

Willis Calender had come to Anton Chico to marry a woman he'd never met except in letters. Three letters from him—the first two to get acquainted, the third to ask her to be his wife. She'd answered all of them, saying, yes, she was interested in the marriage state and finally she thought living down on the Yeso would be just fine. Which was exactly what the marriage broker said she would say. Her name

To discriminating readers, Elmore Leonard's novels of the West seem inordinately few and far between: *The Bounty Hunters, The Law At Randado, Escape From Five Shadows;* only three, but all solid achievements. His short stories, equally well done, have been published in leading magazines. A spare-time writer, Leonard lives and works in Detroit.

was Clare Conway and she was to come over from Tascosa and meet Willis.

He brought Jim along because Jim was eleven, old enough to make the trip without squirming and wanting to stop every second mile, and because he was anxious for Jim to meet this woman before she became his mother. Then, the trip back to Yeso Creek would give the boy time to get used to her. Just bringing her home suddenly and saying, well, Jim, here's your new ma walking in the door, would be expecting too much of the boy; like asking him to pretend everything was still the same. Jim had been good friends with his mother—though he didn't cry at the funeral with all the people around—and he had a picture of her in his mind as fresh as yesterday. Willis Calender knew it, and this was the only thing about remarrying that bothered him.

Little Molly was different. Molly was three when her mother died, and Willis wasn't sure if the little girl even remembered her still. The first few days with the new mother might be difficult, but it would only be a matter of time. It didn't require the kind of getting used to her that it did with Jim; so Molly had been left home with their three-mile-away neighbors, the Granbys. Molly was four now, though, and she needed a mother. She was the main reason Willis Calender had written to the Santa Fe marriage broker, who was said to have the confidence of every eligible woman from the Panhandle to the Sangre de Cristos.

The boy looked about the early-morning street and then to his dad, who was raising his arms to take the mail sack the driver was lowering. He saw the dark suit coat strain across the shoulders and half expected to hear it rip but hoped it wouldn't, because it was his father's only coat that made up a suit. Usually it was hanging with moth balls in the pockets because cattle aren't fussy about how a man looks. It was funny to see his dad wearing it. When was the last time? Then he remembered the bright, silent afternoon of the funeral.

Maybe she won't be here, the boy thought, watching the driver come down off the wheel and take the mail sack and go up the steps of the express office. A man in range clothes was standing there against a post, and as the boy looked that way, their eyes met. The man said, "Hello, Jimmy," his mouth forming a funny half-smile in the beard stubble that covered his mouth and jaw.

As Calender looked up, surprise seemed to sadden his weathered face. He put his big hand behind the boy's shoulder and moved him forward toward the steps and said, "Hello, Dick." Only that.

Dick Maddox was still against the post, his thumbs crooked in his belt. Another man in range clothes was on the other side of the post from him. Maddox nodded and said, "Will." Then added, "I'm surprised you brought your boy along."

"Why would that be?" Calender said.

"Well, it ain't many boys see their dad get married."

"How'd you know about that?"

"Things get around," Maddox said easily. "You know, I was surprised Clare didn't ask one of us fellas to give her away."

Calender looked at the man steadily, trying to hide his surprise, and hesitated so it wouldn't show in his voice. "You know Miss Conway?"

Maddox glanced at the man next to him. "He says do I know *Miss* Conway." Both of them grinned. "Well, I'd say anybody who's followed the Canadian to Tascosa knows *Miss* Conway, and that's just about everybody."

The words came like a slap in the face, but Calender thought: Hold on to yourself. And he kept his voice natural when he said, "What do you mean by that?"

Maddox straightened slightly against the post. "You're marrying her, you must've known she worked at the Casa Grande."

Calender was suddenly conscious of his boy looking up at him. He said, "Come on, Jim." And, glancing at Dick Maddox: "We've got to move along."

They started up the street toward the two-story hotel, and Maddox called, "What time's the wedding?" The man with him laughed. Calender heard them but he didn't look around.

When they were farther up the street, the boy said, "Who was that man?"

"Maddox is his name," Calender said. "He used to be old man Granby's herd boss. Now I guess he works around here."

They were silent, and then the boy said, "Why'd you get mad when he started talking about *her?*"

"Who got mad?"

"Well, it looked like it."

"Most of the time that man doesn't know what he's talking about,"

Will Calender said. "Maybe I looked mad because I had to stand there and be civil while he wasted air."

"All he said was other people knew her," the boy said.

"All right, let's not talk about it any more."

"I didn't see anything wrong in that."

Calender didn't answer.

"Maybe he was good friends with her."

Calender turned on the boy suddenly, but his judgment held him, and after a moment he spoke quietly: "I said let's not talk about it any more."

But it stayed in his mind, and now there was an urgency inside him, an impatience to meet this woman face to face and try to read there what her past had been. It was strange. From the letters he had never doubted she was anything but a good woman, but now— And with this uncertainty the fear began to grow, the fear that he'd see something on her face, some mark of an easy woman.

Damn Maddox! Why'd he have to say it in front of the boy! But he could be just talking, insinuating what isn't so, Calender thought. A man like that ought to have his tongue cut out. All he's good for is drink and talk. Ask old man Granby, he got his bellyful of Maddox and fired him.

They went into the hotel, into the quiet, dim lobby with its high beamed ceiling. Their eyes lifted to the second-floor balcony which extended all the way around, except for the front side, so that all of the hotel's eleven rooms looked down on the lobby, where, around the balcony support posts, were cane-bottom Douglas chairs and cuspidors and here and there parts of newspapers. The room was empty, except for the man behind the desk who watched them indifferently. His hair glistened flat on an angle over his forehead, and a matchstick barely showed in the corner of his mouth.

"Miss Conway," Will Calender said. The name was loud in the high-ceilinged room, and he felt embarrassed hearing himself say it.

"You're Mr. Calender?"

"That's right." Calender thought: How does he know my name? He stared at the room clerk closely. If he starts to grin, I'll hit him.

"Miss Conway is in Number five." The clerk nodded vaguely up to the balcony.

Calender hesitated. "Would she be—up yet?"

The clerk started to grin, and Calender thought: Watch yourself, boy. But the clerk just said, "Why don't you go up and knock on the door?"

The boy frowned, watching his father climb the stairs and move along the balcony. He was walking funny, like his feet hurt. Maybe she won't be there, the boy thought hopefully. Maybe she changed her mind. No, she'll be there. He pictured her coming down the stairs, then smiling and patting his cheek and saying, "So this is *Jimmy*." A smile that would be gone and suddenly come back again. "My, but Jimmy is a fine-looking young man. How old are you, Jimmy?" She'll be fat and smelly like Mrs. Granby and those other ladies down on Yeso Creek. How come all women get so fat? All except Ma. She wasn't fat and she smelled nice and she never called me Jimmy. He felt a funny feeling remembering his mother, the sound of her voice and the easy way she did things without complaining or getting excited. What did Molly have to have a mother for? She's gotten along for a year without one.

He saw the door open, but caught only a glimpse of the woman. His father went inside then, but the door remained open.

The room clerk grinned and winked at the boy. "Now, if that was me, I think I'd close the door."

A moment later they came out of the room. The boy watched his father close the door and follow the woman along the balcony to the stairs and then down. The woman was younger than he'd imagined her, much younger, with a funny hat and blond hair fixed in a bun. And she wasn't fat; if anything, skinny. Her face was slender, the skin pale-clear and her eyes seemed sad. The boy looked at her until she got close.

"This here is my son," Will Calender said. "We left Molly at the Granby's. She's only four years old"—he smiled self-consciously— "like I told you in the letters."

The woman smiled back at him. She seemed ill at ease but she said, "How do you do?" to the boy, and her voice was calm and without the false enthusiasm of Will Calender's.

The boy said, "Ma'am," not looking at her face now but noticing her slender white hands holding the ends of the crocheted shawl in front of her.

A silence followed, and Will Calender suggested that they could get something to eat. He had intended mentioning Maddox's name up in the room then watch her reaction, but there hadn't been time. She didn't look like the kind Maddox hinted she was, did she? Maybe Maddox was just talking. She was better-looking than he'd expected. Those eyes and that low, calm voice. Dick Maddox better watch his mouth.

They went to the café next door for breakfast. Calender and the boy ordered eggs and meat, but Clare Conway just took coffee, because she wasn't very hungry. Most of the time they ate in silence. Every now and then Will Calender could hear himself chewing and he'd move his fork on the plate or stir at his coffee with the spoon scraping the bottom of the cup. Clare said the coffee was very good. And, maybe a minute later: It's going to be a nice day. It's so dry out here you can stand the extra heat.

Then it was Will's turn. Where you from originally? . . . New Orleans. . . . I never been there but I hear it's a nice town. . . . It's all right. . . . Silence. . . . How long'd you live in Tascosa? . . . Five years. My husband was with one of the cattle companies. . . . Oh. . . . He died three years ago. . . . Silence. . . . That's right, you told me in your letter. . . . That's right, I did. . . . Silence. . . . What've you been doing since then? . . . I took a position. . . . Calender's jaw was set. . . . At the Casa Grande? . . . Clare Conway blushed suddenly. She nodded and took a sip of coffee in the silence.

There were two men at a table near them and Will Calender had the feeling one nudged the other, and they both grinned, looking over, then looked away quickly when Calender shot a glance toward them.

Calender passed the back of his hand across his mouth and cleared his throat. "Miss Conway, I planned on ordering some stores this morning, long as I was here. They're hauled down to Puerto de Luna, and I pick 'em up there. Some seed and flour"—he cleared his throat again—"and I have to speak to the justice yet." He looked quickly toward the front window, though it wasn't necessary because Clare's eyes were on her coffee cup.

"Jim, here, will stay with you." The boy looked at him with a plea in his eyes, and Will scowled. Then he rose and walked out without looking at the woman.

Standing in front of the hotel, Dick Maddox looked over toward the café as Calender came out, putting on his hat. Maddox glanced at the three men with him, and they grinned as he looked back toward Calender, who was coming toward them now.

"You married yet, Will?"

Calender glanced at Maddox's closed face, at the beard bristles and the cigarette and the eyes in the shadow of the hat brim. "Not yet," he said, and looked straight ahead again, not slowing his stride.

Maddox waited until he was looking at Calender's back. He drew on the cigarette and exhaled and said slowly, "Some men will marry just about anything."

Calender's boots sounded on the planking one, two, three, then stopped. He came around. "Do you mean me, Dick?"

A smile touched the corner of Dick Maddox's mouth. "Old man Granby used to have a saying: If the shoe fits, wear it."

"You can talk plainer than that."

"How plain, Will?"

"Talk like a man for a change."

"Well, as a man, I'm wondering if you're going to go ahead and marry this—*Miss* Conway." One of the men behind him laughed but cut it off.

"What if I am?"

Maddox shrugged. "Every man to his own taste."

Calender stepped closer to him. "Dick, if I was married to that woman and you said what you have—you'd be dead right now."

"That's opinion, Will." Maddox smiled because he was sure he could take Will Calender and he wanted to make sure the three men with him knew it.

Calender said, "The point is, I'm not married to her yet. Not yet. If you don't come out with what's on your mind now, you better not come out with it about two hours from now."

Maddox shook his head. "You're a warnin' man, Will."

"What did she do in Tascosa?" Calender said bluntly.

Maddox hesitated, grinning. "Worked at the Casa Grande."

"And that's what?"

"You never been to Tascosa?"

"I just never saw the place."

"Well, the Casa Grande's where a sweaty trail hand goes for his drink, gamblin', and girls." Maddox paused. "I could draw you a picture, Will."

"Dick, if you're pullin' a joke——"

"Ask anybody in town."

Calender looked at the hat brim shadow and the eyes, the eyes that held without wavering. Then he turned and went up the street.

From his office window, Hillpiper, the Anton Chico Justice of the Peace, watched Will Calender cross the street. The office was above the jail and offered a view of sun, dust, and adobe; there was nothing else to see in Anton Chico, unless you were looking down the streets east, then you'd see the Pecos.

Hillpiper sat down at his desk, hearing the boots on the stairs, and when the knock came he said, "Come in, Will."

"How'd you know it was me?"

"Sit down." Hillpiper smiled. "You had an appointment for this morning, and I've got a window." Hillpiper wore silver-rim spectacles for close work, but he looked over them to Calender sitting across the desk from him.

Calender said, "You know what everybody in town's saying?"

Hillpiper shook his head. "Not everybody."

"They're talking about this woman I'm to marry."

"I'll say it again. Not everybody."

Calender's raw-boned face was tightening, and his voice was louder. "How can they know so much about her—and me, the man that's to marry her, not know anything?"

"It's happened before," Hillpiper said.

"You heard what they're saying?"

"I heard Maddox in the saloon last night. Is he the everybody you're talking about?"

"He's enough. But it's what she is!" Calender said savagely. "What she didn't tell in her letters!"

"Three letters," Hillpiper said mildly. Calender had told him about it when he made the arrangements and set the date: the marriage broker in Santa Fe writing to him, then writing to the woman. Hillpiper had told him it was all right as far as he was concerned, since he didn't see why two people had to love each other to get along. Love's something that might come, but if it didn't—look at all the marriages getting on without it. And Calender had said, that's right. I never thought of that. See, my little girl's the main reason.

"In three letters," Hillpiper went on, "a woman hardly has time to open up her heart."

"She could have told me what she did!"

"Just what does she do, Will?"

"You heard Maddox."

"I want to hear it from you."

"She worked at the Casa Grande!" Calender flared. "How do you want me to say it?"

Hillpiper put his palms on the desk and leaned forward. "All right, Will, she worked in a saloon. She danced with trail hands, maybe sang a little and smiled more than was natural to get the boys to buy the extra drink they'd a bought anyway. And that's all she's done, regardless of how Maddox makes a dozen words sound like a whole story. Why she did that kind of work, I don't know. Maybe she had to because there was nothing else for a girl to do and she still had to eat like anybody else. Maybe it killed her to do it. Or"—Hillpiper's voice was quieter and he shrugged—"maybe she liked doing it. Maybe she forgot where she carried her morals—assuming what she was doing is morally wrong. By most men's standards it is wrong for a female to work in a saloon, your standards too or you wouldn't be here with your face tied in a knot. But those same men have a hell of a good time with the females when they're at the Casa Grande."

Hillpiper smiled faintly. "You were always a little stricter than most men anyway, Will. Seems like most of your life you've been a hard-working, Bible-reading family man, with no time for places like the Casa Grande. You've sweated your ranch into something pretty nice, something most other men wouldn't have the patience or the guts to do. And I can see you not wanting to chance ruining all you've built—ranch or family. That's why I was a little surprised when you of all people came in with this mail-order romance idea. I suspect, now that I think about it, you had the idea if a girl wants to get married she's the simon-pure family type and nothing else. You had a good woman before, Will; so you expected one just as good this time."

Hillpiper leaned a little closer, his eyes on Calender's weathered face. "Will," Hillpiper said. "You might be shocked a little bit, but when you get to heaven you're going to see a lot of faces you never expected to see. Folks who got up there on God's standards and not man's. For all you know, you're liable to even see Dick Maddox—though I suppose that would be stretching divine mercy a little thin."

Anton Chico's Justice of the Peace leaned back in his swivel chair, his coat opening to show a gold watch chain across his vest. His hand came out of a side pocket with a cigar, and with a match from a vest pocket he lit it, puffing a cloud of smoke. When he looked up, Calender was standing.

"What've you decided, Will?"

"I've got my kids to think about."

"It's your problem." Hillpiper said this in a kindly way, stating a fact. "If you've decided not to go through with it, that's your business."

Will Calender nodded. "I suppose I should pay her stage fare back to Tascosa."

"That would be nice, Will," Hillpiper said mildly.

Calender thanked him and went out, down the stairs and into the street. Crossing to the other side, he felt awkward and self-conscious. The suit coat held tight across the shoulders and he could feel his big hands hanging too far out of the sleeves, and with nothing to hold onto.

It's gotten hot, he thought, pulling his hat lower. Maybe the dryness makes it easier on some people, but it's still hot. And then he thought: I'd better tell her before I buy the stage ticket.

Dick Maddox was still in front of the hotel, but now more men were there. It had gotten around that Maddox was having some fun with Will Calender, so they drifted over casually from here and there, the ones who knew Maddox standing closest to him, laughing at what he said. The rest were all along the hotel's shady ramada. One of the men saw Calender coming and he nudged Maddox, who looked up, then pretended he wasn't concerned, until Calender was close to the hotel entrance.

"You change your mind, Will?"

Calender stopped and breathed out wearily, "If you showed as much concern for your own business, you'd be a well-to-do man."

"You can't take kiddin', can you?"

"Why should I have to?"

"You got a lot to learn, Will."

Calender shrugged, because he was tired of this, and went inside.

The boy was sitting alone, with his heels hooked in the wooden rungs of the chair. When he saw his father he jumped up quickly.

Calender looked about to be certain the woman was not in the lobby.

"Where is she?" he asked the boy.

"She went upstairs. All of a sudden she just started crying and went upstairs."

"What?"

"It was when they started talking. We were sitting here, and then her chin started to shake—you know—and then she run upstairs."

"Who was talking? The men outside?" The boy nodded hurriedly, and Calender could see that he was frightened and trying to hide it and at the same time was not sure what it was all about.

"What did they say?"

"Just one of them, the rest were laughing most of the time. He was telling them"—the boy said it slowly as if he'd memorized it—"he said some women didn't know their place. They think they can live in the gutter then go out when they want and brush against people like nothing's coming off. He was talking loud so we could hear every word and he said a man would be a fool to marry a woman like that and have her brushing against his kids with her gutter ways. It was like that, what he said. Then he spoke your name and he said he'd bet anybody five dollars American you'd changed your mind now about getting married. That's when she run upstairs."

The boy frowned, looking at his father, watching his eyes go up to the room. "Why'd he have to say things like that? We were sitting here talking—getting acquainted."

Calender looked at the boy and saw that he was grinning.

"You know she never once asked me how old I was or if I knew my reader or things like that. She talked to me about affairs and interesting things like I was grown up, like Ma used to do. And, Pa, she called me *Jim!* Can you imagine that? She called me *Jim!* If her hair was darker and her nose a little different, I'd swear she was Ma!"

"Don't say things like that!" Calender was conscious of his voice, and he said quietly, "There's the difference of night and day."

"Well, her voice is different too, and maybe she's a speck taller, though that could be the hat. I never seen Ma in a regular hat. But outside of that, they sure are alike."

"You know what you're saying, comparing this woman with your mother?"

The boy looked at him questioningly, but the trace of a smile was still on his face. "I'm just saying they're alike, that's all. Maybe they don't look so much alike, but they sure are alike." The boy smiled; he was sure his explanation was clear because he understood it so well himself.

Calender was looking at the boy closely now. "What if she's done something bad?"

"Pa, little Molly's doing bad things all the time. That's just the way girls are. Most times they're not doing serious things, so they have more time to get theirselves into trouble."

Calender's eyes remained on the boy. Calender asked: "You think Molly will like her?"

"Couple of bad women like them will get along just fine." The boy grinned.

Calender left him abruptly, going up the stairs. In a few minutes he came back down, and in front of him was Clare Conway.

They walked across the lobby. Nearing the door, the woman hesitated and looked up at Will Calender. She was unsure and afraid. It was in her wide-open eyes, in the way her fingers held the ends of the crocheted shawl. Then she moved on again as if not under her own power—when Will touched her elbow and said to the boy, "Come on, Jim."

And when they were out on the ramada the woman's eyes were looking down at her hands; she could feel Will Calender holding her elbow, she could feel the guiding pressure of his hand, and moved to the right along the ramada, along the line of silent men, hearing only her footsteps and the footsteps of the man at her side. The hand on her elbow tightened. She was being turned gently, and there was no longer the sound of footsteps and when she looked up a man was close in front of her, a man with heavy beard bristles.

"Miss Conway," Calender said. "This is Mr. Maddox. He's had such a keen interest in our business, I thought you might like to meet him."

"Now, Will——" Maddox said, looking at Calender strangely.

"And, Dick," Calender went on, "this is Miss Conway. Isn't there something you wanted to say to her?"

"Will——"

"Maybe you'd just like to tip your hat like a gentleman."

Maddox was staring at Calender almost dumbfounded, but slowly his face relaxed as he realized what Calender was doing in front of all these men and he said mildly, grinning, "Now, Will, I don't know if I want to do that or not."

Calender's fist came around suddenly, unexpectedly, driving against Maddox's jaw, changing the smile to lopsided surprise and sending him back off the ramada into the street. Calender followed, and hit him again and this time Maddox went down, his hat falling off in front of him. Maddox started to rise, but Calender came for him again. Maddox hesitated, then eased down and sat in the street, looking up at Calender.

"One other thing, Dick," Will said. "I hear you're taking bets there isn't going to be a wedding today." He glanced back at the crowd of men in the shade. "Who's holding the stakes?"

There was a silence, then someone called, "Nobody'd bet him."

Calender beckoned to the man. "Come here." He brought a five-dollar gold piece out of his pants pocket and gave it to the man. "Dick Maddox'll give you one just like this. Now you add the two up and have that much ready for me when I get back."

He walked to the ramada. The tension was gone. Some of the men were whispering and talking, some just looking out at Maddox still sitting in the street.

The boy's face was beaming as he watched his father. Clare came toward him.

"You ripped the seam of your coat up the back," she said.

He felt her hand on his back pulling the cloth together. "Gives me a little more room," he said, conscious of the men watching him.

"It's your good coat, though," the woman said. "I'll mend it soon as we get home."

The City of Sin

Noel M. Loomis

PACKER was dead. He had a bullet hole through one cheekbone, and the bullet had come out the back of his head. Choate felt in Packer's pockets. He found a wallet with a few eastern banknotes in it. He put the wallet in a wooden strongbox at the stern of the boat. "He might have some kin somewhere back yonder," he said.

He found a carrot of tobacco with the end chewed out and one side covered with blood. He wiped it off on his leggings and put it in the pocket formed by the lapping over of his moosehide shirt. "We better save this," he said. "It won't be no good by the time we get back."

He lifted Packer's body over the side, lowered it into the water, and held it for a minute. "Packer was a hard fighter—*and* a hell of a hard drinker," he said in eulogy, and let the body go.

He looked over Diah Jones. Diah was seventeen, long and lanky but

One of WWA's scrappiest members, pint-sized Noel Loomis has cut quite a swathe in the Western fiction field since he entered it some years ago with *Rim of the Caprock*. Earlier this year the University of Oklahoma Press published his fine historical study, *The Texan-Santa Fe Pioneers*. A former resident of Minneapolis, Noel, with his writer-wife Dorothy, now lives in southern California.

tough as a willow withe. A bullet had dug into his ear and out the side
of his neck.

Choate said, "The bullet's out. There's not much I can do. Put some
grease on, I reckon. Goin' to be hard to sleep tonight."

Diah grinned. "Whiskey'll take care of that."

"Afraid you won't hear much out of that ear. I feel bad about this,
Diah. I shouldn't of taken you."

"Why should I stay at home all my life?" Diah argued. "My mother
took care of herself before. She can now. It ain't as if I was leavin' her.
I'm just gonna be away a while."

"You won't go back a whole man."

"Won't I, though? Why do men ship out on boats without pay just to
get to New Orleans?"

"A lot do," Choate admitted. "A lot don't come back, though."

"I'll come back. And when I do, my mother won't treat me like a
kid no more."

"A lot of men get killed going to New Orleans—from pirates,
wrecked boats, Indians, fights—just about everything you can mention.
You might not come back home at all."

"*You're going,* I notice," Diah said impatiently. "Smear that grease
on me, and let's be off."

The boat jerked and began to move. Bill Persons had cut the hawser
to the shore with the ax. The ark swung around, and Jeff's crew began
to lash the two together. It wasn't long before they were back in the
middle, floating down with the current.

They tied up at dark. Choate would have liked to keep going, but the
river was too full of danger to risk it.

Jeff said, "We better look for a place to tie up at the lower end of an
island somewhere."

"Any place," said Choate, "where there's young cottonwoods or
willows growing."

The channel split soon after, and they took the right-hand current.
The island was three miles long and covered with a solid growth of
tree and underbrush. They tied up at a sandy beach on the lower end.
The high banks of the river squeezed in tight against them and made a
fast, deep channel with a heavy load of water.

"You're right," said Jeff. "If a boat got away from a man in that
there water at night, he'd be a gone goose."

Bill Persons cooked a mess of old Ned in a big brass pan and a gallon of navy beans in an iron kettle. When the fat pork was half done, he set the pan out in the open. Both crews squatted around and fished out pieces of meat with their scalping knives. There was no bread, and they ate the meat out of their fingers.

Choate looked at Diah Jones. "She's swole up, but I don't think she'll gangrene on you." He brought Rufus a cupful of whiskey to ease the pain in his heel.

"You won't need no guard tonight," said Rufus. "I don't figger on sleepin'."

"You can try," said Choate.

He went back to the fire. Darkness had come down over the river, bringing the swirl of water through the rocks, the chirruping of crickets, the hollow boom of a bullfrog, the far-off howl of a wolf trying to stampede a herd of buffalo. The yellow fire lit up the men's faces strangely and threw distorted shadows against the brush behind them. Choate got himself a cup of steaming coffee and nursed it between big hands. "Whose outfit you reckon that was?" he asked.

Jeff shook his head. "No tellin'. Might be Bully Wilson, Sam Mason, Wiley Harpe, or Colonel Flug—or a hundred others. The river's lousy with 'em." He crushed a leaf of tobacco in his long bony fingers and filled his pipe. "Pretty soon we'll be below Smithland, and it ain't so bad down there. The river's better." He picked up a small branch, glowing on one end, and held it to his pipe. "That's why they concentrate up here—the river's tough to navigate."

Choate examined the carrot of tobacco he had taken from Packer's pocket. The blood had dried. Choate scraped it with his big knife and twisted off a chew with strong white teeth. "Yeah, tomorrow we'll be gettin' into mosquito country," he noted.

Jeff Chandler sat back from the fire, cross-legged. He cocked an ear at a long-drawn howl. "That's varmint," he said finally. "Thought for a minute it might be Indians."

Choate studied him now in the red glow of the fire. Jeff was a wild-looking critter, with black hair long and shaggy under his coonskin cap, his face narrow with chiseled bones. He wore a buckskin shirt and shapeless gray linsey-woolsey pants that were cut off about his boot tops to keep from getting his feet tangled up. Choate figured he was a good man to tie up with.

Rufus got his bad leg out in front of him. "Funny," he said, "I've had bullets and arrows stickin' all over me but I never got hurt till a damn' renegade white man cut me up for meanness."

Choate's muscles made knots at the corners of his jaws. "That was pure, deliberate cussedness. If he'd wanted to keep you from gettin' the ax, he could have stuck you through the back." He spit into the fire. "But he had to cut you up like an Injun—only no Injun ever cut a man that way when he could just as well have killed him."

"It was a cussed stunt," Jeff Chandler agreed.

Choate worked his chew. Rufus filled his pipe, and Bill Persons brought him a light.

"Anyhow," said Rufus, "I still got one good leg."

Choate made Rufus a bed in a grove of sugar trees. He posted Jim Bedley to guard the ark till midnight and told the other, a wiry old man named Hudson, to take over from Bedley. "Call me when it breaks in the east," he said. "We'll get away from this stretch as fast as we can."

Jeff Chandler posted a guard on his own boat. The rest of the men found spots in the sand to sleep. Jeff lighted up his pipe and looked at Choate across the fire. "Mind if I ast you why you come down in the fall instead of waiting for high water in the spring?"

"I don't mind," said Choate. "I—we had a load of skins we didn't get down this spring and we wanted to get rid of them." After a moment he added, "I'd rather come down in low water anyway. You can see the rocks and sawyers better, and there's no danger of losing the channel and getting stranded in that almighty big swamp to the east of the river. They say it's twelve hundred miles long."

Jeff studied him over his pipe. He pushed up the coonskin snout on his cap—on the river, the badge of a white man—and looked into the fire. "Well, me," he said, "I heard they're plenty short of produce in New Orleans, account of taxes stopping the ships from the East, and a man can get his own price—if he can get past the officials."

Choate grunted. "Anything to do with the Spanish officials is a gamble," he said. "One day you can bribe them; the next you can't get close enough to throw a gold eagle into the same parish. Things go along fine for a while, and then the captain-general in Havana or the West Indies sends down an order, and fellers like you and me are caught. I never counted much on bribing myself," he added. "I don't like it when some feller's lookin' for money that way."

In fact, Choate figured, unless Jeff Chandler had some secret arrangement like Wilkinson had fixed up for Rufus, it was a mighty high gamble.

Jeff looked at Choate across the fire. "How you comin' back—up the Trace?"

Choate shook his head. "Soon as I get my money out of the cargo I'm going over into the Tejas country to hunt mustangs."

Jeff considered that. "Seems like right popular work the last few years, trappin' mustangs in Tejas."

Choate didn't answer.

"Man can cover a lot of country lookin' for mustangs," said Jeff. "If he keeps his eyes open, he can find out a lot *about* the country."

Choate still sat silent.

"You don't really figger the gover'ment at Washington gives a whoop and a holler about Tejas, do you?" Jeff asked.

"For that," Choate said finally, "I reckon it does. I come up through Natchez two summers ago and talked to Andrew Ellicott, the U.S. border commissioner, and he said he'd like to know more about the Tejas country."

"What's this about Wilkinson?"

Choate shook his head. "Nobody knows. Everybody's got ideas. Some, like my old man, believe in Wilkinson, even though once he was kicked out of the Army. Leastwise, Wilkinson's stirrin' up a heap of trouble for somebody."

Jeff was silent for a moment. "And you're goin' to Tejas to———"

"I'm goin' to hunt mustangs," Choate said evenly.

Jeff was hollowing out a spot in the sand for his shoulders. "You better stick to that," he said. "Them Spaniards would skin you alive if you did anything else."

"They're good at that," Choate admitted.

"They killed Philip Nolan and cut off his ears. I reckon they figgered *he* wasn't just after mustangs."

Choate looked into the dark. He heard splashes. Jeff lay where he was on one elbow, but watched and listened. The splashing grew. Then came a tremendous big one. The ground trembled beneath them. Choate settled down and looked back at the fire. "Bank fell in," he said.

"Good thing we're here," Jeff observed.

"If there's anything to this secret treaty," Choate went on, "and Spain has to give Louisiana back to France, the Spaniards maybe won't be so fussy about who goes into the Tejas country."

Jeff pulled on his pipe. "I 'low there's plenty to it. The French already got a big army in San Domingo, and they said at the Falls they've got five battalions of infantry and plenty of cannon gathered at Dunkirk to sail for Louisiana as soon as the fall storms are over."

Choate studied the fire. "I heard that," he said. "It don't sound good. That feller Napoleon is out to conquer the world—all the more reason we've got to control the Mississippi."

"Who's goin' to stop him?"

"Not the British."

"Not hardly. They can't even protect Egypt and India. Look what Buonaparte's doin' now—goin' through the British armies like salts through a bloated cow."

"I reckon," said Choate, "it's the same old story. There ain't nobody to look after us but ourselves."

He got to his feet and kicked a little sand against the edges of the fire.

Jeff was watching him. He raised himself on one elbow. "You got a bullet in your leg," he said.

Choate looked down at the ragged four-inch gash across his thigh. The edges of the buckskin were crusted with blood. "Damnation, yes!" he said. "That snake in the grass that was playin' possum on the bank damn near ruined a good pair of leggin's for me." He looked off into the dark. "Someday I'll meet up with that feller," he said, "and when I do"—he glanced up toward where Rufus lay and went on grimly— "when I do, he'll pay for more than a pair of leggin's."

That was the way he'd met up with Jeff Chandler. That was the way of the river—when you needed help, it came, or you quit needing it. Lose one and gain another. When a man is alive he can drink whiskey and do his work; when he's dead you've got to get somebody to take his place.

Choate had lost Packer and gained Pierre. The faces changed, the names were different—but they were all rivermen and they all had one objective: to beat the river. For the river was always the same, always an enemy. . . .

They approached New Orleans on an afternoon, with a sudden rain just over and the rising chorus of a million small birds, rejoicing in the sunlight, coming to them clearly across the tumbling brown water, along with the fragrance of jasmine, olives, and hibiscus, fresh and dainty after the rain. There were also birds with brilliant plumage but harsh voices; there were bayous that smelled of stagnant water, rotting logs, snakes, and alligators; there were great red-brick plantation houses and there were hovels set in malarious wet thickets of willows. There had been highborn ladies riding with attendants in carriages of exotic woods, pulled by high-stepping thoroughbred horses; there were also naked Negro children playing in the dirt; and the levee had been with them from Point Coupee—a huge dirt bank six feet high and twenty feet wide at the top, to keep the river from flooding the plantations in the spring.

They came around a bend and the town was before them, looking clean and bright as its buildings dripped water in the afternoon sun. Jeff got on top of the cargo box to get a better look. Then he gave a shout, "Yippee! She's a city!" and stomped up and down.

"Go easy on them skins," said Choate. "We got to sell 'em before we go back."

"It looks to me," said Diah, "like a bunch of houses on stilts."

"That's on account of the water in the ground—to say nothin' of snakes and reptiles gener'ly."

"New Orleans!" Jeff's eyes were shining. "The City of Sin!"

"Listen," said Choate. "That sin business is no joke. There's Annie Christmas, and they say she's the biggest woman on the river. She's killed thirty-four men and gouged out more eyes and cut off more ears than any man alive. And Apache John, the trickiest knife fighter east of the Rio Bravo. He'd cut your throat to sell your clothes."

"Don't they have police?"

"Yes and no. They got police, but the police don't go into some parts. New Orleans has changed hands too many times. A lot of men have come in lookin' for easy money. There's French and Spanish and Irish and German and niggers from San Domingo and Indians and voodoo doctors."

"You might' near got me scared," said Jeff, pushing the snout of his coonskin cap up on his head.

Choate grinned. "Tell you a secret. There's plenty of people in New Orleans just as scared of you as you are of them—and then some. New Orleans has been taken clean apart by the rivermen so many times they don't even keep count any more."

Jeff got down. "Well," he said, "I reckon onct more won't do any harm, then."

They pulled in along the levee. There were fifty or sixty riverboats anchored to posts, and on down the river the foreign-flag ships were lined up three deep.

"That part down there next to the foreign ships is the official Spanish part of town—the French section, they call it. You never know what's Spanish and what's French around here. Anyway, whatever's south and west of the Spanish gates—that means upriver—is American. The high-class Spanish and French live in the French section or north or east of it. That's downtown for them, but it ain't downtown for us."

"You mean we ain't gonna get to see it?" asked Jeff.

"There's an empty post. We'll pull in there," said Choate. "Sure, you'll see it. But that's about all. Mostly you'll stay in the American section, and your hell-raising better be on this side too. Them Spanish dandies east of the Tchoupitoulas Gate might not like your smell."

Choate cast the hawser around a post that had been hammered into the mud.

"What's about this syndic?" asked Jeff.

"It means," said Rufus, "that now we're pulled up along Tchoupitoulas Street, there'll be a Spanish delegation meet us to inspect boat, crew, and cargo. They'll do their damnedest to find something out of place."

Choate wondered how Rufus was feeling about the tobacco tied up in the skins.

"What happens if they do?"

"They gener'ly do," said Rufus, "and it costs you more to unload your stuff. That's about all. Of course, if you got contraband, they'll seize your cargo."

"See that rowboat comin' up?" asked Choate.

"Yeah. A woman and a girl in it. The woman looks about six feet eight and is totin' the breastworks of Gibraltar. Besides, she's got a mustache."

"And the girl ain't exactly overdressed," Choate said dryly.

"She ain't, at that, by Jupiter! She's got on nothin' but a chemise, and it's——"

"Ahoy, there, you landlubbers!" came the bass voice of the woman. "Kentuckians, ain't you?"

"We come from different places," Jeff said. "I'm from Ohio."

"All Kentuckians down here," boomed the woman, "and all lookin' for the same thing. Bet you ain't seen a woman for a month."

Jeff was staring at the girl, who seemed about to lose her chemise completely.

"We got a barge anchored over here. You got a canoe or a skiff?"

"Sure," said Choate.

"Come on over. Don't wait till dark. We're always open for business."

"On the barge?" Jeff asked incredulously.

"What do you think them pieces of canvas are stretched over the deck for—to keep off the rain?"

Jeff was staring. "I reckon."

"You reckon right," said the madam. "Come on over. Make our place your headquarters. We got liquor too."

"How much for the girl?" asked Choate.

"Her?" The madam looked at the girl in the boat with her. "That's Yvonne. She's a French countess. Very classy. You'd like her."

"How much?" asked Rufus.

"A dollar for Yvonne."

"She's no more French than I am," said Rufus.

"Whatsa difference?" the madam retorted. "French, Irish, Spanish, German, Italian, Eskimo. They're all the same when they take off the wrappers. Anyway, we got all kinds—anything you want."

"We'll see you later," Choate said.

"You boys down on your luck? We got all the way to a picayune— half a real—six cents, American money."

Choate showed his distaste.

"All right!" said the bass-voiced woman. "If you're so damn fussy. But you'll be glad for us before you get through at New Orleans," she added mysteriously.

"*That's* Annie Christmas," said Choate. "The old reprobate."

Another rowboat approached, and the madam and her bait went back to their canvas-covered barge. The new boat was rowed by two Spanish soldiers in uniforms like those at New Madrid. The boat came alongside the lashed broadhorns, and a man stood up. He wore a white frilled shirt, a short black jacket, skin-tight black breeches, and a red silk sash.

"*Señores!* Who is *capitan* of this ship?"

Choate finished wrapping the hawser and went to the edge of the broadhorn. "It's my boat. Are you the syndic to inspect us?"

"I am so sorry to disappoint you, *señor*. There will be no inspection of the crew, cargo, or boat at present."

"What do you mean?"

"*El señor* Morales, the intendant of the port of New Orleans, has issued an order. Have you not heard? But no, this was only two days ago. You would not have heard."

Choate tightened up. He felt the men tense about him. "What order?"

"*El señor* Morales has decreed that you may not deposit your goods in New Orleans."

"We can pay."

"I have sorrow. It is not a question of pay, *señor*. It is the law."

The men crowded around Choate now. "What does that mean?" asked Jeff.

"It means we can't unload our stuff."

"Hmph!" said Rufus. "The same old tricks are back again. This is the way it was before the treaty of 1795."

"I have great sorrow, *señores*," said the Spanish official. "You may, I presume, anchor here for the time being. There will be a small charge, of course—three piastres for each boat of this size, I believe."

"But no unloading," Choate said. "That means we can't sell our stuff."

"Possibly it may mean that, *señor*."

"There are ships being unloaded down the river there."

"Those are Spanish bottoms, *señor*. They are, of course, not affected by the order."

"Looky here," said Choate, losing his temper. "Aren't we as good as any damn' Spaniard?"

"That is hardly the question," the Spaniard said stiffly. "This is Spanish territory—and you are Kentuckians."

Choate clamped his lips together. "All right, we'll see."

"How about leavin' the boat?" asked Jeff.

"There are no restrictions on your personal movements, *señor*."

"Hmph!" said Choate.

The official was rowed away. Choate sat on the edge of the boat, staring at the brown water. Jeff watched the official's back. Rufus glared at the ships farther down the levee. Pierre stood wide-legged before the cargo box and stared hungrily at the city. Bill Persons plumped himself down hard beside Choate. "What the hell do you know about that?" he asked.

"One thing is sure," said Rufus. "Kentucky still needs a free river. How do they feel up around where you come from, Jeff?"

Jeff's deep eyes turned on him. "About the same as they do in Kentucky," he said. "If Jefferson won't do something, we'll do it ourselves."

Rufus moved his leg and grimaced. "How far would they go?"

Jeff's answer was slow but deliberate: "There's talk of seceding and going in with Kentucky and Tennessee."

Rufus's eyes widened a fraction. "If the whole western country would pull together," he said, "we could do it. Not that anybody in the East would greatly care. They got everything they want—no more Indians to fight, no outlaws, no high freight, no Spaniards or Frenchmen to block the river."

Choate lay on one elbow on the deck and watched both of their faces.

Jeff said thoughtfully, "There's others in Ohio that favor joinin' up with the British."

Rufus looked up at him quickly. Then he observed, "Wilkinson says if we throw in with Spain we could have anything we want."

Jeff looked up. "There's people in my country don't think Wilkinson is workin' for anybody but Wilkinson," he said. "Myself, I don't know —only it seems strange to me that Spain could do us any good when she can't even protect the Lower Louisiana country. They're scared of the French and scared of the Americans and they can't handle the Indians. How can they do us any good in the western country?"

"Why are they scared of the Americans?"

Jeff smiled. "Too many Americans got their eye on the Tejas country."

Rufus grunted. "What's good about the Tejas Country?"

"It's big," Jeff said. "Big as a continent might' near—and nobody to defend it but Injuns."

"Ain't no different from Louisiana."

"Sure enough," Jeff agreed. "But I'll tell you what they say in Ohio. They say the Tejas country has got to be taken before we can hold New Orleans. Let the Spanish have New Spain, but we want the Tejas country. And that ain't all: we'll get it, and they know we'll get it."

Rufus cleared his throat but didn't answer. Choate knew what Rufus was thinking. This wasn't quite what Rufus planned—or, for that matter, all the big men of Kentucky and the Cumberland territory who had been listening to Wilkinson.

Jeff Chandler subsided. Some of the fire went out of his eyes. "Anyhow," he said after a while, "that's what they're sayin'. "

A bass voice came across the water. "I said you gents would be glad we're here," said the huge-busted woman. "Come over any time."

Choate looked at the barge absently. "So now they've done it," he said. "They've really stopped us from unloading our goods. I thought about it but somehow I never figgered it would happen."

"That's a trick of Buonaparte's," Jeff said angrily. "He's the one issued that order."

"How could he?" asked Rufus.

"The treaty is signed. New Orleans belongs to Buonaparte now."

"If this is an example of what we're in for under Buonaparte, I say let's fight."

Choate said slowly, "We may have to."

Jeff looked worried. "I got every cent I own tied up in this boat and cargo. I can't even pay off my crew if I can't sell the goods."

"I got an answer," said Choate.

"I'm listenin', " said Jeff.

Choate looked at the city beyond the levee. "Tomorrow's another day. Tomorrow I got to see about selling the cargo to get money for mustangin' in Tejas." He looked at Bill. "I say let's go over to the Swamp and throw an almighty big drunk that the City of Sin will remember for a hundred years."

Bill Persons brightened. "That's the first smart thing you said today."

Rufus spoke up. "I'm older than you fellers and I ain't in no hurry. Besides, I been down here before. I'll stay and watch the boat the first night while the rest of you take the town apart."

They unlashed the broadhorns and tied Jeff's to a separate post. They used the canoe to gather on the levee, and Rufus took it back to the broadhorn.

Choate pulled up his wide belt and said, "Well, gents, what'll it be?"

"I want to see the Swamp and the Sure Enuf Hotel," Jeff said.

"You go tanglin' up with Mother Colby and you'll come home with your throat cut."

"I come down here to see it," Jeff said. "Lead the way."

They went through straight but narrow streets, now muddy from the rain. There were no sidewalks, and they walked in a body in the center, kicking squealing pigs out of the way and avoiding children who ran to their mothers screaming, "The Kaintocks!"

Choate grinned. "They musta heard about us," he said.

Bill Persons eyed a buzzard working on a dog carcass. "They kinda let things take care of themselves, don't they?"

"You might say they take advantage of nature," said Choate. "Why bury anything, anyway? You dig down eighteen inches and you hit water. If you put a coffin in the ground, you have to dig holes in it and have a couple of slaves stand on top till it fills with water."

"Hell of a way to be buried," said Bill Persons.

"You're only dead once," Jeff reminded him.

The houses were made mostly of wood, with weather-gray cypress shingles that looked like slate. Sometimes the outer walls were white-washed—more often they were not. Most houses were four to eight feet off the ground on stilts, with ladders leading to the doors. And it was apparent, with the sun coming out, that garbage was thrown from the houses into the streets.

"Must be different over in the Spanish part of town," said Jeff.

"Not much," said Choate. "Garbage stinks just as much when the sun hits it over there as it does over here."

They kept north on what Choate thought was Girod Street and presently were in a section of dilapidated shacks and flophouses. Some were tied to each other with ropes to keep from falling down. Most of them had red curtains at the windows and red lanterns over the doors.

They found the Sure Enuf Hotel, with the giant Mother Colby in charge. "You can have a bed and a woman for a picayune," she assured them. "What more you want? You just come off the river, didn't you?"

"We don't want our throats cut," said Choate.

Mother Colby shook her head as if very sad. "I run a clean place. It's cheap—but that's what most rivermen want. You got any money at all?" she asked sharply.

Bill Persons's answer was prompt. "We haven't got a sou."

Mother Colby shook her head. "I can fix you up cheap—but not for nothin'. You can sleep under the eaves for a picayune; if you're fussy and have to have the center of the room so you can stand up to take off your clothes, it'll be a bit."

"A woman too?" asked Bill Persons.

Mother Colby laughed loudly. "Never saw a riverman that wanted a bed by himself," she said.

Choate led them away. "Whatever you do, don't go splitting up. At least two men keep together."

Diah Jones strode along in his buckskin breeches, bare from the waist up. A woman came from behind them. *"Messieurs,* you weesh someone?" she asked.

Choate looked at her hard, pinched face, with its too-bright eyes and heavy rouge. "That depends," he said cautiously.

But Diah Jones spoke up: "Gents, the time has come for action. I didn't ride all the way from the Falls of the Ohio River to go to church."

The woman sidled up to him. She was still pretty—if a man didn't look too close. But Choate looked close. She was bareheaded, and in the sunlight her scalp looked filthy. She was drenched with perfume but she looked sidewise at Diah. "You like what you see, Kaintock?"

"If the rest of you is as artificial as your accent," said Choate, "you're in the wrong business."

She turned on him viciously. "You big, fat, blabbermouthed Kentucky son of a bitch!"

But the fire was rising in Diah's eyes, and he didn't hear her hoarse voice. "See you gents later," he said, and took her arm.

Choate looked after him and frowned. "I don't like it," he said.

"It don't look," said Bill Persons, "like you got much to say about it. If he ain't a man yet, he's gonna be mighty soon."

"This is a hell of a place to split up in," said Jeff.

Bill Persons looked back. "I kind of liked Diah," he said. "He was quiet and minded his own business. Did his work."

The sun had gone down, and from the cypress swamps a quarter of a mile away began to rise a droning chorus of crickets, mosquitoes, bullfrogs, and alligators. A red lantern hanging over a door illuminated a weathered sign painted on a piece of oak that had come off of a broadhorn: "House of Rest for Weary Boatmen."

"As good a place to get hijacked as any," said Choate. "In fact, one of the best—if you're alone." He led the way in through the door. They lined up at the bar, eight of them. The bartender was a swarthy man with long black mustaches. "What you want, gents?"

"Evenin', Turk," said Choate.

Turk was alert for an instant. Then he relaxed and gave what probably was intended for a grin. "Choate, you ole soakhead! I t'ought you was headed up the rivaire!"

"That was yesterday," said Choate. "How much for whiskey?"

Turk glanced at the men. "One bit 'piece—a peso all around."

"How much for the whiskey without water in it?"

Turk grinned. "Rivaire water—she's mix good with whiskey." He began to pour it into dirty glasses.

Choate tossed his down. "Our rye is better than this," he said.

Turk shrugged. "You got no women on boat?"

"No."

"I think there is something maybe we got for you." Turk whistled.

"Fill 'em up," said Choate.

Turk set out a brown bottle. "Give me two pesos—you take the whole bottle."

Choate threw out two milled Spanish silver piastres. "These are pesos, aren't they?"

"Sure," Turk swept them up.

Choate pulled the cork and passed it around.

Three women ducked under a heavy red curtain at the far end of the bar and paraded past the men. One was young and hard; the others were old and tough. Choate sighed; rivermen didn't have much choice. "Anybody's got any studdin' to do, git it done while we're all here— and if anybody starts throwin' knives or lead," he told Turk, "we take the place apart and throw it in the river."

Turk said solemnly, "I run a nice clean place. Ask the girls."

Bill Persons, old man Hudson, and Pierre went through the red curtains. Choate and the others had another drink. In a few minutes the three were back and three more went in.

Bill had another drink. "You might as well be next."

Choate shook his head slowly.

"What's the matter? You gittin' old?"

"Maybe." Choate turned the glass in his big fingers. "Last time I was here I seen a Spanish girl in one of them fancy carriages," he said slowly. "I got to thinkin' about her when we come around the bend this afternoon."

"Gittin' pretty snooty, ain't you?"

"I reckon not. She just looked like the kind of a girl I'd like."

"You got no chance to git within speakin' distance of one of them highborn Spanish ladies," said Bill. "I'll grant you they're beautiful, and them who know say they're so passionate they're on fire practically all the time, but you——" He shook his head dolefully. "You better have another drink and take what you can git."

"I'll have the drink," Choate said.

Bill Persons nodded thoughtfully. "Now I know why you didn't fool around in Natchez."

They left. It was dark, and the only light for half a dozen blocks was shed by the red lanterns over the doors. "Diah should be around some-wheres," said Choate.

"Maybe he made a deal to stay all night."

"Maybe, but——"

"Wait a minute," said Bill. His voice was tight. "What's wrong up there?"

A small crowd had gathered—half a dozen men, no women. They were looking at something on the ground.

Choate ran forward. The half-dozen men parted and let him through. Choate looked at the naked corpse of Diah Jones.

Jeff and Pierre and Bill Persons and old man Hudson and the rest came up beside Choate. The half-dozen men disappeared in the night and left the eight rivermen standing and one lying dead in the street. Choate looked down and began to feel a great hardness rise in him. He turned the naked body over with his toe.

"Stabbed in the back," Bill said, "and robbed down to his moccasins. Damn it, we *told* him not to split up."

"Where's the woman?" demanded Choate of anybody who could answer.

"You'd never find her now," said old man Hudson. "She's gone through the gutter with the rest of the rats."

"We could take the Swamp apart," said Bill Persons. His forehead was gleaming with perspiration.

"Is sound right to me," said Pierre.

"Wait a minute," said Choate. "We're practically here on our good behavior. We can't go rippin' up the town."

Bill Persons planted himself squarely in front of Choate. "One man can," he said.

"What do you mean?"

"I looked back and saw where they went in—about two doors down. The Genteel Boarding House, it said."

Choate began to swell up. He strode to the Genteel Boarding House and hammered on the door with his hard fist.

"Come in!" a voice growled.

They marched inside. It was like the rest—crude furnishings, home-made bar lighted by a candle, and a bare "parlor" at one side. "Where's that woman?" Choate demanded.

The man arose. He was bronze-skinned—almost black. He wore a turtle-neck sweater, with stripes running around it, and he was a giant. "What woman?"

Choate had to look up to him. "The woman with a fake French accent who brought my friend in here and tossed him out the door with a knife in his back."

The giant shrugged and yawned. "It's a big place—the Swamp. I can't keep track of ev'rybody."

"You keep track of that woman," Choate said suddenly. "You live with her."

The giant looked at him. He didn't yawn now. "You know?"

"I know," said Choate. "You're Apache John, and the woman is Gorgeous Gertie."

"You know a lot," Apache John said. "Maybe you know where Gertie is."

Bill Persons planted himself before the giant. "We're findin' out— from you."

Apache John laughed. "How would you like to find your guts spilled all over the place?" he asked suddenly.

"Fine," said Bill Persons, and hit him in the stomach. Apache John gasped once. Then he straightened and looked at them all. "Are you man enough to try that again?" he asked Bill.

"No!" said Choate. "But I am!"

"Shut up!" said Bill. "*I* started this fight."

The giant looked at him. "What you fight with?"

"Bare hands," said Bill.

The giant nodded. He went to the far door and turned the key in the lock. He took out the key and tossed it to Choate. "You gents wait outside and watch the front door," he said.

Old man Hudson frowned. "Bill, this is the knife-fightin'est man in New Orleans."

"Then it was him that stuck Diah in the back."

"I fight with the bare hands," said Apache John.

"He's a liar," said Hudson. "The place is full of knives."

Bill Persons grinned. "I fit a full-grown grizzly once with a knife. I reckon I can hold my own with this."

Choate said, "We'll put two men behind that door you just locked, and the rest of us'll stay outside."

Apache John shrugged. "Suit yourself, gents."

Choate took the key and unlocked the door. He stationed Pierre and

Jeff beyond the door. He locked the door and kept the key. He looked at Bill Persons. "I don't think this is smart," he said.

"I been spilin' for a fight ever since we left the Falls."

"That's how you lost that eye," Choate reminded him.

"Sure. I got that to make up. I might as well do it on this feller."

"You better trade places with me."

"Nix. He's my meat."

Apache John looked twice as big as Bill Persons. Choate scowled. Bill could be a hard nut to crack, but he didn't shine against a man like this. Choate said to Apache John, "If there's foul play, I'll be back myself."

The giant looked down at him. "Any time, mister, any time at all."

Choate went out and closed the door behind him. He and Hudson and Pierre and the two others stood before the door under the red lantern. There was a rush of feet from inside, and the flimsy building shook as somebody jumped. The candle must have been extinguished, for abruptly it was dark inside.

"That's Bill's work," said Choate. "He can see like a cat in the dark."

"That's the only thing that'll give him a chance," Hudson said nervously. "This Apache John is absolute murder with a knife. He's killed at least twenty men."

There was another rush of feet, a thud, and a grunt. Silence. Occasionally a board cracked. They were moving around inside.

"Did Bill have a knife?" asked Hudson.

"No."

A third rush. This time heavy feet pounded to meet it. The two men must have locked. There was a moment of straining silence. Then the floor thumped and the building rattled. They had gone to the floor. Choate wiped the sweat off his forehead with the back of his hand.

A crash. The building shivered. Somebody scrambled on the floor. There was the distinctive thud of a knife sinking into wood. Choate sucked in a deep breath.

Again a rush of feet. Choate was relieved. Bill was still in the fight, anyway.

There was a terrible crash. Hudson stood looking at the door. "The bar went over," he said.

A heavy thud against the door. Bodies tangled along the wall. The window crashed and fell in shattered pieces. Grunts, harsh breathing, curses. Silence.

Somebody jumped. The two bodies rolled on the floor. Silence.

A grunt. The unmistakable sound of a sharp knife snicking through meat and gristle. Then a long silence.

Choate swallowed hard. "If that door don't open pretty quick," he called, "I'm comin' in."

The door was flung back. The eerie call of a bobcat startled him. He went inside. He went to the back door and unlocked it. "Get a light," he told Pierre.

Choate started back but stumbled over the fallen bar. Pierre found a candle. Choate stared at the huge form of Apache John lying flat on his back, the handle of a knife sticking up from his chest. Choate looked at the grinning Bill Persons. The side of his head was bloody and one ear was gone, but Bill stepped over the fallen bar and said, "Help yourselves, gents. It's on the house." He opened a bottle of rum and turned it up and took a full swig. "The bear was more sportin'," he announced. "I didn't have to take a knife away from him to git somethin' to fight with."

Pierre whooped as he embraced Bill Persons. "We the two finest fighters on the Mississippi. We the champeens!"

Bill took another drink. "Except for him," he said, and pointed the bottle at Choate. "He can lick you and me and any two other fellers put together."

Pierre looked down at Choate. "Well, I not try it now," he said judiciously.

"Anyway, we got our work cut out for us," said Bill. "We *got* to take the Swamp apart now."

"All right," Choate said suddenly. "We'll start here and work down to the Sure Enuf Hotel."

"And don't forget the House of Rest for Weary Boatmen," said Hudson. "That whiskey he sold us was nothin' but alcohol with creosote dumped in it."

They didn't forget anything. Even the Swamp would always remember the night Choate Wilber's Kentuckians came to New Orleans. In a town that was used to rough doin's, Choate and his men shone some. They took the Genteel Boarding House apart board by board, square nail by square nail, and tossed the pieces into the street. They chased the women into the alley. They threw the liquor bottles into the mud. Then they went next door and started over, up one street and down another.

There had been nothing like it since the tornado of 1723 or the great fire of 1788. Block after block was laid flat, and they staggered back to the boats at daybreak, arms loaded with liquor, weary and sore but happy. Even Bill Persons was satisfied at last.

"There's one good thing about it," said Hudson. "The Spanish don't dare go down there in the Swamp themselves, so they prob'ly won't care too much what happened as long as it didn't happen in their part of town."

Rufus was counting noses. "What happened to Diah?" he asked.

Choate said soberly, "Diah run into a little trouble."

Rufus rubbed his whiskers. "I know'd Diah since he was a pup," he said. "He always said he wanted to git to New Orleans afore he died."

Choate stared at him. "He just made it," he said.

The Sack of Calabasas

John Myers Myers

1
BIG GAME UP WIND

With only buzzards watching as he went
a man jogged up along the Santa Cruz,
a stream whose winter flow had long been spent;
southward he rode, unarmed except with news—
two stringy yards of man hunched up astraddle
a donkey lost beneath an army saddle,
threading a trail which smoldered like a fuse

Born on Long Island, Jack Myers, after college in Vermont and New
Mexico, eventually settled in Tempe, Arizona, where he's a teacher. His
books have included *The Harp and the Blade,* a historical novel: *Silverlock,*
a fantasy in the tradition of Gulliver's Travels; frontier history: *The Alamo,*
The Last Chance, and *Doc Halliday;* and an offbeat Western novel titled
Dead Warrior. He is currently working on a series of narrative poems
depicting the growth of the American frontier, of which "The Sack of
Calabasas" is one.

while winding past the Arizona hills,
as barren as sheet iron in the heat
they caught and threw, or crossing braided rills
atwist amidst the cactus and mesquite;
no water troughs, but each a dusty furrow
to mock the thirsting of the weary burro
and of the one for whom it made a seat.

He was that Western miracle, a man
with neither kindred, ties, nor name, nor past;
each time he moved a different life began
which kept no consulate within the last.
Meanwhiles, as now, he was a formless power,
waiting until the force of his next hour
should clamp him in a mold to be recast.

He went because he had no need to stay:
as self-sufficient as a rolling rock,
he had the strength of nothing to betray—
nothing invested, nothing put in hock
to fortune by ambition or devotion;
he only recognized that life was motion,
desired or forced. Behind him lay a stock

of fifty secret, disregarded years;
ahead lay rawness counting on renown
which drew him as a water hole draws steers
that smell it from the hills and trace it down.
It took new worlds to greet new life and nourish
its sudden growth and give it space to flourish,
like this, the Border's most ingenious town.

Bonanza camps were often known to bloom
like cactus blossoms, blowing over night,
but Calabasas had the goofiest boom
the sagebrush ever saw. Where men alight
to build, some wealth has elsewhere been in season,
but this was tossed together for no reason
except a rumor, bought for truth on sight.

Gold raised up Wickenburg and silver put
Tombstone upon the mesa of Goose Flats;
Bisbee was built by copper under foot—
for men have always swarmed like swamp-hole gnats
at twilight to the site of buried metal,
afire to dig free treasure out and settle
and throw up walls in which to hang their hats—

but Calabasas, Spanish long ago,
revived through someone guessing out of turn
about the railroad's route to Mexico;
he talked, and footloose rogues rejoiced to learn
this greasewood patch would be a national sentry,
a shipping point, a mart, a port of entry,
where men of parts need hardly strive to earn.

And so the frontier gave the place its best:
the boom-town planets, faded by this moon,
paid tribute in the coinage of the West
by losing shifty citizens till soon
the classic cast of gunmen, whores, and gamblers,
land speculators, thieves, and loafing ramblers
were gathered in the Golden Fleece Saloon,

whose elegance was covered by a tent;
the Grand Hotel was canvas patched with duck.
The cash was yet to come which would be spent
by tycoons, there to parlay skill and luck
and for a side dish order up a city
whose denizens could eye New York with pity.
So much was sure, but destiny was stuck

till rail officials should at length concede
that what they must do, they could not avoid:
the line would use the valley—thus to lead
the tracks through Calabasas. Though annoyed
by stalling due to nitwit indecision,
the townsmen did not let it cloud their vision
of better days, when they would be employed

in palming off vast chunks of real estate
and shaking greenhorns down with joyous ease
for everything they used or wore or ate,
or fleecing them with cards, the badger squeeze,
and many another tried and ancient swindle,
some used to make new settlers' purses dwindle
since Jamestown planters watched beneath the trees

for suckers sailing from the mother isle.
So, as the rails rammed nearer, spike by spike
en route from Benson, southwest mile by mile,
they schemed and skinned each other. Or belike
they talked of how Tubac would be deflated
and how Nogales would be populated
by ghosts alone when facts approved their strike.

Or else they took impatience out in death
and dropped on Railroad Street amidst the gore
which turned its dust to mud, or kept their breath
to brag and challenge others. For the roar
of shooting irons, fired in careless fury,
was all their warrant, sheriff, judge, or jury:
they killed for cards, for insults, for a whore;

but most of all to hold their place among
a pack where weakness never met with ruth.
Theirs was a city of the knowing young,
where violence was the arbiter of truth;
yet while engaged in rank, wolf-hearted scheming
they could not keep from softer styles of dreaming
and that too saddle-galled their angry youth.

This was the prey—this hot and ready stag,
this strutting cock whose spurs were set for blood,
this bull whose charge would never wait the rag,
this rearing stallion, savagely in stud—
this was the game the riding man had scented
and now was tracking to its torrid, tented
lair amidst the swirling dust and scud

of wheeling tumbleweeds. He had no plan;
he did not know how he'd confront his prey
or what that prey would face in him, a man
whose only passion was to have his way,
because he had a force of wit and knowledge,
of things beyond the scope of church or college,
which he must use until his mortal clay

was part and parcel of that other earth
whose purpose is less wayward and more sure,
where questing restlessness must find a berth
and make its peace with stillness and endure.
But now, emerging from a mesquite thicket,
he first saw horses, hobbled or at picket,
and then the tents which meant he'd struck his lure.

2

DEATH ON RAILROAD STREET

The year was eighteen hundred eighty-two,
the month July, the hour was first-drink-time
on Sunday morning, and Sedalia Sue
prepared for breakfast with a gin and lime,
while Deuces Wilde and Longhorn Charlie Durben
gnawed quietly at tumblers full of bourbon
on either side of her. Cards, lust, and crime

must wait the issue of the crucial strife,
or rather ritual of somber peace,
when drink, the moon, won back the tide of life:
meanwhile their spirits, pending their release,
lurked motionless within or foraged, stalking
some shadow of the past. There was no talking
as, grimly waiting for the ebb to cease,

each leaned upon the Golden Fleece's bar.

The nearest to the door was Deuces Wilde,
remembered by his kin as Hamilcar,
though none could then have seen in him the child
who'd tired of Illinois and chores and schooling
and said, "I'm going West," and wasn't fooling
some twenty years before. His eyes were mild,

but so are fishes', when the fish are dead;
the only difference was that his would blink
the lids whose stubby lashes once were red,
though they had long been bleached a mushroom pink,
the match of the mustache which blurred concession
to what his mouth might yield toward an expression.
He stood beneath his hat and eyed his drink

as if it were a hand he meant to fill
by bottom dealing, angling in his sleeve
or kindred prestidigitative skill;
all men have credos: Deuces' *I believe*
was luck is for the crooked and the ready
to palm the derringer and hold it steady
and never ask nor proffer a reprieve.

He wore the gambler's black, but just beyond
a sworl of color was his foil, and more.
Sedalia Sue was blond as brass is blond;
her hair shone like a polished cuspidor.
The purple gown below it was a litter
of precious stones, or near enough to glitter
and advertise a first-line frontier whore,

though she was now the seller, not the sold,
postgraduate in harlotry, a bawd,
a matriarch of tarts, purse-proud and cold,
whose rugged dignity was seldom thawed.
Her smiles cost more, they said who'd tried and counted,
than lesser heifers charged for being mounted;
though few essayed her smiles, for most were awed

by either Sue herself or by her mack:
one Longhorn Charlie, dark as she was fair,
and more convincingly. A muddy black,
his eyes took in all comers with a glare
which spoke of energy leased out to meanness;
the face they glowed in was not wrought of cleanness,
though he was not the one to know or care.

The body which it topped showed wide and thick
beneath the gaily colored open vest,
yet he could move demoniacally quick,
which he had proved all up and down the West
as rustler, sheriff, robber, pimp, and marshal;
but some said—not to him—he was not partial
to shooting ready gunmen in the chest

when backs would serve as well. So there they stood,
morosely silent, till a woman screamed,
"You fish-fed bastard, now I'll fix you good!"
And on the instant did as she had schemed
by firing at her enemy or lover.
No matter which, he fell for blood to cover,
while he stared up and neither saw nor dreamed.

The incident destroyed the moody hush
of first-drink-time. The gun-schooled clientele
ducked out the side flaps, jostling in the rush,
or hugged the ground themselves till they were well
assured the frenzied wench was through recruiting
for Boothill's silent witnesses to shooting.
Yet Deuces, Sue, and Longhorn scorned to yell

or dodge or even start. This stuff was old,
and they had seen it often and survived.
Besides, they'd counted five full shots, which told
no more were coming; wherefore they contrived
to gaze with boredom, not unmixed with pleasure
at showing rock-ribbed poise, to prove the measure
of three who'd seen the elephant and thrived.

Deadwood they'd known, Tascosa, Leadville, Dodge,
Fort Griffin Flat and Tombstone and what not:
the roaring chapters of the frontier lodge
whose high degrees they held. Yet, of the lot,
they swore that Calabasas was the roughest,
its citizens the slickest and the toughest,
who dubbed in what the Devil had forgot;

so in a moment Longhorn shrugged and grinned.
"Call in the buzzards, boys; he's drawing flies.
Who is it?" "Schooner Blaine, fresh out of wind,"
said Deuces. "Oh?" Sue looked her mild surprise.
"The dude who's fixin' up the Gloucester Palace
but ain't yet got her stock? Don't worry, Alice."
This to the murderess, whose widened eyes

showed dawning fear. "He didn't have no friends;
he hadn't bought a round yet for the house."
"He'd ought to do it now, to make amends,"
cried Deuces. "Go ahead and frisk the louse!
He's your corpse, Alice; see he does his duty."
And Alice, brightening, took and used the booty,
then tucked away the balance in her blouse

while all the others cheered her, overjoyed
at sharing in this corpse-is-treating wake.
Then Longhorn slapped the bar, his spirits buoyed.
"We've had our man for breakfast; let's have steak.
You coming, Sue?" "You fellows feed your faces;
I won't swap here," she told him, "for no places
until I get my cut of this whore's take.

You hear that, Alice?" But the girl had turned
to watch two bouncers readying to eject,
forever, Schooner Blaine. "I guess I learned
that son of a bitch," she mumbled, "to respect
a lady——Oh!" And then she started bawling.
"Shut up!" said Longhorn. "Hell, the sky ain't falling
because you plugged a man." But the effect

of tears at death, now passing in review—
as Blaine was leaving, soon to be beyond
all reach of fellowship—was to imbue
the moment with the matter of despond,
and quiet put a crusher on their revel.
But Deuces noticed, as the corpse drew level
with him and Longhorn, that the dead was fond,

or had been, of cigars—a taste they shared—
for two fine, long cheroots were sticking out
of Schooner's waistcoat pocket, unimpaired
by blood or bullets. Like a fly-sucked trout,
the gambler's hand moved, snatched them both, and darted
to place one smoke between the slackly parted
jaws of Blaine, wherein it rolled about

as he was hustled to the tent's rear door;
while Deuces snapped aflame a lucifer,
to fire the stogie he had mouthed, before
he called, "Well, thanks, and don't get lost now, sir.
I didn't think to offer matches, knowing
you'd easy find a light where you are going.
But don't you take my roasting place, or fur

will fly when I drift in." Longhorn guffawed
and, forcing more than he, the others laughed;
now keen to show they were not overawed,
they drove their stalling mirth with studied craft
until it gained momentum and recovered
the ground lost when the wraith of horror hovered
so close they'd felt its presence like a draft.

But Deuces' offhand mockery of the cult
of death and mortal sinning's just rewards
had steadied them again, with the result
they once more knew themselves the ribald lords
of antiworlds which outlawed moral beauty
and recognized apostasy as duty;
for by their will they'd severed all the cords

which bound them to the world of ordered homes,
religion, and the hangdog decencies:
the fool's gold some had mined for once as gnomes
enslaved to trades or universities,
before they'd found true wisdom on the Border.
So, seeing that their own house was in order,
the gambler and the gunman hit the breeze.

3

THE CREATION OF ABIMELECH JONES

Along the dusty length of Railroad Street,
symbol of all that Calabasas hoped,
Deuces and Longhorn minced with booted feet
toward Dan's—"The Best Meat Rustlers Ever Roped"—
until their way was blocked by some who'd halted
to watch a traveler, not much exalted
by perching on the animal which moped

down street, a ratty donkey, tired and small.
The man aboard looked glum as he was long,
somehow more helpless too for being tall:
a pilgrim born for rougher souls to wrong.
He called no word and got a Western greeting,
a chorus of blank stares to chill the meeting,
daunting the weak or challenging the strong.

The rider seemed the first. When none gave ground
to let him pass, he whoa'd; the mount obeyed.
"Hello," the stranger said, and blinked around,
uncertain certainly, perhaps afraid.
"Is Calabasas far?" he asked then, pitching
his voice so high it cracked and meanwhile twitching
a long and bony nose on sad parade

beneath the reaches of a floppy hat.

In time a man asked gently, "Far from where?
It's far from 'Frisco or Mount Ararat,
the realm of Prester John or Herald Square,
the Shannon or the Mississippi Valleys;
but not so far from Tubac or Nogales,
and nearer to a jackass. Do you care,

or were you only asking?" For a while
the other seemed to ponder, then his lean
and wrinkled face lit feebly with a smile.
"I think I understand just what you mean;
this place is Calabasas. I am *in* it."
He looked about him, wide-eyed, for a minute,
while winks and snickers were exchanged between

the men who watched. But he who waited felt
the surge of life creep through his nerves and veins,
heating his substance till it yearned to melt,
plastic to circumstance. He took no pains
to force the onset of an inspiration
but made himself a blotter for sensation
as he observed the street awaiting trains

and then the townsmen with their edgy air
of having chewed damnation, fruit and pit,
and fattened on it. Yet he grew aware
that some had shaved, had even spruced a bit
in dim response to what was once a habit
of honoring the Sabbath, though a rabbit
could now match mystic faith with any there.

The rider sensed the place then, also those
who poured in it the force to work on him;
he felt the current tugging at his toes
and guessed it deep enough for him to swim.
The time was near, he knew, when he must wallow,
trusting his genius for what next would follow,
but now, still uncommitted on the brim,

he gauged the speed and temperature. At length
he cleared his throat and spoke. "I'm very glad.
The name is Jones." His voice took on more strength.
"Abimelech." He paused as if to add
those elements, and then he started over.
"The Reverend A. Jones, a humble drover
of straying sheep, though none, I hold, are bad."

And so this western Proteus took the form
which he would use and settled in that shape,
but anything so foreign to the norm
of Calabasas left the rest agape:
a rattlesnake that rode a dromedary,
a Gila monster sipping Tom and Jerry,
a grizzly banking faro for an ape

would not have startled them one half so much
as this that solemnly returned their gaze
and looked paternal, for an added touch.
"Aw, nix!" one watcher mumbled from his daze.
"Go 'way! I just ain't seein' it—a parson!"
But neither man, nor ass he had his arse on
would vanish, so one tried a different phrase:

"I met a fellow back in Vinegaroon
who told me that he once saw General Grant
raped by a Flathead squaw in a balloon,
and I believed it all; but this I can't.
A minister——Ah, hell! A goddamn preacher!
A sin-and-liquor-hating Bible teacher
turned loose in whore-and-rye-land with his rant—

it just won't wash!" "It's true; it has to be,"
a third declared. "It's written on his phiz,
and it's a thing, like trainer to a flea,
a man don't claim to be unless he is—
he'd never think of it. There's no use talking
for facts don't lose their patents through our balking;
we've got a shepherd, and this flock is his,

so let's see what he wants." "I guess I'll ask,"
a fourth said. "Reverend Jones, what's on your mind?"
"The bearing of the Word is all my task,"
the rider told him, "so if I could find
a tent or shack—I don't expect a steeple—
where I could give the Message to you people
which I am duty bound to give all blind

and erring souls, my work here will be done.
Is there a place?" But each one shook his head
till Deuces laughed and answered, "I know one,
if you don't mind saloons." "I do not," said
Abimelech. "A barkeep is my brother,
I humbly own, as much as any other."
"Well," Deuces purred, "a man called Blaine is dead

of cheating on a whore, or some such thing
which he won't do again. He had a bar
he'd not yet opened called the Gloucester King—
no, Gloucester Palace. It's not very far.
Just back down Railroad Street and read the banners,
and when you find the tent, don't stand on manners."
"The Lord," said Jones, "is still my guiding star,

but who will guide me now to a hotel?"
The rest swapped looks before one fellow spoke:
"The Grand should do him." "It should do him well,"
another man agreed. "And if you're broke,"
a third said, "why just tell the Chink your troubles;
he'll bust 'em for you, smooth as poppin' bubbles."
At this some hid their knowledge of a joke

behind a hand, bandanna, or a cough;
but Reverend Jones said, "All men here seem kind."
And after getting bearings, he moved off
to find the Grand Hotel; and there to find
the landlord, Ah Chin Honk, a most unplacid
Oriental, wizened, shrewd, and acid
to all but wealthy patrons. Some assigned

his own wealth to the fact he had the trick
of squeezing coins, not merely till they yelped
but till each eagle yielded forth a chick;
while others claimed a Chinese idol whelped
gold ingots for him while the joss was burning.
True tales or not, his one-track, no-switch yearning
so owned his mind that it could not be helped

if now he marked Jones "enemy—he's poor";
and so he did not bow but sat and shrugged.
"Five dollar cash for bunk; we gots no more
of any room." The parson sadly tugged
upon his lips but did not voice resentment.
"I find the heat infringes on contentment,
don't you?" he asked. And with the words he lugged

a handkerchief in view, as though to mop
the sweat from where his hat had left its mark;
but coins came with the handkerchief to drop
upon the hard-packed floor. And as the dark
is shriveled by a lighting lamp and ceases,
just so did heavy, shiny yellow pieces
erase Ah Chin Honk's gloom. A friendly spark

warmed up his eyes before he rose and bowed.
"I have forgots," he said, "my best of all.
Will you allows me?" "You will be allowed,"
the parson said, and soon was in a stall
with tarpaulin walls, wherein a brazen, burnished
bed stood fast, if hardly level, furnished
with bolster, spread, and quilt against the call

for warmth in desert dawns. There was a stand
for washing and the pottery attached:
four pieces. To the glory of the Grand,
the pitcher, bowl and pot and slop jar matched:
beauty in porcelain, brave with princely towers
seen in the distance through an arch of flowers
whose very stems were gold. The parson scratched

a scar beside his nose as he admired
each separate ceramic work of art.
"No more," he said at last, "could be desired.
Have you a cook?" "Damn goods and velly smart,"
the landlord nodded. "Tell this clever minion,"
the parson urged him, "that in my opinion
fried eggs are best; say, four eggs for a start

and then we'll see." Ah Chin Honk saw and sighed,
for Reverend Jones was diligent and ate
as warrior ants do, not to be denied
while food holds out. At last he mopped his plate,
however, with a biscuit. "Now I'm able,"
he said, "to make a temple of a stable.
Great ventures must be met with strength as great."

4

READYING FOR THE PITCH

With dignity the man of God set forth,
slow as to step but quicker with his eye;
the barren hills ran south, the dry stream north,
and in between them, sat on by a sky
which glowed like brandy flame, the boom town squatted
amid the dust which coated it and blotted
all color out. The lanes ran out awry

through dust to tent, bare camp and wickiup,
or from such residence points they turned and curled
toward Railroad Street, where Lil's, The Gutter Pup,
The One-to-Spare, and Trips-around-the -World,
The Louvre, Beefsteak Dan's, and Dot's-from-Dallas
were all near neighbors of the Gloucester Palace.
Reading the painted bunting there unfurled,

the parson left the street and slowly crossed

the doorless threshold, stopped, and peered around.
The empty bar—where never man had tossed
his snifter off and never gun had downed
a customer or gambler proved his slyness—
seemed waiting any claimant to its dryness:
content but not yet sure of what he'd found,

the parson pottered aimlessly about,
gazing at pictures, fixtures, and spittoons,
the jars for hard-boiled eggs or sauerkraut,
glasses and corkscrews, jiggers, stirring spoons;
but these were messageless, and so he shambled
to tables, custom-built for those who gambled.
He neared the one for craps and read its runes

indifferently before he next perused
the faro table's layout. There he stopped
to fiddle with the dealer's box, bemused
by flaring lips which snarled and fangs that chopped:
traditional, a raging tiger guarded
the thirteen spades whose pips and features larded
the felt expanse. His hands rose up, then dropped.

But up the sun climbed, fiercer as it soared,
and Calabasas, yielding to it, drowsed,
except for one pledged servant of the Lord,
intent to see his congregation housed
as suitably as will and work could make it;
if he had thirst, he did not pause to slake it,
this not withstanding all the dust aroused

by sweeping out the place. He pushed away
the gaming tables to make room for pews,
then sought out Ah Chin Honk anew to say
he needed extra chairs, could even use
the boxes emptied by the trained and artful
chef when cooking beans. There was a cart full,
and when they were installed, he bent his thews

to beating out the dirty canvas flaps
which walled the Gloucester Palace. Though the sign
that styled it so he'd shredded into scraps
with which to scrub and make the fixtures shine
behind the bar—of which he'd wrought a chancel—
with rags to hide the buxom nudes and cancel
the posters billing whiskey, beer, and wine.

And when the legacy of Schooner Blaine
had all been hid or drafted for the church,
the parson, not content to slave in vain,
endured the sun of Railroad Street in search
of souls to save. So girls and macks and matrons,
barkeeps, barflies, the gamblers and their patrons
were startled and amused to see him lurch

into their purlieus, drumming on a pan
and crying, "Sinners saved at half past six
in Blaine's old place, next door to Beefsteak Dan,
the rustlers' friend. Beware the devil's tricks
and learn instead the orders of the Master
from Brother Abimelech, your loving pastor;
admission free." And with that word he'd fix

some listener with a smile and then move on.
But those who heard him only grinned or laughed,
mocking his godliness when he was gone;
or didn't wait for that and crudely chaffed
him to his face with taunts and counter-drumming.
At first, it was agreed, no one was coming
to hear a man so childish and so daft

that he would challenge sin on its home stand.
But still they talked of him and prized a joke
so different from the Border's common brand;
and finally a notion stirred and woke:
the thing to do was not to dodge the fellow
but follow up the fun and hear him bellow;
then get his goat till he went up in smoke

and lost his pious air, or lost his nerve
and quit the game. The idea spread and took—
not fast at first, then jumped upon with verve
by almost every killer, whore, and crook
in town, which meant the cream of Calabasas
would swarm like yellow jackets on molasses
to watch the sucker struggle on the hook.

Sedalia Sue and Longhorn had a spat
about the matter. "Sure, I want to go;
it might be fun," she urged, "to hear him blat.
And trade won't start till dark." "Aw, honey, no!"
he told her. "If the devil heard you praying,
he'd quit the job he's got and take to playing
an end man in a traveling minstrel show

so he could spread the joke." "Is that a fact?"
she asked. "Why, you dry gulcher, I'm as good
as any slut for which you ever macked;
and if I don't do everything I should,
you ain't the one to say so, when you're livin'
on what my girls are makin' and I'm givin'."
"Giving!" he laughed. "You'd keep it, if you could;

but you need me, like I need you. All right;
this ain't a reason we should have a split:
we'll pick up Deuces when we've had a bite,
then watch the pilgrim throw a holy fit.
If he ain't spry enough, my Smith and Wesson
will give the boob a fancy dancing lesson
to start him going like his pants was lit—

it might be fun at that." And so it chanced
that as the hour appointed marked the clock,
Sue with her escorts trailing grandly pranced
inside the tent, now crowded chockablock,
and made for the front row, then calmly waited
till three seats in the center were vacated
when Longhorn showed his gun and slapped the stock.

So all were there but their evangelist,
whose whereabouts nobody could discern;
though at the outset he was hardly missed,
his congregation was so keen to learn,
by dint of signs and gestures, winks and whistles,
just who had brought along what noisome missiles,
produced in handy sizes from the stern

of hens long since or horses, à la carte,
to name two favorites. But the moment came
which brought impatience for the show to start;
the huntsmen started calling for their game
to break from cover. There were shouts and stamping,
whoops, and the imitated snorts and champing
of mustangs not yet ready to be tame,

so like themselves. But Deuces rose and held
a slim cigar aloft until the din
was hushed a little. "Blast your hides," he yelled;
"you'll scare the vicar clean out of his skin!
This is a church, remember, not a riot—
not yet." They got the point then and were quiet,
trying to lure their holy quarry in.

5

THE GOSPEL OF THE PIPS

Deuces had hardly lighted his cigar
when, straightening, the man of God upreared
from where he had sat hunched behind the bar.
He mounted it, while Calabasas cheered,
then stepped upon a box with "Beans" for label
which humped its back above a faro table
to form his pulpit. From this height he peered

a moment at his chuckling flock, then clapped

his hands as loud and sharply as a shot;
and when all jumped, he raised his arms and snapped,
" 'Keno!' you'll cry and claim the doomsday pot
of good or ill, when death calls out your number
and at the end you wake again from slumber
to take your winnings, liking them or not."

Addressed in their own tongue, his hearers stirred
but quieted and dropped their nether jaws.
So Brother Abimelech was clearly heard
as he went on with but the briefest pause:
"I quote no Bible text to start my sermon,
for rather I let where I am determine
the subjects of my little talks, because

no matter where I am, the spot is God's;
and so all places offer me a text.
A temple or a railway stop—what odds?
He sponsors both, and I am not perplexed
to find His power upon a depot landing;
I read His word wherever I am standing—
a gaming table now. Should I be vexed

at what it tells me? Rather the reverse;
the layout there below is near akin
to all of life, for better or for worse.
The tiger which we buck, my friends, is sin;
the devil deals, and we must back or copper
on every turn he thumbs from out the hopper;
nor can we welch or quit the game we're in

until our stack is gone." At this the throng
who'd come to heckle found each other's eyes,
nor hurled the ancient eggs they'd brought along
nor laughed nor mimicked Jones; and there were sighs
from five or six whose recent fatal traffic
with faro made his parable too graphic
for hearts to bear without protesting sighs.

"You who are gamblers!" Brother Abimelech
next shot at them; and everyone sat straight.
"You each have Bibles, if you know your deck.
So learn to read, before it is too late,
the message of the cards you handle nightly;
then, as you play, you will be guided rightly
and be prepared of soul, in case your fate

should overtake you, as it sometimes does
in games of chance, unsparingly and quick."
He showed them cards and waited for the buzz
of talk to quiet. "This is not a trick;
it is the tale of man and sin and glory,
with pips instead of words to tell the story."
He took one card and, giving it a flick,

he let it fall upon the layout. "There.
I played my trust in God. It is my ace."
He dropped one more. "My deuce. God made a pair
of Eve and Adam in a state of grace.
My trey. There stole a third into the Garden,
creating sin past any earthly pardon.
My four. We have four helpers in the race

for our salvation: Matthew, Luke, and Mark
and John, who daily pray for our escape
from Satan's clutch. My five. You ladies, hark:
of some ten virgins of a lovely shape,
though five were wise, yet five were vain and silly,
which means we are not punished willy-nilly
but damned for what we do, and if we ape

the ways of hell. My six. There are six days
for us to gad and jape and do our worst.
My seven. The Sabbath is our day to gaze
upon the sins in which we are immersed,
then choose a better course." The words came slowly,
spoken in tones as soft as they were holy,
but yet all heard distinctly. For a haze

of smoke no longer rose from the cheroot
in Deuces' hand, Sedalia Sue was flushed
and motionless, with no desire to hoot,
and Longhorn merely moved a hand which brushed
a fly away—his gun stayed in its holster,
as harmless as a chicken-feather bolster;
and all the rest were leaning forward, hushed

and wondering, while they watched the falling cards
as though they'd never seen a deck before.
"My eight," the parson said. "You have eight guards
against misdoing and you need no more:
you have two eyes to tell the right from evil,
two feet to crush the serpent head's upheaval,
two hands to thrust temptation from your door,

two ears to sift from Satan's lies the truth.
My nine. Nine days of falling fast divide
the Enemy from God. My ten. In youth
you heard the Ten Commandments; but abide
by these, and Paradise is your assurance.
My knave. The angel fallen into durance:
the Prince of Hell, the devil, horns and hide.

My queen. It is the Church, my children dear,
a royal mother, warding you from harm.
My king. He's God's own mightiness, to fear
and love forever—if you take alarm
in time to earn forgiveness from heaven
and soar aloft with angel wings for leaven.
Yet thirteen cards do not complete the charm

that's spelled out by a deck. My diamonds tell
salvation is a gem above all price,
my clubs say sin is punished down in hell,
my hearts remind us that in Paradise
the Savior's beats for us, while spades give warning
our mortal selves must slumber night and morning
down in the ground, where worms with blood like ice

and carrion maggots wait. So that's four suits.
They tell us of the seasons we enjoy
while we are here and reap the earthly fruits,
so rich and numerous they never cloy,
which God has blessed us with." Abruptly dashing
the ones he still held down, his tones now crashing,
the parson cried out, "Cards are not a toy!

They number fifty-two to match the weeks;
and each week has a Sunday such as this,
when we can show we are not brainless freaks
by paying on account for heavenly bliss.
I'll sing 'Old Hundred' as I take collection.
This is your chance to show the Lord affection
in concrete terms—a chance you must not miss!"

6

BUCKING THE TIGER

The parson had a pleasing baritone
and lungs enough to fill the tent with sound,
though now and then he'd pause enough to drone,
"Let's all put in, to show we're heaven-bound
and are not paying taxes to the devil.
Use faro checks to fill the Stetson level—
if cash is short—before it goes around."

And Calabasas, hypnotized and awed,
reached in its money belts and pocketbooks
to give, with hearts rejoiced at being thawed;
while some, their fervor lighting up their looks,
took up the words that Reverend Jones was singing
and sent "Old Hundred" thunderously ringing
throughout the town. Yet if some softened crooks

forgot themselves and knew not what they were,

Deuces was made of no such flimsy stuff.
He saw a pot which set his blood astir,
and though he fed it carelessly enough
and won a smile from Jones by grandly throwing
a double eagle in, his eyes were glowing
but then went dead, as when he meant to bluff

for major stakes. He watched the cash pile up
until the hat had made the circuit, when
the parson cried, "My friends, you've filled my cup
and that of God, who'll bless you all. Amen.
Now buck the tiger!" When these words were spoken,
the sacred spell he'd wrapped them in was broken,
to let high spirits back. They cheered him then

or whistled, clapped their hands or fired their guns
to let the twilight through the church's roof
and let the angels know who were the ones
that prized religion; then, in further proof
of zeal, they sped to drink to their conversion.
Some women made a similar excursion,
though others, left uneasy, kept aloof

to ponder soberly upon their sins—
made manifest by Jones a little since—
and swore they would not, for a thousand skins,
so lose themselves again. But no mere hints
that after death, that far and dim dry gulcher,
there'd hover Judgment Day, a dimmer vulture,
could alter Sue's intent or make her wince

away from profit. Off to work she went
at Trips-around-the-World, her place of trade;
while Longhorn sought his natural element,
the Golden Fleece. There Deuces also made
his gambling stand; but now the dealer waited,
to join the handful, reverently elated,
who watched the parson count. Then when he'd prayed

and given thanks for heaven's charity,
these eager faithful flocked around to talk.
"By God!" one said, "you done converted me;
I'm harnessed to the Right and I won't balk."
"You sure did cheer me up, sir," Deuces told him.
"You gave the devil hell enough to hold him
but didn't draw too thin a line of chalk

for me to follow. How about a drink?"
The man of God was courteous with his smile
but shook his head. "Why, thank you, but I think
I'd best retire and meditate awhile
in my hotel." "Aw, damn it, come on, vicar,"
another urged him; "just one round of liquor
to get acquainted on. We like your style;

besides, I think you ought to know the town
you're preaching in." "My son, I find you right,
on second thought," said Jones, "and I don't frown
upon a friendly glass. When hearts are light
they're nearer to the Lord, for hell is sorrow."
"Don't worry till you shake your head tomorrow,"
said Deuces. "My treat, gents." No one would fight

at those words in that land of chronic thirst;
docile, they trailed him to his chosen bar.
"A pleasant spot," said Jones, and downed his first.
"A bird," said Deuces, "can't fly very far
on just one wing." "A witty observation."
Brother Abimelech took the next potation.
"And aren't tails needed too?" "You bet they are!"

cried Deuces, slapping him upon the back.
"We'll have one more, then come and watch me deal,
unless you think you'd like to take a crack
at faro playing." "No, I hardly feel,"
said Jones, though hesitating, "I should gamble.
You go ahead, and I'll drink up and amble
to my hotel before I show more zeal

for worldly things than any pastor should.
I fear the whiskey's going to my head
or I should not be tempted." Touching wood
for luck, the gambler gripped his arm and said,
"Suppose you *won,* though, vicar. You could double
or triple your collection take." "The trouble,"
the parson told him, "is that I might tread

the path of folly till I lose it all."
"But think of what," said Deuces, "you might get.
You'll need a stack of checks that's mighty tall
to build a church with. Chance it, and I'll bet
you'll win enough. I've got one of my hunches;
besides, I know that good luck comes in bunches,
and yours got such a start tonight you're set

for quite a run." "But how about yourself?"
the parson asked. "My gain must be your loss.
Are you so large of mind that risking pelf
when you feel certain you can't win the toss
is something you can court to please a stranger?"
"Oh, I am not that generous—no danger,"
said Deuces, "but a gambler learns to cross

bad spots of luck—and I am in one now—
as quickly as he can; and never mind
just what it costs to shake the jinx." "I vow,"
the parson smiled, "you fill me with a kind
of admiration for the gamester's spirit—
unmoved by fortune's whims; Jovelike or near it—
I never thought to own. So now I find

my interest stirred; though you must show me how.
From Hoyle," he said, as Deuces led the way,
"I've learned the terms, but they're just phrases now."
His words were drowned in cries of, "Look!" and "Say!"
"The preacher!" "No!" "Hell, yes!" Then everybody
picked up his shot or highball, beer or toddy
and ganged around, intent to watch the play;

among them Longhorn—well aware—who wished
he had some way to cut in on the game.
He'd watched them wistfully while Deuces fished,
tickling the trout until he'd made it tame;
and now stood waiting for the subtle killing,
half fascinated, also half unwilling
to view a prize on which he had no claim.

The fifty cards from soda down to hock
were slipped, and Deuces patiently explained,
while fumblingly the parson tapped his stock
of checks or added to it as he gained.
But on the whole, he found by careful counting,
that steadily his wealth in hand was mounting;
and he was overjoyed—though later pained

as fortune changed. "Perhaps I'd better quit,"
he said, on finding he'd sustained some loss,
though minor only. "Now's the time to hit!"
the dealer told him. "Show your luck who's boss
by crowding it. Just kite your bets up higher
and bring your money back upon the flyer."
"I'll try," the parson said, and reached across

to scoop the cards his way. "And just for luck
I'll make the deck, my son; I've got to learn.
If I'm to be a gamester, I won't duck
my portion of the work, and it's my turn."
His long, thin fingers dropped the cards and fumbled,
but in a little while he'd somehow jumbled
the deck together well enough to earn

a nod from Deuces Wilde, who cut and filled
the box; the bets were placed; the cards were sprung.
"The Lord," Jones murmured shortly, "must have willed
that I should win." The gambler held his tongue,
but as each card produced a new disaster
his well-drilled face had much ado to master
the urge to show the anguish of the stung

each time the parson raked in all the chips,
then raised his eyes toward heaven to invoke
the powers there before, with prayer-moved lips,
he pushed out stacks so tall they sometimes broke.
They came back bearing gifts, but Deuces dourly
accepted chance until the other surely
called out the turn; and then his wrath awoke.

He yearned to kill. He almost snatched his gun
and shot the parson as he bowed to bless
his winnings; but he heard: "By God! he won."
"The angels do look after him, I guess!"
"He broke the bank!" "Why, gents, we got a preacher
I wouldn't swap, with boot, for old man Beecher!"
To slay this novel, popular success

was more than he could do and not be lynched;
so Deuces, bracing, made his face a mask,
and when Jones shook his hand, he hardly flinched.
"We'll play another time, that's all I ask,"
he said aloud, though in a voice that fluttered.
But in the reaches of his soul he muttered,
"I'll have your blood and stow it in a flask

to use instead of catsup someday soon."
But Reverend Jones meanwhile was on his feet
and called to everyone in the saloon,
"My friends, I've taken note that it is meet
for winners to be hosts, and as a servant
of Heaven should be carefully observant
of cherished customs, it's the Church's treat."

7

THE SQUEEZE AT THE ONE-TO-SPARE

The parson did not have to say it twice;
the invitation started a stampede
which even Deuces, lacking now the price
of soothing bourbon, joined to glut his need.
But Longhorn Charlie, though he blithely started,
in mid-stride left the course his thirst had charted
to sidle out the door and stride with speed

down Railroad Street to Trips-around-the-World,
the bawdyhouse of Sue, who was on deck.
"Wipe off your paint and get your hair uncurled,"
he told her. "This here Brother Abimelech
somehow won Deuces' roll and now he's drinking."
They looked into each other's eyes, unwinking,
and then Sue nodded. "Well, get on his neck

and don't let go. I'll meet you at the Fleece."
But Longhorn shook his head at her. "Not there.
Deuces would spot the game and want a piece.
I'll take the parson to the One-to-Spare
and fill him full of buzzard's milk. Now hustle
and wash that goo off." "Tell it to my bustle,"
she counseled him. "Just go and hold him where

the hair is short until I come along.
Here, take this eagle." Longhorn did and sped
to seek the Golden Fleece and work the prong
into the sucker's mouth before it bled
and warned him he was hooked. Now, as he reckoned,
the parson's guests were working on their second
so, easing into line by Jones, he said,

"A stool must have three legs or it can't stand;
my treat!" He bounced his coin to make it ring.
"Don't mind me, Reverend. I'm a little canned."

"Yet not too drunk," said Jones, "to say a thing—
that phrase about the stool—that's very clever.
Yes, I'll have one more drink, though I should never
imbibe so much." "Go on and have your fling,"

Longhorn advised him. "Reverend, what I like
about you is you're good but you don't itch.
You let me know that heaven's a lucky strike
and that the devil is a son of a bitch
but still don't make me feel that I'm a bastard
for being just a man." "I have not mastered
myself," said Jones, "those dreadful urges which

impel a man to sin. I'm getting drunk
right now, I fear, and must be off to seek
my bed before I play the fool." "Aw, bunk!
You're sober as a stone and you can't sneak
away," said Longhorn. "Look, the house is buying."
"Man strives and falls," said Jones, "but keeps on trying;
the spirit still is strong, though flesh is weak,

which God perhaps will take into account."
"My flesh ain't weak," said Longhorn; "what the hell!
But still, when I've took in the right amount
my shanks get tuckered. Let's sit down a spell,
when these are gone; not here in all this riot
but right next door, say, where it's kind of quiet."
"Indeed," Jones murmured, "it is just as well

that I should sit." He did not stagger but
he wove a little, as they picked a course
outside and in again. "I'll tell you what,"
said Longhorn; "I'll just buy a quart, old horse,
and then we won't be always dry and waiting
for barkeep service." "How I will be hating

tonight tomorrow! though I'm past remorse

just now," said Jones. As Longhorn had declared,
the One-to-Spare was quieter in the sense
that rifle shots are quieter compared
with cannonading. Life was less intense
than at the Golden Fleece but bluffly jolly,
and Jones, admitting pleasure in his folly,
forebore to dwell on sin's sad recompense.

"You know," he said, "I even think I'll smoke."
And when cigars were brought he proffered cash.
"Your dough's no good here, Reverend." Longhorn spoke,
while paying off as if bestowing trash.
"No friend of mine can buy while I've got money."
He turned, then looked annoyed. "Aw, beat it, honey!"
For Sue stood there; a different Sue, not brash

or wanton or aglitter with fake gems
but dressed in white, and shy, and bare of paint.
A tear-soaked handkerchief with lacy hems
concealed one eye. "Oh, please!" Her voice was faint.
"I've got to see you, Charlie—just a minute!"
"Go find a grave," he said, "and then dive in it;
I got no time for crying jags." "I ain't,"

she told him, "tight. Oh, Charlie, don't be mean!"
So Longhorn, groaning, rose. "Well, say it fast."
In pantomime they briefly sketched a scene
where he refused but yielded at the last
and came back to the table, looking harassed.
"That loco heifer there," he said, embarrassed,
"got scared this evening when she heard you blast

at sin. You've got her thinking of the end
when hell and heaven bid in for our souls.
She's keeping hurdy girls but wants to mend
her cat-house ways so she won't fry on coals.
She says she's got to pray or she'll go crazy

and hopes you'll learn her how—ain't that a daisy?"
"She's right to think of death before it tolls

the bell for her," said Jones. He cast a glance
to where Sue filled the contours of her dress.
"It seems a very piteous circumstance
that such a goodly vessel should confess
the Devil's presence. Surely I must aid her,
but I could do no good with the Invader
right here in public; don't you see?" "Hell, yes,

and so does she," said Longhorn. "What she hopes
is that you'll go and see her in the dive
she owns—and so, of course, she pulls the ropes;
you'll have a private room in which to drive
the devil out. But look; there ain't no hurry.
The devil would get in, so let him worry
about the chance of getting out alive.

Let's you and me drink up." "Don't talk like that!"
the parson warned. "I'm drunk, but not so much
that I will countenance such callous chat
or share in mocking anyone in such
distress of heart. And if she feels that learning
to pray will save a soul now doomed to burning,
I must not fail her, so I will not touch

another drop. Poor child! Where does she live?"
"At Trips-around-the-World, just seven tents
down Railroad Street," said Longhorn. "Well, then give
this message to her: I am going hence
to get my Bible, hymnal, and my psalter
but presently will join her and won't falter
until I've taught her something of the sense

of my religion, friend." The parson rose,
somewhat unsteadily, and made the door.
Then Longhorn sprang toward Sue, who shed her pose

of tearful humbleness. "Just what's the score?"
she asked. "He swallowed hook and line and sinker;
what's more, I filled him up, and he's no drinker,"
he whispered to her grinning. "Why the poor
old nut has gone to get his praying books
so he can save the soul that you ain't got.
He'll meet you at your joint; and when your hooks
are in him deep, I'll jump him on the dot;
and there's our pigeon, cooked and carved and salted.
And he's a fat one!" Starting off, she halted.
"What happens, Charlie, if he don't get hot

and keeps on prayin' for me?" "What's the dif?"
he asked. "No matter how he moves, he's tagged.
A preacher in a whore house, stinking stiff,
and you ascreaming that he up and bragged
he'd do you wrong, and him afeared of scandal—
why he'll sweat money like a burning candle
sweats off its wax. Oh, he's as good as bagged.

Now this was my idea, but I'll be fair
and cut you in for thirty." "Ain't you nice?"
she wondered. "I'll take fifty for my share—
I'm doin' half the work—or it's no dice.
It ain't your brains that starts these poor hicks droolin';
it's what *I've* got. God damn you, I ain't foolin'!
I freeze the game unless I get my price."

8

MAN BAIT AND WOMAN BAIT

Assuring Sue her snack would be a half,
Longhorn sat down and poured himself a drink
to brighten waiting time but had to laugh
before he gulped. It tickled him to think
of Deuces Wilde and how his wrath would kindle

at learning that the ancient badger swindle
had snatched away from Jones the very chink

which Wilde had lost at faro, not to name
the church collection money. Longhorn's watch
was out four times before the minute came
wherein he judged it time to slink—a blotch
of deeper shadow on a midway brightened
by only lamplit entryways, which heightened
the darkness in between each gilded splotch

of boot-marked dust. Apachelike in craft,
he slipped through these before some fellow's hail
could warn the victim of impending graft;
and, sure but careful still, he did not fail
to check his draw, so there would be no hitches
to rob him of this chance for easy riches.
He passed six tents, then turned to swing his trail

between another tent and that of Sue's.
He took three steps but did not take the next.
An arm choked off the oaths he tried to use,
its fellow cured him then of being vexed;
it rose and fell just once to end the scuffle,
and Longhorn's hair was thick enough to muffle
the sound of his revolver barrel flexed

across his scalp. The gunless gunman sank
in hushed acceptance of a passive part
in life's great drama—heedless while a lank
and aging parson found the harlots' mart
called Trips-around-the-World. He hesitated
but shambled in where Sue and duty waited,
the former with impatience. "Bless your heart!"

she cried. "I thought you'd maybe changed your mind
or figured I ain't good enough to save."
"Not so," he said, "but I am slow to find

my way through darkness." Bibulously grave,
he peered around. "Is this a dance hall, daughter?"
"We do lots worse things that we hadn't oughter
than dancin'," Sue confessed. She broke and gave
herself to tears she covered with her hands;
yet not so thoroughly she could not peek
to note Jones wore the slack-jawed look which brands
the owner as too lost in drink to seek
for ties of reason linking words and action.
She could spin fast, she saw with satisfaction,
and not alarm a fly with eyes so weak

he'd fail to see the web she wrought upon.
"Regret is half salvation," Jones approved.
"The sin you've learned to hate is all but gone,
and so the penalty may be removed.
But just what have you done that's so unlawful
and ill-beseeming?" "It's," she cried, "too awful
to tell of—but come here." His forehead grooved

with puzzled lines, he let her be his guide
past all the canvas cubicles but one;
and there she motioned him to step inside.
"Here's where I lost my soul," she said, "and done
it every night for pay." "But *how?*" he cried.
"This is no time for mysteries; speak frankly.
The name of sin can never smell as rankly
as wrong's accomplishment." "Oh, I have tried

to say it," she informed him, "but I can't!
I'm too ashamed; but I will show you how,
if you won't scold me." "Why, of course, I shan't,"
he told her, belching. "Well, then watch me now";
and Sue undid the fastening of her placket.
"A guy would come and say he'd like to shack it,
so I'd do this." The parson smote his brow,

collapsing on the bunk meanwhile. "And then?"

Sedalia Sue removed her skirt and blouse,
asnicker, thinking of the moment when
the cat would spring to pin the moron mouse;
for Longhorn, with long practice, was a master
at injured-husband roles and showed a vaster
enragement at the dalliance of his spouse

each time he slashed the canvas with his knife
and stormed, his pistol flashing, on the scene
to threaten the philanderer and the wife
whose honor only blood and death could clean;
though in the end he grudgingly would settle
for all the money—paper stuff or metal—
the man could proffer, borrow, beg, or glean

through selling his effects. Sue's shoes were off,
but still her partner did not take his cue;
and so the parson, blinking, watched her doff
her petticoats. "What further did you do,"
he asked her, "that was sinister and shocking
and fateful for your soul?" She shucked a stocking
and next its mate, then paused when she was through

but nothing happened; so she hid a smile.
"Old Charlie wants this sucker dead to rights,"
she told herself. "O.K." So in a while
she'd shed her corset, bustle, slip, and tights
to stand before the parson in a fashion
which hinted that she felt the call of passion.
"The serpent of temptation once more bites,"

the parson groaned and, rising, gave a shove
which stretched her out full length upon the bunk.
"If sin is wrong, yet it's divine to love,
or so the Scriptures teach." "You horrid skunk,
get out of here!" she mimicked scared confusion;
yet still there was no sign of fierce intrusion
on Longhorn's part. The fear that she was sunk

at last bored in, to make her really scared.
She moved to flee, but something fell to thud
upon the bedding. Furiously she glared,
and then her anger fizzled like a dud;
for in the lamplight, round and richly yellow,
there gleamed a coin—followed by its fellow
and then eight more. And as a golden flood

once rendered Danae pliable to Zeus,
so now one did as much for Reverend Jones;
for Sue was prompt to see there was no use
in letting wealth move off to other zones
of lesser worth. And so she fell back, crying,
"They never shot Methuselah for tryin'.
Get on, old horse, and don't break any bones;

but first blow out the light, so I can't see,
and maybe so I'll never know you're there."
So what was done was done nocturnally;
and light began retreating everywhere
as most, in time, resigned themselves to giving
that kickback, sleep, which death demands for living—
stretched out or sprawling, snoring, in a chair.

Though some, their liquor turned philosopher,
sat leaned together, chattering like birds
in all but empty bars; or still astir
in open camps, they hunched in little herds
between the darkness lurking at each shoulder
and fires they crowded as the night grew colder,
to muse aloud on Jones and on the words

he'd handed down. By one such fire of dung,
left by the Spanish cattle, three conversed
beneath the outsize desert stars which swung
slow-motion over looming hills. "At first,"
one fellow said, "I didn't want to listen,
but he made so much sense I wasn't missin'
a word he threw at us before——" "The worst,"

another interrupted, "of the case
is that each one of us so damn well knew
that what he said hit home and found its place
as slickly as a foot goes in a shoe.
I say it's good he got here." "He was needed,"
the third man nodded, "and I hope he's heeded.
It's time that we gave thought to what we do,

and to the consequences, not alone
for our salvation but for what we owe
to future generations here. The tone
of any town is set by those, you know,
who are its leaders. Blast it, we're the founders!
And if *we* act like rotten, heathen bounders
the rest will follow suit." "By God! that's so,"

the first approved. "Well, they can count on me,
them future generations. I'll be straight
from this on out." Responsibility
so weighed on them, they passed the flask. "I'd hate
to have my kids," the second man admitted,
"raised in a burg like this has been, outfitted
with every mantrap on the devil's slate."

"And with no place for God to swing his loop.
You've called the shot; we got to settle down,"
the first averred, "as soon as we can scoop
our fortunes out." "Oh, when the tracks reach town,"
the third said, yawning, "that part will be simple."
"I'll find a blue-eyed church girl with a dimple,"
the second stated. "Aw, not blue eyes—brown,"

the first said. "Man, if I was married now,
I sure would start my family tonight."
"The method would be pleasing, I'll allow,"
the third said, drinking. "That's my last. I'm tight
enough, I hope, to dream that Calabasas
is populous with pure and dimpled lasses."
They slept then as the stars and sky turned white

above themselves and others of their like:
hard as a loaded pistol, aimed and cocked,
ruthless in action as a hungry shrike
but young enough to keep their hearts unlocked
to hopes of tenderness. They went on sleeping
while down on Railroad Street a man was heaping
his plate so high that Ah Chin Honk was shocked.

9

THE SHERIFF FROM GRIZZLY PAW

The Golden Fleece, although it never closed,
was quiet at the hour of ten to six
on Monday morning. Scattered patrons dozed,
but one could not. His eyes like burnt-out wicks,
his mouth a bloodless furrow, Deuces wondered
about his losses: had he really blundered
into the hands of one more skilled to fix

the cards for paying off than he, or had
the parson hit a streak of bonehead luck,
as sometimes chanced? By then he was half mad;
his mind could neither break nor cease to buck
the wall of mystery which hid the answer,
and one-groove thinking gnawed his nerves like cancer.
He jumped as Longhorn staggered up and struck

the faro table, fumbled for a chair,
and then sat down. "I got to have a peg
and got no dough," he said. "Then we're a pair,"
said Deuces. "Jesus! who pulled off your leg
and hit you in the phiz with it?" The query
was not unapt, for chaos had made merry
with Longhorn's face, resembling now a keg

whose load of wine had leaked from seams and dried,

though first it had been rolled around in dirt.
His hair was long but not enough to hide
the welt upon his head, which throbbed and hurt
at every move; though quiet too was painful.
"Cork it!" said Longhorn, trying to look baneful
but mostly looking cross-eyed. To avert

this strain upon his sight he dropped the lids,
seeking again to conjure up the scene
where, ambuscaded, he had hit the skids.
He could recall his ducking in between
the tents; but who had laid for him and strangled
his cry of protest, struck, and left him mangled?
He searched his pockets one more time. "Picked clean,"

he mumbled. When he'd spoken those words, both
retired to private thoughts, the gambler still,
the gunman sometimes muttering an oath
into the hands which propped his face, until
they heard, "Why here's the double-crossin' flivver!"
And Sue sat down. "God rot your lemon liver!
You welched on me." But yet there was no chill

of anger in her eyes or in her voice;
rather she seemed at peace. "Oh, well, I bet
you didn't go and let me down for choice,"
she said, "so what the devil happened, pet?
I couldn't sleep all night, I was so worried;
that's why I left the hay so soon and hurried;
to look for you and——" "Get your whistle wet,"

said Longhorn. "Here's my alibi." He dropped
his hands to show the carnage. "Christ!" she gasped,
"who scrambled you?" He glared at her, then stopped
because it hurt. "I don't know yet," he rasped.
"Shut up and buy us drinks around. I'm stony,
and so is Deuces." Nodding at his crony
stepped up the pain once more. He bent and clasped

his arms around his head. "Well, I ain't flush,"
she warned him. "We sure done a sickly trade
after the parson handed out that mush
about reform. My punks was so afraid
of being damned, I hardly made a dollar;
but I can buy a round or so." "Then holler
and tell the barkeep," Longhorn said; and stayed

head down and motionless until he heard
the glasses rap the table. "One more round,"
he said when they had drunk. And on the word,
Sue bought again and sighed when she had downed
the double shot. "You know," she said, "I needed
them drinks myself. I'm bushed." She spoke unheeded
and once again the silence was profound,

brooding on their part, comfortable on hers,
until a horseman strode into the place,
dusting himself and jingling pinwheel spurs:
a long, loose-jointed fellow with a face
which told of readiness for fun or killing—
two things or one for him. Slim Parr was willing,
and his obligingness took in more space

than Barkis ever dreamed of. He had been
on both sides of the law like jaws of clamps
and held broad views on statutory sin
which served him well. They told it in the camps
that he'd put in for mileage to the county
to chase himself, then pay himself a bounty
for catching up. With two ground-shaking stamps

he now kicked dust, whisked out his money, crooked
his elbow, downed his whiskey with a snap
and wheeled to gaze; then chuckled as he looked.
"I know," he cried, "that Gila monster map,
warpaint or not. You're Longhorn Charlie Durben;
who you been fightin', what'll you have but bourbon,
and are you on the lam now or on tap,

if I need deputies?" He slapped his star.
"Bring us a quart of forty rod!" he roared;
"I'm dry as buffalo chips in hell." "Slim Parr,"
said Longhorn warmly, as the sheriff poured,
"it's good to see you." But he eyed the liquor.
His eyes were clearer now, his movements quicker
as he tossed off the shot. "It's been——Oh, Lord!

When did I see you last?" "Cheyenne, I guess,
after we pulled that job in Black Hawk or,"
said Slim, "in Silver City, maybe." "Yes,
a year before the Lincoln County War
when we was deputies," said Longhorn, sliding
his empty glass across. "And now I'm ridin'
as one of John Law's hands again, unless"

—the sheriff winked—"you know a better pitch."
Longhorn and Deuces kept their faces blank.
"It's quiet here, and no one's getting rich."
Before continuing, the gambler drank.
"Just whose trail did they sic you on, old-timer?"
The sheriff swallowed half his shot for primer
and then he laughed. "Some bird that cracked a bank

in Bozeman, robbed a stage near San Antone,
and shot a man who recognized his horse
at Jackson's Hole. Them facts ain't really known,
though I suspect he done them things, of course."
His hearers shrugged, for he described the masses;
what normal citizen of Calabasas
might not have such a history? Perforce

their thirst sought amity with such a host;
but he was with, and they were not, the law,
and that was that. They closed their ears almost,
as he went on. *"But* up in Grizzly Paw
this fellow set up shop as an assayer
and sold some salted claims to Smith, the mayor,
and that's who put me on him." "I ain't saw

no renegades in these parts," Longhorn said.
The sheriff grinned. "Each time you've stuck your pan
before a glass, that's all. To scoot ahead:
I think I'm just a day behind my man,
because in Tubac folks was kind of bitter
at havin' just found out a counterfeiter
had boiled a brass bed down to suit his plan

of mintin' double eagles cheap. So——" "What!"
Sue lurched from lazy dreaming with a shriek,
unsnapped a little purse and spilled its glut
of coins upon the layout. Ten were sleak
and brightly yellow twenty-dollar pieces,
"In God We Trust" the double-ended thesis
embossed above each lordly eagle's beak.

With trembling hand she picked one up and let
it fall upon the table's polished edge.
It hit as socks do when they're soaking wet,
to make a sound like dry and rattling sedge
instead of bouncing with a gladsome ringing.
"I didn't get a cent!" she shouted, flinging
the rest away. She beat the rounded wedge

between her breasts and let them have the news:
"He worked me over like I was his farm:
I ain't had such a go since Bearcat Clewes
blew into Medicine Bow." She flashed an arm
across the board to jab a shaking finger
at Longhorn, who recoiled as from the stinger
of a scorpion and blinked in the alarm

of one who's in the wrong but not yet sure
just why or how. "He got to travel free,
as if I was a pinhead amateur!"
Sue rose to scream her anguish at him. *"Me!*
A top price whore in Deadwood and Dodge City,
bought like a squaw with buttons—and I'm pretty
sure *you* helped the weasel rig my fee

and got one of your own from him." "From who?"
Longhorn demanded, goggling and aghast.
"The wolverine you sicked on me," cried Sue,
"and claimed was stewed! The thievin' louse who passed
that counterfeit! That son of a bitch, the parson,
who ain't none, any more than I'm Kit Carson!
You got that through your skull, or must I blast?"

10

LONGHORN MAKES A NOOSE

Deuces' and Longhorn's eyes made bitter tryst;
and only then did either one begin
to trust his ears. But suddenly the mist
of puzzlement which both had floundered in
was burnt away by truth so bright and searing
it hurt to face it. Knowledgeably peering
at each in turn, the sheriff wore a thin

and hardened smile. "I see you know my boy.
Where is he now, and what's his local game
outside of passing queer stuff to annoy
the hurdy girls? And what's his local name?
He's money in the bank for me." But shaking
his head, the gambler rose. "You won't be taking
that fellow back alive," he said. A flame

of savage hope now flared in Longhorn's eyes;
recovered from the shock of shame, he stood.
"We'll get a rope and steer him toward them skies
he likes to preach about." "You mean that? Good!"
Sue cried. A little calmed but still not trusting,
she eyed him as she gave her face a dusting
with powder. "Will you cut me in or would

you rather have me tell the whole damned town

what's goin' on?" "Oh, hell, we'll split three ways,"
said Longhorn. "Four," said Deuces with a frown,
in answer to the sheriff's cough and gaze
of cold reproach. "You see, it ain't the money;
it's just that I get feelin' kind of funny
when I let guys be lynched and no one pays

my conscience back," Slim told them. "And I'll pry
his boots from off him, so I can collect
when I get home and tell how him and I
swapped lead until I blew his soul direct
to hell with my last bullet." "Let's get started!"
the gambler barked. No longer heavyhearted,
Sue fell in step till, pausing to reflect,

she asked, "But where's the rope?" "Why, right outside,"
the sheriff said. "I got one on my bronc."
So first he led them with his rider's stride
and then was led past tented honky-tonk
and shop to where the Grand Hotel's wide portal
showed—burning joss to spirits of immortal
ancestral kin—the landlord, Ah Chin Honk,

whose look of reverence vanished when his ribs
were larruped by the rope in Longhorn's hand.
"Show us," said Deuces, "where his pious nibs
the vicar bunks." "The pleacher give command
when he come ins and eat so big this morning
that he want sleeps and I must stops men horning
ins, and if I do, he pay me grand

when he rise ups again." The landlord bowed
but straightened when the sheriff grabbed his hair
and pointed to his star. Ah Chin Honk, cowed,
then shrugged and led the way in dumb despair
to where big canvas curtains, painted brightly,
marked off the bedrooms. Stepping very lightly,
the landlord entered one and whispered, "There."

On tiptoe the avengers one by one
stole in, exchanging nods and woodchuck grins—
bared teeth and rock-hard eyes which gleamed with fun
at thought of teaching Jones indeed that sins
net retribution. So as Longhorn knotted
Jack Ketch's tie to show their sleep-besotted
bamboozler that the world held other gins

than Satan's, they gazed, gloating, where lay stretched
beneath the jumble of a quilt, their man;
no part was showing but the bulges sketched
the figure well enough to show the plan
from foot to head. The sheriff neared the latter
and jerked the cover off—to start a clatter
of crockery on parade. For in the van

there was the pot; the jar stood next in file,
the pitcher next, and last of all the bowl.
This held a note penned in an ornate style,
and while they cursed the writer, frame and soul,
Sue reached within to find what had been written.
"Dear Friends," she read aloud. "When fate has smitten,
to struggle is to earn a harsher dole

of agony. Be wise, forget, forgive;
though I will never pardon my own self
for one sin of omission while I live.
In Tubac two nights since a jovial elf
revealed a secret which he might not throttle
while with a man he honored—or his bottle.
This town will be left high upon the shelf

where railroads are concerned, a few days hence
when line officials—conning the report
of him who lately drank at my expense
(though cards in turn left him too somewhat short)
make known what they will give as *their* decision,
to prove that it was rather blind misprision
which led you here, not sense of any sort,

as I forgot to tell you yestereve.
My bottle crony was the engineer
who's laying out the road. There's no reprieve;
instead of switching southward it will veer
across this pearl of sucker-haunted valleys
and enter Mexico at twin-Nogales.
I grieve I may not offer better cheer

to you who proffered hospitality
to put the Good Samaritan to shame.
There was no thing which you withheld from me,
and so I'm richer far than when I came,
in cash and memories—and better mounted:
I leave the beast I came on to be counted
among the Calab-asses I could name

who fed me and———" What followed was not heard,
for Ah Chin Honk discharged an eldritch wail
like to the crying of a great sea bird
and bolted from the spot to spread the tale.
So pidgin English launched the tragic story
of broken local hopes of urban glory
and, sadder yet, of Jones and how leg bail

had served to cancel out a monstrous bill
for meals to make an emperor stretch his belt.
The tale, progressing, then grew wilder still,
to end by showing that Ah Chin Honk felt
the sheriff-hunted, lynch-evading preacher
was no mere con man but a darker creature,
a demon lurking in a human pelt.

But while the tortured landlord aired his grief,
the four he'd left behind, though also wracked
by savage anguish, did not seek relief
in vain laments. "My bronc's been too long backed;
I'll need a fresh one," Slim said. Longhorn nodded.
"I've got to get a rod," he snapped, and wadded
the man-stretch rope till it was deftly packed

in coils to loop below the saddle horn.
"I'm heeled," the gambler growled. Sue drew the gun
her flaring skirt concealed from view when worn.
"I'd trail a saint to hell for what he done,
to watch him when the rope chokes off his hollers
and he starts dancin', rattlin' them brass dollars."
"Well, keep up if you can," said Slim, and spun

to glare at her, "but see here, you don't get
to join no posse I'm the sheriff of."
"Oh, she'll get tired," said Longhorn, "don't you fret,
when she gets slappin' leather hard." "Let's shove,
before the breeze," said Deuces, "blows up stronger;
for if we let it dust his tracks much longer
he'll leave a trail like a Sonora dove."

11

THE SLAYING OF THE PARSON

Out of the valley where the Santa Cruz
hitched aridly along the parson went,
leaving the city where his name was news
for parts which neither knew him nor his bent.
He left as he had come there, solitary
and taking nothing difficult to carry
except a swift, black horse, now somewhat spent;

for, wild when mounted, it had lost its taste
for sprinting on the long slope to the ridge
to westward of the river. There it faced
once more the town, now tiny, and each midge
of mankind kicking dust around the city.
The watching rider's lips were also gritty,
and so he spat before he burned the bridge

which linked them to these folk—a big cigar,

one Longhorn Charlie Durben's parting gift.
Detached as though considering a star,
he eyed the town. Betimes he'd be adrift
with no bell buoy of the past to guide him,
but now, while curiosity still tied him,
he slowly smoked and watched smoke also drift

above the camps where men prepared to eat
before surrendering to the suction force
which soon would draw them all to Railroad Street.
But four then took a strongly different course
and left the street of manifold attractions
to ride and stop and show by other actions
they sought the trail of either man or horse.

The lounging parson blew a ring of smoke
and nodded but he did not move as yet.
"The dreamer waxes bitter, once awoke,"
he quoted. "Granted company, I'd bet
I know the names of three but not the other—
who seeks me as I never sought a brother—
unless it's he to whom I stand in debt

for mount and saddle. There! They've cut my trail."
And as he spoke, the distant riders bunched,
then started toward him, carrying the mail.
Not finished smoking yet, the parson munched
the frayed wet end and waited for their nearing
to give them shape and color. Grimly peering,
he saw a tall man leading, riding hunched

to keep his eyes on sign, while just behind
Longhorn and Deuces rode. Behind this pair
in turn came Sue, though mostly riding blind;
she'd shaken loose the pins that held her hair,
which swirled around her face, now seen, now hidden.
"She does not ride so well as she was ridden,"
the parson said. "She's losing ground. Ah, there;

she's turning back, perhaps to make my shroud."
And as he spoke, the ashen skeleton
of his cigar stub fell. His voice endowed
with crispness, he remarked, "That top's been spun";
and threw the butt away, as he was throwing
all thought for any act except his going.
He wheeled his rested horse to flee the sun,

still low above the valley where were pitched
the tents where dreams and viciousness had bloomed
and both alike had sent him off enriched—
and both alike were stricken as there loomed
the shadow of new knowledge. Up it towered
until the boldest read the truth and cowered,
as Ah Chin Honk, twice wretched, moved and gloomed.

His stories spread like ragweed, and which burned
their hearts more cruelly they did not know;
for though their backs were broken when they learned
their railroad was now lost to them, and so
their chance for easy money had been buried
in hope's boot hill—its murdered spirit ferried
trans-Styx to ghost town's limbo—yet the blow

to pride was deep and festering. To think
that they, the tough, the worldly-wise, the fly,
had all been sold down river by a gink
who dealt in gold bricks; yes, and made them buy!
Rubes for a con man! Marks for a thimblerigger!
A flock of pigeons, brainless as a chigger,
who'd let themselves be plucked, then let the guy

who'd trimmed them live to laugh! All good had left
the town where such a thing could come about;
the place was jinxed past salvaging, bereft
of any chance for better luck to sprout.
Prosperity could never round the corner
where Jones' memory, like a hired mourner,
stood by to tell them what they had paid out

to shamming piety. It was too much
for sober men to bear with fortitude,
so all worked in a body for the touch
of Lethe that is found in getting stewed,
before they started pulling stakes or loading
their wagons, mules, and horses, in foreboding
of Calabasas left and not reviewed

in pristine grandeur ever—vanished, lost
with Tara, Ur, Mycenae, Camelot, Tyre,
and Gila City; Calabasas tossed
back to the dusty end of all desire
and crossed by tracks of drowsy lizards only,
never to know the stirring, deep, and lonely
hallooing from those other tracks afire

with snorting engines, clanging with the vim
they used to drag the world down Railroad Street.
The town was ended, then. But what of him—
the one who'd wrought this Ilium's defeat
and forced its folk, Aeneaslike, to travel;
proud loafers now reduced to scratching gravel
or punching cows and hearing woollies bleat

in mines or ranges where they sought a berth
to make a stake and lick their raw wounds clean
in near or far-flung corners of their earth,
stretched east from Angel's Camp to Abilene
and from Canuck to southern border passes—
what of this nemesis of Calabasas?
Nogales, not far distant, was a mean

and not too hopeful boundary-straddling town;
but still it sat athwart the finest road—
a rugged relic of the Spanish crown—
which entered Mexico. The parson slowed
some rods before he reached this point of entry,
then walked his horse to meet the barefoot sentry.
The latter called an officer, who strode

to block the passageway from Gringoland.
"This Mexico," he said. "What do you here?"
In answer to the truculent demand
Jones glanced behind and, seeing no one near,
he raised a hand as though in benediction;
then shook his head, to show a lost conviction,
before he dropped his arm and spoke in sheer,

raw desperation. "Are you loyal, friend,
to old Sonora and the governor
at Hermosillo? Can we both depend
upon your secrecy?" His keen eyes bore
into the startled soldier's, who stood blinking
and gaping back as Jones stared on, unwinking,
before he whispered: "I need say no more;

I see you are a man whom we can trust.
I have a message for His Excellency
and him alone, and if I live, I must
deliver it—though I am trailed by three
who must not pass the border now. Devotion
to duty here will win you a promotion,
if we succeed. Here, drink to Liberty!"

He flipped a yellow coin toward the man,
who caught it on the upswing of salute,
and then sped onward, with no other plan
than finding sanctuary to recruit
his shattered forces, now without a focus.
For by his latest act of hocus-pocus
he'd slain the parson, when he'd found him mute,

his piety unequal to the task
of squeezing past the border. Forced by need,
he'd sketched and donned a flimsy form and mask
to meet the moment's wants but had been freed
at once of their demands and of their guiding.
An empty vessel seeking new providing,
his energies withdrawn into the seed,

his name now Nemo—played completely out—
he blindly moved toward something to attack,
assured of but one fact unpocked with doubt:
there was no point to which he might go back
or wanted to. Then he was overtaken
by sleep at last and, slumping, did not waken—
so fiercely did his body claim its lack—

for miles along the empty road, south bound.
The horse, now pacing slowly, did not jog
the rider from his rest; he rolled around
but held his saddle like a sleeping frog
upon a pad that's teetered by an eddy.
Some miracle of balance held him steady
until he should emerge from slumber's fog,

prepared to build anew with circumstance.
He was not, then; but in this middle while
did he recall the last bequest of chance,
that stricken victim of his force and guile?
It seemed he did so, for a shark-tooth gleaming
flashed to the surface of some depths of dreaming,
as now and then his face cracked with a smile.

Traitor Town

Les Savage, Jr.

UNCLE HONDO found Tony Ferrar playing solitaire at one of the short card tables in the rear of La Fonda. The old man came across the crowded barroom at a hobbling walk, apprehension deepening the furry seams of his face.

"George Manatte is in Number five, asking for you," he told Ferrar. "Don't go in, Tony. Cimarron Garrett is with him."

Ferrar grinned, getting up. "Would you have me hide from that blowhard?"

The old man shook his white head. "Short men and fools, they are recognized from afar."

Chuckling, Ferrar moved through the crowd of peons and trappers that filled the inn this summer evening of 1846. He was a tall man, with curly black hair and startling blue eyes that came from the Irish trapper who had fathered him, and a darkness to his long face, a sharp height to his cheekbones that were the heritage of his Mexican mother.

Les Savage, who died suddenly and tragically while this book was being made, absorbed fiction-writing savvy in the late Stanley Vestal's famous course at the University of Oklahoma. Well-grounded in the now all-but-vanished pulps, Les's stories had a distinctive action-plus-color quality that always fascinated. Later he turned to the wide-canvas historical with good results—witness *Silver Street Woman* and *Royal City*.

The exotic mixture seemed to extend to his whole personality. While his solid-muscled upper body was clothed in padded waistcoat and tailored fustian, he wore elkhide leggings that were black and greasy from years on the trail.

Reaching the door of Number five, he knocked, and was told to enter. George Manatte and his daughter Julia sat at the small deal table, while Cimarron Garrett stood against the wall, arms folded across his massive chest. Ferrar took a chair, tilted it back against the wall, and relaxed immediately into his indolent sprawl. He smiled at Julia, but she did not answer it. Her wide blue eyes were solemn as a child's in her softly rounded face, gazing at him with disturbing fixity. Her cloak was pushed back, revealing deep breasts swelling at a prim calico dress, and her hair spilled like a cascade of honey onto her shoulders.

"You take your daughter into strange places, George," Ferrar said.

"I want her to know what's going on," Manatte said. He put his elbows on the table—a tall man, well in his fifties, with a face scored by the weather and eyes faded by the sun. One of the biggest fur traders in this town of Santa Fe, he still wore a simple broadcloth suit and beaver hat.

"As you probably know, Ferrar, the War with Mexico is going against the Mexicans," he said. "General Kearny has taken Las Vegas. He's going to march on this town in a couple of days. We have one chance to stop the bloodshed, to convince Governor Armijo how useless it is to stand against the American army."

Ferrar's heavy brows raised. "Captain Cordenza is coming from Chihuahua with four companies of cavalry. Add that to Governor Armijo's dragoons and they can cut Kearny to pieces in Apache Canyon."

Manatte shook his head. "Captain Cordenza and his four Chihuahua companies were captured by an American force last week."

Ferrar came forward, chair legs slapping the floor. "How do you know?"

"Cordenza accepted the surrender terms by note. Kearny now has the note. I heard that from my last contact with him. But no more of my men can get through. Governor Armijo was close to Cordenza, he'll know Cordenza's signature and handwriting. Armijo won't be able to stand against Kearny without Cordenza's cavalry. If Armijo knew Cordenza had been captured, he'd capitulate immediately. General Kearny could walk into Santa Fe without a shot. We want you to go to

Las Vegas, Tony, get Cordenza's note of surrender from Kearny, and bring it to Armijo."

Ferrar settled back, frowning deeply. Cimarron Garrett stirred against the wall, speaking disgustedly.

"I told you Ferrar was more greaser than Yankee, George. He wanted Cordenza to get through and help Armijo."

Ferrar's eyes flashed with anger, swinging up to Cimarron. The man was one of Manatte's mule skinners, six feet tall and almost as wide, with a mane of yellow hair and a yellow beard that curled against his keg-chest like foamy hoar frost. His greasy rawhide jacket was fringed with the black hair of a dozen Indian scalps, and his leggin's were held up by a belt of gold pesos.

Manatte leaned farther toward Ferrar. "You know how the Americans in this town have been clamped down on. Any white man who tried to leave town would be shot. Even if he did get out, he'd never make it through that strip between here and Las Vegas. Only a Mexican could get through, but we don't know any Mexicans we can trust. You're the only one, Tony. The Mexicans trust you. You could get through."

Ferrar shook his head. "I'd betray every friend I have if I helped Kearny take this town."

"You don't number the Americans among your friends, then," Manatte said thinly.

"That proves he's a greaser," Cimarron said.

Ferrar stood up, nostrils pinched with anger. "Don't use that word again, Cimarron."

The man grinned evilly. "Why not? Any grea——"

"Never mind, Cimarron." Manatte got up angrily, almost upsetting his chair. "I can see there's no use talking any more. But you've made an unwise choice, Ferrar. It will be hard for those who fought Kearny, when he takes the town."

He turned and stamped to the outer door, swinging it open and stepping out into the alley. With an enigmatic grin, Cimarron followed him. It left only Julia in the room. She had risen and she came slowly around the table to face Ferrar.

"Why did you refuse, Tony? You're more Yankee than Mexican. You've got to help your own people."

He waved his hand toward the noise of the main room. "These are my people as much as the Yankees. I was born here. My life is here. I speak Spanish as easily as English."

"But you'd *help* them by bringing Kearny in! You know what the government has been here."

He shook his dark head. "I admit there's a lot of graft under Armijo's rule——"

"Not Armijo's rule," Julia said. "He's nothing more than a figurehead. Morina Garcia is the power behind the throne, and you know it. She doesn't represent Mexican rule any more than a cat represents a dog. Graft is the smallest part of it, Tony. The kind of life you've led has blinded you to it. Drinking, gambling, living high, off on your trap lines half the time, you have no real picture of what's going on. The people are suffering under that woman's domination. She's gotten Armijo to bleed them dry——"

"Stop it!"

He checked himself, surprised that it had come out so hotly. They stood there, staring at each other a moment, white-faced. Then Julia took a deep breath.

"I've thought for a long time that Morina Garcia had come between us, Tony. Now I know it's true."

He tried to catch her arm, protesting. "Julia——"

She stepped back, her voice shaking a little. "Never mind, Tony. If it's over, it's over. You can't force something like that."

She looked at him for a last instant, with an intense hurt shadowing her eyes, then turned and went out. He stared after her with a sense of deep loss. Then, shaking his head helplessly, he turned back into the outer room.

The bar was filling with *peons* and Taos Indians and young *vaqueros*. Tomas was throwing three-card monte for Uncle Hondo, and Ferrar made his way through the crowd toward their table.

"What did they want, Antonito?" the old man asked.

"Just some fur deal," Ferrar said.

Tomas went on shuffling the cards. He was Morina Garcia's Navajo servant, an enigmatic statue of a man with a face that might have been carved from some dark wood, so little did it change expression. A bright red band held his long black hair, and his pants and shirt were of doeskin, white as milk and always immaculately clean.

Ferrar poured himself some *pulque,* trying to relax, trying to take the pleasure he should in being here with his friends. Life should be like the taste of good wine in the mouth. He should savor the reek of the place as he always had—the piquant scent of chile peppers drying out front and the stable stench drifting in from the rear and the smell of grape wine and rotgut whiskey and sweat and leather and sawdust. He should drink in the soft sound of Spanish and the slap of cards. It was the life he loved.

But somehow he was disturbed. "Uncle Hondo," he said. "You are a *peon*. Are your people happy?"

"They sing all day, they drink all night. I would live no place else in the world."

"How about Armijo?"

The old man looked around him. "Is that wise?"

"You are among friends."

Uncle Hondo leaned forward, wagging his shaggy head from side to side. "The governor he is at times hard. But we are certainly better off than we were under Spanish rule."

"And you don't want the Americans?"

"If the *gringo* is all like that Cimarron Garrett, I would do to them that." Uncle Hondo spat on the floor. Then he turned his wise old eyes up to Ferrar, the wind-wrinkles deepening at their corners. "Something she is troubling you, Antonito. I have been your man since a baby you were and I know that look."

Ferrar shook his head. "Nothing."

Uncle Hondo put a gnarled hand on his arm. "It is sometimes hard to be a child of two races."

Ferrar glanced sharply at him, surprised at his insight, then chuckled softly. "I can't hide anything from you, old one."

Uncle Hondo grinned at him, then glanced over his head, the expression changing in his face. Ferrar turned to see Captain Seguro Ugardes coming through the door. He pushed through the knots of *peons* and *vaqueros,* answering their greetings with a jaunty grin. He made an elegant figure in the round blue jacket of the Mexican dragoons, with its red cuffs and collar. His blue velvet breeches were unbuttoned at the knees to show white stockings above the deerskin boots, and the Golden Cross of Honor glittered brazenly over his heart. He came clear to Ferrar's table, clapping him on the shoulder.

"It is good to see someone who can relax, *amigo*. I have had a trying day."

"Governor Armijo been keeping you busy?" Ferrar asked.

Captain Ugardes took a chair and dropped wearily into it. "The palace is in an uproar. All kinds of rumors. Some say Kearny has ten thousand men. Some say only a handful. Armijo is in one of his rages. Nothing is right. I wish Cordenza and those four Chihuahua companies would get here. It would make us all feel safer."

"Cordenza's coming, then?"

"*Pues,* of course———" Ugardes broke off, studying Ferrar. "You make a point of that. Do you have any information?"

Ferrar frowned, realizing for the first time what a position Manatte had put him in. Ugardes's reaction convinced him that Governor Armijo did not yet know Cordenza had been captured. Thus, Manatte had put Ferrar under an obligation of secrecy by telling him the news. But why had Manatte been so sure he would keep their secret? Captain Ugardes was Ferrar's oldest friend in Santa Fe, they had grown up together. Didn't his loyalty to that kind of friend place a deeper obligation upon him than the mere fact his father was white? Wouldn't Manatte know that?

He looked up, on the point of telling Ugardes. Yet something checked him. Perhaps Ugardes saw the struggle going on within him. He leaned forward and put a hand on Ferrar's arm.

"I have always known it would be hard for you, if something like this ever came up, Antonito. I will not press you. Just remember this. No matter what happens, no matter which side you choose, we will always be *compadres.*"

They stared into each other's eyes a moment. Then the embarrassment of a man who has touched deep emotion flushed Ugardes's face, and he leaned back with a laugh.

"Enough of this. I came here to forget the war. Like the old days, no? Wine and monte and maybe a pretty *doncellita* to amuse us."

They had their drink and wandered to the monte table, and for a short while the laughter and pleasure which only this country could afford filled the two men. Then Ferrar noticed a change in the sound about him. First it was the rough laughter dying out. Then the clink of glasses seemed to diminish.

Ferrar turned to see Cimarron Garrett shouldering his way through the knots of men. With him was Pitch, his swamper. The man was shorter than Garrett but just as broad. The muscles of his chest and shoulders bulged like sides of beef beneath a hickory jacket. A barrel of hot pitch had been dumped over his face while he was doping a hotbox on the trail, many years before. It had burned most of his hair off and left one eye blinded, and the left side of his face was badly scarred.

Behind Garrett and Pitch were three of the buckskinned trappers who worked for Manatte. They were tall, rawboned men from Tennessee and Kentucky, their elkhides black with bear grease and stinking of beaver medicine.

"That fool," Ugardes said under his breath. "Doesn't he know better than to come in here? With the feeling against the Yankees he's liable to be torn apart."

"He's drunk," Ferrar said.

Garrett pushed his way heedlessly through the crowd, ignoring the curses and hateful looks that followed him. He halted before Ferrar's table, hooking thumbs in his waistband and swaggering drunkenly.

"I thought I'd better check on you. Manatte was a fool to trust you. Ran right to your greaser friends with the news."

Ferrar felt his fingers close around the edge of the table. "I haven't said anything you wouldn't, Garrett, and you'd better not stay in here. You're taking too big a chance."

"But you aren't, are you?" Garrett asked, swaying toward Ferrar. "Put you in a bunch of *chilis* and nobody could tell the difference."

Ugardes's voice was a drawn blade. "*Señores,* you are insulting my friend."

"I expect," Garrett said. "Too yellow to dodge for himself. Has to hide behind the Mexican Army."

"Are you blind, as well as a pig?" snapped Ugardes. His face was dead white. "If Ferrar hit you and a fight started in here, you'd be torn to pieces. The feeling is so bad against you the slightest thing will set it off. Ferrar is giving you this chance. Take it and get out."

"Git out, hell," Garrett said. He grabbed Ferrar's shoulder, twisting him around in his chair. "Did you think I wouldn't follow you in here just because this place was filled with Mexicans?"

Ferrar was trembling, unable to contain himself much longer. "I notice you didn't come while you were alone," he said thinly.

Already there was an ominous muttering from the crowd, and Ugardes grabbed Garrett's arm. "They'll kill you if anything starts, *señor.* Will you get out?"

Garrett jerked his arm free. "There ain't enough greasers in all Santa Fe to cause us trouble. You're the one who'd better get out, Ugardes. In a couple of days there won't be any *chili* army left."

"You make a bad mistake," said Ugardes in a voice so low it was barely audible. "I am not so noble as Ferrar. Do not insult my service."

"Service?" snorted Garrett. "A bunch of donkeys in rags with a sheepherder for a general——"

"*Pordiosero*——"

It escaped Ugardes in a hissing curse, as he slapped Garrett across the face. For one instant, the immense mule skinner stared at Ugardes, disbelief in his gaping mouth. Then he made a snarling sound and lunged for the captain. Savage vindication in his face, Ugardes jumped backward, unsheathing his saber. But it caught on the underside of the table, and Garrett reached him before he could bring it into play. Garrett's blow made a sharp, meaty crack in the room. It bent Ugardes back across the *chusa* table like a bow.

Ferrar lunged up out of his chair at Garrett, but Pitch caught his arm, spinning him halfway around. Ferrar saw Garrett snatch the saber from Ugardes's limp hand and swing it high. With only that moment left, Ferrar sank his fist into Pitch's belly with all his weight behind it. Pitch doubled over with a gasp. Ferrar tore free and threw himself bodily at Garrett as the saber swung down.

He smashed heavily into the man, knocking him aside. The sword bit into the edge of the *chusa* table an inch from Ugardes's hip. Ferrar carried Garrett on down the table, and the man had to let go of the saber to catch hold of the edge and stop himself.

Before Ferrar could recover, he felt the man's arm snake around his neck. The great bicep bulged. There was the pop of tendons, a shooting pain in Ferrar's head. Holding Ferrar in the crook of his elbow, Garrett brought his other fist into Ferrar's belly.

The wind left Ferrar in a gasp. He hung there in a moment of limp helplessness, sensing the shift of Garrett's weight as the man brought that fist back for another blow. With the last of his will, Ferrar doubled up and jackknifed a knee to block the fist.

He heard Garrett grunt in pain as his fist cracked against Ferrar's knee. That arm around Ferrar's neck tightened spasmodically. The congestion in Ferrar's head was so great now he thought it would burst. Sound and sense spun. He felt Garrett shifting for another blow.

With a gasp, Ferrar brought his right arm around behind Garrett, into the kidneys. Garrett's grunt was full of pain. Ferrar hit him there again, a vicious hooking blow. This time he felt it slack Garrett's death lock on his head. He tore free. Garrett tried to follow up and grapple again, but Ferrar hit him in the belly. It stopped the giant for a moment, pain twisting his face.

Ferrar knew he would be finished if Garrett could get in close and grapple again. As the big man recovered and took a step toward Ferrar, arms outthrust, Ferrar weaved off to one side, brushing aside the right arm, smashing at his belly again. Garrett grunted sickly and doubled forward. It left his face exposed. Ferrar put all his weight behind the blow. Garrett's head jerked up and his whole body spun. The table caught him waist-high and bent him over. It left the back of his neck open. Ferrar made a hammer of his fist and hit the man there.

Garrett stiffened, then went limp, rolling off the table and onto the floor. Ferrar caught at the table to keep from going down, surprised at how drained he was. Garrett lay unmoving at his feet. The room was filled with wild shouting and cursing, the sound of cracking furniture, and vicious blows.

Ferrar turned to see the *chusa* dealer and the bartender struggling with Pitch against the bar. Ugardes was on his knees astraddle one of the trappers on the floor, slamming his head into the hard adobe.

The other two trappers were struggling in the midst of half a dozen Mexicans, and more *peons* were streaming in the door, drawn by the fight. The bartender broke a bottle over Pitch's head, and the man went to his knees. Ferrar staggered over to Ugardes, pawing at him.

"Stop it, Seguro, we've got to get them out of here before a mob gathers, get off him——"

Ugardes spun over onto one knee, eyes blank with rage. Then his eyes cleared, and he saw who it was. Shaking his head, he got to his feet. His black hair was torn from its queue and hanging down over his eyes.

"Get that one out," he shouted to the bartender. "Get him out before he's killed."

The *chusa* dealer and the barman got the stunned Pitch between them and half dragged him to the rear door. The trapper on the floor rolled over with a groan. The other two broke and ran suddenly before the growing crowd jamming in the front door. Ferrar staggered back to Garrett, rolling him beneath the *chusa* table and standing in front of him.

"That way," he shouted, pointed toward the rear door. The first wave of *peons* streamed past him after the trappers, and there was a momentary break. He caught Garrett by the collar and dragged him over to one of the side doors, rolling him into a small room. There was an outer door here leading onto a back alley. Garrett was coming around as Ferrar dumped him against a wall.

"You'd better get out fast," Ferrar told him. "If they catch you, they'll cut you to pieces."

Garrett got to his feet, sagging heavily against the wall. His eyes were bloodshot and vindictive.

"This isn't the end, Ferrar," he said thickly. "You'd better not stay in this town when Kearny comes."

Ferrar slammed the door on him and went back into the bar. More *peons* were coming in from the front now and milling around Ugardes, who stood at the bar with a big drink. He hailed Ferrar with a grin.

"Are they all safe?" Ferrar asked in a low voice.

"A bunch of *vaqueros* are still chasing the trappers," Ugardes laughed. "But those mountain men have long legs. What a fight, Antonito! We haven't had so much fun since the bull got loose in the palace. I owe you a drink. Garrett would have cut me in two with that sword." He poured Ferrar a drink and then jumped up onto the bar with his own, raising the glass high.

"A toast, *compadres,* a toast to Antonito, the *gringo*-killer. He saved my life. He defended the honor of Santa Fe. Truly he is a *hidalgo* and one of us."

A knot of the men who knew Ferrar gathered around, slapping him on the back and making obscene jokes at the expense of the *gringos.* Their hands were calloused, and the reek of them was strong, and it was the kind of a thing that struck deep at the roots of a man. Ferrar took a drink, smiling around at their sweating, grinning faces. It was as if the old life had returned, with all the strange tensions and conflicts swept away.

CHAPTER TWO

Primitive

San Francisco Street was full of black shadows and thick silences when Ferrar and Ugardes and Uncle Hondo left La Fonda near midnight. They crossed the plaza with a hot little wind rustling tawny dust against them, passed the deserted market place, lonely and ghostly now in the moonlight. Ahead of them lay the Palace of the Governors, the center of Mexican rule for all New Mexico. It was a long building of adobe, with towers at either end. The arcade running the length of its front was supported by a row of peeled *puntales*.

"What do you keep looking around for?" Ferrar asked Uncle Hondo.

"Is somebody following us?" muttered the old Mexican.

"You are an old *burro*," chuckled Captain Ugardes.

"Even a hair casts a shadow," moaned Uncle Hondo. "We had better be careful going home, Antonito. That Cimarron Garrett does not give up so soon——"

He broke off with a sharp intake of breath as a figure suddenly stepped from the black shadows beneath the palace arcade. Ferrar wheeled sharply. But he saw that it was Tomas. His immaculately white doeskins turned him to a pale wraith in the darkness. He stopped before them, staring with enigmatic eyes at Ferrar.

"Señorita Garcia," he murmured.

Ugardes looked with envy at Ferrar. "She wishes to see you, Ferrar. I wish I were so honored."

Ferrar grinned, gripping his hand. "See you tomorrow, Seguro. Uncle Hondo, it'll be safe for you to go home. It isn't you Garrett wants."

Ferrar left them before the Palace and followed the Navajo down past Burro Alley, where a single burro still stood, loaded down with faggots, his master rolled up in a blanket against the wall, fast asleep. The massive oak door of Morina Garcia's gambling *sala* was half a block beyond the alley. It opened into a hall which led to the large gambling rooms at the rear. Ferrar could hear the click of the roulette wheels and the metallic voices of *chusa* dealers. Before reaching the gambling rooms, however, Tomas turned through a door halfway down the hall that opened into the woman's private chambers.

Morina Garcia's parlor was probably the most sumptuous room in Santa Fe. The floor was of red Spanish tile. A polychrome frieze ran around the wall. Hangings of velvet and silk draped corners of pierglass mirrors that reflected the pendants of the cut-glass chandelier in a hundred glittering shards. Diagonally across one corner was a Turkish divan upholstered in jade silk. Upon this sat Morina Garcia.

Light from the candles in their silver sconces caught up a soft blueblack glow in her hair. Bare shoulders gleamed like alabaster against the contrast of a taffeta dress red as blood. A single cabochon emerald rode the deep upper swell of her breast.

Until this woman had come to Santa Fe two years before, Ferrar had thought Julia Manatte was the woman he wanted, had been on the point of asking her to marry him. Then Morina Garcia had come north from Mexico City, filling the whole province with the legends of her fabulous rise from a ragged *peon* to one of the most famous gamblers of the period.

Within a few short days after the establishment of her gambling salon in Santa Fe, every man in town was vying for her affections. A general had fought a duel with a judge and had got but a rose from her hair for his trouble. Captain Ugardes had sworn he would die for her, and all she asked of him was an introduction to Tony Ferrar.

"Antonito."

Just the single, husky word from her. But it sent an excitement through him he had never felt with Julia. Her magnetism seemed to permeate the room.

"*Chica,*" he murmured.

Her eyes became veiled. "You are the only man in Santa Fe who has the right to use that name. Perhaps I should take away the privilege. You have not been to see me for so long."

"Business," he said.

"Like smuggling your furs into the hills pelt by pelt so you can make up a fur train that will run through Armijo's blockade to St. Louis?" she asked.

His eyes widened in surprise. "Do you know everything in this town?"

"Everything." Her ripe lips spread in an indulgent smile, and she rose from the divan. "If I help you get those furs through, will you help me in something?"

He could not help chuckling. "It's a long time since we made a deal."

"Your greatest threat is Armijo's fur patrol, no?"

"If they catch me, I don't have enough men to fight them."

She moved toward him, voice growing husky. "What route were you planning to take?"

"Glorieta Pass, Apache Canyon."

"Don't do it. That is where the patrol will be tonight."

He caught her by the arms, and the satiny feel of them went through him like fire. *"Chica,* you're wonderful. What do you want from St. Louis?"

"Not from St. Louis," she said, looking down at her fine strong hands. "I have helped you, Antonito; now you will help me. Have you heard of the Cordenza note?"

The humor left him in a rush, his hands slid off her arms. Face tight with wariness, he played it close to the vest.

"No. What is it?"

"As you know, Captain Cordenza was bringing four companies of cavalry from Chihuahua to help Governor Armijo here. The Americans now claim Cordenza has been captured and they have his note of surrender as proof. But it is not his note. It is a forgery."

"How can you be sure?"

"My agents inform me that Cordenza was not captured. He is but a day's march from Santa Fe. Have I ever been mistaken before, Antonito?"

"If anybody has the truth, you have."

"I am glad you have so much faith in me," she said. "Governor Armijo is not so easy to convince. You know him under pressure. He is ready to run at the drop of a pin. If that forged note reaches him, he will be convinced Cordenza is captured. He will think he can't stand against Kearny with the dragoons he has here. We are afraid he will capitulate and give Santa Fe to the Americans."

"I thought Armijo knew Cordenza's handwriting."

"The Americans must have taken that into consideration," she said. "Maybe they actually got some of Cordenza's handwriting and copied it. I don't know the details of their plot. All I know is it will lose the war for us if the note reaches Armijo. All the talking we can do in the world won't convince him once he gets it into his head that Cordenza has been captured." She looked up. "I know Manatte sent word to Kearny that he was trying to get you to take the note through to Armijo for them."

"Your spies have been working overtime," he said wryly.

Her chin lifted. "I also know that you refused Manatte. I am proud of you, Antonito. Now you will get the note for us. We will see that it does not fall into Armijo's hands."

Ferrar moved restlessly to a heavily shuttered window. "There must be somebody else who could do as much."

"Nobody!" She rose with a sensuous hiss of taffeta across a full hip.

"You are the one Kearny is expecting. He will not trust another without proper credentials from Manatte, which we can't get. You can't ride the surface any longer, Antonito. It's fine to gamble and drink and sing and be everybody's friend in normal times. But there's a war going on. You are on one side or the other. Think of your people."

"My people?"

She came toward him. "You are more Mexican than Yankee. Perhaps your father was Yankee, but it is where you live, who are your friends that counts. Men like Uncle Hondo and Ugardes would die for you. Will you let them down now? If Kearny takes over we will be nothing but dogs in the dust. You know the Yankee attitude toward us. Greasers——" Her lips writhed on the word. "You know what will happen the minute Santa Fe is in American hands."

He frowned with the picture of Cimarron Garrett before him. Somehow it symbolized what had been brought to his attention so often these last years, the contempt so many Americans seemed to hold for the Mexicans here. And yet something else was trying to resolve itself in his mind.

"It's funny," he said. "I was given the same kind of talk earlier this evening. Only the Mexican rule was represented as despotic then."

"Despotic?" She laughed softly. "Your mother must have told you what went on under the Spanish regime here, before the Mexicans revolted. Haven't we advanced a thousand years from that? You've been listening to the wrong people, Antonito. You know where your heart is. Say you'll do it. Say you'll start tonight and meet me at the old Pecos pueblo tomorrow night after dark, with that note."

He shook his head, realizing how right both Morina and Manatte had been. He had ridden the surface too long. And now, when he wanted to look beneath and see the hidden issues at stake, he couldn't. His indecision must have shown in his face. The woman came closer. Her voice dropped to a husky whisper.

"If you will not do it for your people, Antonito, will you do it for me?"

He felt the blood thickening in his throat. "You, *Chica?*"

"You told me once you'd do anything for me."

"But this——"

"Yes—this."

The kiss started as something rich and ripe; suddenly it was savage. Her lips flared beneath his, the curves of her body flattened to him, he was swept by the passion of it. Finally she pulled her head back, staring heavy-lidded into his eyes.

"If you start tonight, you can reach Kearny at Las Vegas by dawn."

He shook his head, trying to pull away. "I don't know. I can't think with you this close."

"Do you have to think?"

"Yes."

She tried to kiss him again. He pulled free. The pupils of her eyes distended.

"*Tu barrachon,*" she hissed. "I was right. You are nothing but a drunken fool meant to spend his nights in some cantina, swilling and gambling. *Chica!* You shall never use that name again. How could I have ever thought you worthy of my confidence?"

All the primitive, savage force of the Indian blood darkened her face and blazed in her eyes. He could not help the sardonic smile that crossed his face.

"You should have done this in the first place," he said. "I always thought you much more fascinating in your barbaric state."

"*Bribón!*" she panted.

With a husky curse, she wheeled for a tankard of brandy which sat on one of the marquetry tables. He had already reached the door and swung it open by the time she wheeled and threw the tankard. The silver pitcher made a clanging crash against the door as he pulled it shut behind him.

CHAPTER THREE

The Toll of the Bell

Tony's father had been an Irish trapper for Hudson's Bay who had drifted down to Taos and Santa Fe in the early part of the century, establishing a fur business there. Prospering, he had married the daughter of one of the most aristocratic houses in the province. With her had come the dower of a sprawling hacienda on the hills overlooking Santa Fe. The walls were adobe, thick and high, built in the days when Indian attacks necessitated that the home be a fortress. On the death of his parents, Tony had taken over the fur business, using much of the house on the hill as a storage place for the pelts his trappers brought in every spring.

He knocked three times on the immense door of the *zaguan,* and it was opened for him by Uncle Hondo. He rode through this wagon entrance into the patio.

"Troops have been up in the hills half a dozen times today, watching the house," Uncle Hondo said. "They know you make a run for it soon now, Antonito?"

"Do you think they suspect anything?"

"No. The last load of pelts went out in a *carretta,* covered by a load of onions. We unloaded it at the old woodcutter's house. If troops were watching, they will think we were merely giving him his winter's supply of onions, as we always do."

Ferrar nodded in satisfaction. They had been sneaking furs out like that for days now, under loads of vegetables, beneath the cover of faggots on a woodcutter's burro, even under the skirts and *tilmas* of laborers and peasants whose comings and goings around the Ferrar house were so usual they would not arouse suspicion. Each load had been picked up in a safe spot along the road or in the hills and transferred to the train of mules Ferrar's men held back in the mountains.

"And now we are ready, old one," Ferrar said. "Get your horse and we will ride."

North of Santa Fe the cedars filled the hills with their stunted ghosts, and the yucca stood like lonely candles in the pale moonlight. They picked up the Pecuris Trail and followed it for an hour and then turned off for the meeting place in the mountains. Deep in timber, at a deserted and crumbling hacienda, they found the mules. Twenty-five of them, their straw-matted *aparejos* bulging with the swart beaver pelts that had piled up in Tony Ferrar's warehouse since Governor Armijo had closed the Santa Fe Trail to any trade with the United States.

Little Joe was standing by the lead mule, a short, squat, bowlegged man in white cotton shirt and buckskin leggin's. He looked like a gypsy, with the brass ring in his ear and the spotted bandanna drawn over his greasy black hair. But he claimed pure Castilian descent and would cheerfully knife anybody who doubted it.

"Were you followed?" he asked.

"We circled back three times to make sure we weren't," Ferrar said. "I think we can start safely. Morina gave me a tip that the fur patrol would be in Apache Canyon tonight. The only thing we'll have to worry about is the customs troops at Taos."

"I don't know," Uncle Hondo said darkly. "In Santa Cruz it is said that the toll of the bell is not for the dead but to remind us we too may die tomorrow."

"And the time I will really start worrying is when you quit grumbling, you old *bribón*," leered Little Joe. *"Vamanos,* you lazy *burros.* Let's go!"

He swung onto his ratty little pony and the four other drivers stepped into saddle, prodding the mules with their pointed poles. There was a great groaning and grumbling and twitching of ears, and the train was under way.

They found the Pecuris Trail again and turned north. It led through dry washes where *chamiza* turned the sand to gold and primrose lay like patches of blood so red it was almost black in the feeble moonlight. They passed Cuyamangue while it was still dark, a huddle of adobe huts surrounded by fields of alfalfa sighing like a lonely woman in the wind. And beyond that was Pojoaque, with the Indians sleeping in their mud hovels and a dog howling at the cavalcade passing above the town through the hills.

And all the time they were rising toward the mountains around Taos. The hour before dawn was the blackest, with the stars blinking out. Then light began to come, milky at first, finally flushed by a rising sun. They were south of the Pecuris pueblo now, climbing a shelving trail that looked across a vast expanse of timbered ridges and sheltered valleys. It was a country Ferrar loved, but somehow the familiar exhilaration, the sense of freedom did not come. His mind was still on the Cordenza letter.

He had tried to tell himself that he had done right, that he would be gone a month, and it would all be resolved before his return. But that did not satisfy him. Yet, even if he returned now, what could he do? Was Morina right, was his allegiance to the people of Santa Fe? Or was his white heritage too strong? It seemed that he could not turn either way without betraying someone with whom he had ties. It would do no good to go back, with the decision unresolved.

"What are you always looking behind for, old one?" Little Joe asked.

"Didn't something move up there on the hill?" Uncle Hondo said.

"Yes, and we were followed all the way from Santa Fe. By our shadows. You live in dreams, you old *bribón*."

With the full light of the sun came the cry of a great blue fool hen perched beside the trail in one of the spruces. Ferrar's buckskin shied at the sound, and he fought it with numbed hands. The shadows swallowed the canyons and gorges beneath him with hungry mouths.

They reached the top of the cut and began descending. The trail shelved down through a deep canyon, with the silvery flash of a river far below. Ferrar's attention was still turned down when the sound came.

It was like a great clap of thunder. The buckskin reared, bulging shrilly. The mules brayed behind Ferrar and began to bolt, banking up behind the buckskin in wild ranks. One of them was shoved off the edge and crashed down the cliffside like a broken rag doll.

"Let the mules go, Antonito," shouted Little Joe. "They'll all go off the side."

Another shot crashed, its echoes rolling across the gorge. Ferrar put the spurs to his buckskin. The frenzied beast squealed and plunged forward down the rocky trail, with the burros streaming out behind.

All Ferrar could do was let his frantic horse have its head on the narrow shelf. He risked one glance up but could see nothing on the timbered slope above. The trail was getting steeper, dropping swiftly toward the level of the canyon floor. His horse stumbled and almost went down. He knew it was only a matter of time before it spilled or was shot from beneath him. He heard another mule slide off the treacherous shoulder behind him and plummet down the steep escarpment with a lost bray.

He saw a point ahead where the cliff became a talus slope and knew it was his only chance. If he were thrown beyond it, where the wall became sheer again, he would be broken to bits before reaching bottom.

Another volley of shots put his buckskin into a new frenzy. He tried to pull it down before the slope. It fought the bit, stumbled. He realized it was going down and kicked free, diving right over the horse's head. Its impetus threw him far enough to strike a shoulder of the slope. He sprawled flat, stunned, and slipped and flopped through the shale. It seemed as if he slid a thousand feet before he rolled off onto a sandy beach.

He lay there a moment, dazed, bleeding. His shirt had been ripped completely off his back, his body was a mass of bloody bruises and wounds from the rocks, his leggin's hung in shreds. As from far off, he heard the shots begin again. Sand kicked up a foot from him.

Groaning, he rolled over and crawled into the water. It cleansed his wounds and revived him. He threw himself deep into the current and let it carry him down till he reached a rocky shallow where he could cross into the timber on the other bank.

Crouched here, sobbing with exhaustion, he could see the mules just streaming out into the floor of the canyon from the end of the trail. Some plunged into the river, and their pack saddles immediately overturned them and they were swept downstream until the packs were torn off by the rocks and they could start swimming for the opposite side. Others charged on down the other side of the canyon, braying wildly. Little Joe plunged off the trail and into the river. A shot chipped rock off in the face of his horse, and the man had a wild time forcing him into the current.

Ferrar came to his feet and ran toward the point Little Joe would reach. The horse lunged onto the bank, dripping wet. Little Joe saw Ferrar in the timber and reined the squealing animal toward him. He dropped off, holding the reins, and they both hunkered down behind a screen of brush, looking out at the carnage. Then they realized how silent it had become.

"The shots, they have stopped," Little Joe said.

"Sure they have," Ferrar said bleakly. "They've done their job. Half the pelts have been ripped to pieces on the rocks, and the other half will be swept all the way down to Santa Fe in this river."

"Is right," Little Joe said mournfully. "A dozen of them mules must have gone over the side. St. Looey will get no fur this year."

Ferrar shook his head. "What are we thinking of? The hell with the furs. What about the men?"

"I saw Ramirez go over the side with the mules. The others were ahead of me. They were chasing what few mules got into timber, the last I saw."

The clatter of hoofs on the rocky trail brought both their heads up. Uncle Hondo had been at the rear of the column. His frightened horse had settled down to a spooky, skittish trot. The old man was bent over the big saddle horn, hanging on grimly, his wizened body jerked from side to side.

Ferrar's face went white. Both he and Little Joe left the trees at a run, plunging into the creek, fighting its turbulent spring current across to the other side. Ferrar came out a hundred yards farther down from where he had gone in, crouched on the white sand, sobbing for air. The old man's horse clattered from the trail onto the beach.

Gasping, Ferrar rose to his feet and stumbled to catch it before the animal went by. He blocked it up against the canyon wall, got its bit. Little Joe was there to help him lift Uncle Hondo off. They lowered the old man to the ground. His eyes fluttered open, he tried to grin.

"They are right about the bell, in Santa Cruz, no?"

Ferrar clutched his shoulders. "Uncle Hondo, who did it, who was it?"

"I get a look at one of them——" The old man broke off to cough feebly. Blood bubbled from his mouth. He settled back, fighting for breath. Finally the words left him, on a dying whisper: "A man with long yellow hair, and a beard, all yellow—all yellow——"

Ferrar stared down at him with bleak eyes. His voice, when he finally spoke, was barely audible. "Cimarron Garrett."

CHAPTER FOUR

"I Belong to Both."

They got back to Rancho Ferrar near dusk, with Uncle Hondo's body wrapped in his poncho and hung across his horse. Little Joe went to the cathedral in town and came back with the priest, and after a simple service they buried Uncle Hondo by torchlight in the cemetery where Sean Ferrar and his wife lay, and a dozen of the retainers and faithful *peons* who had died in their service.

Before the services were over, Ferrar saw a wagon coming up the road from town, and when he led the procession back to the house, it was waiting before the front door. Julia Manatte had just got down from the front seat, with one of George Manatte's teamsters still up in the wagon, holding the reins.

"I heard Little Joe was in town for the priest," she said. "What happened, Tony? The caretaker at the church said something about Uncle Hondo."

Bitterness and deep fatigue turned his face gaunt, forming shadowy hollows beneath the cheekbones, lending his eyes a sunken, feverish look. He stared down at her without answering, unable to believe she did not know. Her face was thrown into deep shadow by the hood of a cloak that covered her to the knees, but he could see her eyes, guileless and deeply worried.

"I guess your father doesn't tell you the dirtier side of his business," he said. His voice was ugly. "That was Uncle Hondo we buried up on the hill. My fur train was attacked. They couldn't be satisfied with merely making sure the furs were ruined or lost. They had to kill a harmless old man."

"Who had to? Tony, please, who had to——"

"Cimarron Garrett."

Her lips parted, the blood left her face till it had a parchment hue. There was a restless murmur from the people around them. A torch spat softly. Then she began shaking her head.

"Tony, you can't believe that, you can't! Dad had nothing to do with it. If Cimarron did it, Dad didn't know about it."

"What did your father want to do? Make me think Morina attacked me, make me turn on her? Then maybe send you up to convince me when I came back, is that it? So I'd take the letter through for you? Only Cimarron made the mistake of getting seen. Maybe that's why he killed Uncle Hondo. He knew Uncle Hondo had seen him——"

"No, no, Tony——" She was almost crying. "Dad wouldn't do anything like that, he wouldn't." She came up against him, seeming to forget the rest of the people, her thrown-back head tossing off the hood to let the torchlight shine like wet gold in her hair.

"Did I ever lie to you, Tony? Even after that Garcia woman came between us, did I lie to you? Maybe you're right, maybe it was Cimarron Garrett. But he doesn't represent all the Americans here, any more than Morina Garcia represents the Mexicans——"

"Cimarron works for your father, doesn't he?"

"Yes, but——"

"Just how bad does your father want the Americans in Santa Fe?" he asked her.

She pulled away, staring blankly up at him.

"That's what I thought, you're afraid to answer it," he said. "And just how far would he go to bring them in?" He paused, and her lips parted slowly as if she would speak, but she did not.

He said bitterly, "Your father wanted me to get the Cordenza letter of surrender. You tell him I've gone to get it."

She pulled away from him, forcing the words out. "Who—who will you bring it to?"

"Who do you think?"

She grabbed his arm as he tried to wheel away. "You can't do it, you can't betray your own people."

"I guess I didn't really know who my people were, up till now," he said. "You decided for me, by killing one of them."

He tore loose and went inside with long, savage paces. She tried to follow, but the servants blocked her off, coming after him. He told one of them to saddle up his best horse. The powder in his Dragoon cap-and-ball was wet from his swim in the river, and he reloaded the cylinder, primers and all, before buckling the five-shot back on. Then he hooked the powder horn onto the other side of his belt and put the buckskin bullet pouch in a coat pocket and went out into the patio, where the horse was saddled.

Little Joe wanted to go with him, but he knew he could travel with more secrecy alone. Julia's wagon was gone when he rode through the gate in the *zaguan,* and turned down toward the Santa Fe Trail.

Through his bleak fury, his grief at Uncle Hondo's death, one thought drove him. George Manatte had always been highly representative, to Ferrar, of the Americans in Santa Fe. And now what had happened became just as representative of how it would be if the Americans took over. If they were capable of killing one innocent man to gain their ends, they were capable of killing a thousand.

In this bitter mood he reached Glorieta Pass, with the cedars standing like stunted ghosts on the slopes. He passed through Apache Canyon and went by the cutoff to Pecos, the deserted pueblo at which Morina had promised to meet him if he got the letter for her. He knew she would hear of what had happened, would know he was going after the note, and would be waiting at the pueblo for him on his return.

He pushed his horse to the small farm of a *peon* he knew and had something to eat and got another horse. He reached the canyon in the mesa south of Las Vegas about noon of the next day, and a Yankee patrol picked him up there and took him to Las Vegas, a hundred squalid adobes huddled along the west bank of the Gallinas. Kearny and half a dozen officers were gathered in one of the larger buildings in a feeble attempt to escape the heat.

Ferrar had dealt with Kearny several times before in his business along the Trail, and Manatte had already sent word that he was trying to get Ferrar to carry the note, so Kearny accepted him without much question. Cordenza's letter of surrender was a short missive, written in poor Spanish, stipulating two terms beside those offered by the Americans. All the American officers seemed sure that Armijo would either capitulate or surrender once he saw the note and realized his main hope of support was cut off.

They fed Ferrar and replaced his beaten-down animal with an army horse, and a patrol escorted him out as far as the mesa. In the late afternoon he passed Starvation Peak, with its penitente cross stamped forebodingly against the sky, and San Jose, where the dogs set up a howl at the drumming of his horse's hoofs. He was stupefied with fatigue, now, and rocking heavily in the saddle. He lost count of the times he fell asleep and jerked up barely in time to keep from pitching from the horse.

It was already evening when he sighted the turnoff to Pecos ahead. It was here the first shot smashed out. The bullet struck the road directly in front of him, and the excited horse veered and pirouetted and reared high, pitching him off its rump.

He hit heavily on the bank of an arroyo and rolled to its bottom and lay there, stunned. Dimly he could hear the tattoo of the horse's hoofs, racing away into the night. He rolled over, shaking his head, and pulled out his Dragoon.

He could not be sure but he thought the shot had come from the other side of the road. The arroyo he was in pinched off right against the cutoff into Pecos. He lay there a moment, thinking back. He had told Julia where he was going and he knew who this was.

For a moment he had the savage impulse to stop and fight and get Cimarron Garrett for Uncle Hondo. But the Cordenza letter was more important. He had to get it to Morina first.

He crawled to the end of the arroyo and then snaked up into the cover of scrub timber. It was what they had been waiting for. From across the road came the boom of a shot. Lead crackled through piñons a few feet from him. He fired four times at the gun flash and then turned and ran as hard as he could into timber.

His volley had made them seek cover, for the return shot did not come till he was deep in the trees. He reloaded his gun as he ran, measuring powder roughly into each chamber, spilling a little each time, seating the gray lead balls with the ramrod. With the cylinder reloaded, he fumbled for caps in his pocket, thumbing them home on the nipples at the rear of each chamber. He was in broken country by the time he finished, looking down into Pecos.

An early moon had risen, its light making a hazy mystery of the ancient Indian town. Pestilence and war had wiped out its people long ago, and it stood ancient and deserted. He sought vainly in its court-yard for sight of Morina's coach.

He knew he would be foolish to remain in the open, if he had to wait for her, and dropped down a crumbling shale bank to the buildings, stepping into the first door that had not fallen in. The dark-ness was musty with the odor of ancient things. Broken pottery crum-bled beneath his feet.

Then the waiting began. The ghosts of this lost city whispered through its countless chambers. He remembered stories of a sacred fire that never died and of human sacrifices that still went on in hidden *kivas*. Then he realized it was not his imagination causing the whispers in the crumbling buildings. While he had been watching the approach, his ambushers could have moved around and come in from behind.

He heard the distinct crunch of pottery underfoot, from far within the city. He turned to stare achingly into the blackness. No telling how many passages led into this chamber.

Then a new rattling broke into his tension. The coach came up on the crest and clattered down the age-old trail. There were half a dozen outriders in blue jackets and red helmets, their lance tips silvery flickers of light. Captain Seguro Ugardes led them, a proud figure in his high-cantled saddle.

The coach pulled up with a flourish, its matched team stamping, and Tomas jumped from beside the driver to open the door. The troop of lancers formed ranks of their prancing horses and faced the coach at attention as Morina Garcia stepped out.

"Seguro," Ferrar called. *"Chica.* Get out of the open. Manatte's got his men here."

His voice echoed into the crumbling chambers and died. Out in the courtyard, Morina turned toward the sound of his voice. She had on a hooded cloak which dropped her face into black shadow; diamonds glittered on her fingers. Finally she laughed huskily.

"Antonito, how would Manatte know we were here?"

"Move her out of here, Ugardes," Ferrar called desperately. "They hit me on the road, I tell you!"

He saw the sharp toss of her head, the motion of anger he knew so well. There was a pause, then she laughed again. "It is all right, Antonito. We are safe. There has been a mistake. You can come out."

"A mistake?"

"I assure you, you are safe. Come out."

Slowly he moved into the open, gun held tight, peering at the doorways of the buildings that circled the great courtyard. But no shots came. Finally he reached Morina, gazing at her wonderingly. At that instant, there was a faint movement from the first-story roof of a building which formed the balcony of the second story.

"Señor," Morina called sharply, as if to halt something.

But the man had already come into view, sliding over the edge of the balcony, to hang and drop to the earth below. It was Cimarron Garrett, carrying a long Yerger rifle, with the moon making a golden mane of his yellow hair. Then there was a faint crunch of pottery behind Ferrar, and he wheeled to see Pitch emerge from the doorway next to the one he had stood in.

"You are both fools!" Morina said disgustedly.

"How the hell did we know he was coming here?" Cimarron said. "He was seen talking to Julia Manatte last. You told us he'd already refused to get the letter for you."

The whole thing struck Ferrar with a sick shock, as he wheeled back to Morina. "I thought Cimarron and Pitch were Manatte's boys."

"Everybody else in Santa Fe thinks they are too," she said. "It suits me to have it so."

"Then *you* killed Uncle Hondo." It left Ferrar in a thin whisper.

The toss of her head slid the hood off, and moonlight made a blue-black flash in her dark hair. She stepped forward, reaching for his hand.

"Antonito, they didn't mean to. It was an accident. I had to do that, don't you see? I couldn't let you leave with your furs. You were the only one who could get the letter through. But Uncle Hondo was an accident. Cimarron told me. He was shooting at the mules——"

"The hell he was!" Ferrar pulled away from her, face white. "You knew I thought Cimarron was Manatte's man. You knew I'd get that letter for you if I was convinced Manatte killed Uncle Hondo."

"Antonito——"

"No!" He pulled away again, staring at her. His breathing made a thin sound in the moment of silence. "I brought the letter to you because I realized the people who had killed Uncle Hondo would be capable of doing the same thing again to attain their ends. Capable of doing it on any scale, one man or a thousand. But I brought it to the wrong one, didn't I? How many more people do you think you'll kill?"

He wheeled to Ugardes. "Seguro, you aren't going to let her get away with it! Can't you see how she operates now?"

There was a hurt confusion in Ugardes's face as he looked at Morina. She turned swiftly to him, putting more intensity into her voice than Ferrar had ever heard before.

"Seguro, you can see what I had to do. It was only to save our people. Uncle Hondo was an accident, I swear it. But if it had to be, isn't it better to have one suffer that many may be saved?"

Ugardes turned to Ferrar, shaking his head. "She's right, Tony. It was tragic that it had to be Uncle Hondo. But now we must finish it."

Morina faced Ferrar, holding out her hand. "Let us have it, now. Don't try to destroy it in this last moment. You wouldn't have a chance."

Ferrar realized how right she was. Cimarron held that Yerger on him now and Pitch had a big Cherington pistol pointed at his back. Sick with his own helplessness, he took the letter from his pocket, handed it to her. She opened it, read it, smiled triumphantly.

"Hadn't we better destroy it at once?" Ugardes said.

"I want to know whether it is a forgery," she said. "There is a man in Santa Fe who knows Cordenza's handwriting. We will have to leave Ferrar here. You can understand how dangerous it would be to let him go. When it is over, he will go free. Does that suit you, *Segurito?*"

Ferrar saw the captain's young eyes widen. *"Segurito?"*

"Yes," she murmured. "Why not? And there will still be but one man in Santa Fe who calls me *Chica*. That will be you, *Segurito.*"

Ferrar saw a wild flame of adoration light Ugardes's eyes. He wondered if his own eyes had looked that way when Morina told him the same thing, so long ago. The woman had turned to Cimarron, her brows raised in a faint inquisition.

"We'll hold him here till we hear from you," the yellow-haired man said. "We'll do that."

She wheeled and stepped into the coach. The Navajo climbed back onto the seat beside the driver. Ugardes stepped into his saddle, turned to look down at Ferrar. That shine had left his eyes. They were beginning to look puzzled again.

"I'm sorry, *amigo*. I hope we meet again when it is over."

He raised his arm, dropped it, the troop wheeled and broke into a gallop after the coach as it clattered up the rise. Then Cimarron told Pitch to get Ferrar's gun. The man stepped in behind Ferrar, pulled the cap-and-ball from Ferrar's hand.

"Now we'll wait a while, so they won't hear the shots," Cimarron said. "Captain Ugardes didn't look too convinced."

Ferrar's sick defeat deepened as he realized what they meant. He knew it was only a few seconds now. But he couldn't just let them shoot him. Not just bow his head and submit. He felt the sweat start out on his forehead, felt all the muscles of his body contract. A surprised look crossed Cimarron's face. He jerked his rifle up, till it covered Ferrar's chest.

The shot made a great smashing sound. But it did not come from Cimarron's gun. His mouth dropped open, he staggered backward with shock making a grotesque mask of his face and a red hole staining his chest.

At the same time, Pitch swung away from Ferrar, firing his Cherington at the rise of land. He realized his mistake an instant after his shot and tried to wheel back and jerk Ferrar's Dragoon up in his other hand. But Ferrar had already spun around and was lunging into him. He knocked the gun back down as it went off, crashing into Pitch so hard the man fell.

Ferrar went down with him, catching the Dragoon and twisting it from his hand as they fell. He struck the ground on his knees, astraddle Pitch, and raised up, with the heavy cap-and-ball in his hand, and smashed it into the man's face. Pitch made a broken sound and went utterly slack.

Panting, Ferrar got up. Cimarron lay on his back, dead eyes staring emptily at the sky. There was nothing in sight on the rise of land. Ferrar ran heavily up the trail, gun ready. Finally he came into sight of Captain Ugardes, lying on the ground just beyond the crest.

"That Pitch, he's a better shot than I thought," Ugardes chuckled. Then he choked, and blood bubbled from his mouth.

Ferrar dropped to his knees beside the man, trying to ease him. "Why did you come back, Seguro?"

"I got to thinking," the man muttered feebly. "It came to me how quickly Morina had changed from you to me. I had wanted it so long that I couldn't think straight when it happened. But riding back, it came through. She wouldn't have switched so easily if she really cared for you. And if she didn't care, she had only been using you. And if she could use you, she could use me. I had to make sure, Tony, I had to come back."

"Seguro——"

The man's eyes were getting glassy, his voice fading. "You were right, Tony. What happened to Uncle Hondo had been going on a long time, in many different ways. We didn't see it. We only saw the *peons* at the cantinas, drinking, gambling—we thought that represented their life as much as ours. But they were suffering under the rule. And it was her rule. Not Armijo's. She was pulling all the strings. Just like the Cordenza letter. She knew it was real all along. But she wanted Armijo to fight Kearny, so what she had here wouldn't be overthrown by the Americans. She doesn't represent our people—any more than Cimarron and Pitch represent the Yankees. Stop her, Tony. Get the letter—to Armijo—Too much needless bloodshed—already——"

He sagged back. Ferrar called his name. The young captain's eyes were closed. He did not answer.

Ferrar got up, a pale look to his face, a lost feeling inside him. Then he turned and stumbled through the greasewood to where Ugardes had left his horse. He mounted the nervous beast, turning it down the trail. But Ugardes had left his troop where the cutoff ran into the Santa Fe Trail, and they must have heard the gunshots, for the earth began to tremble with their galloping.

Ferrar pulled his horse off into the piñons and watched them sweep by in the darkness, lances down. He thought bitterly that it was a fitting tribute to Ugardes.

Then he turned the horse and rode.

It was a wild ride, over barrancas, into arroyos, seeking short cuts across the loops and switchbacks of the trail. He had cut off the last wide turn in by the road by crossing the ridge and was forcing the lathered horse down through scrub oak when the coach rolled around the point, coming hard. It passed him before he reached the road, and he burst out a few feet behind it, blocked off from the view of Tomas and the driver.

He spurred the stumbling horse into its last run. It gained the rear of the coach, began to veer and weave, unable to keep the pace. Knowing it was his last chance, he rose to a crouch in the saddle and leaped for the coach. His left foot came down on the boot, his right foot caught in the rear window. His hands caught the luggage rail on top.

Tomas must have felt the coach tilt. He turned sharply on the front seat, then rose and climbed back across the top, pulling his knife. Ferrar fought desperately to get on top and meet the man. He had to use both hands, and had no time to draw his gun. He managed to sprawl out on top, belly down, when Tomas reached him. The Navajo lunged up and drove down with the knife.

All Ferrar could do was flop over. The knife drove hilt-deep into the wood of the top. Before Tomas could pull back, Ferrar caught the man around the neck, pulling him down and doubling up at the same time to smash a knee in his downcoming face.

It stunned Tomas, knocking him over Ferrar's body. Wildly he tried to catch the rail, but his impetus carried him over it, and he rolled off the racing coach with a scream.

Ferrar pulled the knife from the top and crawled up behind the driver, who was still fighting to stop the horses. He put the point of the blade against the man's back, disarmed him, waited until the coach was halted, and then ordered him to jump down and walk away from the coach.

As the man reached the ground, Morina shoved open the door and started to step out, calling angrily to the driver, "Juan, what's going on, why did Tomas fall off——?"

She stopped, mouth open in surprise, as Ferrar dropped off to confront her. Then she ripped the Cordenza note from the bosom of her dress. He reached her before she could tear it, putting the point of the knife against her throat.

"Don't destroy it, *Chica*——" He made the word thin and ugly.

Her eyes widened. "You wouldn't."

He pressed the knife harder against her neck. "I'm thinking of Uncle Hondo, *Chica.*"

Her eyes narrowed, her cheeks grew pale. Slowly, the defeat came into her face, making it indefinably gaunt and old. He took the letter from her slack fingers. Then he turned and climbed back into the seat, picking up the reins.

He took one last look at Morina. It was like stirring the ashes of a burned-out fire. The passion he had felt for her, the intense attraction, seemed to have belonged to another life, another man. It had been real enough, in its way. But again he had only been looking at the surface. Now he knew what lay underneath. He lifted the reins and started the horses down the road.

Manatte, Julia, and a dozen Yankee trappers met Ferrar a mile down the road, halting his coach.

"What happened?" Manatte asked him. "We heard the Garcia woman had left town and figured it was to get the letter. Julia wouldn't stay behind. She still couldn't believe you'd take it to Morina."

Ferrar handed down the letter. "She was almost wrong. I'll tell you sometime. Just get this note to Armijo. It will straighten out a lot of things."

Julia was dressed in a man's coat and blue jeans, a flat-topped hat tilted over one eye. Smiling, she climbed off her horse onto the coach seat.

"Take my horse back with you," she told her father. Then she turned to Ferrar, face radiant. "You must have finally found out who your people really are."

"I belong to both," he said. "Your people are my people, and so are the Mexicans. And soon they can all be one people, if men like Cimarron or women like Morina don't get the power in their hands and twist it all into lies for their own sake."

She put a hand on his arm. "I have the feeling you've come back to me, Tony."

He smiled down at her. "Yes," he said. "I've come back to you."

Trail's End in Tombstone

Thomas Thompson

CHAPTER ONE

"She Said 'Ride'!"

HE CAME from San Francisco and before that from the mining camps in the Sierras, and these hills, the Huachuchas, were little more than tired lumps of old land to him. But there was timber here, and the cool shade was a welcome relief from the hot miles of barrenness that lay behind him. North and east were the Dragoons and the Apaches, and between here and there was the valley of the San Pedro and the town

Genial and popular, Tommy Thompson recently served a term as WWA's president, remains one of its most valuable members. His books include a long list of novels—*King of Abilene* and *Gunman Brand,* to name only two—and a collection of shorts (*They Brought Their Guns*) worth any Western fan's careful attention. Screen and TV writing have taken much of his time for the last couple of years, but his recent novel, *Brand of a Man,* indicates he's not forsaking the fiction field. Tommy and his wife, June, have a home in Santa Rosa.

of Tombstone. And in that new and boisterous town was a man—Clayton Rutherford by name.

Ted Gavin rolled the fire from his cigarette between thumb and forefinger, and the muscles along his jaws were hard and his eyes were bleak. If he found what he thought he'd find he'd kill Clayton Rutherford. It was no use covering up for his foster brother any longer.

Solitude and the long ride had brought Ted Gavin an unaccustomed carelessness, and there was a stubble of beard on his usually smooth-shaven face. His clothes, made for riding, were sweat-stained and dusty, and his alertness too had been dulled by inactivity. He didn't see the riders until they had moved out of the timber and were nearly upon him. He rolled his hand against the reins, and his horse stopped obediently, lifting its head, tilting its ears, as glad as the man was for some sign of companionship.

There were six riders in all, cowboys by their dress, and the one moving out in front was the leader. He was a tall, craggy, and ugly man, with sandy brows and a tawny mustache that drooped below the line of his blocky, scarred jaw. He looked at Ted Gavin without friendliness, and his gray-green eyes were hard and cold.

"Start talking," he said, and his hand dropped and rested there on the butt of his six-shooter.

"A pleasure, believe me," Ted Gavin said. "I haven't talked to anybody for two weeks———"

"To hell with him, Nick," one of the cowboys said. "Let's put the rope on him and talk to him later."

Ted's eyes roved swiftly across the line of men. He had seen vigilante justice in Angel's Camp and Hangtown. He knew he was seeing something similar here. He said, "Hold on, boys. I'm just passing through———"

"So was the last rider," the man called Nick said. "But a man was killed. This is Walking M."

There was no time to consider whether this was mistaken identity, a holdup, or just plain meanness. Two of the men had drawn guns and one was taking a rifle from the saddle scabbard. Another tossed a rope, and the loop of it settled around Ted's shoulders. He fought it with his hands, felt it tighten, nearly jerking him from the saddle, and then he saw the two horsemen come out of the timber.

The girl's voice was a whisper in the charged stillness: "What is it, Nick?"

The improbability of hearing a woman in this Arizona solitude was a greater shock than the rope around Ted's shoulders. His eyes whipped across the faces of the men, and even though there wasn't surprise there, there was hesitation and respect. The big man didn't turn his head. His eyes were suddenly troubled, and there was almost softness on his battered face.

"A trespasser, Marjorie. You go on and let us handle it."

The girl reined her high-spirited buckskin alongside Nick. She was a young girl, and when Gavin first glanced at her he couldn't tell whether she was beautiful in her own right or only beautiful because of the unexpectedness of seeing her. She wore a divided skirt and a man's shirt. Her hair was cut shorter than shoulder length but it seemed natural that way, even though he had never seen such a haircut before. Her face was angular, her cheekbones chiseled. There was a matter-of-fact elegance about her that gave her a rich dignity in her rough surroundings.

She met Ted's gaze levelly, studying him, and then she said, "I've never seen him before, Nick. Have you?"

"That don't mean nothin', " Nick said. "They come and go. I'll talk to him." The big man never looked at the girl when he spoke to her.

The girl met Ted's eyes, and he felt a warm glow of pleasure at her candid attention. "What do you have to say for yourself, stranger?" she asked.

Ted forced a smile. He wished he had shaved. "Just traveling, that's all. Wanted to see Tombstone." He started to add that he was looking for Clayton Rutherford, then he thought better of it. It was hard to say what Clayton Rutherford's name might mean to people. It usually depended on how long Rutherford had been in one place. "I heard Tombstone was a rough camp," he said, and now the grin was genuine, "but I didn't expect a welcome like this."

"Let him go, Nick," the girl said.

"Wait a minute, Marjorie," Nick protested. "After what happened and with Luke Bell hiding out——"

"I said let him go."

Nick shrugged and accepted her order by riding close and lifting the slacked rope from Ted's shoulders. Ted got the impression that this man would always accept her orders without question. Perhaps it was almost a religion with him.

"Make sure you go to Tombstone, stranger," Nick said. "Make sure you don't ride this way again."

Ted lowered his hands, and as he did Nick's own hand flashed down and came up with a gun. Ted spread his hands on the pommel of his saddle. "I'd like to say thanks, Miss——"

The girl turned her back. She spoke sharply to her men. "We're after rustlers," she said, "not broken-down drifters."

"You can look in my saddlebags," Ted called, wanting to prolong the conversation. "You won't find any cows——"

She turned quickly, her eyes hard. "Get riding," she said. "We don't like strangers on Walking M. You stick around here and the boys will stretch your neck. You get out of line in Tombstone and the Citizen's Committee will do it for you."

"It's sure a friendly place," Ted said, and now there was a hint of devilment in his eyes. "And me such a likable cuss, once you get to know me." She was riding away, trying to ignore him. He rose in his stirrups. "And I'm not so broken-down, either. I've got money enough to buy you the best meal in Tombstone if you've got nerve enough to accept the offer."

"She said ride, didn't she?" Nick's voice was deep in his throat, and there was more there than dislike for a drifter. This Nick considered this girl his personal responsibility. He glanced toward her, and Ted didn't miss the caress in the big man's eyes.

"I'm riding," Ted said, and he felt less harshly toward Nick.

He touched his heels lightly to his horse's flanks and rode slowly on down the slopes, his casualness the only form of defiance he could show. He heard the men talking behind him and he heard the girl's voice, sharp and clear, and then two riders separated and started following him. It was plain he was going to have an escort to make sure he got off Walking M range. That was all right with Ted Gavin. He was anxious to get to Tombstone.

The riders, who had stayed a hundred yards or so behind him, deserted him at the edge of the town, which was laid out in perfect squares on the little mesa. The air was thin and clean, and a flawless sky looked down on man-made ugliness. The streets were laid out and named, but the town itself was still in the process of building. He followed Allen Street, and at the corner of Third he came to the OK Stable with the corral behind it taking up the entire width of the block. He turned in there, the incident with the girl nearly crowding out the press of bigger things swelling within him.

It was the end of the afternoon shift, and men were coming up into the town from the Tough Nut claims, dirt-stained, bearded men, with the flush of a big strike bright in their eyes.

Ted stabled his horse and asked casually, "Know where I can find Clayton Rutherford?"

The stableman glanced at him quickly, and then his eyes dropped to the gun on Ted's hip. He grinned then. "I don't stick my nose in Clayton Rutherford's business, but I'd say the Oriental would be a good place to start looking. Two blocks down on Allen."

He gave the direction automatically, like a man who is used to meeting many strangers; then he waited expectantly. Ted took a silver dollar from his pocket, flipped it, and the old man caught it with a down sweep of his hand. The stableman grinned.

"My name's Joe," he said. "Just thought I'd tell you that I'm mighty absent-minded. I don't know nothin' and I never see nobody."

"That's fine, Joe," Ted Gavin said. "I'll remember."

He walked down the street, past Hafford's Saloon and the Campbell and Hatch Pool Hall. The Crystal Palace Saloon stood on the corner of Fifth and Allen, and directly across from it was the Oriental. These buildings alone had some semblance of elegance about them.

A dozen horsemen came thundering down Fifth Street, yelling at the top of their lungs, and miners scattered and hit for cover. When the riders were past, Ted crossed the street and entered the Oriental. The place was jammed to the walls. No one paid any attention to his entering. No one noticed the gun on his hip.

It took him five minutes to work his way to the bar; another five minutes to attract the bartender's attention. "I'm looking for Clayton Rutherford," he said.

Two men near him turned quickly and looked at him. One of the men had a frozen frown between his intelligent eyes.

"Friend of Clayton's?" the bartender asked.

"I didn't say that," Ted said. "I said I was looking for him."

The two men moved in closer. Ted felt a pressure against his ribs. He glanced down, and there was a six-shooter pressing his side. He looked at the man who held it—a tall, thin man, the man with the frown.

"Just happens we was goin' to see Clayton Rutherford ourselves," the thin man said. "We'll be glad to take you."

His companion indicated the stairway at the back of the room. They went through the crowd that way, the gun plainly exposed if anyone had looked, but no one paid the slightest bit of attention. Men talked of millions as if they were speaking of dimes for beer, and no one had time for another man's troubles.

There were office rooms on the second floor and one of the men rapped on a door. An old familiar voice—a pleasant voice with a laugh in it, told them to come in. The gunman kneed open the door and the three of them stepped inside and Ted Gavin was looking at Clayton Rutherford.

For a moment the old friendship was strong in him—the feeling of seeing a familiar face in a faraway place after so many strange faces— and then all the double-dealing and crookedness and outright foulness of this man came up and stood like a wall between them. Ted's lips were set, and his voice was hard.

"Hello, Clay," he said. "Surprised to see me?"

Clayton Rutherford stood up slowly. Color left his face and his lips had a bluish cast. He was a young man, no older than Ted. He was handsome, with dark, curly hair that waved in drake's tails above his ears. His eyes were brown and open and pleasant, and his features had an irritating regularity. The color came back in his cheeks.

"No, Ted," he said, "I'm not surprised." He waved a well-kept hand at the two men who had brought Ted in. "It's all right, boys," he said. "Ted Gavin and I are old friends."

CHAPTER TWO

"I'm Glad I Didn't Hang You."

For a moment the two gunmen stood there, looking at Rutherford, and then the taller of the two said, "You're getting a lot of friends, Rutherford. Be careful with 'em." He turned abruptly and left the room. The shorter man took a good, steady look at Ted Gavin before holstering his gun, and then he followed his companion out and closed the door gently.

"I see you still have sweet playmates," Ted Gavin said.

Clayton Rutherford smiled. "In my business, I need them," he said. He leaned back in his chair, pressed the tips of his fingers together, and the smile left his face. "I haven't got a job for you, Ted," he said, "so what else is on your mind?"

Ted Gavin took a straight chair, straddled it backward, leaning his arms on the back, and looked steadily at this man he had known so long. "A lot of things, Clay," he said. "Two thousand dollars, just to start with. That's what it cost me. And I'd thought some of killing you."

Clay Rutherford laughed easily. "Over two thousand dollars?" He shook his head. "That's why you and I weren't any good as partners, Ted. Or as brothers, for that matter. Growing up together didn't make us think alike, did it?"

"I'm thankful for that."

"All right," Clayton said, waving a fleck of dust off his desk. "So I walked out on that mining-stock deal and I took two thousand dollars with me and you made it good. I knew you would. I took that two thousand because I needed it, and what I need I get. It's chicken feed now, and I'll pay you off and you can go home the lily-white hero."

"And cover up for you again?"

"I never asked you to cover up for me," Clayton said.

"But you knew I would."

"So what am I supposed to do?"

"I said I was thinking about killing you, Clay."

There was no fear on Clayton Rutherford's face. There was nothing but confidence. "I don't think you will, Ted. I'm a big man around here. I'm the law. I've got a lot of friends. You haven't."

"That's right, Clay," Gavin said. "I haven't any friends anywhere. I lost them all, covering up for you."

"I've told you before, Ted, you should have been a preacher."

"But I'm not," Gavin said. "There wouldn't be any blemish on my soul if I killed you."

"If I had a violin I'd play soft music," Rutherford said.

"It's taken me a long time to realize just how rotten you are," Gavin said. His eyes never left Rutherford's face. He knew this man like a book. He had grown up with him, accepted him as a foster brother. He had tried to find some good in him——

"I saw Gwen before I left San Francisco," he said. "I guess that helped me decide."

A small worry crossed Rutherford's face. "Gwen took a lot for granted," he said.

"Did she?" Ted said. "She bought a wedding dress with money you gave her.

"She'll use it," Rutherford said. "She's pretty, she has charm. She'll find somebody better than me."

"That won't be hard."

"Then why the tears?"

"Maybe because of the baby; maybe because of a million things," Gavin said. "You spoil everything you touch. You always have. What do you think you've done to my mother?"

"Now wait a minute," Rutherford said quickly. "I've sent Mom money——"

"That was white of you," Gavin said.

"So you think killing me would make her feel better?"

"I wouldn't know," Gavin said. "She died three months ago."

For just a second there was shock on Rutherford's face, and his eyes were as furtive as a rabbit's. "I didn't know——"

"It changes things, doesn't it?" Gavin said. "The club you've held over my head is gone."

Rutherford ran his tongue across his lips, the first sign of real agitation he had shown. "I said I'd give you the two thousand dollars. You can pay off what you owe."

"I think I owe more than money, Clay," Gavin said softly. "I think if a man knows there's a rattlesnake under the house it's a man's duty to get rid of the snake." His hand dropped to his gun.

"Don't be a fool, Ted," Rutherford said, and now he was afraid. His voice was low in his throat. "You'd never get out of this building alive."

"And neither would you, Clay. And you like living. Even more than I do."

Rutherford was perspiring. "What do you want?"

"Nothing from you," Ted said. He had lifted the gun from the holster. "I used to think I did. I stuck with you and took the wrong end of the stick every time. I listened to Mom. Like her, I thought there was something good in you, and with just one more chance it would come out. I liked you, Clay."

"You're breaking my heart." Rutherford's hand was sliding along the top of the desk.

"A gun in the drawer?" Ted asked. "Don't try for it. You know I could beat you."

There was a line of perspiration on Rutherford's upper lip. "You're acting like a damn fool. Listen to me, Ted. I could cut you in on something good."

"Yes," Ted said, "I'll bet you could." He thumbed back the hammer of the gun. "For Mom and Carolyne and Gwen and for a hundred or more people you've touched once and ruined——"

Clayton Rutherford jumped to his feet. "For God's sake, man, you're mad——"

The rapping on the door punctuated his sentence. There was wild hope in Rutherford's eyes, and before either man could move, the door swung inward, and a girl stepped into the room. Ted could just see her from the corner of his eye, but he knew it was the girl he had met with the lynch mob. He half turned, hiding the movement, and dropped the gun into its holster.

The girl stood there with her back against the wall, her eyes, questioning, going from one man to the other. She had changed into a dress, and her short hair was brushed back and caught with a single silver bar. Her eyes were blue, wide, straightforward, her lips full, and the dress accented her maturity.

"Clayton!" she said. "What is it?"

"Nothing, my dear," Clayton Rutherford said. He took a handkerchief from the breast pocket of his coat and dabbed his face. He could regain his composure faster than any man Ted had ever seen. "Here, you haven't met Ted Gavin. My foster brother. I've told you about him—Ted, my fiancée, Marjorie Peterson——"

"We've met," Ted said, and now he was holding the girl with his eyes, trying to read her. Clayton Rutherford had only two kinds of girls in his life. This one was not from a dance hall——

"Good heavens, no!" The girl pressed her hand to her forehead and simulated faintness. "I practically hanged him!"

Rutherford hurried out from behind the desk and put his arm around the girl's shoulders. "What on earth are you talking about?" He shot a warning glance at Gavin.

"It's all right," Ted said. "Anybody can make a mistake."

"Honestly, Clay. He was riding across Walking M range, and Nick and the boys spotted him——"

"Why didn't you tell them you were coming to see me, you fool?" Rutherford said, and there was something that passed for brotherly concern in his voice.

"I thought it might make them want to hang me that much sooner," Ted said.

The girl took it as a joke, and Rutherford covered up with his own laughter.

"We can't be too careful," Rutherford said, and now he was busy, important, explaining things to Ted. "We're not organized as a county yet and we're too isolated to have any formal protection, so we have to make our own laws. There's a certain group run things just about as they please and they've taken a great liking to Miss Peterson's beef, among other things———"

"You tell me about it later," Ted said. "I think I'd like to get cleaned up a bit."

"Certainly, Ted," Rutherford said. "I just can't tell you what it means to me, seeing you again." He reached into his pocket suddenly. "Here, do you need any money?"

"Just the two thousand dollars," Ted said. "That's all." He opened the door and went outside without looking at either of them and he saw the two gunmen standing in the shadows farther down the hall. He walked up to them and said to the tall, thin one, "Take a good look at me, pal. I'm probably your next job."

The toothpick fell from the gunman's mouth, but before he could say anything Ted was hurrying down the stairs.

He pushed his way through the crowd, straight-arming a miner out of the way. The miner whirled, staggering-drunk, trying to focus his eyes. His hand shot out and gripped Ted's shirt.

"Who the hell you think you're pushin'?"

The edge of Ted's hand chopped against the miner's forearm. "You."

"Just thought I'd ask," the miner said, and he reeled off into the crowd.

Ted batted aside the doors and sucked the clean, thin air into his lungs. The street was full of boisterous people, and Ted hurried along, needing physical exercise to calm the turmoil that was in him.

He had faced Clayton Rutherford and he had accomplished nothing. All the old pattern was there—Rutherford in a money-making proposition, a girl trusting him——— And yet for a moment sentiment had quenched the anger that had been blazing like a windblown fire.

It had seemed a simple thing, this decision to exact payment in full from a man who had never paid for anything. And yet, meeting Rutherford face to face, he had had that moment of indecision—almost the old hope that perhaps there was still time for Rutherford to change. He remembered the hurt this man had left behind him, the trusts he had broken. He had wrecked a dozen lives and he would wreck a dozen more, for that was Clayton Rutherford's way. And some of the people he had hurt most had been the first to cover up for him——

There was Carolyne, the girl he had married. The day had come when Clayton Rutherford didn't need her any more, and Carolyne had been cast aside as easily as a worn-out garment, abandoned a thousand miles from home without a cent. And Gwen—so innocently in love that right and wrong ceased to exist. Gwen, staring at the floor with red-rimmed eyes, her fingers fondling a wedding dress that wouldn't be used, thinking of a child who would be born without a name.

And a hundred or more people—old friends, holding worthless stock certificates they had received in exchange for their life savings. And again Ted Gavin had covered up, making the loss good, because these were friends of his mother's and Clay probably hadn't meant any real wrong——

He remembered his mother's last words: "Clayton is a good boy, Ted——" There was no end to a thing like that. Except the end that came with a bullet.

He swung up the street, his boots pounding against the hard earth, and he thought of this new one—Marjorie Peterson, the girl from the Walking M.

He didn't realize he was back at the OK Corral, but it was the only familiar place in this town, and he turned in there and saw Joe, the stableman, currying down a buggy mare. The stableman looked up and grinned his vacant smile.

"Quite a town, ain't she?"

"What does Clayton Rutherford do for it?" Ted demanded. The tone of his voice made the old man slow his currying and glance up apprehensively.

"Like I said," the stableman said, "I don't see nothin' and I forget fast."

Ted took a ten-dollar gold piece from his pocket, flipped it, and caught it on the back of his hand. "Would you say heads or tails?"

Joe licked his lips. "Tails, I'd say."

"You're right," Ted said. He tossed the coin and Joe caught it. "I take it Rutherford's a big man."

"A big man," Joe said. "In real estate and in politics. A hero, I'd call him. Rutherford gets things done. If things don't get done the way Rutherford wants them done, somebody gets hurt. It's a rough show, but Rutherford does good and folks like it." He spat against the horse's side and polished with the brush. "He's law and order hereabouts, and it's good to have him like you. I hear tell he might be governor of the Territory some day, but I ain't sayin' where I heard it. Politics is rough in this town."

"Who's he in with? Who's behind him?" Ted was impatient.

"Ten dollars don't go fer these days, does it, bub?" the old man said.

"To hell with you," Ted said.

He turned and walked back out on the street and turned down Allen. The dirt sidewalk was crowded, and it appeared that half the men he saw were drunk. He glanced around and saw the striped pole and he went that way.

The barber was a talkative Mexican with a sharp razor and a bathroom in the back of his shop. A half hour later Ted was clean and he went to the mercantile down the street and bought himself a new pair of pants, some socks, and a blue shirt. He changed clothes in the storeroom at the back of the building and checked the loads in his gun before strapping it back on.

His mother had accused him once of being jealous of his foster brother. That thought had bothered him often, and it was bothering him now.

He had just gone back outside when he saw the drunk reeling toward him. He stepped aside, and the drunk lurched around and bumped into him, nearly knocking him off his feet. Ted reached to grip the man's arm to straighten him out and he saw the drunk's hand dropping toward a sheathed knife.

Ted's fist came up from his hip and smashed against the man's chin. The drunk went over backward, the knife in his hand, and he sprawled out on the sidewalk. Fifty men, yelling "fight" at the top of their lungs, appeared from nowhere.

But there wasn't to be any fight. Ted's blow had been solid, and the drunk lay just where he had fallen. Ted dropped to one knee and, pretending to lift the man to his feet, he was able to sniff his breath. There wasn't a trace of whiskey on it.

Two men pushed through. "What the hell you doin' to our friend?"

"Standing him up," Ted said. "Here!"

He shoved the unconscious man hard, and the two who called themselves his friends reached out instinctively to catch him. Ted backed into the crowd and out into the street, his hand near his gun, his eyes alert. He nearly collided with the tall, thin gunman who had first taken him to Rutherford's office.

"You know how to take care of yourself, Gavin," the gunman said.

"That's right," Ted said. "You can tell Clay his knife trap didn't work."

A flush of anger twisted the thin man's features. "I don't run errands for Clay Rutherford, friend. Remember that."

"Then I'll tell him myself," Ted said.

He started toward the Oriental and he saw the covered stairway on the outside of the building. That would lead up to the office rooms so that a man wouldn't have to go back through that crowd inside. It was undoubtedly the way Marjorie Peterson had entered; he knew, just by looking at her, that she wouldn't be walking through a saloon.

He walked half turned, his hand on his gun, trying to keep an eye on the tall, thin man, and he was walking that way when he saw the girl come down out of the covered stairway. She saw him immediately and called to him.

"Mr. Gavin!"

He stood there, waiting until she came across the street and, watching her, he wondered how it was that Clayton Rutherford always managed to get such pretty women. He felt a momentary disgust for women in general. And then she was by him and her hand was on his arm.

"Mr. Gavin—— May I call you Ted? I feel I know you, Clay has told me so much about you."

He said the first empty thing that came into his mind. "I hope it was all good."

"Of course it was," she said, and now she had her arm linked through his. "Clay never says anything against anybody." She saw him looking down at her and she laughed. "That wasn't the thing to say, was it?"

"It was all right," he said.

"Don't be angry with me. Please." Her fingers tightened against his arm.

He stopped walking and looked down at her, and her face was turned up toward him, her lips slightly parted, her eyes earnest and pleading. There was a disarming frankness about her that made her seem like a little girl.

He smiled, a full smile he felt.

"I couldn't be," he said.

"I'm glad. After all, we are practically brother and sister. After Clay and I are married next month——"

"In that case," he said, "how about that supper I offered to buy you? Or are you and Clay——?"

"Your offer is accepted," she said. "Clay has another committee meeting tonight. Oh, I'll be so glad when everything is settled and we have a real law-enforcement agency and Clay can get rid of his job as head of the Citizen's Committee." She tightened her grip on his arm again. "Those men he has to have around! That Bat Fenton and his kind, and Gurn Meeker——" She shuddered. "That Gurn Meeker reminds me of a walking skeleton."

Ted thought of the tall, thin gunman and knew who she meant.

"But you have to fight fire with fire, and things are certainly a lot better than they were a few months ago." Now she was smiling, walking along, trying to match her stride with his, trying to make a pleasant occasion of this. "I'm awfully glad I didn't hang you, Ted Gavin."

"Likewise," he said, and he was glad now that he had shaved and bathed and changed his clothes. He liked this girl. She was fresh and sweet and outspoken. Like Carolyne, he thought suddenly, and the thought was bitter and some of the brightness was gone. She was completely trusting. Like Gwen.

"You must be very proud of Clayton," she said, and she was saying something that was an accepted fact to her. She was proud of Clayton and the whole world should share her belief——

"Yeah," Ted Gavin said. He thought of the man who had collided with him, pretending to be drunk as he reached for a knife. "I'm very proud," he said.

CHAPTER THREE

"A Hell of a Big Man."

The supper was no good. The food was tasty, the dining room at the hotel was pleasant, men turned to look at the attractive girl who was dining with the wind-burned stranger. She was pleasant, she made him feel like an old friend, she liked him and she said so. All the elements of a perfect evening were there, and it was all no good.

He thought of the two gunmen who had taken him to see Clayton Rutherford and he put down his fork suddenly and said, "Where do Bat Fenton and Gurn Meeker fit in?"

She looked at him quickly, and a slight irritation was in her eyes, but it was no more than an irritation at discussing an unpleasant subject.

"They're gunmen," she said honestly. "Hired killers, if you want." She saw the question in his eyes and she said, "It's safer to have them on the side of law and order than it is having them on the side of cutthroats and rustlers, isn't it?"

"Maybe," he said. "If you can keep them under control."

"That's Clay's job," she said. "I don't envy him the job, but he does it well. I said before, you had to fight fire with fire."

"A good enough way," he said, "if you don't get your fingers burned."

She looked at him quickly, and he thought that the outstanding thing about this girl was her loyalty. She would give complete loyalty to any man she loved; she would expect that same loyalty from everyone else.

"I would expect you to have confidence in your brother," she said.

"He's not my brother," he said, and he was immediately sorry he had said it. He tried to cover it up. "Clay seems to rate pretty high in this town."

"With those of us who have seen the change, yes," she said. "With women whose children have seen killings on the street, with men who have been dragged out of bed to be beaten half to death because they tried to identify a murderer, with ranchers who have been forced to harbor criminals—"

She looked at him steadily. "My father was killed just six months ago because he wouldn't give his range as a holding ground for a bunch of cattle that had been stolen from Mexico. My foreman, Nick Fears, and two of my boys saw the killing. A so-called judge and a jury called it accidental death and turned the killer loose."

"He's still free?"

She shook her head. "No, the killer is not still free. He's dead. Gurn Meeker saw to that."

"It's not pretty."

"No, it's not," she said. "But it's just. Clayton Rutherford justice. Until something better comes along, it's the kind of justice that works."

"You love Clay, don't you?"

"I wouldn't marry him if I didn't," she said.

He hadn't noticed that Nick Fears, the girl's big foreman, had entered the dining room. Fears came to their table, a seamed and serious man, his mustache like two rope ends drooping around his homely mouth. He looked at Ted Gavin, his gray-green eyes as positive as gun muzzles, and then he looked at the girl and his voice was amazingly tender.

"Luke Bell is in town." He didn't meet the girl's eyes.

The color left the girl's cheeks, and her lips were dim, thin lines. "I can't help him, Nick."

"He was your father's friend."

"He was a friend of my father's killer too."

"He hasn't said so, Marjorie. He hasn't had a chance to talk."

The girl was fighting a battle with herself, forcing herself to accept this brand of law that dealt in hired killers and blood—a brand of law enforced by a man she loved. "Clay knows how I feel about Luke Bell," she said softly. "Clay will do the right thing."

"I'm gonna talk to Luke," Nick Fears said. "I wanted you to know that."

"All right, Nick."

The big foreman left the room, and for a long time the girl sat there, her thin hands gripping the edge of the table, and then she looked up suddenly, her eyes bright and hot, defensive anger in her voice.

"Do you think I like this?" she demanded. "Do you think I like paying for blood with blood? Do you think Clay likes it?" Her voice was high-pitched, and men at the next table quit eating and looked at her. "Don't you think I've sat with him and watched him cry like a woman because of it? Have you ever seen a man cry, Ted Gavin?"

Yes, he thought, *I've seen a man cry. I've seen Clayton Rutherford cry. In a courtroom, once. In front of my mother a dozen times. It's a strong weapon, a man's tears——*

He reached out and touched her hands, and his voice was soft. "I don't want to see *you* cry, Marjorie Peterson. I'd feel like killing the man who made you cry."

He got up abruptly and left the table, knowing he couldn't say any more without saying too much, and he hurried out of the room, leaving the girl sitting there, staring at his back, wondering at the thing she had heard in his voice. A slow flush climbed her throat and found her cheeks and her heart started pulsing slowly, high in her chest.

Ted Gavin left a five-dollar bill to pay for the meals and he went outside and found that night had come to the mesa.

He walked rapidly up toward the OK Corral and he saw the tall bulk of Nick Fears, standing near the corral fence. Nick was talking to a man —a small man, weather-bent and saddle-lean, a man with thin hair showing from beneath his tilted hat. The small man reached up and scratched his head with a rope-burned hand. Nick Fears held out his hand, and the small man took a six-shooter from the waistband of his trousers and handed it over to Nick.

The two of them turned then and started down the street toward Ted Gavin. At the corner they stopped, and Gurn Meeker, the gunman, stepped out of the shadows.

"We want you, Luke Bell," Gurn Meeker said.

"He'll go peaceful, Gurn," Nick Fears said. "Luke's got nothing to hide. He wants a chance to talk to Clayton Rutherford, that's all."

Luke Bell twisted his shoulders in old habit. Ted Gavin had seen a dozen men like him—small ranchers, always scrambling for the big opportunity, never finding it. They lived in a pattern, these men. They did things by habit—— A stray beam of light caught Luke Bell's face, and there was a tired smile twisting his lips.

"Sure, Gurn. I'll go along peaceful. I just want to tell how it was, that's all—"

He spat across the center of his lips, and his hands dropped to hitch at his trousers. That too was old habit. A man with thin hips, hitching his trousers.

Gurn Meeker's hands flashed down, and two guns roared. Two times —four times? Witnesses argued about it later. Luke Bell's thin body turned completely around and it jerked and slammed against the ground from the impact of vigilante lead.

"The damn fool went for his gun," Gurn Meeker whispered to the fast-gathering crowd. "Why did the damn fool go for his gun?"

"What gun?" It was the voice of Nick Fears, a trembling voice, a strong man's voice, weak with rage. Ted Gavin was standing near Nick Fears. Bat Fenton, Gurn Meeker's friend, was kneeling near Luke Bell's riddled body.

"This gun, I reckon," Bat Fenton said. He pointed to the six-shooter that was lying by Luke Bell's body. "Don't you reckon it was this gun, Nick?" Bat Fenton's eyes were brilliantly blue. His face had a bluish cast, and it made his teeth appear white and prominent. He was holding the gun that had lain by Luke's body, holding it pointed at Nick Fears. "I reckon this was the gun he was reaching for."

Nick Fears turned and pushed through the crowd. His huge arms sent men reeling out of the way. Ted Gavin followed.

He had to hurry to match Nick's huge strides. He didn't speak to him until they had turned in at the Crystal Palace and then he shoved men aside so that he could stand by Nick. He motioned for a bottle and took a drink and with the glass in his hand he raised it to Nick and said, "To murder, Nick."

Nick Fears whirled, his lips tight against his teeth, his fists clenched. He saw serious eyes, eyes that had known hurt. And he saw hatred, but it was a different form of hatred from anything Nick Fears had ever known. It was a long-time thing, built, stone upon stone, of injury and injustice and a hopeless knowledge of rottenness. It was bigger than hatred, for hatred is a hot and violent thing, and this thing Nick Fears saw was not like that. This was calm and premeditated and deadly and full of pain.

Nick's hands unclenched. He raised his glass and said, "To a man with guts enough to say so, regardless of his reason for saying it."

"Shall we talk, Nick?" Ted Gavin said.

The big man's gaze never wavered. "Why not?" he said. "Clay Rutherford is a good friend of mine. Why shouldn't I talk to his brother?"

He snatched a bottle from the bar and motioned toward a table in the rear of the room. Ted noticed he kept the bottle and shot glass in his left hand; his right stayed near his gun.

They sat down at the table, and for a long time neither man spoke. Gavin poured a drink and sat there, staring down at the amber liquid. Nick Fears watched the younger man, trying to decide in his own mind where this foster brother of Clayton Rutherford fitted. He wasn't prepared for the thing Ted Gavin said.

"You could kill Clay Rutherford, all right, but if you did you'd never see Marjorie again. That wouldn't do, would it, Nick?"

Nick Fears was like a small boy caught stealing cookies. He had carried a secret for five years now; he had never expected it to show. His broken and seamed face flushed, and his hands knotted there on the table top.

"Watch what you say, Gavin."

"Why?" Ted Gavin said. "Are you ashamed of being in love with her?"

The strength went out of Nick Fears, and he was helpless. He looked up, and there was pain in every line of his expression. "Are you crazy, man?"

"I don't think so," Ted said softly. "It sticks out all over you."

"So suppose it does?" Fears said hotly. "You think anything will ever come of it? She doesn't know about it and she never will." He laughed, and it was a brutal sound. "Me, with a face like a horse. Hell, I'm old enough to be her father."

"So you've set back and watched her fall in love with Clayton Rutherford, knowing he was rotten, knowing he'd hurt her. What kind of love is that, Nick?"

"I just want her to be happy, that's all," Nick Fears said. "She's been alone all her life, see? She's never had anything the way she wanted it. She's been happy since she's known Rutherford." His balled fist crashed against the table top. "Damn it, man, I can love her without having her for myself. I don't have to marry her. She doesn't even have to know how I feel."

"You're a big man if you can do that, Nick Fears," Ted Gavin said. "You're a hell of a big man."

"I'm a fool," Nick said. He hid his face in his hands.

"You're a bigger man than I am, Nick," Gavin said. He stood up and he waited until Nick looked up and met his eyes. "I couldn't be satisfied with just loving a girl like her. Maybe I been looking for someone like her for a long time. I don't know. But I do know I couldn't be satisfied with half a loaf. I'd rather have nothing than half."

He saw the dull pain in Nick's eyes and he saw a hopeless jealousy that would come to nothing. The big man slumped there at the table, his hand gripping the shot glass. He was a bewildered man in love, fully aware that his love was a hopeless thing. Around him the noise of the saloon beat and throbbed and then suddenly it was still, and Ted Gavin looked up and saw Bat Fenton coming through the crowd. There was a little alley opened for him.

"Turn around slow, Nick," Ted said quietly.

Nick caught the warning and he moved his body in his chair. He was that way, half turned, when Bat Fenton went for his gun. Ted dove, his shoulder catching Nick Fears in the ribs, spilling the big man out of his chair. Fenton's gun crashed and the lead furrowed across the top of the table. Men yelled and cursed and dove for cover, and then Ted's gun was blasting and the lights were out—— A man started crying like a baby.

"Let's get out of here, Nick."

Nick led the way toward the back of the saloon. A man collided with them, and Ted's gun barrel chopped once. The clubbed man made a sighing sound.

"Everybody stay where you are! I got a shotgun here!" Ted recognized the voice of the bartender.

A match flickered, and Nick Fears pushed ahead, and there was an oblong of blue light as a door opened in front of them. A gun blasted and lead splattered against the doorjamb as the two men threw themselves out the door. They rolled over twice and were on their feet.

"Get to Marjorie and keep yourself in one piece," Ted Gavin commanded. "You're no good to her dead."

"Where you goin', Gavin?"

"To visit my brother," Ted Gavin said. "You see, it don't make a damn bit of difference to me what Marjorie Peterson thinks of me."

As he crossed the street toward the Oriental he thought he had never done such a poor job of telling a lie.

CHAPTER FOUR

"He Died Bravely."

He climbed the outside stairway and, once under protection of the roofed tunnel, he paused to reload his gun. This was the showdown, the decision he had made two months ago. He had been a fool to hesitate over it just because of memories and sentiment. Clayton Rutherford was no good. He never had been and he never would be and as long as he lived he would go on poisoning everything he touched, ruining the lives of people like Marjorie Peterson.

Ted didn't bother to drop the gun in the holster. He held it in his right hand and as he mounted the stairs he thought of Marjorie and he told himself this wasn't because of her. She was only a symbol— one more thing in a long line of things. And he was lying to himself again.

There were voices inside Clayton's office, and he stopped, pressing himself against the wall, listening. He heard the woman's voice first —high and shrill, a needle of a tongue blunted with compliments:

"You're simply wonderful, Mr. Rutherford, and when we finally do get a county of our own believe me your friends won't forget you."

"Now, Mrs. Tracy——" Clay's voice was full and proud and a bit embarrassed.

"It's the truth, Rutherford," a man's deep baritone said. "I haven't always agreed with your methods, as you well know. But there isn't another man could have done as much as you have in such a short time."

"You're all too kind——"

There was a shuffling of feet and the doorknob turned. Three women, middle-aged, and two men stood in the door saying a dozen good-bys, passing more compliments. A committee of some kind, made up of the most substantial people of the town, by the looks of them. They weren't people who would be involved in graft. They were sincere in their thanks to Clayton Rutherford.

Ted pretended to be looking for a room number while they finally filed down the stairway. He had holstered his gun. He drew it now and opened the door to Clayton's office.

Clayton was standing there, his hands locked behind his back. He was staring out the window.

"Turn around, Clay," Ted Gavin said softly.

There was a smile on Clayton's face—a smile of a man who is satisfied with a job well done. The smile froze when he turned and saw the gun and his hands rose out from his sides.

"Ted! I thought you were having supper with Marjorie—I thought she would have told you about me."

"She told me," Ted said. "I had a chance to see your law at work too."

"Oh," Clayton Rutherford's voice dropped. "You mean Luke Bell—— If you saw it, you must have seen him go for a gun."

"He wasn't wearing a gun, Clay."

"You're lying. You've been listening to talk."

"Have I?" Ted said. "How about the drunk that tried to knife me? And in case you haven't heard yet, Bat Fenton didn't get Nick Fears. Nick's with Marjorie right now, and it's my guess he'll have plenty to say."

The color had left Clayton Rutherford's face. "What in hell are you talking about, Ted? I don't know anything about Nick Fears——"

"Look, Clay, don't play-act with me. I know you, remember? I've known you a long, long time."

But Clayton Rutherford wasn't play-acting. A man could feign surprise, but a man couldn't break out in cold sweat at will. He sat down weakly and stared across the desk at Ted Gavin.

"Damn Gurn Meeker," he said, and he was a man talking to himself. "I told him to leave Fears alone." He stared at Ted and suddenly he was a man in a trap, a wild man. His hand slapped open the desk drawer and reached for the gun that was there.

Ted's voice froze him. "Hold it, Clay." The command was backed by Ted's gun.

They were that way, staring at each other, when the door opened and Gurn Meeker and Bat Fenton came into the room. Both men held cocked guns.

"Drop it, Gavin," Meeker said. "I don't want to kill you here if I can help it."

"Meeker, damn you!" Rutherford screamed. "You've ruined everything. I told you to leave the Walking M out of it!"

"Shut up, Rutherford," Meeker said. "Nick Fears is getting too smart and you know what that means. Besides that, I'm getting sick of your playing big shot while I sit back and see my business go to hell. I don't like your meeting with that committee tonight, Rutherford. I told you to stay away from them."

Rutherford's hands were shaking. "I didn't do anything, Gurn. I'm doing my job. You've got no complaints——"

"I've got five thousand Mexican cattle being held in a patch of sand," Gurn Meeker said. "They need grass; they need water. I'm tired of waiting for you, Rutherford. I'm moving those cows onto Walking M. It was part of the deal. I'm moving them in and you're covering up for me or you're out of a job."

"You can't do it, Gurn."

Meeker moved across the room, the gun in his right hand, and with his left he reached across the desk and jerked Clayton Rutherford toward him. "This is the end of the line then, Rutherford. I'm taking over again. I like it better the way I had it at first. I was a fool for ever letting you talk me into this political tie-up."

"Meeker, listen to me!" Clayton Rutherford was pleading now, his face was contorted, and his voice had that high-pitched whine Ted had hated all his life. "They'll have a county here, I tell you. The old way won't work. You'll need a man like me——"

"I won't need you," Meeker said. "People will vote right if they've got a gun in their ribs."

"I'm not double-crossing you, Gurn," Clayton pleaded. "I had to meet with that committee——"

"Sure you did," Meeker said. "You had to meet with them because you wanted to show your girl what a fine big citzen you are. But you're starting to squeeze people who are friends of mine, Rutherford, and I don't like it. Our deal was that I was to run things and you was to make it look legal. That was our deal."

"It's still our deal, Meeker——"

Ted watched the man cringe and he was sick at his stomach.

"No more, Rutherford. People have been telling you you're a great man and you're beginning to believe it. You're starting to step on my toes, Rutherford, and there ain't no man big enough to step on the toes of Gurn Meeker. You got to find that out, Rutherford, just like Luke Bell found it out. Too bad you had to listen in, Gavin. Just like it's too bad Nick Fears had to start talkin' out of the wrong side of his mouth."

A sudden change had come over Clayton Rutherford. From a cornered animal he was an animal in a trap, fighting for his life. His face had gone chalk-white, and his lips were pulled tight against his teeth. He stepped out from behind the desk.

"You're not getting the girl mixed up in it, Meeker. That's one thing you're not big enough to do. I'll stop you, Meeker."

Ted Gavin had seen Rutherford this way perhaps four times in his life, but he had remembered each one of those times. There was latent dynamite in Clayton Rutherford when he wanted something badly enough. Usually he fought with his wits or he worked for sympathy. But sometimes—only a few times—he had shown his claws this way and Ted had recognized the potential killer. He came around the desk now, straight toward Meeker, and just for a second Ted saw only the man who had been as close to him as a brother, and he was a man who was going to protect Marjorie Peterson in spite of a gun thrust in his face.

He could stand here, Ted knew, and watch it, and Clayton Rutherford would be killed. No man could face a cocked gun and get away with it. And in the confusion of Gurn Meeker's first shot Ted himself might find the break he needed to get out of this alive. He looked at Clayton Rutherford, walking straight toward that gun, and he knew that for once the man was acting for someone other than himself. A thousand old memories flashed across his mind and they were memories unstained by fact.

"Watch it, Clay," Ted said.

He hardly knew he had uttered the words. But Clayton Rutherford heard them and he knew he was going to have help. Ted Gavin stood there, every nerve taut, waiting for Clayton's move, knowing now he was going to side with the man he had come to kill, knowing he couldn't help himself.

"That's all, Rutherford." Meeker's voice was tight in his throat.

Ted shifted weight, and Bat Fenton moved to match his movement, jabbing the gun against his ribs.

"I told you I'd stop you——" Rutherford took one more step.

The gun in Meeker's hand came up. And Ted Gavin yelled.

For that thousandth of a second Gurn Meeker's eyes were flicking toward Ted Gavin, and in that thousandth of a second Ted's elbow came back and jabbed into the pit of Bat Fenton's stomach. At the same time Clayton Rutherford was diving in, both hands gripping the wrist of Meeker's gun hand. Ted dropped to the floor and Bat Fenton's gun blasted, the heat of the muzzle scorching against Ted's shoulder. He rolled, gripped Fenton's legs, and pulled the man down.

He couldn't see the struggle that was going on above him, but he could hear Meeker's grunting curse, and then a gun hit the floor. Ted drove his fist against Bat Fenton's jaw and scooped for the gun. Fenton was on his feet like a cat, his hand clawing inside his shirt. Ted threw himself against the wall, the gun coming up, and he saw Clayton Rutherford vault over the desk. Bat Fenton still had his hand inside his shirt when Rutherford scooped his own gun from the desk drawer and fired.

Bat Fenton slammed back against the wall, stunned by shock, but still game. His hand came out of his shirt holding a small-caliber pistol. He started firing, firing until it was empty, firing wildly at Ted, at Rutherford, at Gurn Meeker, hitting nothing, it seemed——But Rutherford was swaying. He fired once more, and Bat Fenton slid slowly down the wall still squeezing the trigger of the empty gun.

Gurn Meeker, disarmed, had been pinned in the corner trying to escape the hail of lead in the room. He turned now, snatched up a chair, and hurled it across the room. The seat of the chair struck Ted on the side of the head, a stunning blow that dazed him. He heard the roar of a gun and couldn't tell who fired the shot.

He shook his head and he heard Rutherford's voice yelling, "Stop him! Stop him!" He saw the door slam and it seemed the sound came later and then the door was open again and Nick Fears was there. Ted's senses cleared and he looked at Clayton Rutherford.

Clayton was behind the desk, a gun in his hand, and it was obviously an empty gun or he would have stopped Gurn Meeker. Rutherford's face was twisted until it was hard to recognize. There was blood on his shirt and splashes of blood on the desk top and flecks of it on his lips. He was staring at the door, the gun in his hand pointed at Fears.

"Nick, I've got to talk to you———"

The bulk of Nick Fears filled the doorway. His hand dropped smoothly and came up and the gun he held roared and the sound of it filled the room. Clayton Rutherford clutched his stomach with one hand and gripped the desk top with the other. For seconds, it seemed, he stood that way, and then he fell back into the chair behind him. Ted Gavin put an arm around him to keep him from falling.

He was still alive but he wouldn't be for long. Big Nick Fears stood there across the desk, staring down, no malice in him, just bewilderment.

"Ted———" Clayton's voice was barely audible. Ted bent down close to catch it.

"Money in the safe, Ted. Take your two thousand. Want to pay up before I go———"

The harshness faded from his face and again he was handsome, his eyes pleading, his lips trembling slightly, and Ted remembered him as a boy, talking his way out of a jam he was in. He was torn between feeling sorry for the man and hating him, and neither emotion was strong enough to matter.

"I'm better off dead," he said. "No other way—" He raised one hand just enough to motion to Nick Fears. "Listen to me, Nick." Nick Fears nodded. "I would have hurt Marjorie," Clayton said. "I didn't want to hurt her. That was my trouble. I loved her, Nick———"

He died, and Ted Gavin and Nick Fears stood there, knowing they had heard a man telling the truth—perhaps the one truth of his life.

"Damn it," Nick said softly. "Maybe it would have worked out all right———"

"It never would have," Ted said. "I've known him too long." He

thought of the empty gun Clayton had held when Nick shot him and
he kicked it under the desk with his toe. Nick needn't know about it;
anyone checking it later would think nothing of it. He looked at Nick.
"You want to tell Marjorie?"

Nick Fears shook his head. "No, Gavin. You knew him better than
I did. You could lie about him better than I could."

Ted put out his hand, and the two men gripped there over the
body of the dead man and somehow they knew each other's feelings.
A girl could get over the grief of the death of the man she loved.
Especially if the man she loved had died a hero——

They stood there, gripping hands, hardly realizing that the room
was filling with people, then together they slipped out the door.

"You know a lot of people around here, Nick," Ted Gavin said.
"Get the ones you can really trust. Keep the Citizen's Committee
going—just the way Clayton had it. Tell everybody he was getting
ready to clean the rats out of the nest and they got him."

They swung in at the OK Corral, knowing they had to run down
Gurn Meeker before he could talk, and Joe, the stableman was there,
chewing vigorously, his eyes blinking rapidly. Ted Gavin drew his
gun and shoved it in Joe's middle.

"No pay this time, Joe. Just the truth. Gurn Meeker was here.
Which way did he go?"

"I told you before," Joe wailed. "I don't see nothin', I don't hear
nothin'——"

"Talk, damn you."

"I'll do my own talking, Gavin." The voice lashed out and Ted
spun, dropping to one knee. Gurn Meeker stood in the wide door of
the barn, a gun in each hand. Joe screamed and four guns blazed
together. Ted saw Nick Fears go down; he felt the burn of lead across
his own ribs. But Gurn Meeker's guns were silent. The tall, thin,
skeleton of a man tried to take a step. He never made it.

Ted dropped down beside Nick Fears. One of Gurn Meeker's bullets
had found a target. Big Nick Fears would never worry about a hopeless love again.

Marjorie Peterson took the news the way Ted expected her to take
it. There was a splendid strength about the girl; he had sensed it the
first time he saw her. She didn't cry; she made no scene. When he had

told her what he had to say she took his hand and held it a long time. She stood up then and smiled.

"Thank you, Ted," she said. "We both loved him." She left to do her crying alone.

Ted Gavin sat in the hotel room a long time and the night was gone and the morning was gray across the mesa. He thought back, clear to the beginning, to the day his mother had taken Clayton Rutherford after his own parents had been killed. He rebuilt his own life and Clayton's life and he saw that he had known from the first that Clayton Rutherford would have to die. He sighed and took a sheet of paper and a pen.

Dear Gwen, he wrote. *Clayton was doing well and he was going to send for you and the baby. He died bravely, doing his duty. He wanted you to have this——*

He folded the two thousand dollars in bills he had taken from Clayton Rutherford's safe. Tomorrow he'd get a draft from the bank. Tomorrow he'd start doing his part toward building the kind of town Marjorie Peterson thought Clayton Rutherford was building for her. He would be covering up for Clayton Rutherford again, he knew, but that in itself didn't seem to matter much.

The Proud Diggers

William O. Turner

THE SUN shone just barely warm, and a breeze stirred just barely cool, with a kiss in it that made Steve Hartlett want to sing and his horse want to canter. It was the first morning that ever was, he thought. He was the first man that ever was, riding the first horse and leading the first mule. He was the caress of the breeze and the limp response of the pines on the far slope; he was the nagging voice of the stream in the canyon it had been wearing deeper for ten thousand years; he was the energy in the animal between his thighs and he was the fire of the sun. These were thought-up things and he was a thought-up creature; he and they had a common reality in the Mind that thought them up.

This was the comfort, the strange comfort that he found beyond the Ruby Mountains.

One of the most impressive of all newcomers to Western-novel ranks in the past several years has been quiet, serious Bill Turner. Books like *The Proud Diggers* and *The Settler,* good as they are, will surely be succeeded by even finer ones. Writer-to-watch Turner lives and works in Hendersonville, North Carolina.

He had been a week away from Bannack—a week meandering over ground that he could have covered in less than three days of unexploratory travel. He had ridden north around the Rubies, then south up a flat green valley, following the little Ruby River (that was also called the Passamari, translated Stinkingwater, either because it was fed by faintly odoriferous sulphur springs or because at its lower end it was joined by a creek whose banks an Indian tribe had adorned with the bodies of its dead). He had picked his way up a steep and rocky canyon that led to a higher valley, thick with brush and alive with game. He had found still another canyon that led to a still higher valley, mottle-floored with short green grass and patches of melting snow.

He had intended to hunt; but he had killed nothing except a sage hen that first night on the Ruby benchland, shooting it when it strutted stupidly close as he was making camp, beheading it with a shot from his rifle as casually as if he were selecting a delicacy from a pantry shelf. It turned out that the bird had flavored itself with sage to the point of bitterness, and he wished he had chosen bacon after all.

And so he rode aimlessly, in search of nothing and of everything. It was the searching that counted. He wondered if Ellie had finally come to understand that. He wondered if that was why she had wanted to come to Bannack.

He bathed in an icy creek, slept naked in the sun, rode on, camped, rode on. He built a lean-to against the rain and lay snug; he fished in the Ruby with a hook fashioned from a horseshoe nail and caught a trout; he slept a great deal, letting the horse and mule graze. When he came to three forks of the river, he went up the most easterly and got out of the valley into the Gravellies. Now he was headed north again, avoiding the brushy bottoms and letting his horse choose the way over grassy or sage-dappled or barren clay slopes.

As he skirted a hill more massive than its neighbors, darkly bearded at its top with pine, he was puzzled to find the mule pulling off to the left, wanting to climb. Whimsically, Steve turned the horse diagonally upward. After a quarter of an hour of hard going, feeling the straining and the heavy breath of the horse, he leveled off and circled the nipple of the hill. On the western slope he stopped to breathe the animals and stretch his legs.

The mule was excited, eager to begin the mile-long descent into a green-bottomed gulch that lay ahead. Steve could see the lower Ruby valley in the distance to the northwest and he realized that he had come through a modulation in the range—the mountains to the north of him were probably the Tobacco Roots. There was probably a creek down there in the gulch, he thought, a tributary of the Ruby.

He caught a flash of motion in the gulch, but the thing was at once obscured by foliage. He got into the saddle and headed down the gentle slope, having trouble with the mule, who kept trotting up past the horse to the end of the lead rope. A shift of the wind brought the sound of chopping. The sound is unmistakable, yet Steve pondered it, verifying its rhythm by imagining he was swinging an ax.

When he was halfway down the grade, he caught a glimpse of men riding up the gulch. The chopping was suddenly accompanied by the sharper, more rapidly repeated ring of a hammer. A man in a red undershirt came into view from behind a clump of alder and wiped his face on his forearm. And now Steve could see a sort of cabin in the alder, a shoulder-high cubicle roofed with brush.

After a week in the mountains without seeing a human being, he had a dreamy feeling that he was the dupe of a conspiracy between nature and his senses. But it was a simple fact that he was riding into a remote gulch that was alive with humanity.

Men dotted the creek bank, but none of them paid him the slightest heed as he rode up. They were hunched over prospecting pans, swinging picks, sawing logs into lumber, nailing together sluice boxes. He rode to the bank and watched a man who stood knee-deep in water, panning. A piece of deerskin the size of a handkerchief was spread on the ground, anchored by a rock at each of its corners. At its center, there was a little pile of pale, gleaming granules.

"How you making out?" Steve asked the man.

Bloodshot eyes surveyed him from a grimy face; they moved to the pack mule and back to Steve. The sifting motion of the pan never faltered.

"This ground all along here is staked, mister. I reckon there still might be good ground down the gulch—dry claims, anyways."

"Thanks. How you making out?"

"About two dollars the pan, mostly—though I've had 'em up to ten."

Steve caught his breath. "Are there many claims that good?"

The man, intent on the mucky swirl in the pan, didn't seem to hear.

"How's the pay other places?" Steve demanded.

"I couldn't say for sure, mister. From what I hear, it's good everywhere."

"How long you been here?"

"Come yesterday noon with the stampede. Worked most of the night—till my lantern burned out."

"How's the quality?"

"It's in flakes, mister—little flakes pure as God's own light and just as pretty. Now, why don't you move along mister? No offense, but a man don't like a stranger on his claim—you ought to know that. There's already been two shootin's."

"Sure," Steve said. He turned the horse down the gulch.

Gold fever. The old fever—as old as civilization. The man had it bad, a killing case of it. *And I'm getting it too,* Steve thought. *One look at that pile of grit and I was infected.*

He rode along the creek, questioning other men. He learned that the narrow gulch curved upward for thirteen miles from the Ruby valley. Practically everybody everywhere in it was panning pay. At this end of the gulch, a mining district had already been formed. Claims were fifty feet along the creek and a man was allowed to stake two.

Thirteen miles of high-pay placer gulch! This was a big strike— bigger than anything he had seen in California as a kid. Bannack was a mere camp compared to the civilization that tortuous new roads would pour into Alder Gulch. Clay-calked cabins would replace tents and wickiups; then houses of stone and lumber would toe hilly streets; saloons and dance halls would be followed by schools and churches. A city would mushroom in this crease of desolate, unfertile, and treasure-laden earth.

I'll stay, Steve thought. *I have gold fever and I'll stay. Gold is neither a purpose nor a goal; it is merely part of the seeking. And yet I have gold fever.*

Three miles down the gulch he found a rocky stretch that was unclaimed, he was told, because it was poor ground and alive with rattlesnakes. He paced off a hundred feet of it, staked it, and tethered the horse and mule on the gentle east slope of the gulch.

He borrowed a shovel from a neighbor, found that he was close to bedrock, and for a while bent his back to the accumulation of a pile of likely-looking muck. He returned the shovel and began to pan, using an iron skillet that was too shallow for the purpose, awkward and wasteful. He panned thirty dollars by sundown. And never saw a snake.

As he ate his supper of bacon and beans out of the same skillet, word came down the gulch that Walt Dance had arrived at a place called Daylight Gulch with four wagonloads of goods. So Steve saddled the horse and rode up-gulch in the twilight, leading the mule.

Daylight Gulch turned out to lie alongside the slope down which he had ridden that morning. Several ridges focused here, not quite coming together at Alder Gulch but ending at a little open space like spokes around a hub. Steve was amazed to see that in the half day since he had been here a camp had sprung up: lean-tos, tents, bedrolls spread in the open. A tarpaulin sagged above a bar formed of wooden boxes. A knot of men around a large dry goods box solemnly played monte by lantern light—standing up. The seductive chants of faro dealers floated from a big tent with eerie inner shadows playing on its luminous canvas.

Steve rode slowly through the camp. Not one trader but three had arrived—Walt Dance with four wagons of grub and hardware; Nat Langford with two loads of lumber; and a Mormon trader with a wagon of sardines (at a dollar a can) and another of gallon jugs of Valley Tan—a sort of liquid fire distilled in Salt Lake Valley for Gentile consumption. Beyond the wagons a stagecoach was pulled up, the long-haired driver unhitching the horses and swearing at a group of bystanders.

It was here that the city would be—up this little side gulch where the ridges focused. The traders had stopped here instinctively.

He dismounted and visited the wagons. Dance was auctioning his goods. Steve spent the dust he had panned and as much more in coin for bread, bacon, flour, potatoes, a pick, shovel, hammer, nails, enough lumber for a long Tom, and a gold-sifting apparatus that consisted of three nesting pans of different depths, with the bottoms of two of them colandered. He packed this plunder on the mule and rode back downcreek through the campfire-infested blackness of the gulch.

He found two men camped on his claim, sitting in the glow of a fire and drinking from a jug. He got off his horse, felt the derringer in his pocket, and went up to them. In the fluid firelight they were shaggy, shadowy, dark-faced figures without individuality.

"Good evening," Steve said.

One of them grunted. They watched him with two pairs of eyes that were made identical by wariness.

"Camping here?"

"What does it look like?" one of them said.

"Just asking. You're on my claim."

"*Your* claim?"

"That's right."

"Want to start something?"

"You're welcome to camp here," Steve said.

"Like to try to run us off?" the second man said viciously. As he spoke, Steve recognized him. He was the man who had shouted from the walk when Steve and Ellie had driven into Bannack, the fighter who had gone for a gun and friends. The man who——His name was Brice Hall.

"You can at least be civil, Hall," Steve said.

The eyes narrowed. Steve had a week's growth of beard. He looked as shadowy nondescript as they did, he thought, and Hall didn't recognize him——if he had ever known him.

"Civil be damned!" Hall said. "You talk like a filthy Yankee. The Yankee ain't been borned that I'll be civil to—nor can run me off a claim."

"I said you're welcome to camp here. But I could pick a better place. This ground is lousy with rattlers."

He lingered to enjoy the flutter of fear, the inevitable searching glance at the ground.

"Rattlers and Yankees," Hall said. "This is a hell of a gulch!"

Steve led the horse and mule up the slope. He unpacked, unsaddled, and picketed them. He built a fire of brush and spread his blankets and buffalo robe. The white handle of the pick he had bought caught his eye and he lifted it, liking its end-heavy efficiency—its promise that, once raised, it contained within itself the strength for the downward blow. He fondled it, swung it, and left it stuck into the ground. He added fuel to the fire and hided up for the night.

He lay a long time without sleeping, snug in the buffalo robe. He lay looking at the garnished sky, trying to feel at one with it and with Ellie and with everything, and not succeeding. There was no order in the stars, he thought. Perhaps if he could find order in them he would not want to kill a man that slept fifty yards below on the creek bank.

He drifted into sleep without seeming to lose awareness of the stars. He was startled by the blinding rim of the sun lifting from behind the Tobacco Roots.

The two men were no longer camped on his claim. When he passed the ashes of their fire on his way to the creek, he saw their whisky jug lying broken on some rocks. He touched it with his boot—and jerked back reflexively. Among the rocks lay the death-twisted pattern of a rattlesnake, its head smashed by the jug.

Steve spent that day and half the next building a short sluice that ran from the creek onto the bank and emptied into a ditch that returned the water to the creek. The afternoon of the second day he tried it out. He shoveled gravel into it for an hour; then he removed the cleated bottom and scraped some of the sandy residue into the pan he had bought. Kneeling by the creek, he cautiously swished away all but the pale, pure dust. After several pans, he had perhaps half a teaspoonful of gold. From this, he estimated that he could make better than a hundred dollars a day with the sluice.

Late in the afternoon he saddled up and rode up-gulch to Daylight —which was hardly recognizable. More traders had arrived. Dance had laid the ground logs for a store. By some miracle of energy, a small building of finished lumber stood where two days before there had been only rocky hillside. It was a grim, square building with iron rods barring paneless windows. Its door displayed a freshly painted sign.

A. J. OLIVER & CO.
EXPRESS & MAIL

Letters to Bannack	
or Cottonwood	50¢
To the U.S.	$1.00
Treasure	
To Bannack	5%
To Salt Lake	10%

Steve mingled with groups of men, chattering and asking questions. He learned that every foot of Alder Gulch and all side gulches was claimed. Very few spots on the creek weren't producing. Some dry miners had tunneled into rich ground in the hillsides. There was a new strike in a small gulch off the Ruby valley.

He recognized Jerry Willows, working with two other men to set a log in place on an oblong structure that had risen to knee height. Jerry responded to Steve's greeting with a curt nod.

"Another restaurant?" Steve asked.

"Yes. I'm going to bring the folks over." Jerry turned away and then turned back nervously. "I have claims too. Nine and ten above discovery. I've hired men to work them for me."

"Wages must be high."

"Sixteen dollars a day. And I have to pay these fellows the same—just to put up a building!" Jerry tossed his head in the direction of his helpers and smiled, as if to turn the remark into good-natured banter. The men exchanged a cynical glance, and one of them spat.

"You get a claim, Hartlett?" Jerry said quickly, as if to change the subject. He had a challenging way of saying Steve's last name.

"Down-gulch. In Granite District."

"By the way," Jerry said, "we caught up with a rascal that came into this country with your train. Fellow by the name of Sam Turkey. He tried to jump a claim. We had a miners' meeting this afternoon and banished him from the gulch. He's lucky he didn't hang."

"Sam Turkey? Sam wouldn't jump a claim."

"He jumped this one, all right. The sooner we run trash like that out of the gulch, the better off we'll be."

Steve suppressed his irritation. "You happen to know where Sam is now?"

"A few minutes ago he was over by Dance's wagon. He has until morning to get out of the gulch."

Steve walked over to Dance's wagon, saw no one he knew. He turned into a tent saloon and found X. Biedler standing at the bar over a plate of ham and beans and a tin cup brimful of whiskey. Biedler was glad to see him.

"You will have a drink with me now?" the bull-chested Dutchman demanded, speaking with the strange precision that suggested that long ago he had learned English from a book.

"I'll have some of that food and a man-size drink," Steve said. "Not an X-size."

It turned out that Biedler knew all about Sam Turkey.

"Sam is over in Judge Doc Bissell's tent now. Walt Dance is with him. Anybody gets in trouble, big-hearted Walt always tries to help."

"Who's Bissell?"

"You haven't heard of Bissell? The man who named this town? Some secessionists had named it Varina—after the wife of Jefferson Davis. When Doc made out the first court order, they told him to write Varina City at the top. 'I'll see you damned first,' Doc said, and he wrote Virginia. 'That is the name of this little corner of hell,' he said, 'by judicial fiat!' "

"Varina would have been better," Steve said. "There's already a Virginia City in Nevada."

"Now there's one in Idaho."

When they had paid for their meal, Biedler led Steve to a tent whose faded canvas was scarred with dirty, pitch-treated patches. Inside, they found a bespectacled little man lacing out big Sam Turkey. Walt Dance looked on silently, his jaw set so that his square beard seemed to stick almost straight out.

"You don't tell a straight story!" Bissell stormed, glaring over his spectacles. "Now you get to tarnation out of the gulch like the court ordered!"

Sam Turkey saw Steve then and grabbed his hand.

"Cap'n Hartlett! Thank the Lord you come! You can tell me rightly what to do."

"I don't know, Sam. What happened?"

"Cap'n, I hit it. Got here with the first stampeders and got a good claim. And now they taken it away from me."

"I want to hear this from the beginning," Steve said.

"Yesterday, couple fellers come a-ridin' up the gulch and stopped to talk," Sam said. "Asked how much I was pannin', and I told 'em. Asked was I a slave man, and I said no. They was slave men and they cussed me right out plain. I wanted no trouble and I laughed it off, and pretty soon they moved on. They talked a while with the feller to the south of me—he's from Georgia. Then they come back past me and talked a long time with the feller to the north of me—he's from Mississippi. Then they rode off down the gulch—the direction they come from.

"The feller to the north of me, the Mississippi feller, he come over after while. He says let's go git a jug of liquor. I'd been a-workin' without no let-up for three days and I felt the need of a drink. So we come up here to Daylight and bought a jug of Valley Tan. I got drunk, Cap'n Hartlett. I own to that. I got blind, rollin', dirty-pants drunk. When I woke up this mornin' I didn't know where I was at and couldn't find my way back. The poke of dust I had round my neck was gone. When I finally did git back to my claim, there was these two fellers on it, a-settin' up a long Tom.

"We had a argyment, all right. They say they had staked the ground two days ago and gone off for supplies. Left a pick and shovel on the claim to hold it, they says, like the rule is. That was a lie, 'cause I had been on that claim three days myself. Well, they run me off'n my own claim with a six-gun. I reckon what they really had in mind was to kill me then and there, but Mr. Dance here was passin' up the gulch and stopped to listen to the argyment. He'd of been a witness if they shot me in cold blood, so they dasn't to do it.

"I didn't know who to go to. Everybody I talked to was too busy gittin' rich to listen. Then I run onto Judge Doctor Bissell here, and he listened. Called a meetin' of the Fairweather court. And they told me I was the claim jumper!"

"The men on both sides of that claim confirmed the stories of the other parties," Doc Bissell said. "You couldn't produce a single witness that saw you on that claim three days ago."

"Judge, them two feller was a-lyin' as fast as they could wag their tongues. That Mississippi feller even denied gittin' drunk with me. He's the one got my poke too, I reckon."

"Sam," Steve said, "are you sure you weren't drunk more than one night?"

"I'm certain, Cap'n. I worked that claim three days."

"Damn it!" Bissell exploded. "You haven't got the dust to prove it!"

"I tell you that Mississippi feller——"

"Bah!"

"This man is telling the truth," Steve said.

"What! How d'you know?"

"I know Sam."

"You know Sam! Well, sir, I don't know you!"

"This is Captain Hartlett," X. Biedler said. "Steve Hartlett."

"What do you say about this, X?" Bissell demanded.

"Steve's opinion is good with me."

Bissell reddened, then exploded again. "God knows, I want to see justice done. But even if this man is telling the truth, what in tarnation can I do about it? Hall and Hucko may have bought those two damned secesh neighbors of his, but how can you prove that?"

Steve caught his breath. "Hall and Hucko!" he said.

"Brice Hall," Biedler said.

"I remember now," Doc Bissell said, studying Steve. "I heard about your wife. My God! Hall was the man——I didn't place this Hall. A tragic thing, sir!"

"That has nothing to do with this," Steve said.

"Doc," X. Biedler said, "this is one of the six Hall brothers. Murderers, all of them. And this Brice—he is the oldest and the worst. He is a cannibal, they say. They say——"

"Well!" Bissell said. "Well! Why wasn't that brought out at the trial?"

Walt Dance spoke for the first time. "It seems plain that those two cutthroats conspired with Turkey's neighbors. I suppose they really intended to kill Turkey and be rid of him once and for all. What went wrong was that I would have been a witness."

"I could call a general meeting of the miners," Doc Bissell said. "And what good would that do? You gentlemen could talk yourselves blue in the face. You could say the witnesses were liars and Hall and Hucko claim jumpers. And what would you have? You'd have a North-South fight that might involve the whole gulch!"

Steve felt X. Biedler's steady little eyes. Even before he met them, he knew the message that would be in them. When he met them the decision was made.

"Bissell, do you believe this man now?" Steve said.

"I don't know what in tarnation I believe."

"According to miners' law, a man has a right to run a jumper off his claim, hasn't he?"

"You're damned right he has!" Bissell said.

"All right, Sam," Steve said. "Let's run those bastards clear out of the gulch."

Sam Turkey and X. Biedler followed him out of the tent. As they left, Doc Bissell said tiredly, "I don't blame you much, men. My court isn't the best in the world. I'm not even a lawyer—I'm a doctor!"

"You got a gun, Turkey?" Biedler asked, as they strode down the grade toward the creek in the twilight.

"No. They taken that too—while I was drunk."

"Steve?"

"I've got a derringer."

"A derringer! A peashooter! We'll stop at one of these traders' and buy two Colts."

"We'll buy one," Steve said. "For Sam." He was aware of Biedler's curious glance but he didn't feel like explaining that he had carried his little double-barreled derringer for years and could handle it better than any revolver ever made.

Sam's claim was a short walk up Alder Gulch from Daylight. When they were in sight of it, they could see Hall and Hucko working close together at the edge of the creek.

"How we a-goin' about this?" Sam said, touching the butt of the new navy Colt that was tucked into the top of his pants. "Seems like we ought to make up a plan."

"Pshoo!" Biedler said. "A plan will get us mixed up."

Steve laughed, grateful for Biedler. You went into a thing like this without plans. You made them fast as you went along. You let yourself be carried by your instinct and your anger. And your luck. You would come out all right because whatever happened was all right. The matter was already decided. You made up your mind to that before you went into it.

Hall and Hucko were making their cleanup, appraising bright residue in a prospecting pan. Hall set the pan gently on the ground and straightened. There was a big revolver in his belt. Hucko's revolver lay on his coat, five yards up the bank.

"This is Turkey's claim," Steve said. "Get off."

Brice Hall's eyes swept the three men who were descending on him. Hucko warily estimated the distance to his coat.

"Get off!"

"The court give it to us," Hall said. "You ——ing Yankees get off."

Steve could see how it was going to be now. He walked straight up to Hall and lunged for his hand as it leaped to the big revolver. He let Hall draw and forced his bent arm up past his shoulder in a continuation of the drawing motion that sent the gun flying into the creek. Still forcing the arm backward, stepping forward and stooping suddenly, he felt Hall pivot over his hip, saw him splash into the shallow water after the gun.

But he had underestimated Hucko's speed, and a big fist caught him on the side of the head before he could straighten. He hit the ground hard, thinking that he must roll in order to avoid a kick but sprawling helplessly in the gravel. Raising himself, he saw Biedler throw a fist at Hucko, miss, lose his balance, and go down from a clublike haymaker.

Hucko, amazingly agile for a thick, solid man, closed with Sam Turkey, kneeing him, spinning him in the direction of the coat and gun, and falling with him on top of them. Steve staggered to his feet and almost fell again dodging a rock that Hall hurled at him as he climbed out of the creek. Hall then dived at Biedler, who was on his knees, drawing his Navy.

Hucko knelt behind the prone Sam Turkey, cocking a revolver— his own or Turkey's—leveling it at Steve.

Steve's hand was in his pocket, grasping the derringer. He didn't remember putting it there; it was just there, cocking the gun, thrusting it forward, firing it through the cloth. He marveled at the neat and tiny hole that appeared in Hucko's forehead and felt himself go limp and weak in a strange sympathetic reaction as Hucko pitched forward. He suppressed the weakness, breathing deeply, and turned to see Biedler tap Hall on the head with the barrel of his revolver.

Other men were converging on them, running up and then standing back a little, gaping. Hall lay on his back, wet and pale but with a scalding hatred in his eyes.

"Get up," Steve said. "Gather your plunder and get out of the gulch."

Hall got up, reeling. He climbed slowly up the slope to where two horses were tethered and led them back to the claim. A bystander, of which there were dozens now, helped him saddle them and secure Hucko's body face down across one of the saddles. Hall mounted unsteadily and, leading the other animal, rode down-gulch.

Biedler and some others were bent over Sam Turkey, who was half paralyzed with pain and nausea from the kneeing he had taken. There wasn't much they could do for him but bathe his face and loosen his clothing. It was some little time before he could stand.

"Look around, Sam," Steve said. "Is the man here who got you drunk and lied against you at miners' court?"

Sam looked painfully at the faces around him. The men stared back at him defiantly.

"That's him." Sam nodded at an emaciated man who was nervously chewing tobacco. "I don't see t'other feller—the one from Georgia."

"Mister, come here," Steve said. It was going to turn out very well, he thought. There would be no doubts about Sam's proprietorship. The only thing that bothered him was the surge of weakness he had felt at Hucko's death. He wanted to get off by himself and try to figure out what caused it.

The man stepped forward, spitting, trying to look amused.

"I ain't stole nothin', Cap."

"I'm going to run you out of the gulch," Steve said.

"I guess you could do it if you wanted, Cap. I seen the fight."

"You've got one chance. Tell these men the truth. Now."

"Well, I reckon I'll swear to most anything a fighter like you says. You tell what you want, and I'll swear to it."

"Get out of the gulch!" Steve found that his hand was in his pocket again, holding the derringer. "Now."

"I'm a-tryin' to please you, Cap." The man's insolent talk was over. His face had gone loose. There was more than fear in it; there was a hopelessness that was ugly and embarrassing to see, an acceptance of inferiority. Tobacco juice trickled from one side of his mouth.

"Then tell the truth, the exact truth, with no prompting from me."

The man talked. He made a rambling story of it, telling of his wife and four children back in Clay County. He swore that Hall and Hucko had threatened to kill him unless he did as they said. But he told the essential facts. He had got Sam Turkey drunk. He had robbed Sam. He had lied at miners' court. He had Sam's dust buried on his claim and he would get it right now and give it to Sam.

The miners listened. When the man brought Sam's poke, they muttered angrily. One of them spoke up.

"If Captain Hartlett don't run you out of the gulch, the rest of us ought to. You damned yellow-back secesh."

Steve turned to the man who had spoken. "Anybody who talks like that ought to go back to the States and get into the war."

He said it mildly because he was not angry. The man knew now that this was Sam's claim. All the miners knew it.

Riding shotgun on the stage to Bannack the next day, Biedler told the driver about the fight. He told it again that night in Skinner's Oro Fino Saloon. "This Hartlett is crazy and smart and lucky all at once," he said.

And others who had seen it told it. And others took it up and told it.